THE CRISIS

BY

WINSTON CHURCHILL

THE MACMILLAN COMPANY

THIRTEENTH PRINTING 1969

The Macmillan Company
Collier-Macmillan Canada Ltd, Toronto, Ontario

Printed in the United States of America

To
J.B.G.
AND
L.M.G.

CONTENTS

BOOK I

BOOK III

THE CRISIS

THE CRISIS

BOOK I

CHAPTER I

WHICH DEALS WITH ORIGINS

FAITHFULLY to relate how Eliphalet Hopper came to St. Louis is to betray no secret. Mr. Hopper is wont to tell the story now, when his daughter-in-law is not by; and sometimes he tells it in her presence, for he is a shameless and determined old party who denies the divine right of Boston, and has taken again to chewing tobacco.

When Eliphalet came to town, his son's wife, Mrs. Samuel D. (or S. Dwyer, as she is beginning to call herself), was not born. Gentlemen of Cavalier and Puritan descent had not yet begun to arrive at the Planters' House, to buy hunting shirts and broad rims, belts and bowies, and depart quietly for Kansas, there to indulge in that most pleasurable of Anglo-Saxon pastimes, a free fight. Mr. Douglas had not thrown his bone of Local Sovereignty to the sleeping dogs of war.

To return to Eliphalet's arrival,—a picture which has much that is interesting in it. Behold the friendless boy as he stands in the prow of the great steamboat *Louisiana* of a scorching summer morning, and looks with something of a nameless disquiet on the chocolate waters of the Mississippi. There have been other sights, since passing Louisville, which might have disgusted a Massachusetts lad more. A certain deck on the *Paducah*, which took him as far as Cairo, was devoted to cattle— black cattle. Eliphalet possessed a fortunate temperament. The deck was dark, and the smell of the wretches confined there was worse than it should have been. And the incessant weeping of some of the women was annoying, inasmuch as it drowned many of the profane communications of the overseer who was showing Eliphalet the sights. Then a fine-linened planter from down river had come in during the conversation, and pay-

1

ing no attention to the overseer's salute cursed them all into silence, and left.

Eliphalet had ambition, which is not a wholly undesirable quality. He began to wonder how it would feel to own a few of these valuable fellow-creatures. He reached out and touched lightly a young mulatto woman who sat beside him with an infant in her arms. The peculiar dumb expression on her face was lost on Eliphalet. The overseer had laughed coarsely.

"What, skeered on 'em?" said he. And seizing the girl by the cheek, gave it a cruel twinge that brought a cry out of her.

Eliphalet had reflected upon this incident after he had bid the overseer good-bye at Cairo, and had seen that pitiful coffle piled aboard a steamer for New Orleans. And the result of his reflections was, that some day he would like to own slaves.

A dome of smoke like a mushroom hung over the city, visible from far down the river, motionless in the summer air. A long line of steamboats—white, patient animals—was tethered along the levee, and the *Louisiana* presently swung in her bow toward a gap in this line, where a mass of people was awaiting her arrival. Some invisible force lifted Eliphalet's eyes to the upper deck, where they rested, as if by appointment, on the trim figure of the young man in command of the *Louisiana*. He was very young for the captain of a large New Orleans packet. When his lips moved, something happened. Once he raised his voice, and a negro stevedore rushed frantically aft, as if he had received the end of a lightning-bolt. Admiration burst from the passengers, and one man cried out Captain Brent's age—it was thirty-two.

Eliphalet snapped his teeth together. He was twenty-seven, and his ambition actually hurt him at such times. After the boat was fast to the landing stage he remained watching the captain, who was speaking a few parting words to some passengers of fashion. The body-servants were taking their luggage to the carriages. Mr. Hopper envied the captain his free and vigorous speech, his ready jokes, and his hearty laugh. All the rest he knew for his own—in times to come. The carriages, the trained servants, the obsequiousness of the humbler passengers. For of such is the Republic.

Then Eliphalet picked his way across the hot stones of the levee, pushing hither and thither in the rough crowd of river men; dodging the mules on the heavy drays, or making way for the carriages of the few people of importance who arrived on the boat. If any recollections of a cool, white farmhouse amongst barren New England hills disturbed his thoughts, this is not recorded. He gained the mouth of a street between the low houses which crowded on the broad river front. The black mud was thick under his feet from an overnight shower, and already steaming in the sun. The brick pavement was lumpy from much travel and near as dirty as the street. Here, too, were drays blocking the way, and sweaty negro teamsters swinging cowhides over the mules. The smell of many wares poured through the open doors, mingling with the perspiration of the porters. On every side of him were busy clerks, with their suspenders much in evidence, and Eliphalet paused once or twice to listen to their talk. It was tinged with that dialect he had heard since leaving Cincinnati.

Turning a corner, Eliphalet came abruptly upon a prophecy. A great drove of mules was charging down the gorge of the street, and straight at him. He dived into an entrance, and stood looking at the animals in startled wonder as they thundered by, flinging the mud over the pavements. A cursing lot of drovers on ragged horses made the rear guard.

Eliphalet mopped his brow. The mules seemed to have aroused in him some sense of his atomity, where the sight of the pillar of smoke and of the black cattle had failed. The feeling of a stranger in a strange land was upon him at last. A strange land, indeed! Could it be one with his native New England? Did Congress assemble from the antipodes? Wasn't the great, ugly river and dirty city at the end of the earth, to be written about in Boston journals?

Turning in the doorway, he saw to his astonishment a great store, with high ceilings supported by columns. The floor was stacked high with bales of dry goods. Beside him was a sign in gold lettering, "Carvel and Company, Wholesale Dry Goods." And lastly, looking down upon him with a quizzical expression, was a gentleman. There was no mistaking the gentleman. He was cool, which Eliphalet was not. And the fact is the more remarkable because the gentleman was attired according to the fashion of the day for men of his age, in a black coat with a deal of ruffled shirt showing, and a heavy black stock wound around his collar. He had a white mustache, and a goatee, and white hair under his black felt hat. His face was long, his nose straight, and the sweetness of his smile had a strange effect upon Eliphalet, who stood on one foot.

"Well, sonny, scared of mules, are you?" The speech is a stately drawl very different from the nasal twang of Eliphalet's bringing up. "Reckon you don't come from anywhere round here?"

"No, sir," said Eliphalet. "From Willesden, Massachusetts."

"Come in on the *Louisiana?*"

"Yes, sir." But why this politeness?

The elderly gentleman lighted a cigar. The noise of the rushing mules had now become a distant roar, like a whirlwind which has swept by. But Eliphalet did not stir.

"Friends in town?" inquired the gentleman at length.

"No, sir," sighed Mr. Hopper.

At this point of the conversation a crisp step sounded from behind, and the wonderful smile came again on the surface.

"Mornin', Colonel," said a voice which made Eliphalet jump. And he swung around to perceive the young captain of the *Louisiana*.

"Why, Captain Lige," cried the Colonel, without ceremony, "and how do you find yourself to-day, suh? A good trip from Orleans? We did not look for you so soon."

"Tolluble, Colonel, tolluble," said the young man, grasping the Colonel's hand. "Well, Colonel, I just called to say that I got the seventy bales of goods you wanted."

"Ephum!" cried the Colonel, diving toward a counter where glasses were set out,—a custom new to Eliphalet,—"Ephum, some of that very particular Colonel Crittenden sent me over from Kentucky last week."

An old darkey, with hair as white as the Colonel's, appeared from behind the partition.

"I 'lowed you'd want it, Marse Comyn, when I seed de Cap'n comin'," said he, with the privilege of an old servant. Indeed, the bottle was beneath his arm.

The Colonel smiled.

"Hope you'se well, Cap'n," said Ephum, as he drew the cork.

"Tolluble, Ephum," replied the Captain. "But, Ephum! Say, Ephum!"

"Yes, *sah.*"

"How's my little sweetheart, Ephum?"

"Bress your soul, sah," said Ephum, his face falling perceptibly, "bress your soul, sah, Miss Jinny's done gone to Halcyondale, in Kaintuck, to see her grandma. Ole Ephum ain't de same nigger when she's away."

The young Captain's face showed as much disappointment as the darkey's.

"Cuss it!" said he, strongly, "if that ain't too bad! I brought her a

Creole doll from New Orleans, which Madame Claire said was dressed finer than any one she'd ever seen. All lace and French gewgaws, Colonel. But you'll send it to her?"

"That I will, Lige," said the Colonel, heartily. "And she shall write you the prettiest note of thanks you ever got."

"Bless her pretty face," cried the Captain. "Her health, Colonel! Here's a long life to Miss Virginia Carvel, and may she rule forever! How old did you say this was?" he asked, looking into the glass.

"Over half a century," said Colonel Carvel.

"If it came from the ruins of Pompeii," cried Captain Brent, "it might be worthy of her!"

"What an idiot you are about that child, Lige," said the Colonel, who was not hiding his pleasure. The Colonel could hide nothing. "You ruin her!"

The bluff young Captain put down his glass to laugh.

"Ruin her!" he exclaimed. "Her pa don't ruin her! eh, Ephum? Her pa don't ruin her!"

"Lawsy, Marse Lige, I reckon he's wuss'n any."

"Ephum," said the Colonel, pulling his goatee thoughtfully, "you're a damned impertinent nigger. I vow I'll sell you South one of these days. Have you taken that letter to Mr. Rénault?" He winked at his friend as the old darkey faded into the darkness of the store, and continued: "Did I ever tell you about Willson Peale's portrait of my grandmother, Dorothy Carvel, that I saw this summer at my brother Daniel's, in Pennsylvania? Jinny's going to look something like her, sir. Um! She was a fine woman. Black hair, though. Jinny's is brown, like her Ma's." The Colonel handed a cigar to Captain Brent, and lit one himself. "Daniel has a book my grandfather wrote, mostly about her. Lord, I remember her! She was the queen-bee of the family while she lived. I wish some of us had her spirit."

"Colonel," remarked Captain Lige, "what's this I heard on the levee just now about your shootin' at a man named Babcock on the steps here?"

The Colonel became very grave. His face seemed to grow longer as he pulled his goatee.

"He was standing right where you are, sir," he replied (Captain Lige moved), "and he proposed that I should buy his influence."

"What did you do?"

Colonel Carvel laughed quietly at the recollection. "Shucks," said he, "I just pushed him into the street, gave him a little start, and put a bullet past his ear, just to let the trash know the sound of it. Then Russell went down and bailed me out."

The Captain shook with laughter. But Mr. Eliphalet Hopper's eyes were glued to the mild-mannered man who told the story, and his hair rose under his hat.

"By the way, Lige, how's that boy, Tato? Somehow after I let you have him on the *Louisiana,* I thought I'd made a mistake to let him run the river. Easter's afraid he'll lose the little religion she taught him."

It was the Captain's turn to be grave.

"I tell you what, Colonel," said he; "we have to have hands, of course. But somehow I wish this business of slavery had never been started!"

"Sir," said the Colonel, with some force, "God made the sons of Ham the servants of Japheth's sons forever and forever."

"Well, well, we won't quarrel about that, sir," said Brent, quickly. "If they all treated slaves as you do, there wouldn't be any cry from Boston-way. And as for me, I need hands. I shall see you again, Colonel."

"Take supper with me to-night, Lige," said Mr. Carvel. "I reckon you'll find it rather lonesome without Jinny."

"Awful lonesome," said the Captain. "But you'll show me her letters, won't you?"

He started out, and ran against Eliphalet.

"Hello!" he cried. "Who's this?"

"A young Yankee you landed here this morning, Lige," said the Colonel. "What do you think of him?"

"Humph!" exclaimed the Captain.

"He has no friends in town, and he is looking for employment. Isn't that so, sonny?" asked the Colonel, kindly.

"Yes."

"Come, Lige, would you take him?" said Mr. Carvel.

The young Captain looked into Eliphalet's face. The dart that shot from his eyes was of an aggressive honesty; and Mr. Hopper's, after an attempt at defiance, were dropped.

"No," said the Captain.

"Why not, Lige?"

"Well, for one thing, he's been listening," said Captain Lige, as he departed.

Colonel Carvel began to hum softly to himself:—

> " 'One said it was an owl, and the other he said nay,
> One said it was a church with the steeple torn away,
> Look a' there now!'

"I reckon you're a rank abolitionist," said he to Eliphalet, abruptly.

"I don't see any particular harm in keepin' slaves," Mr. Hopper replied, shifting to the other foot.

Whereupon the Colonel stretched his legs apart, seized his goatee, pulled his head down, and gazed at him for some time from under his eyebrows, so searchingly that the blood flew to Mr. Hopper's fleshy face. He mopped it with a dark-red handkerchief, stared at everything in the place save the gentleman in front of him, and wondered whether he had ever in his life been so uncomfortable. Then he smiled sheepishly, hated himself, and began to hate the Colonel.

"Ever hear of the *Liberator?*"

"No, sir," said Mr. Hopper.

"Where *do* you come from?" This was downright directness, from which there was no escape.

"Willesden, Massachusetts."

"Umph! And never heard of Mr. Garrison?"

"I've had to work all my life."

"What can you do, sonny?"

"I callate to sweep out a store. I have kept books," Mr. Hopper vouchsafed.

"Would you like work here?" asked the Colonel, kindly.

The green eyes looked up swiftly, and down again.

"What'll you give me?"

The good man was surprised. "Well," said he, "seven dollars a week."

Many a time in after life had the Colonel reason to think over this scene. He was a man the singleness of whose motives could not be questioned. The one and sufficient reason for giving work to a homeless boy, from the hated state of the *Liberator,* was charity. The Colonel had his moods, like many another worthy man.

The small specks on the horizon sometimes grow into the hugest of thunder clouds. And an act of charity, out of the wisdom of God, may produce on this earth either good or evil.

Eliphalet closed with the bargain. Ephum was called and told to lead the recruit to the presence of Mr. Hood, the manager. And he spent the remainder of a hot day checking invoices in the shipping entrance on Second Street.

It is not our place here to chronicle Eliphalet's faults. Whatever he may have been, he was not lazy. But he was an anomaly to the rest of the young men in the store, for those were days when political sentiments decided fervent loves or hatreds. In two days was Eliphalet's reputation for wisdom made. During that period he opened his mouth to speak but twice. The first was in answer to a pointless question of Mr. Barbo's (*ætat* 25), to the effect that he, Eliphalet Hopper, was a Pierce Democrat, who looked with complacency on the extension of slavery. This was wholly satisfactory, and saved the owner of these sentiments a broken head. The other time Eliphalet spoke was to ask Mr. Barbo to direct him to a boarding-house.

"I reckon," Mr. Barbo reflected, "that you'll want one of them Congregational boarding-houses. We've got a heap of Yankees in the town, and they all flock together and pray together. I reckon you'd ruther go to Miss Crane's nor anywhere."

Forthwith to Miss Crane's Eliphalet went. And that lady, being a Greek herself, knew a Greek when she saw one. The kind-hearted Barbo lingered in the gathering darkness to witness the game which ensued, a game dear to all New Englanders, comical to Barbo. The two contestants *calculated*. Barbo *reckoned,* and put his money on his new-found fellow-clerk. Eliphalet, indeed, never showed to better advantage. The shyness he had used with the Colonel, and the taciturnity practised on his fellow-clerks, he slipped off like coat and waistcoat for the battle. The scene was in the front yard of the third house in Dorcas Row. Everybody knows where Dorcas Row was. Miss Crane, tall, with all the severity of side curls and bombazine, stood like a stone lioness at the gate. In the background, by the steps, the boarders sat, an interested group. Eliphalet girded up his loins, and sharpened his nasal twang to cope with hers. The preliminary sparring was an exchange of compliments, and deceived neither party. It seemed rather to heighten mutual respect.

"You be from Willesden, eh?" said Crane. "I calculate you know the Salters."

If the truth were known, this evidence of an apparent omniscience rather staggered Eliphalet. But training stood by him, and he showed no dismay. Yes, he knew the Salters, and had drawed many a load out of Hiram Salters' wood-lot to help pay for his schooling.

"Let me see," said Miss Crane, innocently; "who was it one of them

Salters girls married, and lived across the way from the meetin'-house?"

"Spauldin'," was the prompt reply.

"Wal, I want t' know!" cried the spinster; "not Ezra Spauldin'?"

Eliphalet nodded. That nod was one of infinite shrewdness which commended itself to Miss Crane. These courtesies, far from making awkward the material discussion which followed, did not affect it in the least.

"So you want me to board you?" said she, as if in consternation.

Eliphalet calculated, if they could come to terms. And Mr. Barbo keyed himself to enjoyment.

"Single gentlemen," said she, "pay as high as twelve dollars." And she added that they had no cause to complain of her table.

Eliphalet said he guessed he'd have to go somewhere else. Upon this the lady vouchsafed the explanation that those gentlemen had high positions and rented her large rooms. Since Mr. Hopper was from Willesden and knew the Salters, she would be willing to take him for less. Eliphalet said bluntly he would give three and a half. Barbo gasped. This particular kind of courage was wholly beyond him.

Half an hour later Eliphalet carried his carpet-bag up three flights and put it down in a tiny bedroom under the eaves, still pulsing with heat waves. Here he was to live, and eat at Miss Crane's table for the consideration of four dollars a week.

Such is the story of the humble beginning of one substantial prop of the American Nation. And what a hackneyed story it is! How many other young men from the East have travelled across the mountains and floated down the rivers to enter those strange cities of the West, the growth of which was like Jonah's gourd.

Two centuries before, when Charles Stuart walked out of a window in Whitehall Palace to die; when the great English race was in the throes of a Civil War; when the Stern and the Gay slew each other at Naseby and Marston Moor, two currents flowed across the Atlantic to the New World. Then the Stern men found the stern climate, and the Gay found the smiling climate.

After many years the streams began to move again,—westward, ever westward. Over the ever blue mountains from the wonderland of Virginia into the greater wonderland of Kentucky. And through the marvels of the Inland Seas, and by white conestogas threading flat forests and floating over wide prairies, until the two tides met in a maelstrom as fierce as any in the great tawny torrent of the strange Father of Waters. A city founded by Pierre Laclede, a certain adventurous subject of Louis who dealt in furs, and who knew not Marly or Versailles, was to be the place of the mingling of the tides. After cycles of separation, Puritan and Cavalier united on this clay-bank in the Louisiana Purchase, and swept westward together. Like the struggle of two great rivers when they meet, the waters for a while were dangerous.

So Eliphalet was established, among the Puritans, at Miss Crane's. The dishes were to his taste. Brown bread and beans and pies were plentiful, for it was a land of plenty. All kinds of Puritans were there, and they attended Mr. Davitt's Congregational Church. And may it be added in justice to Mr. Hopper, that he became not the least devout of the boarders.

CHAPTER II

THE MOLE

FOR some years, while Stephen A. Douglas and Franklin Pierce and other gentlemen of prominence were playing at bowls on the United States of America; while Kansas was furnishing excitement free of charge to any citizen who loved sport, Mr. Eliphalet Hopper was at work like the industrious mole, underground. It is safe to affirm that Colonel Carvel forgot his new hand as soon as he had turned him over to Mr. Hood, the manager. As for Mr. Hopper, he was content. We can ill afford to dissect motives. Genius is willing to lay the foundations of her structure unobserved.

At first it was Mr. Barbo alone who perceived Eliphalet's greatness, —Mr. Barbo, whose opinions were so easily had that they counted for nothing. The other clerks, to say the least, found the newcomer uncompanionable. He had no time for skylarking, the heat of the day meant nothing to him, and he was never sleepy. He learned the stock as if by intuition, and such was his strict attention to business that Mr. Hood was heard to say, privately, he did not like the looks of it. A young man should have other interests. And then, although he would not hold it against him, he had heard that Mr. Hopper was a teacher in Mr. Davitt's Sunday School.

Because he did not discuss his ambitions at dinner with the other clerks in the side entry, it must not be thought that Eliphalet was without other interests. He was likewise too shrewd to be dragged into political discussions at the boarding-house table. He listened imperturbably to the outbursts against the Border Ruffian, and smiled when Mr. Abner Reed, in an angry passion, asked him to declare whether or not he was a friend of the Divine Institution. After a while they forgot about him (all save Miss Crane), which was what Mr. Hopper of all things desired.

One other friend besides Miss Crane did Eliphalet take unto himself, wherein he showed much discrimination. This friend was none other than Mr. Davitt, minister for many years of the Congregational Church. For Mr. Davitt was a good man, zealous in his work, unpretentious, and

11

kindly. More than once Eliphalet went to his home to tea, and was pressed to talk about himself and his home life. The minister and his wife were invariably astonished, after their guest was gone, at the meagre result of their inquiries.

If Love had ever entered such a discreet soul as that into which we are prying, he used a back entrance. Even Mr. Barbo's inquiries failed in the discovery of any young person with whom Eliphalet "kept company." Whatever the notions abroad concerning him, he was admittedly a model. There are many kinds of models. With some young ladies at the Sunday School, indeed, he had a distant bowing acquaintance. They spoke of him as the young man who knew the Bible as thoroughly as Mr. Davitt himself. The only time that Mr. Hopper was discovered showing embarrassment was when Mr. Davitt held his hand before them longer than necessary on the church steps. Mr. Hopper was not sentimental.

However fascinating the subject, I do not propose to make a whole book about Eliphalet. Yet sidelights on the life of every great man are interesting. And there are a few incidents in his early career which have not gotten into the subscription biographical Encyclopædias. In several of these volumes, to be sure, we may see steel engravings of him, true likenesses all. His was the type of face which is the glory of the steel engraving,—square and solid, as a corner-stone should be. The very clothes he wore were made for the steel engraving, stiff and wiry in texture, with sharp angles at the shoulders, and sombre in hue, as befit such grave creations.

Let us go back to a certain fine morning in the September of the year 1857, when Mr. Hopper had arrived, all unnoticed, at the age of two and thirty. Industry had told. He was now the manager's assistant; and, be it said in passing, knew more about the stock than Mr. Hood himself. On this particular morning, about nine o'clock, he was stacking bolts of woollen goods near that delectable counter where the Colonel was wont to regale his principal customers, when a vision appeared in the door. Visions were rare at Carvel & Company's. This one was followed by an old negress with leathery wrinkles, whose smile was joy incarnate. They entered the store, paused at the entrance to the Colonel's private office, and surveyed it with dismay.

"'Clar t' goodness, Miss Jinny, yo' pa ain't heah! An' whah's Ephum, dat black good-fo'-nuthin'!"

Miracle number one,—Mr. Hopper stopped work and stared. The vision was searching the store with her eyes, and pouting.

"How mean of Pa!" she exclaimed, "when I took all this trouble to surprise him, not to be here! Where are they all? Where's Ephum? Where's Mr. Hood?"

The eyes lighted on Eliphalet. His blood was sluggish, but it could be made to beat faster. The ladies he had met at Miss Crane's were not of this description. As he came forward, embarrassment made him shamble, and for the first time in his life he was angrily conscious of a poor figure. Her first question dashed out the spark of his zeal.

"Oh," said she, "are you employed here?"

Thoughtless Virginia! You little know the man you have insulted by your haughty drawl.

"Yes."

"Then find Mr. Carvel, won't you, please? And tell him that his daughter has come from Kentucky, and is waiting for him."

"I callate Mr. Carvel won't be here this morning," said Eliphalet. He went back to the pile of dry goods, and began to work. But he was unable to meet the displeasure in her face.

"What is your name?" Miss Carvel demanded.

"Hopper."

"Then, Mr. Hopper, please find Ephum, or Mr. Hood."

Two more bolts were taken off the truck. Out of the corner of his eye he watched her, and she seemed very tall, like her father. She was taller than he, in fact.

"I ain't a servant, Miss Carvel," he said, with a meaning glance at the negress.

"Laws, Miss Jinny," cried she, "I may's 'ell find Ephum. I knows he's loafin' somewhar hereabouts. An' I ain't seed him dese five month." And she started for the back of the store.

"Mammy!"

The old woman stopped short. Eliphalet, electrified, looked up and instantly down again.

"You say you are employed by Mr. Carvel, and refuse to do what I ask?"

"I ain't a servant," Mr. Hopper repeated doggedly. He felt that he was in the right,—and perhaps he was.

It was at this critical juncture in the proceedings that a young man stepped lightly into the store behind Miss Jinny. Mr. Hopper's eye was on him, and had taken in the details of his costume before realizing the import of his presence. He was perhaps twenty, and wore a coat that sprung in at the waist, and trousers of a light buff-color that gathered at the ankle and were very copious above. His features were of the straight type which has been called from time immemorial *patrician*. He had dark hair which escaped in waves from under his hat, and black eyes that snapped when they perceived Miss Virginia Carvel. At sight of her, indeed, the gold-headed cane stopped in its gyrations in midair.

"Why, Jinny!" he cried—"Jinny!"

Mr. Hopper would have sold his soul to have been in the young man's polished boots, to have worn his clothes, and to have been able to cry out to the young lady, "Why, Jinny!"

To Mr. Hopper's surprise, the young lady did not turn around. She stood perfectly still. But a red flush stole upon her cheek, and laughter was dancing in her eyes. Yet she did not move. The young man took a step forward, and then stood staring at her with such a comical expression of injury on his face as was too much for Miss Jinny's serenity. She laughed. That laugh also struck minor chords upon Mr. Hopper's heart-strings.

But the young gentleman very properly grew angry.

"You've no right to treat me the way you do, Virginia," he cried. "Why didn't you let me know that you were coming home?" His tone was one of authority. "You didn't come from Kentucky alone!"

"I had plenty of attendance, I assure you," said Miss Carvel. "A governor, and a senator, and two charming young gentlemen from New Orleans as far as Cairo, where I found Captain Lige's boat. And Mr. Brinsmade brought me here to the store. I wanted to surprise Pa," she continued rapidly, to head off the young gentleman's expostulations. "How mean of him not to be here!"

"Allow me to escort you home," said he, with ceremony.

"Allow me to decline the honah, Mr. Colfax," she cried, imitating him. "I intend to wait here until Pa comes in."

Then Eliphalet knew that the young gentleman was Miss Virginia's first cousin. And it seemed to him that he had heard a rumor, amongst the clerks in the store, that she was to marry him one day.

"Where is Uncle Comyn?" demanded Mr. Colfax, swinging his cane with impatience.

Virginia looked hard at Mr. Hopper.

"I don't know," she said.

"Ephum!" shouted Mr. Colfax. "Ephum! Easter, where the deuce is that good-for-nothing husband of yours?"

"I dunno, Marse Clarence. 'Spec he whah he oughtn't ter be."

Mr. Colfax spied the stooping figure of Eliphalet.

"Do you work here?" he demanded.

"I callate."

"What?"

"I callate to," responded Mr. Hopper again, without rising.

"Please find Mr. Hood," directed Mr. Colfax, with a wave of his cane, "and say that Miss Carvel is here—"

Whereupon Miss Carvel seated herself upon the edge of a bale and giggled, which did not have a soothing effect upon either of the young men. How abominably you were wont to behave in those days, Virginia.

"Just say that Mr. Colfax sent you," Clarence continued, with a note of irritation. "There's a good fellow."

Virginia laughed outright. Her cousin did not deign to look at her. His temper was slipping its leash.

"I wonder whether you hear me," he remarked.

No answer.

"Colonel Carvel hires you, doesn't he? He pays you wages, and the first time his daughter comes in here you refuse to do her a favor. By thunder, I'll see that you are dismissed."

Still Eliphalet gave him no manner of attention, but began marking the tags at the bottom of the pile.

It was at this unpropitious moment that Colonel Carvel walked into the store, and his daughter flew into his arms.

"Well, well," he said, kissing her, "thought you'd surprise me, eh, Jinny?"

"Oh, Pa," she cried, looking reproachfully up at his face. "You knew —how mean of you!"

"I've been down on the *Louisiana,* where some inconsiderate man told me, or I should not have seen you to-day. I was off to Alton. But what are these goings-on?" said the Colonel, staring at young Mr. Colfax, rigid as one of his own gamecocks. He was standing defiantly over the stooping figure of the assistant manager.

"Oh," said Virginia, indifferently, "it's only Clarence. He's so tiresome. He's always wanting to fight with somebody."

"What's the matter, Clarence?" asked the Colonel, with the mild concern which deceived so many of the undiscerning.

"This person, sir, refused to do a favor for your daughter. She told him, and I told him, to notify Mr. Hood that Miss Carvel was here, and he refused."

Mr. Hopper continued his occupation, which was absorbing. But he was listening.

Colonel Carvel pulled his goatee, and smiled.

"Clarence," said he, "I reckon I can run this establishment without any help from you and Jinny. I've been at it now for a good many years."

If Mr. Barbo had not been constitutionally unlucky, he might have perceived Mr. Hopper, before dark that evening, in conversation with Mr. Hood about a certain customer who lived up town, and presently leave the store by the side entrance. He walked as rapidly as his legs would carry him, for they were a trifle short for his body; and in due time, as the lamps were flickering, he arrived near Colonel Carvel's large double residence, on Tenth and Locust streets. Then he walked slowly along Tenth, his eyes lifted to the tall, curtained windows. Now and anon they scanned passers-by for a chance acquaintance.

Mr. Hopper walked around the block, arriving again opposite the Carvel house, and beside Mr. Rénault's, which was across from it. Eliphalet had inherited the principle of mathematical chances. It is a fact that the discreet sometimes take chances. Towards the back of Mr. Rénault's residence, a wide area was sunk to the depth of a tall man, which was apparently used for the purpose of getting coal and wood into the cellar. Mr. Hopper swept the neighborhood with a glance. The coast was clear, and he dropped into the area.

Although the evening was chill, at first Mr. Hopper perspired very freely. He crouched in the area while the steps of pedestrians beat above his head, and took no thought but of escape. At last, however, he grew cooler, removed his hat, and peeped over the stone coping. Colonel Carvel's house—*her* house—was now ablaze with lights, and the shades not yet drawn. There was the dining room, where the negro butler was moving about the table; and the pantry, where the butler went occasionally; and the kitchen, with black figures moving about. But upstairs on the two streets was the sitting room. The straight figure of the

Colonel passed across the light. He held a newspaper in his hand. Suddenly, full in the window, he stopped and flung away the paper. A graceful shadow slipped across the wall. Virginia laid her hands on his shoulders, and he stooped to kiss her. Now they sat between the curtains, she on the arm of his chair and leaning on him, together looking out of the window.

How long this lasted Mr. Hopper could not say. Even the wise forget themselves. But all at once a wagon backed and bumped against the curb in front of him, and Eliphalet's head dropped as if it had been struck by the wheel. Above him a sash screamed as it opened, and he heard Mr. Rénault's voice say, to some person below:—

"Is that you, Capitaine Grant?"

"The same," was the brief reply.

"I am charmed that you have brought the wood. I thought that you had forgotten me."

"I try to do what I say, Mr. Rénault."

"Attendez—wait!" cried Mr. Rénault, and closed the window.

Now was Eliphalet's chance to bolt. The perspiration had come again, and it was cold. But directly the excitable little man, Rénault, had appeared on the pavement above him. He had been running.

"It is a long voyage from Gravois with a load of wood. Capitaine—I am very grateful."

"Business is business, Mr. Rénault," was the self-contained reply.

"Alphonse!" cried Mr. Rénault, "Alphonse!" A door opened in the back wall. "Du vin pour Monsieur le Capitaine."

"Oui, M'sieu."

Eliphalet was too frightened to wonder why this taciturn handler of wood was called Captain, and treated with such respect.

"Guess I won't take any wine to-night, Mr. Rénault," said he. "You go inside, or you'll take cold."

Mr. Rénault protested, asked about all the residents of Gravois way, and finally obeyed. Eliphalet's heart was in his mouth. A bolder spirit would have dashed for liberty. Eliphalet did not possess that kind of bravery. He was waiting for the Captain to turn toward his wagon.

He looked down the area instead, with the light from the street lamp on his face. Fear etched an ineffaceable portrait of him on Mr. Hopper's mind, so that he knew him instantly when he saw him years afterward. Little did he reckon that the fourth time he was to see him this man was to be President of the United States. He wore a close-cropped beard, an old blue army overcoat, and his trousers were tucked into a pair of muddy cowhide boots.

Swiftly but silently the man reached down and hauled Eliphalet to the sidewalk by the nape of the neck.

"What were you doing there?" demanded he of the blue overcoat, sternly.

Eliphalet did not answer. With one frantic wrench he freed himself, and ran down Locust Street. At the corner, turning fearfully, he perceived the man in the overcoat calmly preparing to unload his wood.

CHAPTER III

THE UNATTAINABLE SIMPLICITY

To Mr. Hopper the being caught was the unpardonable crime. And indeed, with many of us, it is humiliation and not conscience which makes the sting. He walked out to the end of the city's growth westward, where the new houses were going up. He had reflected coolly on consequences, and found there were none to speak of. Many a moralist, Mr. Davitt included, would have shaken his head at this. Miss Crane's whole Puritan household would have raised their hands in horror at such a doctrine.

Some novelists I know of, who are in reality celebrated surgeons in disguise, would have shown a good part of Mr. Eliphalet Hopper's mental insides in as many words as I have taken to chronicle his arrival in St. Louis. They invite us to attend a clinic, and the horrible skill with which they wield the scalpel holds us spellbound. For God has made all of us, rogue and saint, burglar and burgomaster, marvellously alike. We read a patent medicine circular and shudder with seven diseases. We peruse one of Mr. So and So's intellectual tonics and are sure we are complicated scandals, fearfully and wonderfully made.

Alas, I have neither the skill nor the scalpel to show the diseases of Mr. Hopper's mind; if, indeed, he had any. Conscience, when contracted, is just as troublesome as croup. Mr. Hopper was thoroughly healthy. He had ambition, as I have said. But he was not morbidly sensitive. He was calm enough when he got back to the boarding-house, which he found in as high a pitch of excitement as New Englanders ever reach.

And over what?

Over the prospective arrival that evening of the Brices, mother and son, from Boston. Miss Crane had received the message in the morning. Palpitating with the news, she had hurried rustling to Mrs. Abner Reed, with the paper in her hand.

"I guess you don't mean Mrs. Appleton Brice," said Mrs. Reed.

19

"That's just who I mean," answered Miss Crane, triumphantly,—nay, aggressively.

Mrs. Abner shook her curls in a way that made people overwhelm her with proofs.

"Mirandy, you're cracked," said she. "Ain't you never been to Boston?"

Miss Crane bridled. This was an uncalled-for insult.

"I guess I visited down Boston-way oftener than you, Eliza Reed. You never had any clothes."

Mrs. Reed's strength was her imperturbability.

"And you never set eyes on the Brice house, opposite the Common, with the swelled front? I'd like to find out where you were a-visitin'. And you've never heard tell of the Brice homestead, at Westbury, that was Colonel Wilton Brice's, who fought in the Revolution? I'm astonished at you, Mirandy. When I used to be at the Dales', in Mount Vernon Street, in thirty-seven, Mrs. Charles Atterbury Brice used to come there in her carriage, a-callin'. She was Appleton's mother. Severe! Save us," exclaimed Mrs. Reed, "but she was stiff as starched crepe. His father was minister to France. The Brices were in the India trade, and they had money enough to buy the whole of St. Louis."

Miss Crane rattled the letter in her hand. She brought forth her reserves.

"Yes, and Appleton Brice lost it all, in the panic. And then he died, and left the widow and son without a cent."

Mrs. Reed took off her spectacles.

"I want to know!" she exclaimed. "The durned fool! Well, Appleton Brice didn't have the family brains, and he was kind of soft-hearted. I've heard Mehitabel Dale say that." She paused to reflect. "So they're coming here?" she added. "I wonder why."

Miss Crane's triumph was not over.

"Because Silas Whipple was some kin to Appleton Brice, and he has offered the boy a place in his law office."

Miss Reed laid down her knitting.

"Save us!" she said. "This is a day of wonders, Mirandy. Now Lord help the boy if he's goin' to work for the Judge."

"The Judge has a soft heart, if he is crabbed," declared the spinster. "I've heard say of a good bit of charity he's done. He's a soft heart."

"Soft as a green quince!" said Mrs. Abner, scornfully. "How many friends has he?"

"Those he has are warm enough," Miss Crane retorted. "Look at Colonel Carvel, who has him to dinner every Sunday."

"That's plain as your nose, Mirandy Crane. They both like quarrellin' better than anything in this world."

"Well," said Miss Crane, "I must go make ready for the Brices."

Such was the importance of the occasion, however, that she could not resist calling at Mrs. Merrill's room, and she knocked at Mrs. Chandler's door to tell that lady and her daughter.

No Burke has as yet arisen in this country of ours to write a Peerage. Fame awaits him. Indeed, it was even then awaiting him, at the time of the panic of 1857. With what infinite pains were the pedigree and possessions of the Brice family pieced together that day by the scattered residents from Puritan-land in the City of St. Louis. And few buildings would have borne the wear and tear of many house-cleanings of the kind Miss Crane indulged in throughout the morning and afternoon.

Mr. Eliphalet Hopper, on his return from business, was met on the steps and requested to wear his Sunday clothes. Like the good republican that he was, Mr. Hopper refused. He had ascertained that the golden charm which made the Brices worthy of tribute had been lost. Commercial supremacy,—that was Mr. Hopper's creed. Family is a good thing, but of what use is a crest without the panels on which to paint it? Can a diamond brooch shine on a calico gown? Mr. Hopper deemed church the place for worship. He likewise had his own idol in his closet.

Eliphalet at Willesden had heard a great deal of Boston airs and graces and intellectuality, of the favored few of that city who lived in mysterious houses, and who crossed the sea in ships. He pictured Mrs. Brice asking for a spoon, and young Stephen sniffing at Mrs. Crane's boarding-house. And he resolved with democratic spirit that he would teach Stephen a lesson, if opportunity offered. His own discrepancy between the real and the imagined was no greater than that of the rest of his fellow-boarders.

Barring Eliphalet, there was a dress parade that evening,—silks and bombazines and broadcloths, and Miss Crane's special preserves on the tea-table. Alas, that most of the deserved honors of this world should fall upon barren ground!

The quality which baffled Mr. Hopper, and some other boarders, was simplicity. None save the truly great possess it (but this is not generally known). Mrs. Brice was so natural, that first evening at tea, that all were disappointed. The hero upon the reviewing stand with the halo of the Unknown behind his head is one thing; the lady of Family who sits beside you at a boarding-house and discusses the weather and the journey is quite another. They were prepared to hear Mrs. Brice rail at the dirt of St. Louis and the crudity of the West. They pictured her referring with sighs to her Connections, and bewailing that Stephen could not have finished his course at Harvard.

She did nothing of the sort.

The first shock was so great that Mrs. Abner Reed cried in the privacy of her chamber, and the Widow Crane confessed her disappointment to the confiding ear of her bosom friend, Mrs. Merrill. Not many years later a man named Grant was to be in Springfield, with a carpet bag, despised as a vagabond. A very homely man named Lincoln went to Cincinnati to try a case before the Supreme Court, and was snubbed by a man named Stanton.

When we meet the truly great, several things may happen. In the first place, we begin to believe in their luck, or fate, or whatever we choose to call it, and to curse our own. We begin to respect ourselves the more, and to realize that they are merely clay like us, that we are great men without Opportunity. Sometimes, if we live long enough near the Great, we begin to have misgivings. Then there is hope for us.

Mrs. Brice, with her simple black gowns, quiet manner, and serene face, with her interest in others and none in herself, had a wonderful effect upon the boarders. They were nearly all prepared to be humble. They grew arrogant and pretentious. They asked Mrs. Brice if she knew this and that person of consequence in Boston, with whom they claimed relationship or intimacy. Her answers were amiable and self-contained.

But what shall we say of Stephen Brice? Let us confess at once that it is he who is the hero of this story, and not Eliphalet Hopper. It would be so easy to paint Stephen in shining colors, and to make him a first-class prig (the horror of all novelists), that we must begin with the drawbacks. First and worst, it must be confessed that Stephen had at that time what has been called "the Boston manner." This was not Stephen's fault, but Boston's. Young Mr. Brice possessed that wonderful power of expressing distance in other terms besides ells and furlongs,—and yet he was simple enough with it all.

Many a furtive stare he drew from the table that evening. There were one or two of discernment present, and they noted that his were the generous features of a marked man,—if he chose to become marked. He inherited his mother's look; hers was the face of a strong woman, wide of sympathy, broad of experience, showing peace of mind amid troubles— the touch of femininity was there to soften it.

Her son had the air of the college-bred. In these surroundings he escaped arrogance by the wonderful kindliness of his eye, which lighted when his mother spoke to him. But he was not at home at Miss Crane's table, and he made no attempt to appear at his ease.

This was an unexpected pleasure for Mr. Eliphalet Hopper. Let it not be thought that he was the only one at that table to indulge in a little secret rejoicing. But it was a peculiar satisfaction to him to reflect that these people, who had held up their heads for so many generations, were humbled at last. To be humbled meant, in Mr. Hopper's philosophy, to lose one's money. It was thus he gauged the importance of his acquaintances; it was thus he hoped some day to be gauged. And he trusted and believed that the time would come when he could give his fillip to the upper rim of fortune's wheel, and send it spinning downward.

Mr. Hopper was drinking his tea and silently forming an estimate. He concluded that young Brice was not the type to acquire the money which his father had lost. And he reflected that Stephen must feel as strange in St. Louis as a cod might amongst the cat-fish in the Mississippi. So the assistant manager of Carvel & Company resolved to indulge in the pleasure of patronizing the Bostonian.

"Callatin' to go to work?" he asked him, as the boarders walked into the best room.

"Yes," replied Stephen, taken aback. And it may be said here that, if Mr. Hopper underestimated him, certainly he underestimated Mr. Hopper.

"It ain't easy to get a job this Fall," said Eliphalet. "St. Louis houses have felt the panic."

"I am sorry to hear that."

"What business was you callatin' to grapple with?"

"Law," said Stephen.

"Gosh!" exclaimed Mr. Hopper, "I want to know." In reality he was a bit chagrined, having pictured with some pleasure the Boston aristocrat going from store to store for a situation. "You didn't come here figurin' on makin' a pile, I guess."

"A what?"

"A pile."

Stephen looked down and over Mr. Hopper attentively. He took in the blocky shoulders and the square head, and he pictured the little eyes at a vanishing-point in lines of a bargain. Then humor—blessed humor—came to his rescue. He had entered the race in the West, where all start equal. He had come here, like this man who was succeeding, to make his living. Would he succeed?

Mr. Hopper drew something out of his pocket, eyed Miss Crane, and bit off a corner.

"What office was you going into?" he asked genially.

Mr. Brice decided to answer that.

"Judge Whipple's—unless he has changed his mind."

Eliphalet gave him a look more eloquent than words.

"Know the Judge?"

"No."

Silent laughter.

"If all the Fourth of Julys we've had was piled into one," said Mr. Hopper, slowly and with conviction, "they wouldn't be a circumstance to Silas Whipple when he gets mad. My boss, Colonel Carvel, is the only man in town who'll stand up to him. I've seen 'em begin a quarrel in the store and carry it all the way up the street. I callate you won't stay with him a great while."

CHAPTER IV

BLACK CATTLE

LATER that evening Stephen Brice was sitting by the open windows in his mother's room, looking silently down on the street-lights below.

"Well, my dear," asked the lady, at length, "what do you think of it all?"

"They are kind people," he said.

"Yes, they are kind," she assented, with a sigh. "But they are not—they are not from among our friends, Stephen."

"I thought that one of our reasons for coming West, mother," answered Stephen.

His mother looked pained.

"Stephen, how can you! We came West in order that you might have more chance for the career to which you are entitled. Our friends in Boston were more than good."

He left the window and came and stood behind her chair, his hands clasped playfully beneath her chin.

"Have you the exact date about you, mother?"

"What date, Stephen?"

"When I shall leave St. Louis for the United States Senate. And you must not forget that there is a youth limit in our Constitution for senators."

Then the widow smiled,—a little sadly, perhaps. But still a wonderfully sweet smile. And it made her strong face akin to all that was human and helpful.

"I believe that you have the subject of my first speech in that august assembly. And, by the way, what was it?"

"It was on 'The Status of the Emigrant,' " she responded instantly, thereby proving that she was his mother.

"And it touched the Rights of Privacy," he added, laughing, "which do not seem to exist in St. Louis boarding-houses."

"In the eyes of your misguided profession, statesmen and authors and emigrants and other public charges have no Rights of Privacy," said

25

she. "Mr. Longfellow told me once that they were to name a brand of flour for him, and that he had no redress."

"Have you, too, been up before Miss Crane's Commission?" he asked, with amused interest.

His mother laughed.

"Yes," she said quietly.

"They have some expert members," he continued. "This Mrs. Abner Reed could be a shining light in any bar. I overheard a part of her cross-examination. She—she had evidently studied our case—"

"My dear," answered Mrs. Brice, "I suppose they know all about us." She was silent a moment—"I had so hoped that they wouldn't. They lead the same narrow life in this house that they did in their little New England towns. They—they pity us, Stephen."

"Mother!"

"I did not expect to find so many New Englanders here—I wish that Mr. Whipple had directed us elsewhere—"

"He probably thought that we should feel at home among New Englanders. I hope the Southerners will be more considerate. I believe they will," he added.

"They are very proud," said his mother. "A wonderful people,—born aristocrats. You don't remember those Randolphs with whom we travelled through England. They were with us at Hollingdean, Lord Northwell's place. You were too small at the time. There was a young girl, Eleanor Randolph, a beauty. I shall never forget the way she entered those English drawing-rooms. They visited us once in Beacon Street, afterwards. And I have heard that there are a great many good Southern families here in St. Louis."

"You did not glean that from Judge Whipple's letter, mother," said Stephen, mischievously.

"He was very frank in his letter," sighed Mrs. Brice.

"I imagine he is always frank, to put it delicately."

"Your father always spoke in praise of Silas Whipple, my dear. I have heard him call him one of the ablest lawyers in the country. He won a remarkable case for Appleton here, and he once said that the Judge would have sat on the Supreme Bench if he had not been pursued with such relentlessness by rascally politicians."

"The Judge indulges in a little relentlessness now and then, himself. He is not precisely what might be termed a mild man, if what we hear is correct."

Mrs. Brice started.

"What have you heard?" she asked.

"Well, there was a gentleman on the steamboat who said that it took more courage to enter the Judge's private office than to fight a Border Ruffian. And another, a young lawyer, who declared that he would rather face a wild cat than ask Whipple a question on the new code. And yet he said that the Judge knew more law than any man in the West. And lastly, there is a polished gentleman named Hopper here from Massachusetts who enlightened me a little more."

Stephen paused and bit his tongue. He saw that she was distressed by these things. Heaven knows that she had borne enough trouble in the last few months.

"Come, mother," he said gently, "you should know how to take my jokes by this time. I didn't mean it. I am sure the Judge is a good man, —one of those aggressive good men who make enemies. I have but a single piece of guilt to accuse him of."

"And what is that?" asked the widow.

"The cunning forethought which he is showing in wishing to have it said that a certain Senator and Judge Brice was trained in his office."

"Stephen—you goose!" she said.

Her eye wandered around the room—Widow Crane's best bedroom. It was dimly lighted by an extremely ugly lamp. The hideous stuffy bed curtains and the more hideous imitation marble mantel were the two objects that held her glance. There was no change in her calm demeanor. But Stephen, who knew his mother, felt that her little elation over her arrival had ebbed. Neither would confess dejection to the other.

"I—even I—" said Stephen, tapping his chest, "have at least made the acquaintance of one prominent citizen, Mr. Eliphalet D. Hopper. According to Mr. Dickens, he is a true American gentleman, for he chews tobacco. He has been in St. Louis five years, is now assistant manager of the largest dry goods house, and still lives in one of Miss Crane's four-dollar rooms. I think we may safely say that he will be a millionaire before I am a senator."

He paused.

"And mother?"

"Yes, dear."

He put his hands in his pockets and walked over to the window.

"I think that it would be better if I did the same thing."

"What do you mean, my son—"

"If I went to work,—started sweeping out a store, I mean. See here, mother, you've sacrificed enough for me already. After paying father's debts, we've come out here with only a few thousand dollars, and the nine hundred I saved out of this year's Law School allowance. What shall we do when that is gone? The honorable legal profession, as my friend reminded me to-night, is not the swiftest road to millions."

With a mother's discernment she guessed the agitation he was striving to hide; she knew that he had been gathering courage for this moment for months. And she knew that he was renouncing thus lightly, for her sake, an ambition he had had from his school days.

The widow passed her hand over her brow. It was a space before she answered him.

"My son," she said, "let us never speak of this again. It was your father's dearest wish that you should become a lawyer, and—and his wishes are sacred. God will take care of us."

She rose and kissed him good-night.

"Remember, my dear, when you go to Judge Whipple in the morning, remember his kindness, and—"

"And keep my temper. I shall, mother."

A while later he stole gently back into her room again. She was on her knees by the walnut bedstead.

At nine the next morning Stephen left Miss Crane's, girded for the struggle with the redoubtable Silas Whipple. He was not afraid, but a poor young man as an applicant to a notorious dragon is not likely to be handled with velvet, even though the animal had been a friend of his father. Dragons as a rule have had a hard time in their youth, and believe in others' having a hard time.

To a young man, who as his father's heir in Boston had been the subject of marked consideration by his elders, the situation was keenly distasteful. But it had to be gone through. So presently, after inquiry, he came to the open square where the new Court House stood, the dome of which was indicated by a mass of staging, and one wing still to be completed. Across from the building, on Market Street, and in the middle of the block, what had once been a golden hand pointed up a narrow dusty stairway. Here was a sign, "Law office of Silas Whipple."

Stephen climbed the stairs, and arrived at a ground-glass door, on which the sign was repeated. Behind that door was the future: so he opened it fearfully, with an impulse to throw his arm above his head.

But he was struck dumb on beholding, instead of a dragon, a good-natured young man who smiled a broad welcome. The reaction was as great as though one entered a dragon's den, armed to the teeth, to find a St. Bernard doing the honors.

Stephen's heart went out to this young man,—after that organ had jumped back into its place. This keeper of the dragon looked the part. Even the long black coat which custom then decreed could not hide the bone and sinew under it. The young man had a broad forehead, placid Dresden-blue eyes, flaxen hair, and the German coloring. Across one of his high cheek-bones was a great jagged scar which seemed to add distinction to his appearance. That caught Stephen's eye, and held it. He wondered whether it were the result of an encounter with the Judge.

"You wish to see Mr. Whipple?" he asked, in the accents of an educated German.

"Yes," said Stephen, "if he isn't busy."

"He is out," said the other, with just a suspicion of a *a* in the word. "You know he is much occupied now, fighting election frauds. You read the papers?"

"I am a stranger here," said Stephen.

"Ach!" exclaimed the German, "now I know you, Mr. Brice. The young one from Boston the Judge spoke of. But you did not tell him of your arrival."

"I did not wish to bother him," Stephen replied, smiling.

"My name is Richter—Carl Richter, sir."

The pressure of Mr. Richter's big hands warmed Stephen as nothing else had since he had come West. He was moved to return it with a little more fervor than he usually showed. And he felt, whatever the Judge might be, that he had a powerful friend near at hand—Mr. Richter's welcome came near being an embrace.

"Sit down, Mr. Brice," he said; "mild weather for November, eh? The Judge will be here in an hour."

Stephen looked around him: at the dusty books on the shelves, and the still dustier books heaped on Mr. Richter's big table; at the cuspidors; at the engravings of Washington and Webster; at the window in the jog which looked out on the court-house square; and finally at another ground-glass door on which was printed:—

SILAS WHIPPLE

PRIVATE

This, then, was the den,—the arena in which was to take place a memorable interview. But the thought of waiting an hour for the dragon to appear was disquieting. Stephen remembered that he had something over nine hundred dollars in his pocket (which he had saved out of his last year's allowance at the Law School). So he asked Mr. Richter, who was dusting off a chair, to direct him to the nearest bank.

"Why, certainly," said he; "Mr. Brinsmade's bank on Chestnut Street." He took Stephen to the window and pointed across the square. "I am sorry I cannot go with you," he added, "but the Judge's negro, Shadrach, is out, and I must stay in the office. I will give you a note to Mr. Brinsmade."

"His negro!" exclaimed Stephen. "Why, I thought that Mr. Whipple was an Abolitionist."

Mr. Richter laughed.

"The man is free," said he. "The Judge pays him wages."

Stephen thanked his new friend for the note to the bank president, and went slowly down the stairs. To be keyed up to a battle-pitch, and then to have the battle deferred, is a trial of flesh and spirit.

As he reached the pavement, he saw people gathering in front of the wide entrance of the Court House opposite, and perched on the copings. He hesitated, curious. Then he walked slowly toward the place, and buttoning his coat, pushed through the loafers and passers-by dallying on the outskirts of the crowd. There, in the bright November sunlight, a sight met his eyes which turned him sick and dizzy.

Against the walls and pillars of the building, already grimy with soot, crouched a score of miserable human beings waiting to be sold at auction. Mr. Lynch's slave pen had been disgorged that morning. Old and young, husband and wife,—the moment was come for all and each. How hard the stones! and what more pitiless than the gaze of their fellow-creatures in the crowd below! O friends, we who live in peace and plenty amongst our families, how little do we realize the terror and the misery and the dumb heart-aches of those days. Stephen thought with agony of seeing his own mother sold before his eyes, and the building in front of him was lifted from its foundation and rocked even as shall the temples on the judgment day.

The oily auctioneer was inviting the people to pinch the wares. Men came forward to feel the creatures and look into their mouths, and one brute, unshaven and with filthy linen, snatched a child from its mother's lap. Stephen shuddered with the sharpest pain he had ever known. An ocean-wide tempest arose in his breast,—a Samson's strength to break the pillars of the temple, to slay these men with his bare hands. Seven generations of stern life and thought had their focus here in him,—from Oliver Cromwell to John Brown.

Stephen was far from prepared for the storm that raged within him. He had not been brought up an Abolitionist,—far from it. Nor had his father's friends—who were deemed at that time the best people in Boston—been Abolitionists. Only three years before, when Boston had been aflame over the delivery of the fugitive Anthony Burns, Stephen had gone out of curiosity to the mass meeting at Faneuil Hall. How well he remembered his father's indignation when he confessed it, and in his anger Mr. Brice had called Phillips and Parker "agitators." But his father, nor his father's friends in Boston, had never been brought face to face with this hideous traffic.

Hark! Was that the sing-song voice of the auctioneer? He was selling the cattle. High and low, caressing and menacing, he teased and exhorted them to buy. They were bidding, yes, for the possession of souls, bidding in the currency of the Great Republic. And between the eager shouts came a moan of sheer despair. What was the attendant doing now? He was tearing two of them from a last embrace.

Three—four were sold while Stephen was in a dream.

Then came a lull, a hitch, and the crowd began to chatter gayly. But the misery in front of him held Stephen in a spell. Figures stood out from the group. A white-haired patriarch, with eyes raised to the sky; a flat-breasted woman whose child was gone, whose weakness made her valueless. Then two girls were pushed forth, one a quadroon of great beauty, to be fingered. Stephen turned his face away,—to behold Mr. Eliphalet Hopper looking calmly on.

"Wal, Mr. Brice, this is an interesting show now, ain't it? Something *we* don't have. I generally stop here to take a look when I'm passing." And he spat tobacco juice on the coping.

Stephen came to his senses.

"And you are from New England?" he said.

Mr. Hopper laughed.

"Tarnation!" said he, "you get used to it. When I come here, *I* was a sort of an Abolitionist. But after you've lived here awhile you get to know that niggers ain't fit for freedom."

Silence from Stephen.

"Likely gal, that beauty," Eliphalet continued unrepressed. "There's

a well-known New Orleans dealer named Jenkins after her. I callate
she'll go down river."

"I reckon you're right, Mistah," a man with a matted beard chimed
in, and added with a wink: "She'll find it pleasant enough—fer a while.
Some of those other niggers will go too, and they'd ruther go to hell.
They do treat 'em nefarious daown thah on the wholesale plantations.
Household niggers! there ain't none better off than them. But seven
years in a cotton swamp,—seven years it takes; that's all, Mistah."

Stephen moved away. He felt that to stay near the man was to be
tempted to murder. He moved away, and just then the auctioneer yelled,
"Attention!"

"Gentlemen," he cried, "I have heah two sisters, the prope'ty of the
late Mistah Robe't Benbow, of St. Louis, as fine a pair of wenches as
was ever offe'd to the public from these heah steps—"

"Speak for the handsome gal," cried a wag.

"Sell off the cart hoss fust," said another.

The auctioneer turned to the darker sister.

"Sal ain't much on looks, gentlemen," he said, "but she's the best
nigger for *work* Mistah Benbow had." He seized her arm and squeezed
it, while the girl flinched and drew back. "She's solid, gentlemen, and
sound as a dollar, and she kin sew and cook. Twenty-two years old.
What am I bid?"

Much to the auctioneer's disgust, Sal was bought in for four hundred
dollars, the interest in the beautiful sister having made the crowd impatient. Stephen, sick at heart, turned to leave. Halfway to the corner
he met a little elderly man who was the color of a dried gourd. And just
as Stephen passed him, this man was overtaken by an old negress, with
tears streaming down her face, who seized the threadbare hem of his
coat. Stephen paused involuntarily.

"Well, Nancy," said the little man, "we had marvellous luck. I was
able to buy your daughter for you with less than the amount of your
savings."

"T'ank you, Mistah Cantah," wailed the poor woman, "t'ank you,
suh. Praised be de name of de Lawd. He gib me Sal again. Oh, Mistah
Cantah" (the agony in that cry), "is you gwineter stan' heah an' see her
sister Hester sol' to—to—oh, ma little chile! De little chile dat I nussed,
dat I raised up in God's 'ligion. Mistah Cantah, save her, suh, f'om dat
wicked life o' sin. De Lawd Jesus'll rewa'd you, suh. Dis ole woman'll
wuk fo' you twell de flesh drops off'n her fingers, suh."

And had he not held her, she would have gone down on her knees on the stone flagging before him. Her suffering was stamped on the little man's face,—and it seemed to Stephen that this was but one trial more which adversity had brought to Mr. Canter.

"Nancy," he answered (how often, and to how many, must he have had to say the same thing), "I haven't the money, Nancy. Would to God that I had, Nancy!"

She had sunk down on the bricks. But she had not fainted. It was not so merciful as that. It was Stephen who lifted her, and helped her to the coping, where she sat with her head bowed between her knees, the scarlet bandanna awry.

Stephen Brice was not of a descent to do things upon impulse. But the tale was told in after days that one of his first actions in St. Louis was of this nature. The waters stored for ages in the four great lakes, given the opportunity, rush over Niagara Falls into Ontario.

"Take the woman away," said Stephen, in a low voice, "and I will buy the girl,—if I can."

The little man looked up, dazed.

"Give me your card,—your address. I will buy the girl, if I can, and set her free."

He fumbled in his pocket and drew out a dirty piece of pasteboard. It read: "R. Canter, Second Hand Furniture, 20 Second Street." And still he stared at Stephen, as one who gazes upon a mystery. A few curious pedestrians had stopped in front of them.

"Get her away, if you can, for God's sake," said Stephen again. And he strode off toward the people at the auction. He was trembling. In his eagerness to reach a place of vantage before the girl was sold, he pushed roughly into the crowd.

But suddenly he was brought up short by the blocky body of Mr. Hopper, who grunted with the force of the impact.

"Gosh," said that gentleman, "but you *are* inters'ted. They ain't begun to sell her yet—he's waitin' for somebody. Callatin' to buy her?" asked Mr. Hopper, with genial humor.

Stephen took a deep breath. If he knocked Mr. Hopper down, he certainly could not buy her. And it was a relief to know that the sale had not begun.

As for Eliphalet, he was beginning to like young Brice. He approved of any man from Boston who was not too squeamish to take pleasure in a little affair of this kind.

As for Stephen, Mr. Hopper brought him back to earth. He ceased trembling, and began to think.

"Tarnation!" said Eliphalet. "There's my boss, Colonel Carvel, across the street. Guess I'd better move on. But what d'ye think of him for a real Southern gentleman? The young dandy is his nephew, Clarence Colfax. He callates to own this town." Eliphalet was speaking leisurely, as usual, while preparing to move. "That's Virginia Carvel, in red. Any gals down Boston-way to beat her? Guess you won't find many as proud."

He departed. And Stephen glanced absently at the group. They were picking their way over the muddy crossing toward him. Was it possible that these people were coming to a slave auction? Surely not. And yet here they were on the pavement at his very side.

She wore a long Talma of crimson cashmere, and her face was in that most seductive of frames, a scoop bonnet of dark green velvet. For a fleeting second her eyes met his, and then her lashes fell. But he was aware, when he had turned away, that she was looking at him again. He grew uneasy. He wondered whether his appearance betrayed his purpose, or made a question of his sanity.

Sanity! Yes, probably he was insane from her point of view. A sudden anger shook him that she should be there calmly watching such a scene.

Just then there was a hush among the crowd. The beautiful slave-girl was seized roughly by the man in charge and thrust forward, half fainting, into view. Stephen winced. But unconsciously he turned, to see the effect upon Virginia Carvel.

Thank God! There were tears upon her lashes.

Here was the rasp of the auctioneer's voice:—

"Gentlemen, I reckon there ain't *never* been offered to bidders such an opportunity as this heah. Look at her well, gentlemen. I ask you, ain't she a splendid creature?"

Colonel Carvel, in annoyance, started to move on. "Come Jinny," he said, "I had no business to bring you over."

But Virginia caught his arm. "Pa," she cried, "it's Mr. Benbow's Hester. Don't go, dear. Buy her for me. You know that I always wanted her. Please!"

The Colonel halted, irresolute, and pulled his goatee. Young Colfax stepped in between them.

"I'll buy her for you, Jinny. Mother promised you a present, you know, and you shall have her."

Virginia had calmed.

"Do buy her, one of you," was all she said.

"You may do the bidding, Clarence," said the Colonel, "and we'll settle the ownership afterward." Taking Virginia's arm, he escorted her across the street.

Stephen was left in a quandary. Here was a home for the girl, and a good one. Why should he spend the money which meant so much to him? He saw the man Jenkins elbowing to the front. And yet—suppose Mr. Colfax did not get her? He had promised to buy her if he could, and to set her free.

Stephen had made up his mind. He shouldered his way after Jenkins.

CHAPTER V

THE FIRST SPARK PASSES

"Now, gentlemen," shouted the auctioneer, when he had finished his oration upon the girl's attractions, "what am I bid? Eight hundred?"

Stephen caught his breath. There was a long pause. No one cared to start the bidding.

"Come, gentlemen, come! There's my friend Alf Jenkins. He knows what she's worth to a cent. What'll you give, Alf? Is it eight hundred?"

Mr. Jenkins winked at the auctioneer, and the crowd joined in the laugh.

"Three hundred!" he said.

The auctioneer was mortally offended. Then some one cried:—

"Three hundred and fifty!"

It was young Colfax. He was recognized at once, by name, evidently as a person of importance.

"Thank you, Mistah Colfax, suh," said the auctioneer, with a servile wave of the hand in his direction, while the crowd twisted their necks to see him. He stood very straight, very haughty, as if entirely oblivious to his conspicuous position.

"Three seventy-five!"

"That's better, Mistah Jenkins," said the auctioneer, sarcastically. He turned to the girl, who might have stood to a sculptor for a figure of despair. Her hands were folded in front of her, her head bowed down. The auctioneer put his hand under her chin and raised it roughly. "Cheer up, my gal," he said, "you ain't got nothing to blubber about now."

Hester's breast heaved, and from her black eyes there shot a magnificent look of defiance. He laughed. That was the white blood.

The white blood!

Clarence Colfax had his bid taken from his lips. Above the heads of the people he had a quick vision of a young man with a determined face, whose voice rang clear and strong,—

"Four hundred!"

Even the auctioneer, braced two ways, was thrown off his balance by the sudden appearance of this new force. Stephen grew red over the sensation he made. Apparently the others present had deemed competition with such as Jenkins and young Colfax the grossest folly. He was treated to much liberal staring before the oily salesman arranged his wits to grapple with the third factor.

"Four hundred from—from—from that gentleman." And the chubby index seemed the finger of scorn.

"Four hundred and fifty!" said Mr. Colfax, defiantly.

Whereupon Mr. Jenkins, the New Orleans dealer, lighted a very long cigar and sat down on the coping. The auctioneer paid no attention to this manœuvre. But Mr. Brice and Mr. Colfax, being very young, fondly imagined that they had the field to themselves, to fight to a finish.

Here wisdom suggested in a mild whisper to Stephen that there was a last chance to pull out. And let Colfax have the girl? Never. That was pride, and most reprehensible. But second he thought of Mr. Canter and old Nancy, and that was not pride.

"Four seventy-five!" he cried.

"Thank *you*, suh."

"Now fur it, young uns!" said the wag, and the crowd howled with merriment.

"Five hundred!" snapped Mr. Colfax.

He was growing angry. But Stephen was from New England, and poor, and he thought of the size of his purse. A glance at his adversary showed that his blood was up. Money was plainly no consideration to him, and young Colfax did not seem to be the kind who would relish returning to a young lady and acknowledge a defeat.

Stephen raised the bid by ten dollars. The Southerner shot up fifty. Again Stephen raised it ten. He was in full possession of himself now, and proof against the thinly veiled irony of the oily man's remarks in favor of Mr. Colfax. In an incredibly short time the latter's impetuosity had brought them to eight hundred and ten dollars.

Then several things happened very quickly.

Mr. Jenkins got up from the curb and said, "Eight hundred and twenty-five," with his cigar in his mouth. Scarcely had the hum of excitement died when Stephen, glancing at Colfax for the next move, saw that young gentleman seized from the rear by his uncle, the tall Colonel. And across the street was Miss Virginia Carvel, tapping her foot on the pavement.

"What are you about, sir?" the Colonel cried. "The wench isn't worth it."

Mr. Colfax shook himself free.

"I've got to buy her now, sir," he cried.

"I reckon not," said the Colonel. "You come along with me."

Naturally Mr. Colfax was very angry. He struggled, but he went. And so, protesting, he passed Stephen, at whom he did not deign to glance. The humiliation of it must have been great for Mr. Colfax. "Jinny wants her, sir," he said, "and I have a right to buy her."

"Jinny wants everything," was the Colonel's reply. And in a single look of curiosity and amusement his own gray eyes met Stephen's. They seemed to regret that this young man, too, had not a guardian. Then uncle and nephew recrossed the street, and as they walked off the Colonel was seen to laugh. Virginia had her chin in the air, and Clarence's was in his collar.

The crowd, of course, indulged in roars of laughter, and even Stephen could not repress a smile,—a smile not without bitterness. Then he wheeled to face Mr. Jenkins. Out of respect for the personages involved, the auctioneer had been considerately silent during the event. It was Mr. Brice who was now the centre of observation.

"Come, gentlemen, come! this here's a joke—eight twenty-five. She's worth two thousand. I've been in the business twenty yea's, and I neve' seen her equal. Give me a bid, Mr.—Mr.—you have the advantage of me, suh."

"Eight hundred and thirty-five!" said Stephen.

"Now, Mr. Jenkins, now, suh! we've got twenty mo' to sell."

"Eight fifty!" said Mr. Jenkins.

"Eight sixty!" said Stephen, and they cheered him.

Mr. Jenkins took his cigar out of his teeth, and stared.

"Eight seventy-five!" said he.

"Eight eighty-five!" said Stephen.

There was a breathless pause.

"Nine hundred!" said the trader.

"Nine hundred and ten!" cried Stephen.

At that Mr. Jenkins whipped his hat from off his head, and made Stephen a derisive bow.

"She's youahs, suh," he said. "These here are panic times. I've struck my limit. I can do bettah in Louisville fo' less. Congratulate you, suh— reckon you want her wuss'n I do."

At which sally Stephen grew scarlet, and the crowd howled with joy.

"What!" yelled the auctioneer. "Why, gentlemen, this heah's a joke. Nine hundred and ten dollars, gents, nine hundred and ten. We've just begun, gents. Come, Mr. Jenkins, that's giving her away."

The trader shook his head, and puffed at his cigar.

"Well," cried the oily man, "this *is* a slaughter. Going at nine hundred an' ten—nine ten—going—going—" down came the hammer—"gone at nine hundred and ten to Mr.—Mr.—you have the advantage of me, suh."

An attendant had seized the girl, who was on the verge of fainting, and was dragging her back. Stephen did not heed the auctioneer, but thrust forward regardless of stares.

"Handle her gently, you blackguard!" he cried.

The man took his hands off.

"Suttinly, sah," he said.

Hester lifted her eyes, and they were filled with such gratitude and trust that suddenly he was overcome with embarrassment.

"Can you walk?" he demanded, somewhat harshly.

"Yes, massa."

"Then get up," he said, "and follow me."

She rose obediently. Then a fat man came out of the Court House, with a quill in his hand, and a merry twinkle in his eye that Stephen resented.

"This way, please, sah," and he led him to a desk, from the drawer of which he drew forth a blank deed.

"Name, please!"

"Stephen Atterbury Brice."

"Residence, Mr. Brice!"

Stephen gave the number. But instead of writing it down, the man merely stared at him, while the fat creases in his face deepened and deepened. Finally he put down his quill, and indulged in a gale of laughter, hugely to Mr. Brice's discomfiture.

"Shucks!" said the fat man, as soon as he could. "What are you givin' us? That the's a Yankee boa'din'-house."

"And I suppose that that is part of your business, too," said Stephen, acidly.

The fat man looked at him, pressed his lips, wrote down the number, shaken all the while with a disturbance which promised to lead to another explosion. Finally, after a deal of pantomime, and whispering and laughter with the notary behind the wire screen, the deed was made out, signed, attested, and delivered. Stephen counted out the money grimly, in gold and Boston drafts.

Out in the sunlight on Chestnut Street, with the girl by his side, it all seemed a nightmare. The son of Appleton Brice of Boston the owner of a beautiful quadroon girl! And he had bought her with his last cent.

Miss Crane herself opened the door in answer to his ring. Her keen eyes instantly darted over his shoulder, and dilated. But Stephen, summoning all his courage, pushed past her to the stairs, and beckoned Hester to follow.

"I have brought this—this person to see my mother," he said.

The spinster bowed from the back of her neck. She stood transfixed on a great rose in the hall carpet until she heard Mrs. Brice's door open and slam, and then she strode up the stairs and into the apartment of Mrs. Abner Reed. As she passed the first landing, the quadroon girl was waiting in the hall.

CHAPTER VI

SILAS WHIPPLE

THE trouble with many narratives is that they tell too much. Stephen's interview with his mother was a quiet affair, and not historic. Miss Crane's boarding-house is not an interesting place, and the tempest in that teapot is better imagined than described. Out of consideration for Mr. Stephen Brice, we shall skip likewise a most affecting scene at Mr. Canter's second-hand furniture store.

That afternoon Stephen came again to the dirty flight of steps which led to Judge Whipple's office. He paused a moment to gather courage, and then, gripping the rail, he ascended. The ascent required courage now, certainly. He halted again before the door at the top. But even as he stood there came to him, in low, rich tones, the notes of a German song. He entered. And Mr. Richter rose in shirt-sleeves from his desk to greet him, all smiling.

"Ach, my friend!" said he, "but you are late. The Judge has been awaiting you."

"Has he?" inquired Stephen, with ill-concealed anxiety.

The big young German patted him on the shoulder. Suddenly a voice roared from out the open transom of the private office, like a cyclone rushing through a gap.

"Mr. Richter!"

"Sir!"

"Who is that?"

"Mr. Brice, sir."

"Then why in thunder doesn't he come in?"

Mr. Richter opened the private door, and in Stephen walked. The door closed again, and there he was in the dragon's den, face to face with the dragon, who was staring him through and through. The first objects that caught Stephen's attention were the grizzly gray eyebrows, which seemed as so much brush to mark the fire of the deep-set battery of the eyes. And that battery, when in action, must have been truly terrible.

The Judge was shaven, save for a shaggy fringe of gray beard around his chin, and the size of his nose was apparent even in the full face.

Stephen felt that no part of him escaped the search of Mr. Whipple's glance. But it was no code or course of conduct that kept him silent. Nor was it fear—entirely.

"So you are Appleton Brice's son," said the Judge, at last. His tone was not quite so gruff as it might have been.

"Yes, sir," said Stephen.

"Humph!" said the Judge, with a look that scarcely expressed approval. "I guess you've been patted on the back too much by your father's friends." He leaned back in his wooden chair. "How I used to detest people who patted boys on the back and said with a smirk, 'I know your father.' I never had a father whom people could say that about. But, sir," cried the Judge, bringing down his fists on the litter of papers that covered his desk, "I made up my mind that one day people should know *me*. *That* was my spur. And you'll start fair here, Mr. Brice. They won't know your father here—"

If Stephen thought the Judge brutal, he did not say so. He glanced around the little room,—at the bed in the corner, in which the Judge slept, and which during the day did not escape the flood of books and papers; at the washstand, with a roll of legal cap beside the pitcher.

"I guess you think this town pretty crude after Boston, Mr. Brice," Mr. Whipple continued. "From time immemorial it has been the pleasant habit of old communities to be shocked at newer settlements, built by their own countrymen. Are you shocked, sir?"

Stephen flushed. Fortunately the Judge did not give him time to answer.

"Why didn't your mother let me know that she was coming?"

"She didn't wish to put you to any trouble, sir."

"Wasn't I a good friend of your father's? Didn't I ask you to come here and go into my office?"

"But there was a chance, Mr. Whipple—"

"A chance of what?"

"That you would not like me. And there is still a chance of it," added Stephen, smiling.

For a second it looked as if the Judge might smile, too. He rubbed his nose with a fearful violence.

"Mr. Richter tells me you were looking for a bank," said he, presently.

Stephen quaked.

"Yes, sir, I was, but—"

But Mr. Whipple merely picked up the *Counterfeit Bank Note Detector*.

"Beware of Western State Currency as you would the devil," said he. "That's one thing we don't equal the East in—yet. And so you want to become a lawyer?"

"I intend to become a lawyer, sir."

"And so you shall, sir," cried the Judge, bringing down his yellow fist upon the *Bank Note Detector*. "I'll make you a lawyer, sir. But my methods ain't Harvard methods, sir."

"I am ready to do anything, Mr. Whipple."

The Judge merely grunted. He scratched among his papers, and produced some legal cap and a bunch of notes.

"Go out there," he said, "and take off your coat and copy this brief. Mr. Richter will help you to-day. And tell your mother I shall do myself the honor to call upon her this evening."

Stephen did as he was told, without a word. But Mr. Richter was not in the outer office when he returned to it. He tried to compose himself to write, although the recollection of each act of the morning hung like a cloud over the back of his head. Therefore the first sheet of legal cap was spoiled utterly. But Stephen had a deep sense of failure. He had gone through the ground-glass door with the firm intention of making a clean breast of the ownership of Hester. Now, as he sat still, the trouble grew upon him. He started a new sheet, and ruined that. Once he got as far as his feet, and sat down again. But at length he had quieted to the extent of deciphering ten lines of Mr. Whipple's handwriting when the creak of a door shattered his nerves completely.

He glanced up from his work to behold—none other than Colonel Comyn Carvel.

Glancing at Mr. Richter's chair, and seeing it empty, the Colonel's eye roved about the room until it found Stephen. There it remained, and the Colonel remained in the middle of the floor, his soft hat on the back of his head, one hand planted firmly on the gold head of his stick, and the other tugging at his goatee, pulling down his chin to the quizzical angle.

"Whoopee!" he cried.

The effect of this was to make one perspire freely. Stephen perspired. And as there seemed no logical answer, he made none.

Suddenly Mr. Carvel turned, shaking with a laughter he could control, and strode into the private office. The door slammed behind him. Mr. Brice's impulse was flight. But he controlled himself.

First of all there was an eloquent silence. Then a ripple of guffaws. Then the scratch-scratch of a quill pen, and finally the Judge's voice.

"Carvel, what the devil's the matter with you, sir?"

A squall of guffaws blew through the transom, and the Colonel was heard slapping his knee.

"Judge Whipple," said he, his voice vibrating from suppressed explosions, "I am happy to see that you have overcome some of your ridiculous prejudices, sir."

"What prejudices, sir?" the Judge was heard to shout.

"Toward slavery, Judge," said Mr. Carvel, seeming to recover his gravity. "You are a broader man than I thought, sir."

An unintelligible gurgle came from the Judge. Then he said:—

"Carvel, haven't you and I quarrelled enough on that subject?"

"You didn't happen to attend the nigger auction this morning when you were at the court?" asked the Colonel, blandly.

"Colonel," said the Judge, "I've warned you a hundred times against the stuff you lay out on your counter for customers."

"You weren't at the auction, then," continued the Colonel, undisturbed. "You missed it, sir. You missed seeing this young man you've just employed buy the prettiest quadroon wench I ever set eyes on."

Now indeed was poor Stephen on his feet. But whether to fly in at the one entrance or out at the other, he was undecided.

"Colonel," said Mr. Whipple, "is that true?"

"Sir!"

"MR. BRICE!"

It did not seem to Stephen as if he was walking when he went toward the ground glass door. He opened it. There was Colonel Carvel seated on the bed, his goatee in his hand. And there was the Judge leaning forward from his hips, straight as a ramrod. Fire was darting from beneath his bushy eyebrows. "Mr. Brice," said he, "there is one question I always ask of those whom I employ. I omitted it in your case because I have known your father and your grandfather before you. What is your opinion, sir, on the subject of holding human beings in bondage?"

The answer was immediate,—likewise simple.

"I do not believe in it, Mr. Whipple."

The Judge shot out of his chair like a long Jack-in-the-box, and towered to his full height.

"Mr. Brice, did you, or did you not, buy a woman at auction to-day?"

"I did, sir."

Mr. Whipple literally staggered. But Stephen caught a glimpse of the Colonel's hand slipping from his chin over his mouth.

"Good God, sir!" cried the Judge, and he sat down heavily. "You say that you are an Abolitionist?"

"No, sir, I do not say that. But it does not need an Abolitionist to condemn what I saw this morning."

"Are you a slave-owner, sir?" said Mr. Whipple.

"Yes, sir."

"Then get your coat and hat and leave my office, Mr. Brice."

Stephen's coat was on his arm. He slipped it on, and turned to go. He was, if the truth were told, more amused than angry. It was Colonel Carvel's voice that stopped him.

"Hold on, Judge," he drawled, "I reckon you haven't got all the packing out of that case."

Mr. Whipple looked at him in a sort of stupefaction. Then he glanced at Stephen.

"Come back here, sir," he cried. "I'll give you a hearing. No man shall say that I am not just."

Stephen looked gratefully at the Colonel.

"I did not expect one, sir," he said.

"And you don't deserve one, sir," cried the Judge.

"I think I do," replied Stephen, quietly.

The Judge suppressed something.

"What did you do with this person?" he demanded.

"I took her to Miss Crane's boarding-house," said Stephen.

It was the Colonel's turn to explode. The guffaw which came from him drowned every other sound.

"Good God!" said the Judge, helplessly. Again he looked at the Colonel, and this time something very like mirth shivered his lean frame. "And what do you intend to do with her?" he asked in strange tones.

"To give her freedom, sir, as soon as I can find somebody to go on her bond."

Again silence. Mr. Whipple rubbed his nose with more than customary violence, and looked very hard at Mr. Carvel, whose face was inscrutable. It was a solemn moment.

"Mr. Brice," said the Judge, at length, "take off your coat, sir. I will go her bond."

It was Stephen's turn to be taken aback. He stood regarding the Judge curiously, wondering what manner of man he was. He did not know that this question had puzzled many before him.

"Thank you, sir," he said.

His hand was on the knob of the door, when Mr. Whipple called him back abruptly. His voice had lost some of its gruffness.

"What were your father's ideas about slavery, Mr. Brice?"

The young man thought a moment, as if seeking to be exact.

"I suppose he would have put slavery among the necessary evils, sir," he said, at length. "But he never could bear to have the *Liberator* mentioned in his presence. He was not at all in sympathy with Phillips, or Parker, or Sumner. And such was the general feeling among his friends."

"Then," said the Judge, "contrary to popular opinion in the West and South, Boston is not all Abolition."

Stephen smiled.

"The conservative classes are not at all Abolitionists, sir."

"The conservative classes!" growled the Judge, "the conservative classes!. I am tired of hearing about the conservative classes. Why not come out with it, sir, and say the moneyed classes, who would rather see souls held in bondage than risk their worldly goods in an attempt to liberate them?"

Stephen flushed. It was not at all clear to him then how he was to get along with Judge Whipple. But he kept his temper.

"I am sure that you do them an injustice, sir," he said, with more feeling than he had yet shown. "I am not speaking of the rich alone, and I think that if you knew Boston you would not say that the conservative class there is wholly composed of wealthy people. Many of my father's friends were by no means wealthy. And I know that if he had been poor he would have held the same views."

Stephen did not mark the quick look of approval which Colonel Carvel gave him. Judge Whipple merely rubbed his nose.

"Well, sir," he said, "what were his views, then?"

"My father regarded slaves as property, sir. And conservative people" (Stephen stuck to the word) "respect property the world over. My father's argument was this: If men are deprived by violence of one kind of property which they hold under the law, all other kinds of property will be endangered. The result will be anarchy. Furthermore, he recognized that the economic conditions in the South make slavery necessary to prosperity. And he regarded the covenant made between the states of the two sections as sacred."

There was a brief silence, during which the uncompromising expression of the Judge did not change.

"And do you, sir?" he demanded.

"I am not sure, sir, after what I saw yesterday. I—I must have time to see more of it."

"Good Lord," said Colonel Carvel, "if the conservative people of the North act this way when they see a slave sale, what will the Abolitionists do? Whipple," he added slowly, but with conviction, "this means war."

Then the Colonel got to his feet, and bowed to Stephen with ceremony.

"Whatever you believe, sir," he said, "permit me to shake your hand. You are a brave man, sir. And although my own belief is that the black race is held in subjection by a divine decree, I can admire what you have done, Mr. Brice. It was a noble act, sir,—a right noble act. And I have more respect for the people of Boston, now, sir, than I ever had before, sir."

Having delivered himself of this somewhat dubious compliment (which he meant well), the Colonel departed.

Judge Whipple said nothing.

CHAPTER VII

CALLERS

IF the Brices had created an excitement upon their arrival, it was as nothing to the mad delirium which raged at Miss Crane's boarding-house during the second afternoon of their stay. Twenty times was Miss Crane on the point of requesting Mrs. Brice to leave, and twenty times, by the advice of Mrs. Abner Reed, she desisted. The culmination came when the news leaked out that Mr. Stephen Brice had bought the young woman in order to give her freedom. Like those who have done noble acts since the world began, Stephen that night was both a hero and a fool. The cream from which heroes is made is very apt to turn.

"Phew!" cried Stephen, when they had reached their room after tea, "wasn't that meal a fearful experience? Let's find a hovel, mother, and go and live in it. We can't stand it here any longer."

"Not if you persist in your career of reforming an Institution, my son," answered the widow, smiling.

"It was beastly hard luck," said he, "that I should have been shouldered with that experience the first day. But I have tried to think it over calmly since, and I can see nothing else to have done." He paused in his pacing up and down, a smile struggling with his serious look. "It was quite a hot-headed business for one of the staid Brices, wasn't it?"

"The family has never been called impetuous," replied his mother. "It must be the Western air."

He began his pacing again. His mother had not said one word about the money. Neither had he. Once more he stopped before her.

"We are at least a year nearer the poor-house," he said; "you haven't scolded me for that. I should feel so much better if you would."

"Oh, Stephen, don't say that!" she exclaimed. "God has given me no greater happiness in this life than the sight of the gratitude of that poor creature, Nancy. I shall never forget the old woman's joy at the sight of her daughter. It made a palace out of that dingy furniture shop. Hand me my handkerchief, dear."

Stephen noticed with a pang that the lace of it was frayed and torn at the corner.

There was a knock at the door.

"Come in," said Mrs. Brice, hastily putting the handkerchief down. Hester stood on the threshold, and old Nancy beside her.

"Evenin', Mis' Brice. De good Lawd bless you, lady, an' Miste' Brice," said the old negress.

"Well, Nancy?"

Nancy pressed into the room. "Mis' Brice!"

"Yes?"

"Ain' you gwineter 'low Hester an' me to wuk fo' you?"

"Indeed I should be glad to, Nancy. But we are boarding."

"Yassm, yassm," said Nancy, and relapsed into awkward silence. Then again, "Mis' Brice!"

"Yes, Nancy?"

"Ef you 'lows us t' come heah an' straighten out you close, an' mend 'em—you dunno how happy you mek me an' Hester—des to do dat much, Mis' Brice."

The note of appeal was irresistible. Mrs. Brice rose and unlocked the trunks.

"You may unpack them, Nancy," she said.

With what alacrity did the old woman take off her black bonnet and shawl! "Whaffor you stannin' dere, Hester?" she cried.

"Hester is tired," said Mrs. Brice, compassionately, and tears came to her eyes again at the thought of what they had both been through that day.

"Tired!" said Nancy, holding up her hands. "No'm, she ain' tired. She des kinder stupefied by you' goodness, Mis' Brice."

A scene was saved by the appearance of Miss Crane's hired girl.

"Mr. and Mrs. Cluyme, in the parlor, mum," she said.

If Mr. Jacob Cluyme sniffed a little as he was ushered into Miss Crane's best parlor, it was perhaps because of the stuffy dampness of that room. Mr. Cluyme was one of those persons the effusiveness of whose greeting does not tally with the limpness of their grasp. He was attempting, when Stephen appeared, to get a little heat into his hands by rubbing them, as a man who kindles a stick of wood for a visitor. The gentleman had red chop-whiskers,—to continue to put his worst side foremost,—which demanded a ruddy face. He welcomed Stephen to St. Louis with neighborly effusion; while his wife, a round little woman, bubbled over to Mrs. Brice.

"My dear sir," said Mr. Cluyme, "I used often to go to Boston in the forties. In fact—ahem—I may claim to be a New Englander. Alas, no, I never met your father. But when I heard of the sad circumstances of his death, I felt as if I had lost a personal friend. His probity, sir, and his religious principles were an honor to the Athens of America. I have listened to my friend, Mr. Atterbury,—Mr. Samuel Atterbury,—eulogize him by the hour."

Stephen was surprised.

"Why, yes," said he, "Mr. Atterbury was a friend."

"Of course," said Mr. Cluyme, "I knew it. Four years ago, the last business trip I made to Boston, I met Atterbury on the street. Absence makes no difference to some men, sir, nor the West, for that matter. They never change. Atterbury nearly took me in his arms. 'My dear fellow,' he cried, 'how long are you to be in town?' I was going the next day. 'Sorry I can't ask you to dinner,' says he, 'but step into the Tremont House and have a bite.'—Wasn't that like Atterbury?"

Stephen thought it was. But Mr. Cluyme was evidently expecting no answer.

"Well," said he, "what I was going to say was that we heard you were in town; 'Friends of Samuel Atterbury, my dear,' I said to my wife. We are neighbors, Mr. Brice. You must know the girls. You must come to supper. We live very plainly, sir, very simply. I am afraid that you will miss the luxury of the East, and some of the refinement, Stephen. I hope I may call you so, my boy. We have a few cultured citizens, Stephen, but all are not so. I miss the atmosphere. I seemed to live again when I got to Boston. But business, sir,—the making of money is a sordid occupation. You will come to supper?"

"I scarcely think that my mother will go out," said Stephen.

"Oh, be friends! It will cheer her. Not a dinner-party, my boy, only a plain, comfortable meal, with plenty to eat. Of course she will. Of course she will. Not a Boston social function, you understand. Boston, Stephen, I have always looked upon as the centre of the universe. *Our* universe, I mean. America for Americans is a motto of mine. Oh, no," he added quickly, "I don't mean a Know Nothing. Religious freedom, my boy, is part of our great Constitution. By the way, Stephen—Atterbury always had such a respect for your father's opinions—"

"My father was not an Abolitionist, sir," said Stephen, smiling.

"Quite right, quite right," said Mr. Cluyme.

"But I am not sure, since I have come here, that I have not some sympathy and respect for the Abolitionists."

Mr. Cluyme gave a perceptible start. He glanced at the heavy hangings on the windows and then out of the open door into the hall. For a space his wife's chatter to Mrs. Brice, on Boston fashions, filled the room.

"My dear Stephen," said the gentleman, dropping his voice, "that is all very well in Boston. But take a little advice from one who is old enough to counsel you. You are young, and you must learn to temper yourself to the tone of the place which you have made your home. St. Louis is full of excellent people, but they are not precisely Abolitionists. We are gathering, it is true, a small party who are for gradual emancipation. But our New England population here is small yet compared to the Southerners. And they are very violent, sir."

Stephen could not resist saying, "Judge Whipple does not seem to have tempered himself, sir."

"Silas Whipple is a fanatic, sir," cried Mr. Cluyme. "His hand is against every man's. He denounces Douglas on the slightest excuse, and would go to Washington when Congress opens to fight with Stephens and Toombs and Davis. But what good does it do him? He might have been in the Senate, or on the Supreme Bench, had he not stirred up so much hatred. And yet I can't help liking Whipple. Do you know him?"

A resounding ring of the door-bell cut off Stephen's reply, and Mrs. Cluyme's small talk to Mrs. Brice. In the hall rumbled a familiar voice, and in stalked none other than Judge Whipple himself. Without noticing the other occupants of the parlor he strode up to Mrs. Brice, looked at her for an instant from under the grizzled brows, and held out his large hand.

"Pray, ma'am," he said, "what have you done with your slave?"

Mrs. Cluyme emitted a muffled shriek, like that of a person frightened in a dream. Her husband grasped the curved back of his chair. But Stephen smiled. And his mother smiled a little, too.

"Are you Mr. Whipple?" she asked.

"I am, madam," was the reply.

"My slave is upstairs, I believe, unpacking my trunks," said Mrs. Brice.

Mr. and Mrs. Cluyme exchanged a glance of consternation. Then

Mrs. Cluyme sat down again, rather heavily, as though her legs had refused to hold her.

"Well, well, ma'am!" The Judge looked again at Mrs. Brice, and a gleam of mirth lighted the severity of his face. He was plainly pleased with her—this serene lady in black, whose voice had the sweet ring of women who are well born and whose manner was so self-contained. To speak truth, the Judge was prepared to dislike her. He had never laid eyes upon her, and as he walked hither from his house he seemed to foresee a helpless little woman who, once he had called, would fling her Boston pride to the winds and dump her woes upon him. He looked again, and decidedly approved of Mrs. Brice, and was unaware that his glance embarrassed her.

"Mr. Whipple," she said, "do you know Mr. and Mrs. Cluyme?"

The Judge looked behind him abruptly, nodded ferociously at Mr. Cluyme, and took the hand that fluttered out to him from Mrs. Cluyme.

"Know the Judge!" exclaimed that lady, "I reckon we do. And my Belle is so fond of him. She thinks there is no one equal to Mr. Whipple. Judge, you must come round to a family supper. Belle will surpass herself."

"Umph!" said the Judge, "I think I like Edith best of your girls, ma'am."

"Edith is a good daughter, if I do say it myself," said Mrs. Cluyme. "I have tried to do right by my children." She was still greatly flustered, and curiosity about the matter of the slave burned upon her face. Neither the Judge nor Mrs. Brice were people one could catechise. Stephen, scanning the Judge, was wondering how far he regarded the matter as a joke.

"Well, madam," said Mr. Whipple, as he seated himself on the other end of the horsehair sofa, "I'll warrant when you left Boston that you did not expect to own a slave the day after you arrived in St. Louis."

"But I do not own her," said Mrs. Brice. "It is my son who owns her."

This was too much for Mr. Cluyme.

"What!" he cried to Stephen. "You own a slave? You, a mere boy, have bought a negress?"

"And what is more, sir, I approve of it," the Judge put in, severely. "I am going to take the young man into my office."

Mr. Cluyme gradually retired into the back of his chair, looking at Mr. Whipple as though he expected him to touch a match to the window curtains. But Mr. Cluyme was elastic.

"Pardon me, Judge," said he, "but I trust that I may be allowed to congratulate you upon the abandonment of principles which I have considered a clog to your career. They did you honor, sir, but they were Quixotic. I, sir, am for saving our glorious Union at any cost. And we have no right to deprive our brethren of their property—of their very means of livelihood."

The Judge grinned diabolically. Mrs. Cluyme was as yet too stunned to speak. Only Stephen's mother sniffed gunpowder in the air.

"This, Mr. Cluyme," said the Judge, mildly, "is an age of shifting winds. It was not long ago," he added reflectively, "when you and I met in the Planters' House, and you declared that every drop of Northern blood spilled in Kansas was in a holy cause. Do you remember it, sir?"

Mr. Cluyme and Mr. Cluyme's wife alone knew whether he trembled.

"And I repeat that, sir," he cried, with far too much zeal. "I repeat it here and now. And yet I was for the Omnibus Bill, and I am with Mr. Douglas in his local sovereignty. I am willing to bury my abhorrence of a relic of barbarism, for the sake of union and peace."

"Well, sir, I am not," retorted the Judge, like lightning. He rubbed the red spot on his nose, and pointed a bony finger at Mr. Cluyme. Many a criminal had grovelled before that finger. "I, too, am for the Union. And the Union will never be safe until the greatest crime of modern times is wiped out in blood. Mind what I say, Mr. Cluyme, in *blood,* sir," he thundered.

Poor Mrs. Cluyme gasped.

"But the slave, sir? Did I not understand you to approve of Mr. Brice's ownership?"

"As I never approved of any other. Good night, sir. Good night, madam." But to Mrs. Brice he crossed over and took her hand. It has been further claimed that he bowed. This is not certain.

"Good night, madam," he said. "I shall call again to pay my respects when you are not occupied."

CHAPTER VIII

BELLEGARDE

Miss Virginia Carvel came down the steps in her riding-habit. And Ned, who had been waiting in the street with the horses, obsequiously held his hand while his young mistress leaped into Vixen's saddle. Leaving the darkey to follow upon black Calhoun, she cantered off up the street, greatly to the admiration of the neighbors. They threw open their windows to wave at her, but Virginia pressed her lips and stared straight ahead. She was going out to see the Russell girls at their father's country place on Bellefontaine Road, especially to proclaim her detestation for a certain young Yankee upstart. She had unbosomed herself to Anne Brinsmade and timid Eugénie Rénault the day before.

It was Indian summer, the gold and purple season of the year. Frost had come and gone. Wasps were buzzing confusedly about the eaves again, marvelling at the balmy air, and the two Misses Russell, Puss and Emily, were seated within the wide doorway at needlework when Virginia dismounted at the horseblock.

"Oh, Jinny, I'm so glad to see you," said Miss Russell. "Here's Elise Saint Simon from New Orleans. You must stay all day and to-night."

"I can't, Puss," said Virginia, submitting impatiently to Miss Russell's warm embrace. She was disappointed at finding the stranger. "I only came—to say that I am going to have a birthday party in a few weeks. You must be sure to come, and bring your guest."

Virginia took her bridle from Ned, and Miss Russell's hospitable face fell.

"You're not going?" she said.

"To Bellegarde for dinner," answered Virginia.

"But it's only ten o'clock," said Puss. "And, Jinny?"

"Yes."

"There's a new young man in town, and they do say his appearance is very striking—not exactly handsome, you know, but strong-looking."

"He's horrid!" said Virginia. "He's a Yankee."

"How do you know?" demanded Puss and Emily in chorus.

54

"And he's no gentleman," said Virginia.

"But how do you know, Jinny?"

"He's an upstart."

"Oh. But he belongs to a very good Boston family, they say."

"There are no good Boston families," replied Virginia, with conviction, as she separated her reins. "He has proved that. Who ever heard of a good Yankee family?"

"What has he done to you, Virginia?" asked Puss, who had brains.

Virginia glanced at the guest. But her grievance was too hot within her for suppression.

"Do you remember Mr. Benbow's Hester, girls? The one I always said I wanted. She was sold at auction yesterday. Pa and I were passing the Court House, with Clarence, when she was put up for sale. We crossed the street to see what was going on, and there was your strong-looking Yankee standing at the edge of the crowd. I am quite sure that he saw me as plainly as I see you, Puss Russell."

"How could he help it?" said Puss, slyly.

Virginia took no notice of the remark.

"He heard me ask Pa to buy her. He heard Clarence say that he would bid her in for me. I know he did. And yet he goes in and outbids Clarence, and buys her himself. Do you think any gentleman would do that, Puss Russell?"

"He bought her himself!" cried the astonished Miss Russell. "Why, I thought that all Bostonians were Abolitionists."

"Then he set her free," said Miss Carvel, contemptuously. "Judge Whipple went on her bond to-day."

"Oh, I'm just crazy to see him now," said Miss Russell. "Ask him to your party, Virginia," she added mischievously.

"Do you think I would have him in my house?" cried Virginia.

Miss Russell was likewise courageous—"I don't see why not. You have Judge Whipple every Sunday to dinner, and he's an Abolitionist."

Virginia drew herself up.

"Judge Whipple has never insulted me," she said, with dignity.

Puss gave way to laughter. Whereupon, despite her protests and prayers for forgiveness, Virginia took to her mare again and galloped off. They saw her turn northward on the Bellefontaine Road.

Presently the woodland hid from her sight the noble river shining far below, and Virginia pulled Vixen between the gateposts which marked the entrance to her aunt's place, Bellegarde. Half a mile through the cool forest, the black dirt of the driveway flying from Vixen's hoofs, and there was the Colfax house on the edge of the gentle slope; and beyond it the orchard, and the blue grapes withering on the vines,—and beyond that fields and fields of yellow stubble. The silver smoke of a steamboat hung in wisps above the water. A young negro was busily washing the broad veranda, but he stopped and straightened at sight of the young horsewoman.

"Sambo, where's your mistress?"

"Clar t' goodness, Miss Jinny, she was heah leetle while ago."

"Yo' git atter Miss Lilly, yo' good-fo'-nuthin' niggah," said Ned, warmly. "Ain't yo' be'n raised better'n to stan' theh wif yo' mouf open?"

Sambo was taking the hint, when Miss Virginia called him back.

"Where's Mr. Clarence?"

"Young Masr? I'll fotch him, Miss Jinny. He jest come home f'um seein' that thar trottin' hoss he's gwine to race nex' week."

Ned, who had tied Calhoun and was holding his mistress's bridle, sniffed. He had been Colonel Carvel's jockey in his younger days.

"Shucks!" he said contemptuously. "I hoped to die befo' the day a gemman'd own er trottah, Jinny. On'y runnin' hosses is fit fo' gemmen."

"Ned," said Virginia, "I shall be eighteen in two weeks and a young lady. On that day you must call me 'Miss Jinny.' "

Ned's face showed both astonishment and inquiry.

"Jinny, ain't I nussed you always? Ain't I come upstairs to quiet you when yo' mammy ain't had no power ovah yo'? Ain't I cooked fo' yo', and ain't I followed you everywheres since I quit ridin' yo' pa's hosses to vict'ry? Ain't I one of de fambly? An' yit yo' ax me to call yo' Miss Jinny?"

"Then you've had privileges enough," Virginia answered. "One week from to-morrow you are to say 'Miss Jinny.' "

"I'se tell you what, Jinny," he answered mischievously, with an emphasis on the word, "I'se call you Miss Jinny ef you'll call me *Mistah Johnson. Mistah Johnson.* You ain't gwinter forget? *Mistah Johnson.*"

"I'll remember," she said. "Ned," she demanded suddenly, "would you like to be free?"

The negro started.

"Why you ax me dat, Jinny?"

"Mr. Benbow's Hester is free," she said.

"Who done freed her?"

Miss Virginia flushed. "A detestable young Yankee, who has come out here to meddle with what doesn't concern him. I wanted Hester, Ned. And you should have married her, if you behaved yourself."

Ned laughed uneasily.

"I reckon I'se too ol' fo' Heste'." And added with privileged impudence, "There ain't no cause why I can't marry her now."

Virginia suddenly leaped to the ground without his assistance.

"That's enough, Ned," she said, and started toward the house.

"Jinny! *Miss Jinny!*" The call was plaintive.

"Well, what?"

"Miss Jinny, I seed that thar young gemman. Lan' sakes, he ain' look like er Yankee—"

"Ned," said Virginia, sternly, "do you want to go back to cooking?"

He quailed. "Oh, no'm. Lan' sakes, no'm. I didn't mean nuthin'."

She turned, frowned, and bit her lip. Around the corner of the veranda she ran into her cousin. He, too, was booted and spurred. He reached out, boyishly, to catch her in his arms. But she drew back from his grasp.

"Why, Jinny," he cried, "what's the matter?"

"Nothing, Max." She often called him so, his middle name being Maxwell. "But you have no right to do that."

"To do what?" said Clarence, making a face.

"You know," answered Virginia, curtly. "Where's Aunt Lillian?"

"Why haven't I the right?" he asked, ignoring the inquiry.

"Because you have not, unless I choose. And I don't choose."

"Are you angry with me still? It wasn't my fault. Uncle Comyn made me come away. You should have had the girl, Jinny, if it took my fortune."

"You have been drinking this morning, Max," said Virginia.

"Only a julep or so," he replied apologetically. "I rode over to the race track to see the new trotter. I've called him Halcyon, Jinny," he continued, with enthusiasm. "And he'll win the handicap sure."

She sat down on the veranda steps, with her knees crossed and her chin resting on her hands. The air was heavy with the perfume of the grapes and the smell of late flowers from the sunken garden near by. A blue haze hung over the Illinois shore.

"Max, you promised me you wouldn't drink so much."

"And I haven't been, Jinny, 'pon my word," he replied. "But I met old Sparks at the Tavern, and he started to talk about the horses, and—and he insisted."

"And you hadn't the strength of character," she said, scornfully, "to refuse."

"Pshaw, Jinny, a gentleman must be a gentleman. I'm no Yankee."

For a space Virginia answered nothing. Then she said, without changing her position:—

"If you were, you might be worth something."

"Virginia!"

She did not reply, but sat gazing toward the water. He began to pace the veranda, fiercely.

"Look here, Jinny," he cried, pausing in front of her. "There are some things you can't say to me, even in jest."

Virginia rose, flicked her riding-whip, and started down the steps.

"Don't be a fool, Max," she said.

He followed her, bewildered. She skirted the garden, passed the orchard, and finally reached a summer house perched on a knoll at the edge of the wood. Then she seated herself on a bench, silently. He took a place on the opposite side, with his feet stretched out, dejectedly.

"I'm tired trying to please you," he said. "I have been a fool. You don't care *that* for me. It was all right when I was younger, when there was no one else to take you riding, and jump off the barn for your amusement, Miss. Now you have Tom Catherwood and Jack Brinsmade and the Russell boys running after you, it's different. I reckon I'll go to Kansas. There are Yankees to shoot in Kansas."

He did not see her smile as he sat staring at his feet.

"Max," said she, all at once, "why don't you settle down to something? Why don't you work?"

Young Mr. Colfax's arm swept around in a circle.

"There are twelve hundred acres to look after here, and a few niggers. That's enough for a gentleman."

"Pooh!" exclaimed his cousin, "this isn't a cotton plantation. Aunt Lillian doesn't farm for money. If she did, you would have to check your extravagances mighty quick, sir."

"I look after Pompey's reports, I do as much work as my ancestors," answered Clarence, hotly.

"Ah, that is the trouble," said Virginia.

"What do you mean?" her cousin demanded.

"We have been gentlemen too long," said Virginia.

The boy straightened up and rose. The pride and wilfulness of generations was indeed in his handsome face. And something else went with it. Around the mouth a grave tinge of indulgence.

"What has your life been?" she went on, speaking rapidly. "A mixture of gamecocks and ponies and race horses and billiards, and idleness at the Virginia Springs, and fighting with other boys. What do you know? You wouldn't go to college. You wouldn't study law. You can't write a decent letter. You don't know anything about the history of your country. What can you do—?"

"I can ride and fight," he said. "I can go to New Orleans to-morrow to join Walker's Nicaragua expedition. We've got to beat the Yankees, —they'll have Kansas away from us before we know it."

Virginia's eye flashed appreciation.

"Do you remember, Jinny," he cried, "one day long ago when those Dutch ruffians were teasing you and Anne on the road, and Bert Russell and Jack and I came along? We whipped 'em, Jinny. And my eye was closed. And you were bathing it here, and one of my buttons was gone. And you counted the rest."

"Rich man, poor man, beggarman, thief,—doctor, lawyer, merchant, *chief*," she recited, laughing. She crossed over and sat beside him, and her tone changed. "Max, can't you understand? It isn't that. Max, if you would only work at something. That is why the Yankees beat us. If you would learn to weld iron, or to build bridges, or railroads. Or if you would learn business, and go to work in Pa's store."

"You do not care for me as I am?"

"I knew that you did not understand," she answered passionately. "It is because I care for you that I wish to make you great. You care too much for a good time, for horses, Max. You love the South, but you think too little how she is to be saved. If war is to come, we shall want men like that Captain Robert Lee who was here. A man who can turn the forces of the earth to his own purposes."

For a moment Clarence was moodily silent.

"I have always intended to go into politics, after Pa's example," he said at length.

"Then—" began Virginia, and paused.

"Then—?" he said.

"Then—you must study law."

He gave her the one keen look. And she met it, with her lips tightly pressed together. Then he smiled.

"Virginia, you will never forgive that Yankee, Brice."

"I shall never forgive any Yankee," she retorted quickly. "But **we** are not talking about him. I am thinking of the South, and of you."

He stooped toward her face, but she avoided him and went back to the bench.

"Why not?" he said.

"You must prove first that you are a man," she said.

For years he remembered the scene. The vineyard, the yellow stubble, and the river rushing on and on with tranquil power, and the slow panting of the steamboat. A doe ran out of the forest, and paused, her head raised, not twenty feet away.

"And then you will marry me, Jinny?" he asked finally.

"Before you may hope to control another, we shall see whether you can control yourself, sir."

"But it has all been arranged," he exclaimed, "since we played here together years ago!"

"No one shall arrange that for me," replied Virginia, promptly. "And I should think that you would wish to have some of the credit for yourself."

"Jinny!"

Again she avoided him by leaping the low railing. The doe fled into the forest, whistling fearfully. Virginia waved her hand to him and started toward the house. At the corner of the porch she ran into her aunt.

Mrs. Colfax was a beautiful woman. Beautiful when Addison Colfax married her in Kentucky at nineteen, beautiful still at three and forty. This, I am aware, is a bald statement. "Prove it," you say. "We do not believe it. It was told you by some old beau who lives upon the memory of the past."

Ladies, a score of different daguerreotypes of Lillian Colfax are in existence. And whatever may be said of portraits, daguerreotypes do not flatter. All the town admitted that she was beautiful. All the town knew that she was the daughter of old Judge Colfax's overseer at Halcyondale. If she had not been beautiful, Addison Colfax would not have run away with her. That is certain. He left her a rich widow at five and twenty, mistress of the country place he had bought on the Bellefontaine Road, near St. Louis. And when Mrs. Colfax was not dancing off to the Virginia watering-places, Bellegarde was a gay house.

"Jinny," exclaimed her aunt, "how you scared me! What on earth is the matter?"

"Nothing," said Virginia—

"She refused to kiss me," put in Clarence, half in play, half in resentment.

Mrs. Colfax laughed musically. She put one of her white hands on each of her niece's cheeks, kissed her, and then gazed into her face until Virginia reddened.

"Law, Jinny, you're quite pretty," said her aunt. "I hadn't realized it—but you must take care of your complexion. You're horribly sunburned, and you let your hair blow all over your face. It's barbarous not to wear a mask when you ride. Your Pa doesn't look after you properly. I would ask you to stay to the dance to-night if your skin were only white, instead of red. You're old enough to know better, Virginia. Mr. Vance was to have driven out for dinner. Have you seen him, Clarence?"

"No, mother."

"He is so amusing," Mrs. Colfax continued, "and he generally brings candy. I shall die of the blues before supper." She sat down with a grand air at the head of the table, while Alfred took the lid from the silver soup-tureen in front of her. "Jinny, can't you say something bright? Do I have to listen to Clarence's horse talk for another hour? Tell me some gossip. Will you have some gumbo soup?"

"Why do you listen to Clarence's horse talk?" said Virginia. "Why don't you make him go to work?"

"Mercy!" said Mrs. Colfax, laughing, "what could he do?"

"That's just it," said Virginia. "He hasn't a serious interest in life."

Clarence looked sullen. And his mother, as usual, took his side.

"What put that into your head, Jinny," she said. "He has the place here to look after, a very gentlemanly occupation. That's what they do in Virginia."

"Yes," said Virginia, scornfully, "we're all gentlemen in the South. What do we know about business and developing the resources of the country? Not *that*."

"You make my head ache, my dear," was her aunt's reply. "Where did you get all this?"

"You ask me because I am a girl," said Virginia. "You believe that women were made to look at, and to play with,—not to think. But if we are going to get ahead of the Yankees, we shall have to think. It was all very well to be a gentleman in the days of my great-grandfather. But now we have railroads and steamboats. And who builds them? The Yankees. We of the South think of our ancestors, and drift deeper and deeper into debt. We know how to fight, and we know how to command. But we have been ruined by—" here she glanced at the retreating form of Alfred, and lowered her voice, "by niggers."

Mrs. Colfax's gaze rested languidly on her niece's face, which glowed with indignation.

"You get this terrible habit of argument from Comyn," she said. "He ought to send you to boarding-school. How mean of Mr. Vance not to come! You've been talking with that old reprobate Whipple. Why does Comyn put up with him?"

"He isn't an old reprobate," said Virginia, warmly.

"You really ought to go to school," said her aunt. "Don't be eccentric. It isn't fashionable. I suppose you wish Clarence to go into a factory."

"If I were a man," said Virginia, "and going into a factory would teach me how to make a locomotive or a cotton press, or to build a bridge, I should go into a factory. We shall never beat the Yankees until we meet them on their own ground."

"There is Mr. Vance now," said Mrs. Colfax, and added fervently, "Thank the Lord!"

CHAPTER IX

A QUIET SUNDAY IN LOCUST STREET

IF the truth were known where Virginia got the opinions which she expressed so freely to her aunt and cousin, it was from Colonel Carvel himself. The Colonel would rather have denounced the Dred Scott decision than admit to Judge Whipple that one of the greatest weaknesses of the South lay in her lack of mechanical and manufacturing ability. But he had confessed as much in private to Captain Elijah Brent. The Colonel would often sit for an hour or more, after supper, with his feet tucked up on the mantel and his hat on the back of his head, buried in thought. Then he would saunter slowly down to the Planters' House bar, which served the purposes of a club in those days, in search of an argument with other prominent citizens. The Colonel had his own particular chair in his own particular corner, which was always vacated when he came in at the door. And then he always had three fingers of the best Bourbon whiskey, no more and no less, every evening.

He never met his bosom friend and pet antagonist at the Planters' House bar. Judge Whipple, indeed, took his meals upstairs, but he never descended,—it was generally supposed because of the strong slavery atmosphere there. However, the Judge went periodically to his friend's for a quiet Sunday dinner (so called in derision by St. Louisans), on which occasions Virginia sat at the end of the table and endeavored to pour water on the flames when they flared up too fiercely.

The Sunday following her ride to Bellegarde was the Judge's Sunday. Certain tastes which she had inherited had hitherto provided her with pleasurable sensations while these battles were in progress. More than once had she scored a fair hit on the Judge for her father,—to the mutual delight of both gentlemen. But to-day she dreaded being present at the argument. Just why she dreaded it is a matter of feminine psychology best left to the reader for solution.

The argument began, as usual, with the tearing apart limb by limb of the unfortunate Franklin Pierce, by Judge Whipple.

"What a miserable exhibition in the eyes of the world," said the

63

Judge. "Franklin Pierce of New Hampshire" (he pronounced this name with infinite scorn) "managed by Jefferson Davis of Mississippi!"

"And he was well managed, sir," said the Colonel.

"What a pliant tool of your Southern slaveholders! I hear that you are to give him a plantation as a reward."

"No such thing, sir."

"He deserves it," continued the Judge, with conviction. "See the magnificent forts he permitted Davis to build up in the South, the arsenals he let him stock. The country does not realize this. But the day will come when they will execrate Pierce before Benedict Arnold, sir. And look at the infamous Kansas-Nebraska act! That is the greatest crime, and Douglas and Pierce the greatest criminals, of the century."

"Do have some more of that fried chicken, Judge," said Virginia.

Mr. Whipple helped himself fiercely, and the Colonel smiled.

"You should be satisfied now," said he. "Another Northern man is in the White House."

"Buchanan!" roared the Judge, with his mouth full. "Another traitor, sir. Another traitor worse than the first. He swallows the Dred Scott decision, and smirks. What a blot on the history of this Republic! O Lord!" cried Mr. Whipple, "what are we coming to? A Northernman, he could gag and bind Kansas and force her into slavery against the will of her citizens. He packs his Cabinet to support the ruffians you send over the borders. The very governors he ships out there, his henchmen, have their stomachs turned. Look at Walker, whom they are plotting against in Washington. He can't stand the smell of this Lecompton Constitution Buchanan is trying to jam down their throats. Jefferson Davis would have troops there, to be sure that it goes through, if he had his way. Can't you see how one sin leads to another, Carvel? How slavery is rapidly demoralizing a free people?"

"It is because you won't let it alone where it belongs, sir," retorted the Colonel. It was seldom that he showed any heat in his replies. He talked slowly, and he had a way of stretching forth his hand to prevent the more eager Judge from interrupting him.

"The welfare of the whole South, as matters now stand, sir, depends upon slavery. Our plantations could not exist a day without slave labor. If you abolished that institution, Judge Whipple, you would ruin millions of your fellow-countrymen,—you would reduce sovereign states to a situation of disgraceful dependence. And all, sir," now he raised his voice lest the Judge break in, "all, sir, for the sake of a low breed that ain't fit for freedom. You and I, who have the Magna Charta and the Declaration of Independence behind us, who are descended from a race that has done nothing but rule for ten centuries and more, may well establish a Republic where the basis of stability is the self-control of the individual—as long as men such as you and I form its citizens. Look at the South Americans. How do Republics go there? And the minute you and I let in niggers, who haven't any more self-control than dogs, on an equal basis, with as much of a vote as you have,—niggers, sir, that have lived like wild beasts in the depths of the jungle since the days of Ham, —what's going to become of our Republic?"

"Education," cried the Judge.

But the word was snatched out of his mouth.

"Education isn't a matter of one generation. No, sir, nor two, nor three, nor four. But of centuries."

"Sir," said the Judge, "I can point out negroes of intelligence and learning."

"And I reckon you could teach some monkeys to talk English, and recite the catechism, and sing emotional hymns, if you brought over a couple of million from Africa," answered the Colonel, dryly, as he rose to put on his hat and light a cigar.

It was his custom to offer a cigar to the Judge, who invariably refused, and rubbed his nose with scornful violence.

Virginia, on the verge of leaving, stayed on, fascinated by the turn the argument had taken.

"Your prejudice is hide-bound, sir," said Mr. Whipple.

"No, Whipple," said the Colonel, "when God washed off this wicked earth, and started new, He saw fit to put the sons of Ham in subjection. They're slaves of each other in Africa, and I reckon they're treated no better than they are here. Abuses can't be helped in any system, sir, though we are bettering them. Were the poor in London in the days of the Edwards as well off as our niggers are to-day?"

The Judge snorted.

"A divine institution!" he shouted. "A black curse! Because the world has been a wicked place of oppression since Noah's day, is that any reason why it should so continue until the day of Judgment?"

The Colonel smiled, which was a sign that he was pleased with his argument.

"Now, see here, Whipple," said he. "If we had any guarantee that you would let us alone where we are, to manage our slaves and to cultivate our plantations, there wouldn't be any trouble. But the country keeps on growing and growing, and you're not content with half. You want everything,—all the new states must abolish slavery. And after a while you will overwhelm us, and ruin us, and make us paupers. Do you wonder that we contend for our rights, tooth and nail? They are our rights."

"If it had not been for Virginia and Maryland and the South, this nation would not be in existence."

The Colonel laughed.

"First rate, Jinny," he cried. "That's so."

But the Judge was in a revery. He probably had not heard her.

"The nation is going to the dogs," he said, mumbling rather to himself than to the others. "We shall never prosper until the curse is shaken off, or wiped out in blood. It clogs our progress. Our merchant marine, of which we were so proud, has been annihilated by these continued disturbances. But, sir," he cried, hammering his fist upon the table until the glasses rang, "the party that is to save us was born at Pittsburgh last year on Washington's birthday. The Republican Party, sir."

"Shucks!" exclaimed Mr. Carvel, with amusement. "The *Black* Republican Party, made up of old fools and young Anarchists, of Dutchmen and nigger-worshippers. Why, Whipple, that party's a joke. Where's your leader?"

"In Illinois," was the quick response.

"What's his name?"

"*Abraham Lincoln*, sir," thundered Mr. Whipple. "And to my way of thinking he has uttered a more significant phrase on the situation than any of your Washington statesmen. '*This government*,' said he to a friend of mine, '*cannot exist half slave and half free.*' "

So impressively did Mr. Whipple pronounce these words that Mr. Carvel stirred uneasily, and in spite of himself, as though he were listening to an oracle. He recovered instantly.

"He's a demagogue, seeking for striking phrases, sir. You're too intelligent a man to be taken in by such as he."

"I tell you he is not, sir."

"I know him, sir," cried the Colonel, taking down his feet. "He's an obscure lawyer. Poor white trash! Torn down poor! My friend Mr. Richardson of Springfield tells me he is low down. He was born in a log cabin, and spends most of his time in a drug-store telling stories that you would not listen to, Judge Whipple."

"I would listen to anything he said," replied the Judge. "Poor white

trash, sir! The greatest men rise from the people. A demagogue!" Mr.
Whipple fairly shook with rage. "The nation doesn't know him yet. But
mark my words, the day will come when it will. He was ballotted for
Vice-President in the Philadelphia convention last year. Nobody paid
any attention to that. If the convention had heard him speak at Bloomington, he would have been nominated instead of Frémont. If the nation
could have heard him, he would be President to-day instead of that
miserable Buchanan. I happened to be at Bloomington. And while the
idiots on the platform were drivelling, the people kept calling for Lincoln. I had never heard of him then. I've never forgot him since. He came
ambling out of the back of the hall, a lanky, gawky-looking man, ridicu-
lously ugly, sir. But the moment he opened his mouth he had us spellbound. The language which your low-down lawyer used was that of a
God-sent prophet, sir. He had those Illinois bumpkins all worked up,—
the women crying, and some of the men, too. And mad! Good Lord, they
were mad—'We will say to the Southern disunionists,' he cried,—'we
will say to the Southern disunionists, we won't go out of the Union, *and
you shan't.*' "

There was a silence when the Judge finished. But presently Mr. Carvel took a match. And he stood over the Judge in his favorite attitude,—
with his feet apart,—as he lighted another cigar.

"I reckon we're going to have war, Silas," said he, slowly; "but don't
you think that your Mr. Lincoln scares me into that belief. I don't count
his bluster worth a cent. No sirree! It's this youngster who comes out
here from Boston and buys a nigger with all the money he's got in the
world. And if he's an impetuous young fool, I'm no judge of men."

"Appleton Brice wasn't precisely impetuous," remarked Mr. Whipple.
And he smiled a little bitterly, as though the word had stirred a memory.

"I like that young fellow," Mr. Carvel continued. "It seems to be a
kind of fatality with me to get along with Yankees. I reckon there's a
screw loose somewhere, but Brice acted the man all the way through.
He got a fall out of you, Silas, in your room, after the show. Where are
you going, Jinny?"

Virginia had risen, and she was standing very erect, with a flush on
her face, waiting for her father to finish.

"To see Anne Brinsmade," she said. "Good-by, Uncle Silas."

She had called him so from childhood. Hers was the one voice that
seemed to soften him—it never failed. He turned to her now with a

movement that was almost gentle. "Virginia, I should like you to know my young Yankee," said he.

"Thank you, Uncle Silas," said the girl, with dignity, "but I scarcely think that he would care to know me. He feels so strongly."

"He feels no stronger than I do," replied the Judge.

"You have gotten used to me in eighteen years, and besides," she flashed, "you never spent all the money you had in the world for a principle."

Mr. Whipple smiled as she went out of the door.

"I have spent pretty near all," he said. But more to himself than to the Colonel.

That evening, some young people came in to tea, two of the four big Catherwood boys, Anne Brinsmade and her brother Jack, Puss Russell and Bert, and Eugénie Rénault. But Virginia lost her temper. In an evil moment Puss Russell started the subject of the young Yankee who had deprived her of Hester. Puss was ably seconded by Jack Brinsmade, whose reputation as a tormentor extended far back into his boyhood. In vain did Anne, the peacemaker, try to quench him, while the big Catherwoods and Bert Russell laughed incessantly. No wonder that Virginia was angry. She would not speak to Puss as that young lady bade her good night. And the Colonel, coming home from an evening with Mr. Brinsmade, found his daughter in an armchair, staring into the sitting-room fire. There was no other light in the room. Her chin was in her hand, and her lips were pursed.

"Heigho!" said the Colonel, "what's the trouble now?"

"Nothing," said Virginia.

"Come," he insisted, "what have they been doing to my girl?"

"Pa!"

"Yes, honey."

"I don't want to go to balls all my life. I want to go to boarding-school, and learn something. Emily is going to Monticello after Christmas. Pa, will you let me?"

Mr. Carvel winced. He put an arm around her. He thought of his lonely widowhood, of her whose place Virginia had taken.

"And what shall I do?" he said, trying to smile.

"It will only be for a little while. And Monticello isn't very far, Pa."

"Well, well, there is plenty of time to think it over between now and January," he said. "And now I have a little favor to ask of you, honey."

"Yes?" she said.

The Colonel took the other armchair, stretched his feet toward the blaze, and stroked his goatee. He glanced covertly at his daughter's profile. Twice he cleared his throat.

"Jinny?"

"Yes, Pa" (without turning her head).

"Jinny, I was going to speak of this young Brice. He's a stranger here, and he comes of a good family, and—and I like him."

"And you wish me to invite him to my party," finished Virginia.

The Colonel started. "I reckon you guessed it," he said.

Virginia remained immovable. She did not answer at once. Then she said:—

"Do you think, in bidding against me, that he behaved like a gentle-man?"

The Colonel blundered.

"Lord, Virginia," he said, "I thought you told the Judge this after·noon that it was done out of principle."

Virginia ignored this. But she bit her lip.

"He is like all Yankees, without one bit of consideration for a woman. He knew I wanted Hester."

"What makes you imagine that he thought of you at all, my dear?" asked her father, mildly. "He does not know you."

This time the Colonel scored certainly. The firelight saved Virginia.

"He overheard our conversation," she answered.

"I reckon that he wasn't worrying much about us. And besides, he was trying to save Hester from Jennings."

"I thought that you said that it was to be my party, Pa," said Virginia, irrelevantly.

The Colonel looked thoughtful, then he began to laugh.

"Haven't we enough Black Republican friends?" she asked.

"So you won't have him?" said the Colonel.

"I didn't say that I wouldn't have him," she answered.

The Colonel rose, and brushed the ashes from his coat.

"By Gum!" he said. "Women beat me."

CHAPTER X

THE LITTLE HOUSE

WHEN Stephen attempted to thank Judge Whipple for going on Hester's bond, he merely said, "Tut, tut."

The Judge rose at six, so his man Shadrach told Stephen. He had his breakfast at the Planters' House at seven, read the *Missouri Democrat,* and returned by eight. Sometimes he would say good morning to Stephen and Richter, and sometimes he would not. Mr. Whipple was out a great part of the day, and he had many visitors. He was a very busy man. Like a great specialist (which he was), he would see only one person at a time. And Stephen soon discovered that his employer did not discriminate between age or sex, or importance, or condition of servitude. In short, Stephen's opinion of Judge Whipple altered very materially before the end of that first week. He saw poor women and disconsolate men go into the private room ahead of rich citizens, who seemed content to wait their turn on the hard wooden chairs against the wall of the main office. There was one incident in particular, when a well-dressed gentleman of middle age paced impatiently for two mortal hours after Shadrach had taken his card into the sanctum. When at last he had been admitted, Mr. Richter whispered to Stephen his name. It was that of a big railroad man from the East. The transom let out the true state of affairs.

"See here, Callender," the Judge was heard to say, "you fellows don't like me, and you wouldn't come here unless you had to. But when your road gets in a tight place, you turn up and expect to walk in ahead of my friends. No, sir, if you want to see me, you've got to wait."

Mr. Callender made some inaudible reply.

"Money!" roared the Judge, "take your money to Stetson, and see if you win your case."

Mr. Richter smiled at Stephen, as if in sheer happiness at this vindication of an employer who had never seemed to him to need a defence.

Stephen was greatly drawn toward this young German with the great scar on his pleasant face. And he was itching to know about that scar.

70

Every day, after coming in from dinner, Richter lighted a great brown meerschaum, and read the St. Louis *Anzeiger* and the *Westliche Post.* Often he sang quietly to himself:—

> "Deutschlands Söhne
> Laut ertöne
> Euer Vaterlandgesang.
> Vaterland! Du Land des Ruhmes,
> Weih' zu deines Heiligthumes
> Hütern, uns und unser Schwert."

There were other songs, too. And some wonderful quality in the German's voice gave you a thrill when you heard them, albeit you could not understand the words. Richter never guessed how Stephen, with his eyes on his book, used to drink in those airs. And presently he found out that they were inspired.

The day that the railroad man called, and after he and the Judge had gone out together, the ice was broken.

"You Americans from the North are a queer people, Mr. Brice," remarked Mr. Richter, as he put on his coat. "You do not show your feelings. You are ashamed. The Judge, at first I could not comprehend him —he would scold and scold. But one day I see that his heart is warm, and since then I love him. Have you ever eaten a German dinner, Mr. Brice? No? Then you must come with me, now."

It was raining, the streets ankle-deep in mud, and the beer-garden by the side of the restaurant to which they went was dreary and bedraggled. But inside the place was warm and cheerful. Inside, to all intents and purposes, it was Germany. A most genial host crossed the room to give Mr. Richter a welcome that any man might have envied. He was introduced to Stephen.

"We were all *Streber* together, in Germany," said Richter.

"You were all what?" asked Stephen, interested.

"Strivers, you might call it in English. In the *Vaterland* those who seek for higher and better things—for liberty, and to be rid of oppression—are so called. That is why we fought in '48 and lost. And that is why we came here, to the Republic. *Ach!* I fear I will never be the great lawyer—but the striver, yes, always. We must fight once more to be rid of the black monster that sucks the blood of freedom—vampire. Is it not so in English?"

Stephen was astonished at this outburst.

"You think it will come to war?"

"I fear,—yes, I fear," said the German, shaking his head. "We fear. We are already preparing."

"Preparing? You would fight, Richter? You, a foreigner?"

"A foreigner!" cried Richter, with a flash of anger in his blue eyes that died as suddenly as it came,—died into reproach. "Call me not a foreigner—we Germans will show whether or not we are foreigners when the time is ripe. This great country belongs to all the oppressed. Your ancestors founded it, and fought for it, that the descendants of mine might find a haven from tyranny. My friend, one-half of this city is German, and it is they who will save it if danger arises. You must come with me one night to South St. Louis, that you may know us. Then you will perhaps understand, Stephen. You will not think of us as foreign swill, but as patriots who love our new *Vaterland* even as you love it. You must come to our Turner Halls, where we are drilling against the time when the Union shall have need of us."

"You are drilling now?" exclaimed Stephen, in still greater astonishment. The German's eloquence had made him tingle, even as had the songs.

"Prosit deine Blume!" answered Richter, smiling and holding up his glass of beer. "You will come to a *commerce,* and see. This is not our blessed Lichtenhainer, that we drink at Jena. One may have a pint of Lichtenhainer for less than a groschen at Jena. *Aber,"* he added as he rose, with a laugh that showed his strong teeth, "we Americans are rich."

As Stephen's admiration for his employer grew, his fear of him waxed greater likewise. The Judge's methods of teaching law were certainly not Harvard's methods. For a fortnight he paid as little attention to the young man as he did to the messengers who came with notes and cooled their heels in the outer office until it became the Judge's pleasure to answer them. This was a trifle discouraging to Stephen. But he stuck to his Chitty and his Greenleaf and his Kent. It was Richter who advised him to buy Whittlesey's "Missouri Form Book," and warned him of Mr. Whipple's hatred for the new code. Well that he did! There came a fearful hour of judgment. With the swiftness of a hawk Mr. Whipple descended out of a clear sky, and instantly the law terms began to rattle in Stephen's head like dried peas in a can. It was the Old Style of Pleading this time, without a knowledge of which the Judge declared with vehemence that a lawyer was not fit to put pen to legal cap.

"Now, sir, the pleadings?" he cried.

"First," said Stephen, "was the Declaration. The answer to that was the Plea. The answer to that was the Replication. Then came the Rejoinder, then the Surrejoinder, then the Rebutter, then the Surrebutter. But they rarely got that far," he added unwisely.

"A good principal in Law, sir," said the Judge, "is not to volunteer information."

Stephen was somewhat cast down when he reached home that Saturday evening. He had come out of his examination with feathers drooping. He had been given no more briefs to copy, nor had Mr. Whipple vouchsafed even to send him on an errand. He had not learned how common a thing it is with young lawyers to feel that they are of no use in the world. Besides, the rain continued. This was the fifth day.

His mother, knitting before the fire in her own room, greeted him with her usual quiet smile of welcome. He tried to give her a humorous account of his catechism of the morning, but failed.

"I am quite sure that he doesn't like me," said Stephen.

His mother continued to smile.

"If he did, he would not show it," she answered.

"I can feel it," said Stephen, dejectedly.

"The Judge was here this afternoon," said his mother.

"What?" cried Stephen. "Again this week? They say he never calls in the daytime, and rarely in the evening. What did he say?"

"He said that some of this Boston nonsense must be gotten out of you," answered Mrs. Brice, laughing. "He said that you were too stiff. That you needed to rub against the plain men who were building up the West. Who were making a vast world-power of the original little confederation of thirteen states. And Stephen," she added more earnestly, "I am not sure but what he is right."

Then Stephen laughed. And for a long time he sat staring into the fire.

"What else did he say?" he asked, after a little while.

"He told me about a little house which we might rent very cheaply. Too cheaply, it seems. The house is on this street, next door to Mr. Brinsmade, to whom it belongs. And Mr. Whipple brought the key, that we might inspect it to-morrow."

"But a servant," objected Stephen, "I suppose that we must have a servant."

His mother's voice fell.

"That poor girl whom you freed is here to see me every day. Old Nancy does washing. But Hester has no work, and she is a burden to

Judge Whipple. Oh, no," she continued, in response to Stephen's glance, "the Judge did not mention that, but I think he had it in mind that Hester might come. And I am sure that she would."

Sunday dawned brightly. After church Mrs. Brice and Stephen walked down Olive Street, and stood looking at a tiny house wedged in between two large ones with scrolled fronts. Sad memories of Beacon Street filled them both as they gazed, but they said nothing of this to each other. As Stephen put his hand on the latch of the little iron gate, a gentleman came out of the larger house next door. He was past the middle age, somewhat scrupulously dressed in the old fashion, in swallowtail coat and black stock. Benevolence was in the generous mouth, in the large nose that looked like Washington's, and benevolence fairly sparkled in the blue eyes. He smiled at them as though he had known them always, and the world seemed brighter that very instant. They smiled in return, whereupon the gentleman lifted his hat. And the kindliness and the courtliness of that bow made them very happy.

"Did you wish to look at the house, madam?" he asked.

"Yes, sir," said Mrs. Brice.

"Allow me to open it for you," he said, graciously taking the key from her. "I fear that you will find it inconvenient and incommodious, ma'am. I should be fortunate, indeed, to get a good tenant."

He fitted the key in the door, while Stephen and his mother smiled at each other at the thought of the rent. The gentleman opened the door, and stood aside to let them enter, very much as if he were showing them a palace for which he was the humble agent.

They went into the little parlor, which was nicely furnished in mahogany and horsehair. And it had back of it a bit of a dining room, with a little porch overlooking the back yard. Mrs. Brice thought of the dark and stately high-ceiled dining-room she had known throughout her married days: of the board from which a royal governor of Massachusetts Colony had eaten, and some governors of the Commonwealth since. Thank God, she had not to sell that, nor the Brice silver which had stood on the high sideboard with the wolves and the shield upon it. The widow's eyes filled with tears. She had not hoped again to have a home for these things, nor the father's armchair, nor the few family treasures that were to come over the mountains.

The gentleman, with infinite tact, said little, but led the way through the rooms. There were not many of them. At the door of the kitchen he stopped, and laid his hand kindly on Stephen's shoulder:—

"Here we may not enter. This is your department, ma'am," said he.

Finally, as they stood without waiting for the gentleman, who insisted upon locking the door, they observed a girl in a ragged shawl hurrying up the street. As she approached them, her eyes were fixed upon the large house next door. But suddenly, as the gentleman turned, she caught sight of him, and from her lips escaped a cry of relief. She flung open the gate, and stood before him.

"Oh, Mr. Brinsmade," she cried, "mother is dying. You have done so much for us, sir,—couldn't you come to her for a little while? She thought if she might see you once more, she would die happy." The voice was choked by a sob.

Mr. Brinsmade took the girl's hand in his own, and turned to the lady with as little haste, with as much politeness, as he had shown before.

"You will excuse me, ma'am," he said, with his hat in his hand.

The widow had no words to answer him. But she and her son watched him as he walked rapidly down the street, his arm in the girl's, until they were out of sight. And then they walked home silently.

Might not the price of this little house be likewise a piece of the Brinsmade charity?

CHAPTER XI

THE INVITATION

MR. ELIPHALET HOPPER in his Sunday-best broadcloth was a marvel of propriety. It seemed to Stephen that his face wore a graver expression on Sunday when he met him standing on Miss Crane's doorstep, picking the lint from his coat. Stephen's intention was not to speak. But he remembered what the Judge had said to his mother, and nodded. Why, indeed, should he put on airs with this man who had come to St. Louis unknown and unrecommended and poor, who by sheer industry had made himself of importance in the large business of Carvel & Company? As for Stephen Brice, he was not yet earning his salt, but existing by the charity of Judge Silas Whipple.

"Howdy, Mr. Brice," said Mr. Hopper, his glance caught by the indefinable in Stephen's costume. This would have puzzled Mr. Hopper's tailor more.

"Very well, thanks."

"A fine day after the rain."

Stephen nodded, and Mr. Hopper entered the house after him.

"Be you asked to Virginia Carvel's party?" he asked abruptly.

"I do not know Miss Carvel," said Stephen, wondering how well the other did. And if the truth be told, he was a little annoyed at Mr. Hopper's free use of her name.

"That shouldn't make no difference," said Eliphalet, with just a shade of bitterness in his tone. "They keep open house, like all Southerners,—" Mr. Hopper hesitated,—"for such as come well recommended. I 'most forgot," said he. "I callate you're not any too well recommended. I 'most forgot that little transaction down to the Court House. They do say that she wanted that gal almighty bad,—she was most awful cut up not to get her. Served her right, though. I'm glad you did. Show her she can't have everything her own way. And say," he added, with laughter, "how you did fix that there stuck-up Colfax boy! *He'll* never forgive you no more than she. But," said Mr. Hopper, meditatively, "it was a durned-fool trick."

I think Stephen's critics will admit that he had a good right to be angry, and that they will admire him just a little bit because he kept his temper. But Mr. Hopper evidently thought he had gone too far.

"She ain't got no use for me, neither," he said.

"She shows poor judgment," answered Stephen.

"She's not long sighted, that's sure," replied Eliphalet, with emphasis.

At dinner Stephen was tried still further. And it was then he made the determination to write for the newspapers in order to pay the rent on Mr. Brinsmade's house. Miss Carvel's coming-out party was the chief topic.

"They do say the Colonel is to spend a sight of money on that ball," said Mrs. Abner Reed. "I guess it won't bankrupt him." And she looked hard at Mr. Hopper.

"I callate he ain't pushed for money," that gentleman vouchsafed.

"He's a good man, and done well by you, Mr. Hopper."

"So-so," answered Eliphalet. "But I will say that I done something for the Colonel. I've saved him a hundred times my pay since I showed old Hood the leaks. And I got a thousand dollar order from Wright & Company this week for him."

"I dare say you'd keep a tight hand enough on expenses," said Miss Crane, half in sarcasm, half in approval.

"If Colonel Carvel was doin' business in New England," said Eliphalet, "he'd been bankrupt long ago."

"That young Clarence Colfax," Mrs. Abner Reed broke in, "he'll get a right smart mint o' money when he marries Virginia. They do say her mother left her independent. How now, Mr. Hopper?"

Eliphalet looked mysterious and knowing. He did not reply.

"And young Colfax ain't precisely a pauper," said Miss Crane.

"I'll risk a good deal that she don't marry Colfax," said Mr. Hopper.

"What on earth do you mean?" cried Mrs. Abner. "It ain't broke off?"

"No," he answered, "it ain't broke off. But I callate she won't have him when the time comes. She's got too much sense."

Heavy at heart, Stephen climbed the stairs, thanking heaven that he had not been drawn into the controversy. A partial comprehension of Mr. Hopper was dawning upon him. He suspected that gentleman of an aggressive determination to achieve wealth, and the power which goes with it, for the purpose of using that power upon those beneath him. Nay, when he thought over his conversation, he suspected him of more, —of the intention to marry Virginia Carvel.

It will be seen whether Stephen was right or wrong.

He took a walk that afternoon, as far out as a place called Lindell's Grove, which afterward became historic. And when he returned to the house, his mother handed him a little white envelope.

"It came while you were out," she said.

He turned it over, and stared at his name written across the front in a feminine hand. In those days young ladies did not write in the bold and masculine manner now deemed proper. Stephen stared at the note, manlike, and pondered.

"Who brought it, mother?"

"Why don't you open it, and see?" asked his mother, with a smile.

He took the suggestion. What a funny, formal little note we should think it now! It was not funny to Stephen—then. He read it, and he read it again, and finally he walked over to the window, still holding it in his hand.

Some mothers would have shown their curiosity. Mrs. Brice did not, wherein she proved herself their superiors in the knowledge of mankind.

Stephen stood for a long while looking out into the gathering dusk. Then he went over to the fireplace and began tearing the note into little bits. Only once did he pause, to look again at his name on the envelope.

"It is an invitation to Miss Carvel's party," he said.

By Thursday of that week the Brices, with thanksgiving in their hearts, had taken possession of Mr. Brinsmade's little house.

CHAPTER XII

"MISS JINNY"

THE years have sped indeed since that gray December day when Miss Virginia Carvel became eighteen. Old St. Louis has changed from a pleasant Southern town to a bustling city, and a high building stands on the site of that wide and hospitable home of Colonel Carvel. And the Colonel's thoughts that morning, as Ned shaved him, flew back through the years to a gently rolling Kentucky countryside, and a pillared white house among the oaks. He was riding again with Beatrice Colfax in the springtime. Again he stretched out his arm as if to seize her bridle-hand, and he felt the thoroughbred rear. Then the vision faded, and the memory of his dead wife became an angel's face, far—so far away.

He had brought her to St. Louis, and with his inheritance had founded his business, and built the great double house on the corner. The child came, and was named after the noble state which had given so many of her sons to the service of the Republic.

Five simple, happy years—then war. A black war of conquest which, like many such, was to add to the nation's fame and greatness. Glory beckoned, honor called—or Comyn Carvel felt them. With nothing of the profession of arms save that born in the Carvels, he kissed Beatrice farewell and steamed down the Mississippi, a captain in a Missouri regiment. The young wife was ailing. Anguish killed her. Had Comyn Carvel been selfish?

Ned, as he shaved his master's face, read his thoughts by the strange sympathy of love. He had heard the last pitiful words of his mistress. Had listened, choking, to Dr. Posthlewaite as he read the sublime service of the burial of the dead. It was Ned who had met his master, the Colonel, at the levee, and had fallen sobbing at his feet.

Long after he was shaved that morning, the Colonel sat rapt in his chair, while the faithful servant busied himself about the room, one eye on his master the while. But presently Mr. Carvel's revery is broken by the swift rustle of a dress, and a girlish figure flutters in and plants itself on the wide arm of his mahogany barber chair, Mammy Easter in the door behind her. And the Colonel, stretching forth his hands, strains her to him, and then holds her away that he may look and look again into her face.

"Honey," he said, "I was thinking of your mother."

Virginia raised her eyes to the painting on the wall over the marble mantel. The face under the heavy coils of brown hair was sweet and gentle, delicately feminine. It had an expression of sorrow that seemed a prophecy.

The Colonel's hand strayed upward to Virginia's head.

"You are not like her, honey," he said. "You may see for yourself. You are more like your Aunt Bess, who lived in Baltimore, and she—"

"I know," said Virginia, "she was the image of the beauty, Dorothy Manners, who married my great-grandfather."

"Yes, Jinny," replied the Colonel, smiling. "That is so. You are somewhat like your great-grandmother."

"Somewhat!" cried Virginia, putting her hand over his mouth, "I like that. You and Captain Lige are always afraid of turning my head. I need not be a beauty to resemble her. I know that I am like her. When you took me on to Calvert House to see Uncle Daniel that time, I remember the picture by, by—"

"Sir Joshua Reynolds."

"Yes, Sir Joshua."

"You were only eleven," says the Colonel.

"She is not a difficult person to remember."

"No," said Mr. Carvel, laughing, "especially if you have lived with her."

"Not that I wish to be that kind," said Virginia, meditatively,—"to take London by storm, and keep a man dangling for years."

"But he got her in the end," said the Colonel. "Where did you hear all this?" he asked.

"Uncle Daniel told me. He has Richard Carvel's diary."

"And a very honorable record it is," exclaimed the Colonel. "Jinny, we shall read it together when we go a-visiting to Calvert House. I remember the old gentleman as well as if I had seen him yesterday."

Virginia appeared thoughtful.

"Pa," she began, "Pa, did you ever see the pearls Dorothy Carvel wore on her wedding day? What makes you jump like that? Did you ever see them?"

"Well, I reckon I did," replied the Colonel, gazing at her steadfastly.

"Pa, Uncle Daniel told me that I was to have that necklace when I was old enough."

"Law!" said the Colonel, fidgeting, "your Uncle Daniel was just fooling you."

"He's a bachelor," said Virginia; "what use has he got for it?"

"Why," says the Colonel, "he's a young man yet, your uncle, only fifty-three. I've known older fools than he to go and do it. Eh, Ned?"

"Yes, marsa. Yes, suh. I've seed 'em at seventy, an' shufflin about peart as Marse Clarence's gamecocks. Why, dar was old Marse Ludlow—"

"Now, *Mister* Johnson," Virginia put in severely, "no more about old Ludlow."

Ned grinned from ear to ear, and in the ecstasy of his delight dropped the Colonel's clothes-brush. "Lan' sakes!" he cried, "ef she ain't recommembered." Recovering his gravity and the brush simultaneously, he made Virginia a low bow. "Mornin', *Miss* Jinny. I sholy is gwinter s'lute you dis day. May de good Lawd make you happy, Miss Jinny, an' give you a good husban'—"

"Thank you, Mister Johnson, thank you," said Virginia, blushing.

"How come she recommembered, Marse Comyn? Dat's de quality. Dat's why. Doan't you talk to Ned 'bout de quality, Marsa."

"And when did I ever talk to you about the quality, you scalawag?" asks the Colonel, laughing.

"Th' ain't none 'cept de bes' quality keep they word dat-a-way," said Ned, as he went off to tell Uncle Ben in the kitchen.

Was there ever, in all this wide country, a good cook who was not a tyrant? Uncle Ben Carvel was a veritable emperor in his own domain; and the Colonel himself, had he desired to enter the kitchen, would have been obliged to come with humble and submissive spirit. As for Virginia, she had had since childhood more than one passage at arms with Uncle Ben. And the question of who had come off victorious had been the subject of many a debate below stairs.

There were a few days in the year, however, when Uncle Ben permitted the sanctity of his territory to be violated. One was the seventh of December. On such a day it was his habit to retire to the broken chair beside the sink (the chair to which he had clung for five-and-twenty years). There he would sit, blinking, and carrying on the while an undercurrent of protests and rumblings, while Miss Virginia and other young ladies mixed and chopped and boiled and baked and gossiped. But woe to the unfortunate Rosetta if she overstepped the bounds of respect! Woe to Ned or Jackson or Tato, if they came an inch over the threshold from the hall beyond! Even Aunt Easter stepped gingerly, though she was wont to affirm, when assisting Miss Jinny in her toilet, an absolute contempt for Ben's commands.

"So Ben ordered you out, Mammy?" Virginia would say mischievously.

"Order me out! Hugh! think I'se skeered o' him, honey? Reckon I'd frail 'em good ef he cotched hole of me with his black hands. Jes' let him try to come up-stairs once, honey, an' see what I say to 'm."

Nevertheless Ben had, on one never-to-be-forgotten occasion, ordered Mammy Easter out, and she had gone. And now, as she was working the beat biscuits to be baked that evening, Uncle Ben's eye rested on her with suspicion.

What mere man may write with any confidence of the delicacies which were prepared in Uncle's kitchen that morning? No need in those days of cooking schools. What Southern lady, to the manner born, is not a cook from the cradle? Even Ben noted with approval Miss Virginia's scorn for pecks and pints, and grunted with satisfaction over the accurate pinches of spices and flavors which she used. And he did Miss Eugénie the honor to eat one of her praleens.

That night came Captain Lige Brent, the figure of an eager and determined man swinging up the street, and pulling out his watch under every lamp-post. And in his haste, in the darkness of a mid-block, he ran into another solid body clad in high boots and an old army overcoat, beside a wood wagon.

"Howdy, Captain," said he of the high boots.

"Well, I just *thought* as much," was the energetic reply; "minute I seen the rig I knew Captain Grant was behind it."

He held out a big hand, which Captain Grant clasped, just looking at his own with a smile. The stranger was Captain Elijah Brent of the *Louisiana*.

"Now," said Brent, "I'll just bet a full *cargo* that you're off to the Planters' House, and smoke an El Sol with the boys."

Mr. Grant nodded. "You're keen, Captain," said he.

"I've got something here that'll outlast an El Sol a whole *day*," continued Captain Brent, tugging at his pocket and pulling out a six-inch cigar as black as the night. "Just you try that."

The Captain instantly struck a match on his boot and was puffing in a silent enjoyment which delighted his friend.

"Reckon *he* don't bring out cigars when you make him a call," said the steamboat captain, jerking his thumb up at the house. It was Mr. Jacob Cluyme's.

Captain Grant did not reply to that, nor did Captain Lige expect him to, as it was the custom of this strange and silent man to speak ill of no one. He turned rather to put the stakes back into his wagon.

"Where are you off to, Lige?" he asked.

"Lord bless my soul," said Captain Lige, "to think that I could *forget!*" He tucked a bundle tighter under his arm. "Grant, did you ever see my little sweetheart, Jinny Carvel?" The Captain sighed. "She ain't little any more, and she eighteen to-day."

Captain Grant clapped his hand to his forehead.

"Say, Lige," said he, "that reminds me. A month or so ago I pulled a fellow out of Rénault's area across from there. First I thought he was a thief. After he got away I saw the Colonel and his daughter in the window—"

Instantly Captain Lige became excited, and seized Captain Grant by the cape of his overcoat.

"Say, Grant, what kind of appearing fellow was he?"

"Short, thick-set, blocky face."

"I reckon I know," said Brent, bringing down his fist on the wagon board; "I've had my *eye* on him for some little time."

He walked around the block twice after Captain Grant had driven down the muddy street, before he composed himself to enter the Carvel mansion. He paid no attention to the salutations of Jackson, the butler, who saw him coming and opened the door, but climbed the stairs to the sitting-room.

"Why, Captain Lige, you must have put wings on the *Louisiana*," said Virginia, rising joyfully from the arm of her father's chair to meet him. "We had given you up."

"What?" cried the Captain. "Give me up? Don't you know better than that? What, give me up when I never missed a birthday,—and this the best of all of 'em? If your pa had got sight of me shovin' in wood and cussin' the pilot for slowin' at the crossin's, he'd never let you ride in my boat again. Bill Jenks said: 'Are you plum *crazy*, Brent? Look at them cressets.' 'Five dollars!' says I; 'I wouldn't go in for five hundred. To-morrow's Jinny Carvel's birthday, and I've just *got* to be there.' I reckon the time's come when I've got to say Miss Jinny," he added ruefully.

The Colonel rose, laughing, and hit the Captain on the back.

"Drat you, Lige, why don't you kiss the girl? Can't you see she's waiting?"

The honest Captain stole one glance at Virginia, and turned red copper color.

"Shucks, Colonel, I can't be kissing her always. What'll her husband say?"

For an instant Mr. Carvel's brow clouded.

"We'll not talk of husbands yet awhile, Lige."

Virginia went up to Captain Lige, deftly twisted into shape his black tie, and kissed him on the cheek. How his face burned when she touched him.

"There!" said she, "and don't you ever dare to treat me as a young lady. Why, Pa, he's blushing like a girl. I know. He's ashamed to kiss me now. He's going to be married at last to that Creole girl in New Orleans."

The Colonel slapped his knee, winked slyly at Lige, while Virginia began to sing:—

> "I built me a house on the mountain so high,
>   To gaze at my true love as she do go by."

"There's only one I'd ever marry, Jinny," protested the Captain, soberly, "and I'm a heap too old for her. But I've seen a youngster that might mate with her, Colonel," he added mischievously. "If he just wasn't a Yankee. Jinny, what's the story I hear about Judge Whipple's young man buying Hester?"

Mr. Carvel looked uneasy. It was Virginia's turn to blush, and she grew red as a peony.

"He's a tall, hateful, Black Republican Yankee!" she said.

"Phee-ew!" whistled the Captain. "Any more epithets?"

"He's a nasty Abolitionist!"

"There you do him wrong, honey," the Colonel put in.

"I hear he took Hester to Miss Crane's," the Captain continued, filling the room with his hearty laughter. "That boy has *sand* enough, Jinny; I'd like to know him."

"You'll have that priceless opportunity to-night," retorted Miss Virginia, as she flung herself out of the room. "Pa has made me invite him to my party."

"Here, Jinny! Hold on!" cried the Captain, running after her. "I've got something for you."

She stopped on the stairs, hesitating. Whereupon the Captain hastily ripped open the bundle under his arm and produced a very handsome India shawl. With a cry of delight Virginia threw it over her shoulders and ran to the long glass between the high windows.

"Who spoils her, Lige?" asked the Colonel, fondly.

"Her father, I reckon," was the prompt reply.

"Who spoils you, Jinny?"

"Captain Lige," said she, turning to him. "If you had only kept the presents you have brought me from New Orleans, you might sell out your steamboat and be a rich man."

"He is a rich man," said the Colonel, promptly. "Did you ever miss bringing her a present, Lige?" he asked.

"When the *Cora Anderson* burnt," answered the Captain.

"Why," cried Virginia, "you brought me a piece of her wheel, with the char on it. You swam ashore with it."

"So I did," said Captain Brent. "I had forgotten that. It was when the French dress, with the furbelows, which Madame Pitou had gotten me from Paris for you, was lost."

"And I think I liked the piece of wheel better," says Virginia. "It was brought me by a brave man, the last to leave his boat."

"And who *should* be the last to leave, but the captain? I saw the thing in the water, and I just thought we ought to have a relic."

"Lige," said the Colonel, putting up his feet, "do you remember the French toys you used to bring up here from New Orleans?"

"Colonel," replied Brent, "do you recall the rough and uncouth young citizen who came over from Cincinnati, as clerk on the *Vicksburg?*"

"I remember, sir, that he was so promising that they made him provisional captain the next trip, and he was not yet twenty-four years of age."

"And do you remember buying the *Vicksburg* at the sheriff's sale for twenty thousand dollars, and handing her over to young Brent, and saying, 'There, my son, she's your boat, and you can pay for her when you like'?"

"Shucks, Brent!" said Mr. Carvel, sternly, "your memory's too good.

But I proved myself a good business man, Jinny; he paid for her in a year."

"You don't mean that you made him pay you for the boat?" cried Jinny. "Why, Pa, I didn't think you were that mean!"

The two men laughed heartily.

"I was a heap meaner," said her father. "I made him pay interest."

Virginia drew in her breath, and looked at the Colonel in amazement.

"He's the meanest man I *know*," said Captain Lige. "He made me pay interest, and a mint *julep*."

"Upon my word, Pa," said Miss Virginia, soberly, "I shouldn't have believed it of you."

Just then Jackson, in his white jacket, came to announce that supper was ready, and they met Ned at the dining-room door, fairly staggering under a load of roses.

"Marse Clarence done send 'em in, des picked out'n de hothouse dis afternoon, Miss Jinny. Jackson, fotch a bowl!"

"No," said Virginia. She took the flowers from Ned, one by one, and to the wonderment of Captain Lige and her father strewed them hither and thither upon the table until the white cloth was hid by the red flowers. The Colonel stroked his goatee and nudged Captain Lige.

"Look-a-there, now," said he. "Any other woman would have spent two mortal hours stickin' 'em in china."

Virginia, having critically surveyed her work, amid exclamations from Ned and Jackson, had gone around to her place. And there upon her plate lay a pearl necklace. For an instant she clapped her palms together, staring at it in bewilderment. And once more the little childish cry of delight, long sweet to the Colonel's ears, escaped her.

"Pa," she said, "is it—?" And there she stopped, for fear that it might not be. But he nodded encouragingly.

"Dorothy Carvel's necklace! No, it can't be."

"Yes, honey," said the Colonel. "Your Uncle Daniel sent it, as he promised. And when you go upstairs, if Easter has done as I told her, you will see a primrose dress with blue corn-flowers on your bed. Daniel thought you might like that, too, for a keepsake. Dorothy Manners wore it in London, when she was a girl."

And so Virginia ran and threw her arms about her father's neck, and kissed him again and again. And lest the Captain feel badly, she laid his India shawl beside her, and the necklace upon it.

What a joyful supper they had,—just the three of them! And as the fresh roses filled the room with fragrance, Virginia filled it with youth and spirits, and Mr. Carvel and the Captain with honest, manly merriment. And Jackson plied Captain Brent (who was a prime favorite in that house) with broiled chicken and hot beat biscuits and with waffles, until at length he lay back in his chair and heaved a sigh of content, lighting a cigar. And then Virginia, with a little curtsey to both of them, ran off to dress for the party.

"Well," said Captain Brent, "I reckon there'll be gay goings-on here to-night. I wouldn't miss the sight of 'em, Colonel, for all the cargoes on the Mississippi. Ain't there anything I can do?"

"No, thank you, Lige," Mr. Carvel answered. "Do you remember, one morning some five years ago, when I took in at the store a Yankee named Hopper? You didn't like him, I believe."

Captain Brent jumped, and the ashes of his cigar fell on his coat. He had forgotten his conversation with Captain Grant.

"I reckon I do," he said dryly.

For a moment he was on the point of telling the affair. Then he desisted. He could not be sure of Eliphalet from Grant's description. So he decided to await a better time. Captain Brent was one to make sure of his channel before going ahead.

"Well," continued the Colonel, "I have been rather pushed the last week, and Hopper managed things for this dance. He got the music, and saw the confectioner. But he made such a close bargain with both of 'em that they came around to me afterward," he added, laughing.

"Is *he* coming here to-night?" demanded the Captain, looking disgusted.

"Lige," replied the Colonel, "you never do get over a prejudice. Yes, he's coming, just to oversee things. He seems to have mighty little pleasure, and he's got the best business head I ever did see. A Yankee," said Mr. Carvel, meditatively, as he put on his hat, "a Yankee, when he will work, works like all possessed. Hood don't like him any more than you do, but he allows Hopper is a natural-born business man. Last month Samuels got tight, and Wright & Company were going to place the largest order in years. I called in Hood. 'Go yourself, Colonel,' says he 'I'm too old to solicit business, Hood,' said I. 'Then there's only one man to send,' says he; 'young Hopper. He'll get the order, or I'll give up this place I've had for twenty years.' Hopper 'callated' to get it, and another small one pitched in. And you'd die laughing, Lige, to hear how he did it."

"Some *slickness*, I'll gamble," grunted Captain Lige.

"Well, I reckon 'twas slick," said the Colonel, thoughtfully. "You know old man Wright hates a solicitor like poison. He has his notions. And maybe you've noticed signs stuck up all over his store, 'No Solicitors nor Traveling Men Allowed Here!"

The Captain nodded.

"But Hopper—Hopper walks in, sir, bold as you please, right past the signs till he comes to the old man's cage. 'I want to see Mr. Wright,' says he to the clerk. And the clerk begins to grin. 'Name, please,' says he. Mr. Hopper whips out his business card. 'What!' shouts old Wright, flying 'round in his chair, 'what the devil does this mean? Can't you read, sir?' 'I callate to,' says Mr. Hopper. 'And you dare to come in here?' 'Business is business,' says Hopper. 'You "callate"!' bellowed the old man; 'I reckon you're a damned Yankee. I reckon I'll upset your "callations" for once. And if I catch you in here again, I'll wring your neck like a roostah's. Git!' "

"Who told you this?" asked Captain Brent.

"Wright himself,—afterward," replied Mr. Carvel, laughing. "But listen, Lige. The old man lives at the Planters' House, you know. What does Mr. Hopper do but go 'round there that very night and give a nigger two bits to put him at the old man's table. When Wright comes and sees him, he nearly has one of his apoplectic fits. But in marches Hopper the next morning with twice the order. The good Lord knows how he did it."

There was a silence. Then the door-bell rang.

"He's *dangerous*," said the Captain, emphatically. "That's what I call him."

"The Yankees are changing business in this town," was the Colonel's answer. "We've got to keep the pace, Lige."

CHAPTER XIII

THE PARTY

To gentle Miss Anne Brinsmade, to Puss Russell of the mischievous eyes, and even to timid Eugénie Rénault, the question that burned was: Would he come, or would he not? And, secondarily, how would Virginia treat him if he came? Put our friend Stephen for the subjective, and Miss Carvel's party for the objective in the above, and we have the clew. For very young girls are given to making much out of a very little in such matters. If Virginia had not gotten angry when she had been teased a fortnight before, all would have been well.

Even Puss, who walked where angels feared to tread, did not dare to go too far with Virginia. She had taken care before the day of the party to beg forgiveness with considerable humility. It had been granted with a queenly generosity. And after that none of the bevy had dared to broach the subject to Virginia. Jack Brinsmade had. He told Puss afterward that when Virginia got through with him, he felt as if he had taken a rapid trip through the wheel-house of a large steamer. Puss tried, by various ingenious devices, to learn whether Mr. Brice had accepted his invitation. She failed.

These things added a zest to a party long looked forward to amongst Virginia's intimates. In those days young ladies did not "come out" so frankly as they do now. Mothers did not announce to the world that they possessed marriageable daughters. The world was supposed to know that. And then the matrimonial market was feverishly active. Young men proposed as naturally as they now ask a young girl to go for a walk, —and were refused quite as naturally. An offer of marriage was not the fearful and wonderful thing—to be dealt with gingerly—which it has since become. Seventeen was often the age at which they began. And one of the big Catherwood boys had a habit of laying his heart and hand at Virginia's feet once a month. Nor did his vanity suffer greatly when she laughed at him.

It was with a flutter of excitement, therefore, that Miss Carvel's guests flitted past Jackson, who held the door open obsequiously. The boldest of them took a rapid survey of the big parlor, before they put foot on the stairs, to see whether Mr. Brice had yet arrived. And if their curiosity held them too long, they were usually kissed by the Colonel.

Mr. Carvel shook hands heartily with the young men and called them by their first names, for he knew most of their fathers and grandfathers. And if an older gentleman arrived, perhaps the two might be seen going down the hall together, arm in arm. So came his beloved enemy, Judge Whipple, who did not make an excursion to the rear regions of the house with the Colonel; but they stood and discussed Mr. President Buchanan's responsibility for the recent panic, until the band, which Mr. Hopper had stationed under the stairs, drowned their voices.

As we enter the room, there stands Virginia under the rainbowed prisms of the great chandelier, receiving. But here was suddenly a woman of twenty-eight, where only this evening we knew a slip of a girl. It was a trick she had, to become majestic in a ball-gown. She held her head high, as a woman should, and at her slender throat glowed the pearls of Dorothy Manners.

The result of all this was to strike a little awe into the souls of many of her playmates. Little Eugénie nearly dropped a curtsey. Belle Cluyme was so impressed that she forgot for a whole hour to be spiteful. But Puss Russell kissed her on both cheeks, and asked her if she really wasn't nervous.

"Nervous!" exclaimed Jinny; "why?"

Miss Russell glanced significantly towards the doorway. But she said nothing to her hostess, for fear of marring an otherwise happy occasion. She retired with Jack Brinsmade to a corner, where she recited:—

> "Oh young Lochinvar is come out of the East;
> Of millions of Yankees I love him the least."

"What a joke if he should come!" cried Jack.

Miss Russell gasped.

Just as Mr. Clarence Colfax, resplendent in new evening clothes just arrived from New York, was pressing his claim for the first dance with his cousin in opposition to numerous other claims, the chatter of the guests died away. Virginia turned her head, and for an instant the pearls trembled on her neck. There was a young man cordially and unconcernedly shaking hands with her father and Captain Lige. Her memory of that moment is, strangely, not of his face (she did not deign to look at that), but of the muscle of his shoulder half revealed as he stretched forth his arm.

Young Mr. Colfax bent over to her ear.

"Virginia," he whispered earnestly, almost fiercely, "Virginia, who invited him here?"

"I did," said Virginia, calmly, "of course. Who invites any one here?"

"But!" cried Clarence, "do you know who he is?"

"Yes," she answered, "I know. And is that any reason why he should not come here as a guest? Would you bar any gentleman from your house on account of his convictions?"

Ah, Virginia, who had thought to hear that argument from your lips? What would frank Captain Lige say of the consistency of women, if he heard you now? And how give an account of yourself to Anne Brinsmade? What contrariness has set you so intense against your own argument?

Before one can answer this, before Mr. Clarence can recover from his astonishment and remind her of her vehement words on the subject at Bellegarde, Mr. Stephen is making thither with the air of one who conquers. Again the natural contrariness of women. What bare-faced impudence! Has he no shame that he should hold his head so high? She feels her color mounting, even as her resentment rises at his self-possession, and yet she would have despised him had he shown self-consciousness in gait or manner in the sight of her assembled guests. Nearly as tall as the Colonel himself, he is plainly seen, and Miss Puss in her corner does not have to stand on tiptoe. Mr. Carvel does the honors of the introduction.

But a daughter of the Carvels was not to fail before such a paltry situation as this. Shall it be confessed that curiosity stepped into the breach? As she gave him her hand she was wondering how he would act.

As a matter of fact he acted detestably. He said nothing whatever, but stood regarding her with a clear eye and a face by far too severe. The thought that he was meditating on the incident of the auction sale crossed through her mind, and made her blood simmer. How dared he behave so! The occasion called for a little small talk. An evil spirit took possession of Virginia. She turned.

"Mr. Brice, do you know my cousin, Mr. Colfax?" she said.

Mr. Brice bowed. "I know Mr. Colfax by sight," he replied.

Then Mr. Colfax made a stiff bow. To this new phase his sense of humor did not rise. Mr. Brice was a Yankee and no gentleman, inasmuch as he had overbid a lady for Hester.

"Have you come here to live, Mr. Brice?" he asked.

The Colonel eyed his nephew sharply. But Stephen smiled.

"Yes," he said, "if I can presently make enough to keep me alive." Then turning to Virginia, he said, "Will you dance, Miss Carvel?"

The effrontery of this demand quite drew the breath from the impatient young gentlemen who had been waiting their turn. Several of them spoke up in remonstrance. And for the moment (let one confess it who knows), Virginia was almost tempted to lay her arm in his. Then she made a bow that would have been quite as effective the length of the room.

"Thank you, Mr. Brice," she said, "but I am engaged to Mr. Colfax."

Abstractedly he watched her glide away in her cousin's arms. Stephen had a way of being preoccupied at such times. When he grew older he would walk the length of Olive Street, look into face after face of acquaintances, not a quiver of recognition in his eyes. But most probably the next week he would win a brilliant case in the Supreme Court. And so now, indifferent to the amusement of some about him, he stood staring after Virginia and Clarence. Where had he seen Colfax's face before he came West? Ah, he knew. Many, many years before he had stood with his father in the mellow light of the long gallery at Hollingdean, Kent, before a portrait of the Stuarts' time. The face was that of one of Lord Northwell's ancestors, a sporting nobleman of the time of the second Charles. It was a head which compelled one to pause before it. Strangely enough,—it was the head likewise of Clarence Colfax.

The image of it Stephen had carried undimmed in the eye of his memory. White-haired Northwell's story, also. It was not a story that Mr. Brice had expected his small son to grasp. As a matter of fact Stephen had not grasped it then—but years afterward. It was not a pleasant story,—and yet there was much of credit in it to the young rake its subject,—of dash and courage and princely generosity beside the profligacy and incontinence.

The face had impressed him, with its story. He had often dreamed of it, and of the lace collar over the dull-gold velvet that became it so well. And here it was at last, in a city west of the Mississippi River. Here were the same delicately chiselled features, with their pallor, and satiety engraved there at one and twenty. Here was the same lazy scorn in the eyes, and the look which sleeplessness gives to the lids: the hair, straight

and fine and black; the wilful indulgence—not of one life, but of generations—about the mouth, the pointed chin. And yet it was a face to
dare anything, and to do anything.

One thing more ere we have done with that which no man may explain.
Had he dreamed, too, of the girl? Of Virginia? Stephen might not tell,
but thrice had the Colonel spoken to him before he answered.

"You must meet some of these young ladies, sir."

It was little wonder that Puss Russell thought him dull on that first
occasion. Out of whom condescension is to flow is a matter of which
Heaven takes no cognizance. To use her own words, Puss thought him
"stuck up," when he should have been grateful. We know that Stephen
was not stuck up, and later Miss Russell learned that likewise. Very
naturally she took preoccupation for indifference. It is a matter worth
recording, however, that she did not tease him, because she did not dare.
He did not ask her to dance, which was rude. So she passed him back to
Mr. Carvel, who introduced him to Miss Rénault and Miss Saint Cyr,
and other young ladies of the best French families. And finally, drifting
hither and thither with his eyes on Virginia, in an evil moment he was
presented to Mrs. Colfax. Perhaps it has been guessed that Mrs. Colfax
was a very great lady indeed, albeit the daughter of an overseer. She
bore Addison Colfax's name, spent his fortune, and retained her good
looks. On this particular occasion she was enjoying herself quite as
much as any young girl in the room, and, while resting from a waltz,
was regaling a number of gentlemen with a humorous account of a
scandal at the Virginia Springs.

None but a great lady could have meted out the punishment admin-
istered to poor Stephen. None but a great lady could have conceived it.
And he, who had never been snubbed before, fell headlong into her trap.
How was the boy to know that there was no heart in the smile with
which she greeted him? It was all over in an instant. She continued to
talk about Virginia Springs. "Oh, Mr. Brice, of course you have been
there. Of course you know the Edmunds. No? You haven't been there?
You don't know the Edmunds? I thought *everybody* had been there.
Charles, you look as if you were just dying to waltz. Let's have a turn
before the music stops."

And so she whirled away, leaving Stephen forlorn, a little too angry
to be amused just then. In that state he spied a gentleman coming
towards him—a gentleman the sight of whom he soon came to associate
with all that is good and kindly in this world, Mr. Brinsmade. And now

he put his hand on Stephen's shoulder. Whether he had seen the incident just past, who can tell?

"My son," said he, "I am delighted to see you here. Now that we are such near neighbors, we must be nearer friends. You must know my wife, and my son Jack, and my daughter Anne."

Mrs. Brinsmade was a pleasant little body, but plainly not a fit mate for her husband. Jack gave Stephen a warm grasp of the hand, and an amused look. As for Anne, she was more like her father, she was Stephen's friend from that hour.

"I have seen you quite often, going in at your gate, Mr. Brice. And I have seen your mother, too. I like her," said Anne. "She has such a wonderful face." And the girl raised her truthful blue eyes to his.

"My mother would be delighted to know you," he ventured, not knowing what else to say. It was an effort for him to reflect upon their new situation as poor tenants to a wealthy family.

"Oh, do you think so?" cried Anne. "I shall call on her to-morrow, with mother. Do you know, Mr. Brice," she continued, "do you know that your mother is just the person I should go to if I were in trouble, whether I knew her or not?"

"I have found her a good person in trouble," said Stephen, simply. He might have said the same of Anne.

Anne was enchanted. She had thought him cold, but these words belied that. She had wrapped him in that diaphanous substance with which young ladies (and sometimes older ones) are wont to deck their heroes. She had approached a mystery to find it human, as are many mysteries. But thank Heaven that she found a dignity, a seriousness,— and these more than satisfied her. Likewise, she discovered something she had not looked for, an occasional way of saying things that made her laugh. She danced with him, and passed him back to Miss Puss Russell, who was better pleased this time; she passed him on to her sister, who also danced with him, and sent him upstairs for her handkerchief.

Nevertheless, Stephen was troubled. As the evening wore on, he was more and more aware of an uncompromising attitude in his young hostess, whom he had seen whispering to various young ladies from behind her fan as they passed her. He had not felt equal to asking her to dance a second time. Honest Captain Lige Brent, who seemed to have taken a fancy to him, bandied him on his lack of courage with humor that was a little rough. And, to Stephen's amazement, even Judge Whipple had pricked him on.

It was on his way upstairs after Emily Russell's handkerchief that he ran across another acquaintance. Mr. Eliphalet Hopper, in Sunday broadcloth, was seated on the landing, his head lowered to the level of the top of the high door of the parlor. Stephen caught a glimpse of the picture whereon his eyes were fixed. Perhaps it is needless to add that Miss Virginia Carvel formed the central figure of it.

"Enjoyin' yourself?" asked Mr. Hopper.

Stephen countered.

"Are you?" he asked.

"So so," said Mr. Hopper, and added darkly: "I ain't in no hurry. Just now they callate I'm about good enough to manage the business end of an affair like this here. I guess I can wait. But some day," said he, suddenly barring Stephen's way, "some day I'll give a party. And hark to me when I tell you that these here aristocrats 'll be glad enough to get invitations."

Stephen pushed past coldly. This time the man made him shiver. The incident was all that was needed to dishearten and disgust him. Kindly as he had been treated by others, far back in his soul was a thing that rankled. Shall it be told crudely why he went that night? Stephen Brice, who would not lie to others, lied to himself. And when he came downstairs again and presented Miss Emily with her handkerchief, his next move was in his mind. And that was to say good-night to the Colonel, and more frigidly to Miss Carvel herself. But music has upset many a man's calculations.

The strains of the Jenny Lind waltz were beginning to float through the rooms. There was Miss Virginia in a corner of the big parlor, for the moment alone with her cousin. And thither Stephen sternly strode. Not a sign did she give of being aware of his presence until he stood before her. Even then she did not lift her eyes. But she said:—

"So you have come at last to try again, Mr. Brice?"

And Mr. Brice said:—

"If you will do me the honor, Miss Carvel."

She did not reply at once. Clarence Colfax got to his feet. Then she looked up at the two men as they stood side by side, and perhaps swept them both in an instant's comparison.

The New Englander's face must have reminded her more of her own father, Colonel Carvel. It possessed, from generations known, the power to control itself. She afterwards admitted that she accepted him to tease Clarence. Miss Russell, whose intuitions are usually correct, does not believe this.

"I will dance with you," said Virginia.

But, once in his arms, she seemed like a wild thing, resisting. Although her gown brushed his coat, the space between them was infinite, and her hand lay limp in his, unresponsive of his own pressure. Not so her feet; they caught the step and moved with the rhythm of the music, and round the room they swung. More than one pair paused in the dance to watch them. Then, as they glided past the door, Stephen was disagreeably conscious of some one gazing down from above, and he recalled Eliphalet Hopper and his position. The sneer from Eliphalet's face seemed to penetrate like a chilly draught.

All at once, Virginia felt her partner gathering up his strength, and by some compelling force, more of will than of muscle, draw her nearer. Unwillingly her hand tightened under his, and her blood beat faster and her color came and went as they two moved as one. Anger—helpless anger—took possession of her as she saw the smiles on the faces of her friends, and Puss Russell mockingly throwing a kiss as she passed her. And then, strange in the telling, a thrill as of power rose within her which she strove against in vain. A knowledge of him who guided her so swiftly, so unerringly, which she had felt with no other man. Faster and faster they stepped, each forgetful of self and place, until the waltz came suddenly to a stop.

"By gum!" said Captain Lige to Judge Whipple, "you can whollop me on my own forecastle if they ain't the *handsomest* couple I ever *did* see."

BOOK II

CHAPTER I

RAW MATERIAL

SUMMER, intolerable summer, was upon the city at last. The families of its richest citizens had fled. Even at that early day some braved the long railroad journey to the Atlantic coast. Amongst these were our friends the Cluymes, who come not strongly into this history. Some went to the Virginia Springs. But many, like the Brinsmades and the Russells, the Tiptons and the Hollingsworths, retired to the local paradise of their country places on the Bellefontaine road, on the cool heights above the river. Thither, as a respite from the hot office, Stephen was often invited by kind Mr. Brinsmade, who sometimes drove him out in his own buggy. Likewise he had visited Miss Puss Russell. But Miss Virginia Carvel he had never seen since the night he had danced with her. This was because, after her return from the young ladies' school at Monticello, she had gone to Glencoe,—Glencoe, magic spot, perched high on wooded highlands. And under these the Meramec, crystal pure, ran lightly on sand and pebble to her bridal with that turbid tyrant, the Father of Waters.

To reach Glencoe you spent two dirty hours on that railroad which (it was fondly hoped) would one day stretch to the Pacific Ocean. You generally spied one of the big Catherwood boys in the train, or their tall sister Maude. The Catherwoods likewise lived at Glencoe in the summer. And on some Saturday afternoons a grim figure in a linen duster and a silk skull-cap took a seat in the forward car. That was Judge Whipple, on his way to spend a quiet Sunday with Colonel Carvel.

To the surprise of many good people, the Judge had recently formed another habit. At least once a week he would drop in at the little house on Olive Street next to Mr. Brinsmade's big one, which was shut up, and take tea with Mrs. Brice. Afterward he would sit on the little porch over the garden in the rear, or on the front steps, and watch the bob-tailed horse-cars go by. His conversation was chiefly addressed to the widow.

Rarely to Stephen, whose wholesome respect for his employer had in no wise abated.

Through the stifling heat of these summer days Stephen sat in the outer office, straining at the law. Had it not been for the fact that Mr. Whipple went to his mother's house, despair would have seized him long since. Apparently his goings-out and his comings-in were noted only by Mr. Richter. Truly the Judge's methods were not Harvard methods. And if there were pride in the young Bostonian, Mr. Whipple thought he knew the cure for it.

It was to Richter Stephen owed a debt of gratitude in these days. He would often take his midday meal in the down-town beer garden with the quiet German. Then there came a Sunday afternoon (to be marked with a red letter) when Richter transported him into Germany itself. Stephen's eyes were opened. Richter took him across the Rhine. The Rhine was Market Street, and south of that street was a country of which polite American society took no cognizance.

Here was an epic movement indeed, for South St. Louis was a great sod uprooted from the Fatherland and set down in all its vigorous crudity in the warm black mud of the Mississippi Valley. Here lager beer took the place of Bourbon, and black bread and sausages of hot rolls and fried chicken. Here were quaint market-houses squatting in the middle of wide streets; Lutheran churches, square and uncompromising, and bulky Turner Halls, where German children were taught the German tongue. Here, in a shady grove of mulberry and locust, two hundred families were spread out at their ease.

For a while Richter sat in silence, puffing at a meerschaum with a huge brown bowl. A trick of the mind opened for Stephen one of the histories in his father's library in Beacon Street, across the pages of which had flitted the ancestors of this blue-eyed and great-chested Saxon. He saw them in cathedral forests, with the red hair long upon their bodies. He saw terrifying battles with the Roman Empire surging back and forth through the low countries. He saw a lad of twenty at the head of rugged legions clad in wild skins, sweeping Rome out of Gaul. Back in the dim ages Richter's fathers must have defended grim Eresburg. And it seemed to him that in the end the new Republic must profit by this rugged stock, which had good women for wives and mothers, and for fathers men in whose blood dwelt a fierce patriotism and contempt for cowardice.

This fancy of ancestry pleased Stephen. He thought of the forefathers of those whom he knew, who dwelt north of Market Street. Many, though this generation of the French might know it not, had bled at Calais and at Agincourt, had followed the court of France in clumsy coaches to Blois and Amboise, or lived in hovels under the castle walls. Others had charged after the Black Prince at Poictiers, and fought as serf or noble in the war of the Roses, had been hatters or tailors in Cromwell's armies, or else had sacrificed lands and fortunes for Charles Stuart. These English had toiled, slow but resistless, over the misty Blue Ridge after Boone and Harrod to this old St. Louis of the French, their enemies, whose fur traders and missionaries had long followed the veins of the vast western wilderness. And now, on to the structure builded by these two, comes Germany to be welded, to strengthen or to weaken.

Richter put down his pipe on the table.

"Stephen," he said suddenly, "you do not share the prejudice against us here?"

Stephen flushed. He thought of some vigorous words that Miss Puss Russell had used on the subject of the "Dutch."

"No," said he, emphatically.

"I am glad," answered Richter, with a note of sadness in his voice. "Do not despise us before you know more of us. We are still feudal in Germany—of the Middle Ages. The peasant is a serf. He is compelled to serve the lord of the land every year with so much labor of his hands. The small farmers, the *Gross* and *Mittel Bauern*, we call them, are also mortgaged to the nobles who tyrannize our Vaterland. Our merchants are little merchants—shopkeepers, you would say. My poor father, an educated man, was such. They fought our revolution."

"And now," said Stephen, "why do they not keep their hold?"

Richter sighed.

"We were unused to ruling," he answered. "We knew not how to act— what to do. You must remember that we were not trained to govern ourselves, as are you of the English race, from children. Those who have been for centuries ground under heel do not make practical parliamentarians. No, your heritage is liberty—you Americans and English; and we Germans must desert our native land to partake of it."

"And was it not hard to leave?" asked Stephen, gently.

The eyes of the German filled at the recollection, nor did he seem ashamed of his tears.

"I had a poor old father whose life was broken to save the Vaterland, but not his spirit," he cried, "no, not that. My father was born in 1797. God directed my grandfather to send him to the Kölnisches gymnasium, where the great Jahn taught. Jahn was our Washington, the father of Germany that is to be.

"Then our Fatherland was French. Our women wore Parisian clothes, and spoke the language; French immorality and atheism had spread like a plague among us; Napoleon the vile had taken the sword of our Frederick from Berlin. It was Father Jahn (so we love to call him), it was Father Jahn who founded the *Turnschulen* that the generations to come might return to simple German ways,—plain fare, high principles, our native tongue, and the development of the body. The downfall of the fiend Napoleon and the Vaterland united—these two his scholars must have written in their hearts. All summer long, in their black caps and linen pantaloons, they would trudge after him, begging a crust here and a cheese there, to spread his teachings far and wide under the thatched roofs.

"Then came 1811. I have heard my father tell how in the heat of that year a great red comet burned in the sky, even as that we now see, my friend. God forbid that this portends blood. But in the coming spring the French conscripts filled our sacred land like a swarm of locusts, devouring as they went. And at their head, with the pomp of Darius, rode that destroyer of nations and homes, Napoleon. What was Germany then? Ashes. But the red embers were beneath, fanned by Father Jahn. Napoleon at Dresden made our princes weep. Never, even in the days of the Frankish kings, had we been so humbled. He dragged our young men with him to Russia, and left them to die moaning on the frozen wastes, while he drove off in his sledge.

"It was the next year that Germany rose. High and low, rich and poor, *Jaeger* and *Landwehr,* came flocking into the army, and even the old men, the *Landsturm.* Russia was an ally, and later, Austria. My father, a lad of sixteen, was in the *Landwehr,* under the noble Blücher in Silesia, when they drove the French into the Katzbach and the Neisse, swollen by the rains into torrents. It had rained until the forests were marshes. Powder would not burn. But Blücher, ah, there was a man! He whipped his great sabre from under his cloak, crying '*Vorwärts! Vorwärts!*' And the *Landwehr* with one great shout slew their enemies with the butts of their muskets until their arms were weary and the bodies were tossed like logs in the foaming waters. They called Blücher *Marschall Vorwärts!*

"Then Napoleon was sent to Elba. But the victors quarrelled amongst themselves, while Talleyrand and Metternich tore our Vaterland into strips, and set brother against brother. And our blood, and the grief for the widows and the fatherless, went for nothing."

Richter paused to light his pipe.

"After a while," he continued presently, "came the German Confederation, with Austria at the head. Rid of Napoleon, we had another despot in Metternich. But the tree which Jahn had planted grew, and its branches spread. The great master was surrounded by spies. My father had gone to Jena University, when he joined the *Burschenschaft*, or Students' League, of which I will tell you later. It was pledged to the rescue of the Vaterland. He was sent to prison for dipping his handkerchief in the blood of Sand, beheaded for liberty at Mannheim. Afterwards he was liberated, and went to Berlin and married my mother, who died when I was young. Twice again he was in prison because the societies met at his house. We were very poor, my friend. You in America know not the meaning of that word. His health broke, and when '48 came, he was an old man. His hair was white, and he walked the streets with a crutch. But he had saved a little money to send me to Jena.

"He was proud of me. I was big-boned and fair, like my mother. And when I came home at the end of a *Semester*—I can see him now, as he would hobble to the door, wearing the red and black and gold of the *Burschenschaft*. And he would keep me up half the night—telling him of our *Schläger* fights with the aristocrats. My father had been a noted swordsman in his day."

He stopped abruptly, and colored. For Stephen was staring at the jagged scar. He had never summoned the courage to ask Richter how he came by it.

"*Schläger* fights?" he exclaimed.

"Broadswords," answered the German, hastily. "Some day I will tell you of them, and of the struggle with the troops in the *Breite Strasse* in March. We lost, as I told you, because we knew not how to hold what we had gained. I left Germany, hoping to make a home here for my poor father. How sad his face as he kissed me farewell! And he said to me: 'Carl, if ever your new Vaterland, the good Republic, be in danger, sacrifice all. I have spent my years in bondage, and I say to you that life without liberty is not worth the living.' Three months I was gone, and he was dead, without that for which he had striven so bravely. He never knew what it is to have an abundance of meat. He never knew from one day to the other when he would have to embrace me, all he owned, and march away to prison, because he was a patriot." Richter's voice had fallen low, but now he raised it. "Do you think, my friend," he cried, "do you think that I would not die willingly for this new country if the time should come? Yes, and there are a million like me, once German, now American, who will give their lives to preserve this Union. For without it the world is not fit to live in."

Stephen had food for thought as he walked northward through the strange streets on that summer evening. Here indeed was a force not to be reckoned, and which few had taken into account.

CHAPTER II

ABRAHAM LINCOLN

I⊤ is sometimes instructive to look back and see how Destiny gave us a kick here, and Fate a shove there, that sent us in the right direction at the proper time. And when Stephen Brice looks backward now, he laughs to think that he did not suspect the Judge of being an ally of the two who are mentioned above. The sum total of Mr. Whipple's words and advices to him that summer had been these. Stephen was dressed more carefully than usual, in view of a visit to Bellefontaine Road. Whereupon the Judge demanded whether he were contemplating marriage. Without waiting for a reply he pointed to a rope and a slab of limestone on the pavement below, and waved his hand unmistakably toward the Mississippi.

Miss Russell was of the opinion that Mr. Whipple had once been crossed in love.

But we are to speak more particularly of a put-up job, although Stephen did not know this at the time.

Towards five o'clock of a certain afternoon in August of that year, 1858, Mr. Whipple emerged from his den. Instead of turning to the right, he strode straight to Stephen's table. His communications were always a trifle startling. This was no exception.

"Mr. Brice," said he, "you are to take the six forty-five train on the St. Louis, Alton, and Chicago road to-morrow morning for Springfield, Illinois."

"Yes, sir."

"Arriving at Springfield, you are to deliver this envelope into the hands of Mr. Abraham Lincoln, of the law firm of Lincoln & Herndon."

"Abraham Lincoln!" cried Stephen, rising and straddling his chair. "But, sir—"

"Abraham Lincoln," interrupted the Judge, forcibly. "I try to speak plainly, sir. You are to deliver it into Mr. Lincoln's hands. If he is not in Springfield, find out where he is and follow him up. Your expenses will be paid by me. The papers are important. Do you understand, sir?"

Stephen did. And he knew better than to argue the matter with Mr. Whipple. He had read in the Missouri *Democrat* of this man Lincoln, a country lawyer who had once been to Congress, and who was even now disputing the senatorship of his state with the renowned Douglas. In spite of their complacent amusement, he had won a little admiration from conservative citizens who did not believe in the efficacy of Judge Douglas's Squatter Sovereignty. Likewise this Mr. Lincoln, who had once been a rail-splitter, was uproariously derided by Northern Democrats because he had challenged Mr. Douglas to seven debates, to be held at different towns in the state of Illinois. David with his sling and his smooth round pebble must have had much of the same sympathy and ridicule.

For Mr. Douglas, Senator and Judge, was a national character, mighty in politics, invulnerable in the armor of his oratory. And he was known far and wide as the Little Giant. Those whom he did not conquer with his logic were impressed by his person.

Stephen remembered with a thrill that these debates were going on now. One, indeed, had been held, and had appeared in fine print in a corner of the *Democrat*. Perhaps this Lincoln might not be in Springfield; perhaps he, Stephen Brice, might, by chance, hit upon a debate, and see and hear the tower of the Democracy, the Honorable Stephen A. Douglas.

But it is greatly to be feared that our friend Stephen was bored with his errand before he arrived at the little wooden station of the Illinois capital. Standing on the platform after the train pulled out, he summoned up courage to ask a citizen with no mustache and a beard, which he swept away when he spat, where was the office of Lincoln & Herndon. The stranger spat twice, regarded Mr. Brice pityingly, and finally led him in silence past the picket fence and the New England-looking meeting-house opposite until they came to the great square on which the State House squatted. The State House was a building with much pretension to beauty, built in the classical style, of a yellow stone, with solid white blinds in the high windows and mighty columns capped at the gently slanting roof. But on top of it was reared a crude wooden dome, like a clay head on a marble statue.

"That there," said the stranger, "is whar we watches for the County Delegations when they come in to a meetin'." And with this remark, pointing with a stubby thumb up a well-worn stair, he departed before Stephen could thank him. Stephen paused under the awning, of which there were many shading the brick pavement, to regard the straggling line of stores and houses which surrounded and did homage to the yellow pile. The brick house in which Mr. Lincoln's office was had decorations above the windows. Mounting the stair, Stephen found a room bare enough, save for a few chairs and law books, and not a soul in attendance. After sitting awhile by the window, mopping his brow with a handker-chief, he went out on the landing to make inquiries. There he met another citizen in shirt sleeves, like unto the first, in the very act of sweeping his beard out of the way of a dexterous expectoration.

"Wal, young man," said he, "who be you lookin' for here?"

"For Mr. Lincoln," said Stephen.

At this the gentleman sat down on the dirty top step, and gave vent to quiet but annoying laughter.

"I reckon you come to the wrong place."

"I was told this was his office," said Stephen, with some heat.

"Whar be you from?" said the citizen, with interest.

"I don't see what that has to do with it," answered our friend.

"Wal," said the citizen, critically, "if you was from Philadelphy or Boston, you might stand acquitted."

Stephen was on the point of claiming Boston, but wisely hesitated.

"I'm from St. Louis, with a message for Mr. Lincoln," he replied.

"Ye talk like ye was from down East," said the citizen, who seemed in the humor for conversation. "I reckon 'old Abe's' too busy to see you. Say, young man, did you ever hear of Stephen Arnold Douglas, *alias* the Little Giant, *alias* the Idol of our State, sir?"

This was too much for Stephen, who left the citizen without the com-pliment of a farewell. Continuing around the square, inquiring for Mr. Lincoln's house, he presently got beyond the stores and burning pave-ments on to a plank walk, under great shade trees, and past old brick mansions set well back from the street. At length he paused in front of a wooden house of a dirty grayish brown, too high for its length and breadth, with tall shutters of the same color, and a picket fence on top of the retaining wall which lifted the yard above the plank walk. It was an ugly house, surely. But an ugly house may look beautiful when sur-rounded by such heavy trees as this was. Their shade was the most in-viting thing Stephen had seen. A boy of sixteen or so was swinging on the gate, plainly a very mischievous boy, with a round, laughing, sun-burned face and bright eyes. In front of the gate was a shabby carriage with top and side curtains, hitched to a big bay horse.

"Can you tell me where Mr. Lincoln lives?" inquired Stephen.

"Well, I guess," said the boy. "I'm his son, and he lives right here when he's at home. But that hasn't been often lately."

"Where is he?" asked Stephen, beginning to realize the purport of his conversations with citizens.

Young Mr. Lincoln mentioned the name of a small town in the northern part of the state, where he said his father would stop that night. He told Stephen that he looked wilted, invited him into the house to have a glass of lemonade, and to join him and another boy in a fishing excursion with the big bay horse. Stephen told young Mr. Lincoln that he should have to take the first train after his father.

"Jiminy!" exclaimed the other, enviously, "then you'll hear the Freeport debate."

Now it has been said that the day was scorching hot. And when Stephen had got back to the wooden station, and had waited an hour for the Bloomington express, his anxiety to hear the Freeport debate was not as keen as it might have been. Late in the afternoon he changed at Bloomington to the Illinois Central Railroad. The sun fell down behind the cardboard edge of the prairie, the train rattled on into the north, wrapped in its dust and smoke, and presently became a long comet, roaring red, to match that other comet which flashed in the sky.

By this time it may be said that our friend was heartily sick of his mission. He tried to doze; but two men, a farmer and a clerk, got in at a way station, and sat behind him. They began to talk about this man Lincoln.

"Shucks," said the clerk, "think of him opposing the Little Giant."

"He's right smart, Sam," said the farmer. "He's got a way of sayin' things that's clear. We boys can foller him. But Steve Douglas, he only mixes you up."

His companion guffawed.

"Because why?" he shouted. "Because you ain't had no education. What does a rail-splitter like Abe know about this government? Judge Douglas has worked it all out. He's smart. Let the territories take care of themselves. Besides, Abe ain't got no dignity. The fust of this week I seen him side-tracked down the road here in a caboose, while Doug went by in a special."

"Abe is a plain man, Sam," the farmer answered solemnly. "But you watch out for him."

It was ten o'clock when Stephen descended at his destination. Merciful night hid from his view the forlorn station and the ragged town. The baggage man told him that Mr. Lincoln was at the tavern.

That tavern! Will words describe the impression it made on a certain young man from Boston! It was long and low and ramshackly, and hot that night as the inside of a brick-kiln. As he drew near it on the single plank walk over the black prairie-mud, he saw countrymen and politicians swarming its narrow porch and narrower hall. Discussions in all keys were in progress, and it was with vast difficulty that our distracted young man pushed through and found the landlord. This personage was the coolest of the lot. Confusion was but food for his smiles, importunity but increased his suavity. And of the seeming hundreds that pressed him, he knew and utilized the Christian name of all. From behind a corner of the bar he held them all at bay, and sent them to quarters like the old campaigner he was.

"Now, Ben, 'tain't no use gettin' mad. You, and Joshway, an' Will, an' Sam, an' the Cap'n, an' the four Beaver brothers, will all sleep in number ten. What's that, Franklin? No, sirree, the Honerable Abe, and Mister Hill, and Jedge Oglesby is sleepin' in seven." The smell of perspiration was stifling as Stephen pushed up to the master of the situation. "What's that? Supper, young man? Ain't you had no supper? Gosh, I reckon if you can fight your way to the dinin' room, the gals'll give you some pork and a cup of coffee."

After a preliminary scuffle with a drunken countryman in mud-caked boots, Mr. Brice presently reached the long table in the dining-room. A sense of humor not quite extinct made him smile as he devoured pork chops and greasy potatoes and heavy apple pie. As he was finishing the pie, he became aware of the tavern keeper standing over him.

"Are you one of them flip Chicagy reporters?" asked that worthy, with a suspicious eye on Stephen's clothes.

Our friend denied this.

"You didn't talk jest like 'em. Guess you'll be here to-night."

"Yes," said Stephen, wearily. And he added, out of force of habit, "Can you give me a room?"

"I reckon," was the cheerful reply. "Number ten. There ain't nobody in there but Ben Billings, and the four Beaver brothers, an' three more. I'll have a shakedown for ye next the north window."

Stephen's thanks for the hospitality perhaps lacked heartiness. But perceiving his host still contemplating him, he was emboldened to say:—

"Has Mr. Lincoln gone to bed?"

"Who? Old Abe, at half-past ten? Wal, I reckon you don't know him."

Stephen's reflections here on the dignity of the Senatorial candidate of the Republican Party in Illinois were novel, at any rate. He thought of certain senators he had seen in Massachusetts.

"The only reason he ain't down here swappin' yarns with the boys, is because he's havin' some sort of confab with the Jedge and Joe Medill of the *Chicagy Press and Tribune.*"

"Do you think he would see me?" asked Stephen, eagerly. He was emboldened by the apparent lack of ceremony of the candidate. The landlord looked at him in some surprise.

"Wal, I reckon. Jest go up an' knock at the door of number seven, and say Tom Wright sent ye."

"How shall I know Mr. Lincoln?" asked Stephen.

"Pick out the ugliest man in the room. There ain't nobody I kin think of uglier than Abe."

Bearing in mind this succinct description of the candidate, Stephen climbed the rickety stairs to the low second story. All the bedroom doors were flung open except one, on which the number 7 was inscribed. From within came bursts of uproarious laughter, and a summons to enter.

He pushed open the door, and as soon as his eyes became accustomed to the tobacco smoke, he surveyed the room. There was a bowl on the floor, the chair where it belonged being occupied. There was a very inhospitable-looking bed, two shake-downs, and four Windsor chairs in more or less state of dilapidation—all occupied likewise. A country glass lamp was balanced on a rough shelf, and under it a young man sat absorbed in making notes, and apparently oblivious to the noise around him. Every gentleman in the room was collarless, coatless, tieless, and vestless. Some were engaged in fighting gnats and June bugs, while others battled with mosquitoes—all save the young man who wrote, he being wholly indifferent.

Stephen picked out the homeliest man in the room. There was no mistaking him. And, instead of a discussion of the campaign with the other gentlemen, Mr. Lincoln was defending—what do you think? Mr. Lincoln was defending an occasional and judicious use of swear words.

"Judge," said he, "you do an almighty lot of cussing in your speeches, and perhaps it ain't a bad way to keep things stirred up."

"Well," said the Judge, "a fellow will rip out something once in a while before he has time to shut it off."

Mr. Lincoln passed his fingers through his tousled hair. His thick lower lip crept over in front of the upper one. A gleam stirred in the deep-set gray eyes.

"Boys," he asked, "did I ever tell you about Sam'l, the old Quaker's apprentice?"

There was a chorus of "No's" and "Go ahead, Abe!" The young man who was writing dropped his pencil. As for Stephen, this long, uncouth man of the plains was beginning to puzzle him. The face, with its crude features and deep furrows, relaxed into intense soberness. And Mr. Lincoln began his story with a slow earnestness that was truly startling, considering the subject.

"This apprentice, Judge, was just such an incurable as you." (Laughter.) "And Sam'l, when he wanted to, could get out as many cusses in a second as his anvil shot sparks. And the old man used to wrastle with him nights and speak about punishment, and pray for him in meeting. But it didn't do any good. When anything went wrong, Sam'l had an appropriate word for the occasion. One day the old man got an inspiration when he was scratching around in the dirt for an odd-sized iron.

" 'Sam'l,' says he, 'I want thee.'

"Sam'l went, and found the old man standing over a big rat hole, where the rats came out to feed on the scraps.

" 'Sam'l,' says he, 'fetch the tongs.'

"Sam'l fetched the tongs.

" 'Now, Sam'l,' says the old man, 'thou wilt sit here until thou hast a rat. Never mind thy dinner. And when thou hast him, if I hear thee swear, thou wilt sit here until thou hast another. Dost thou mind?' "

Here Mr. Lincoln seized two cotton umbrellas, rasped his chair over the bare floor into a corner of the room, and sat hunched over an imaginary rat hole, for all the world like a gawky Quaker apprentice. And this was a candidate for the Senate of the United States, who on the morrow was to meet in debate the renowned and polished Douglas!

"Well," Mr. Lincoln continued, "that was on a Monday, I reckon, and the boys a-shouting to have their horses shod. Maybe you think they didn't have some fun with Sam'l. But Sam'l sat there, and sat there, and sat there, and after a while the old man pulled out his dinnerpail. Sam'l never opened his mouth. First thing you know, *snip* went the tongs." Mr. Lincoln turned gravely around. "What do you reckon Sam'l said, Judge?"

The Judge, at random, summoned up a good one, to the delight of the audience.

"Judge," said Mr. Lincoln, with solemnity, "I reckon that's what you'd have said. Sam'l never said a word and the old man kept on eating his dinner. One o'clock came, and the folks began to drop in again, but Sam'l, he sat there. 'Long towards night the boys collected 'round the door. They were getting kind of interested. Sam'l, he never looked up." Here Mr. Lincoln bent forward a little, and his voice fell to a loud, drawling whisper. "First thing you know, here come the whiskers peeping up, then the pink eyes a-blinking at the forge, then—!"

Suddenly he brought the umbrellas together with a whack.

" 'By God,' yells Sam'l, 'I have thee at last!' "

Amid the shouts, Mr. Lincoln stood up, his long body swaying to and fro as he lifted high the improvised tongs. They heard a terrified squeal, and there was the rat squirming and wriggling,—it seemed before their very eyes. And Stephen forgot the country tavern, the country politician, and was transported straightway into the Quaker's smithy.

CHAPTER III

IN WHICH STEPHEN LEARNS SOMETHING

It was Mr. Lincoln who brought him back. The astonishing candidate for the Senate had sunk into his chair, his face relaxed into sadness save for the sparkle lurking in the eyes. So he sat, immobile, until the laughter had died down to silence. Then he turned to Stephen.

"Sonny," he said, "did you want to see me?"

Stephen was determined to be affable and kind, and (shall we say it?) he would not make Mr. Lincoln uncomfortable either by a superiority of English or the certain frigidity of manner which people in the West said he had. But he tried to imagine a Massachusetts senator, Mr. Sumner, for instance, going through the rat story, and couldn't. Somehow, Massachusetts senators hadn't this gift. And yet he was not quite sure that it wasn't a fetching gift. Stephen did not quite like to be called "Sonny." But he looked into two gray eyes, and at the face, and something curious happened to him. How was he to know that thousands of his countrymen were to experience the same sensation?

"Sonny," said Mr. Lincoln again, "did you want to see me?"

"Yes, sir." Stephen wondered at the "sir." It had been involuntary. He drew from his inner pocket the envelope which the Judge had given him.

Mr. Lincoln ripped it open. A document fell out, and a letter. He put the document in his tall hat, which was upside down on the floor. As he got deeper into the letter, he pursed his mouth, and the lines of his face deepened in a smile. Then he looked up, grave again.

"Judge Whipple told you to run till you found me, did he, Mr. Brice?"

"Yes, sir."

"Is the Judge the same old criss-cross, contrary, violent fool that he always was?"

Providence put an answer in Stephen's mouth.

"He's been very good to me, Mr. Lincoln."

Mr. Lincoln broke into laughter.

"Why, he's the biggest-hearted man I know. You know him, Oglesby, —Silas Whipple. But a man has to be a Daniel or a General Putnam to

111

venture into that den of his. There's only one man in the world who can beard Silas, and he's the finest states-right Southern gentleman you ever saw. I mean Colonel Carvel. You've heard of him, Oglesby. Don't they quarrel once in a while, Mr. Brice?"

"They do have occasional arguments," said Stephen, amused.

"Arguments!" cried Mr. Lincoln; "well, I couldn't come as near to fighting every day and stand it. If my dog and Bill's dog across the street walked around each other and growled for half a day, and then lay down together, as Carvel and Whipple do, by Jing, I'd put pepper on their noses—"

"I reckon Colonel Carvel isn't a fighting man," said some one, at random.

Strangely enough, Stephen was seized with a desire to vindicate the Colonel's courage. Both Mr. Lincoln and Judge Oglesby forestalled him.

"Not a fighting man!" exclaimed the Judge. "Why, the other day—"

"Now, Oglesby," put in Mr. Lincoln, "I wanted to tell that story."

Stephen had heard it, and so have we. But Mr. Lincoln's imitation of the Colonel's drawl brought him a pang like homesickness.

" 'No, suh, I didn't intend to shoot. Not if he had gone off straight. But he wriggled and twisted like a rattlesnake, and I just couldn't resist, suh. Then I sent my nigger Ephum to tell him not to let me catch sight of him 'round the Planters' House. Yes, suh, that's what he was. One of these damned Yankees who come South and go into nigger-deals and politics.' "

Mr. Lincoln glanced at Stephen, and then again at the Judge's letter. He took up his silk hat and thrust that, too, into the worn lining, which was already filled with papers. He clapped the hat on his head, and buttoned on his collar.

"I reckon I'll go for a walk, boys," he said, "and clear my head, so as to be ready for the Little Giant to-morrow at Freeport. Mr. Brice, do you feel like walking?"

Stephen, taken aback, said that he did.

"Now, Abe, this is just durned foolishness," one of the gentlemen expostulated. "We want to know if you're going to ask Douglas that question."

"If you do, you kill yourself, Lincoln," said another, who Stephen afterwards learned was Mr. Medill, proprietor of the great *Press and Tribune*.

"I guess I'll risk it, Joe," said Mr. Lincoln, gravely. Suddenly comes the quiver about the corners of his mouth and the gray eyes respond. "Boys," said he, "did you ever hear the story of Farmer Bell, down in Egypt? I'll tell it to you, boys, and then perhaps you'll know why I'll ask Judge Douglas that question. Farmer Bell had the prize Bartlett pear tree, and the prettiest gal in that section. And he thought about the same of each of 'em. All the boys were after Sue Bell. But there was only one who had any chance of getting her, and his name was Jim Rickets. Jim was the handsomest man in that section. He's been hung since. But Jim had a good deal out of life,—all the appetites, and some of the gratifications. He liked Sue, and he liked a luscious Bartlett. And he intended to have both. And it just so happened that that prize pear tree had a whopper on that year, and old man Bell couldn't talk of anything else.

"Now there was an ugly galoot whose name isn't worth mentioning. He knew he wasn't in any way fit for Sue, and he liked pears about as well as Jim Rickets. Well, one night here comes Jim along the road, whistling to court Susan, and there was the ugly galoot a-yearning on the bank under the pear tree. Jim was all fixed up, and he says to the galoot, 'Let's have a throw.' Now the galoot knew old Bell was looking over the fence. So he says, 'All right,' and he gives Jim the first shot. Jim fetched down the big pear, got his teeth in it, and strolled off to the house, kind of pitiful of the galoot for a half-witted ass. When he got to the door, there was the old man. 'What are you here for?' says he. 'Why,' says Rickets, in his off-hand way, for he always had great confidence, 'to fetch Sue.' "

"The old man used to wear brass toes to keep his boots from wearing out," said Mr. Lincoln, dreamily.

"You see," continued Mr. Lincoln, "you see the galoot knew that Jim Rickets wasn't to be trusted with Susan Bell."

Some of the gentlemen appeared to see the point of this political parable, for they laughed uproariously. The others laughed, too. Then they slapped their knees, looked at Mr. Lincoln's face, which was perfectly sober, and laughed again, a little fainter. Then the Judge looked as solemn as his title.

"It won't do, Abe," said he. "You commit suicide."

"You'd better stick to the pear, Abe," said Mr. Medill, "and fight Stephen A. Douglas here and now. This isn't any picnic. Do you know who he is?"

"Why, yes, Joe," said Mr. Lincoln, amiably. "He's a man with tens of thousands of *blind followers*. It's my business to make some of those blind followers *see*."

By this time Stephen was burning to know the question that Mr. Lincoln wished to ask the Little Giant, and why the other gentlemen were against it. But Mr. Lincoln surprised him still further in taking him by the arm. Turning to the young reporter, Mr. Hill, who had finished his writing, he said:—

"Bob, a little air will do you good. I've had enough of the old boys for a while, and I'm going to talk to somebody my own age."

Stephen was halfway down the corridor when he discovered that he had forgotten his hat. As he returned he heard somebody say:—

"If that ain't just like Abe. He stopped to pull a flea out of his stocking when he was going to fight that duel with Shields, and now he's walking with boys before a debate with the smartest man in this country. And there's heaps of things he ought to discuss with us."

"Reckon we haven't got much to do with it," said another, half laughing, half rueful. "There's some things Abe won't stand."

From the stairs Stephen saw Mr. Lincoln threading his way through the crowd below, laughing at one, pausing to lay his hand on the shoulder of another, and replying to a rough sally of a third to make the place a tumult of guffaws. But none had the temerity to follow him. When Stephen caught up with him in the little country street, he was talking earnestly to Mr. Hill, the young reporter of the *Press and Tribune*. And what do you think was the subject? The red comet in the sky that night. Stephen kept pace in silence with Mr. Lincoln's strides, another shock in store for him. This rail-splitter, this postmaster, this flatboatman, whom he had not credited with a knowledge of the New Code, was talking Astronomy. And strange to say, Mr. Brice was *learning*.

"Bob," said Mr. Lincoln, "can you élucidate the problem of the three bodies?"

To Stephen's surprise, Mr. Hill élucidated.

The talk then fell upon novels and stories, a few of which Mr. Lincoln seemed to have read. He spoke, among others, of the "Gold Bug." "The story is grand," said he, "but it might as well have been written of Robinson Crusoe's island. What a fellow wants in a book is to *know where he is*. There are not many novels, or ancient works for that matter, that put you down anywhere."

"There is that genuine fragment which Cicero has preserved from a last work of Aristotle," said Mr. Hill slyly. " 'If there were beings who lived in the depths of the earth, and could emerge through the open fissures and could suddenly behold the earth, the sea, and the vault of heaven—' "

"But you—you impostor," cried Mr. Lincoln, interrupting, "you're giving us Humboldt's Cosmos."

Mr. Hill owned up, laughing.

It is remarkable how soon we accustom ourselves to a strange situation. And to Stephen it was no less strange to be walking over a muddy road of the prairie with this most singular man and a newspaper correspondent, than it might have been to the sub-terrestrial inhabitant to emerge on the earth's surface. Stephen's mind was in the process of a chemical change: Suddenly it seemed to him as if he had known this tall Illinoisan always. The whim of the senatorial candidate in choosing him for a companion he did not then try to account for.

"Come, Mr. Stephen," said Mr. Lincoln, presently, "where do you hail from?"

"Boston," said Stephen.

"No!" said Mr. Lincoln, incredulously. "And how does it happen that you come to me with a message from a rank Abolitionist lawyer in St. Louis?"

"Is the Judge a friend of yours, sir?" Stephen asked.

"What!" exclaimed Mr. Lincoln, "didn't he tell you he was?"

"He said nothing at all, sir, except to tell me to travel until I found you."

"I call the Judge a friend of mine," said Mr. Lincoln. "He may not claim me because I do not believe in putting all slave-owners to the sword."

"I do not think that Judge Whipple is precisely an Abolitionist, sir."

"What! And how do you feel, Mr. Stephen?"

Stephen replied in figures. It was rare with him, and he must have caught it from Mr. Lincoln.

"I am not for ripping out the dam suddenly, sir. That would drown the nation. I believe that the water can be drained off in some other way."

Mr. Lincoln's direct answer to this was to give Stephen a stinging slap between the shoulder-blades.

"God bless the boy!" he cried. "He *has* thought it out. Bob, take that down for the *Press and Tribune* as coming from a rising young politician of St. Louis."

"Why," Stephen blurted out, "I—I thought you were an Abolitionist, Mr. Lincoln."

"Mr. Brice," said Mr. Lincoln, "I have as much use for the Boston *Liberator* as I have for the Charleston *Courier*. You may guess how much that is. The question is not whether we shall or shall not have slavery, but whether slavery shall stay where it is, or be extended according to Judge Douglas's ingenious plan. The Judge is for breeding worms. I am for cauterizing the sore so that it shall not spread. But I tell you, Mr. Brice, that this nation cannot exist half slave and half free."

Was it the slap on the back that opened Stephen's eyes? It was certain that as they returned to the tavern the man at his side was changed. He need not have felt chagrined. Men in high places underestimated Lincoln, or did not estimate him at all. Affection came first. The great warm heart had claimed Stephen as it claimed all who came near it.

The tavern was deserted save for a few stragglers. Under the dim light at the bar Mr. Lincoln took off his hat and drew the Judge's letter from the lining.

"Mr. Stephen," said he, "would you like to come to Freeport with me to-morrow and hear the debate?"

An hour earlier he would have declined with thanks. But now! Now his face lighted at the prospect, and suddenly fell again. Mr. Lincoln guessed the cause. He laid his hand on the young man's shoulder, and laughed.

"I reckon you're thinking of what the Judge will say."

Stephen smiled.

"I'll take care of the Judge," said Mr. Lincoln. "I'm not afraid of him." He drew forth from the inexhaustible hat a slip of paper, and began to write.

"There," said he, when he had finished, "a friend of mine is going to Springfield in the morning, and he'll send that to the Judge."

And this is what he had written:—

"I have borrowed Steve for a day or two, and guarantee to return him a good Republican.

"A. LINCOLN."

It is worth remarking that this was the first time Mr. Brice had been called "Steve" and had not resented it.

Stephen was embarrassed. He tried to thank Mr. Lincoln, but that gentleman's quizzical look cut him short. And the next remark made him gasp.

"Look here, Steve," said he, "you know a parlor from a drawing-room. What did you think of me when you saw me to-night?"

Stephen blushed furiously, and his tongue clave to the roof of his mouth.

"I'll tell you," said Mr. Lincoln, with his characteristic smile, "you thought that you wouldn't pick me out of a bunch of horses to race with the Senator."

CHAPTER IV

THE QUESTION

MANY times since Abraham Lincoln has been called to that mansion which God has reserved for the patriots who have served Him also, Stephen Brice has thought of that steaming night in the low-ceiled room of the country tavern, reeking with the smell of coarse food and hot humanity. He remembers vividly how at first his gorge rose, and recalls how gradually there crept over him a forgetfulness of the squalidity and discomfort. Then came a space gray with puzzling wonder. Then the dawning of a worship for a very ugly man in a rumpled and ill-made coat.

You will perceive that there was hope for Stephen. On his shakedown that night, oblivious to the snores of his companions and the droning of the insects, he lay awake. And before his eyes was that strange, marked face, with its deep lines that blended both humor and sadness there. It was homely, and yet Stephen found himself reflecting that honesty was just as homely, and plain truth. And yet both were beautiful to those who had learned to love them. Just so this Mr. Lincoln.

He fell asleep wondering why Judge Whipple had sent him.

It was in accord with nature that reaction came with the morning. Such a morning, and such a place!

He was awakened, shivering, by the beat of rain on the roof, and stumbling over the prostrate forms of the four Beaver brothers, reached the window. Clouds filled the sky, and Joshway, whose pallet was under the sill, was in a blessed state of moisture.

No wonder some of his enthusiasm had trickled away! He made his toilet in the wet under the pump outside where he had to wait his turn. And he rather wished he were going back to St. Louis. He had an early breakfast of fried eggs and underdone bacon, and coffee which made him pine for Hester's. The dishes were neither too clean nor too plentiful, being doused in water as soon as ever they were out of use.

But after breakfast the sun came out, and a crowd collected around the tavern, although the air was chill and the muck deep in the street.

Stephen caught glimpses of Mr. Lincoln towering above the knots of country politicians who surrounded him, and every once in a while a knot would double up with laughter. There was no sign that the senatorial aspirant took the situation seriously; that the coming struggle with his skilful antagonist was weighing him down in the least. Stephen held aloof from the groups, thinking that Mr. Lincoln had forgotten him. He decided to leave for St. Louis on the morning train, and was even pushing toward the tavern entrance with his bag in his hand, when he was met by Mr. Hill.

"I had about given you up, Mr. Brice," he said. "Mr. Lincoln asked me to get hold of you, and bring you to him alive or dead."

Accordingly Stephen was led to the station, where a long train of twelve cars was pulled up, covered with flags and bunting. On entering one of these, he perceived Mr. Lincoln sprawled (he could think of no other word to fit the attitude) on a seat next the window, and next him was Mr. Medill of the *Press and Tribune*. The seat just in front was reserved for Mr. Hill, who was to make any notes necessary. Mr. Lincoln looked up. His appearance was even less attractive than the night before, as he had on a dirty gray linen duster.

"I thought you'd got loose, Steve," he said, holding out his hand. "Glad to see you. Just you sit down there next to Bob, where I can talk to you."

Stephen sat down, diffident, for he knew that there were others in that train who would give ten years of their lives for that seat.

"I've taken a shine to this Bostonian, Joe," said Mr. Lincoln to Mr. Medill. "We've got to catch 'em young to do anything with 'em, you know. Now, Steve, just give me a notion how politics are over in St. Louis. What do they think of our new Republican party? Too bran' new for old St. Louis, eh?"

Stephen saw expostulation in Mr. Medill's eyes, and hesitated. And Mr. Lincoln seemed to feel Medill's objections, as by mental telepathy. But he said:—

"We'll come to that little matter later, Joe, when the cars start."

Naturally, Stephen began uneasily. But under the influence of that kindly eye he thawed, and forgot himself. He felt that this man was not one to feign an interest. The shouts of the people on the little platform interrupted the account, and the engine staggered off with its load.

"I reckon St. Louis is a nest of Southern Democrats," Mr. Lincoln remarked, "and not much opposition."

"There are quite a few Old Line Whigs, sir," ventured Stephen, smiling.

"Joe," said Mr. Lincoln, "did you ever hear Warfield's definition of an Old Line Whig?"

Mr. Medill had not.

"A man who takes his toddy regularly, and votes the Democratic ticket occasionally, and who wears ruffled shirts."

Both of these gentlemen laughed, and two more in the seat behind, who had an ear to the conversation.

"But, sir," said Stephen, seeing that he was expected to go on, "I think that the Republican party will gather a considerable strength there in another year or two. We have the material for powerful leaders in Mr. Blair and others" (Mr. Lincoln nodded at the name). "We are getting an ever increasing population from New England, mostly of young men who will take kindly to the new party." And then he added, thinking of his pilgrimage the Sunday before: "South St. Louis is a solid mass of Germans, who are all antislavery. But they are very foreign still, and have all their German institutions."

"The Turner Halls?" Mr. Lincoln surprised him by inquiring.

"Yes. And I believe that they drill there."

"Then they will the more easily be turned into soldiers, if the time should come," said Mr. Lincoln. And he added quickly, "I pray that it may not."

Stephen had cause to remember that observation, and the acumen it showed, long afterward.

The train made several stops, and at each of them shoals of country people filled the aisles, and paused for a most familiar chat with the senatorial candidate. Many called him Abe. His appearance was the equal in roughness to theirs, his manner if anything was more democratic,—yet in spite of all this Stephen in them detected a deference which might almost be termed a homage. There were many women among them. Had our friend been older, he might have known that the presence of good women in a political crowd portends something. As it was, he was surprised. He was destined to be still more surprised that day.

When they had left behind them the shouts of the little town of Dixon,

Mr. Lincoln took off his hat, and produced a crumpled and not too immaculate scrap of paper from the multitude therein.

"Now, Joe," said he, "here are the four questions I intend to ask Judge Douglas. I am ready for you. Fire away."

"We don't care anything about the others," answered Mr. Medill. "But I tell you this. If you ask that second one, you'll never see the United States Senate."

"And the Republican party in this state will have had a blow from which it can scarcely recover," added Mr. Judd, chairman of the committee.

Mr. Lincoln did not appear to hear them. His eyes were far away over the wet prairie.

Stephen held his breath. But neither he, nor Medill, nor Judd, nor Hill guessed at the pregnancy of that moment. How were they to know that the fate of the United States of America was concealed in that Question,—was to be decided on a rough wooden platform that day in the town of Freeport, Illinois?

But Abraham Lincoln, the uncouth man in the linen duster with the tousled hair, knew it. And the stone that was rejected of the builders was to become the corner-stone of the temple.

Suddenly Mr. Lincoln recalled himself, glanced at the paper, and cleared his throat. In measured tones, plainly heard above the rush and roar of the train, he read the Question:—

"Can the people of a United States Territory, in any lawful way, against the wish of any citizen of the United States, exclude slavery from its limits prior to the formation of a State Constitution?"

Mr. Medill listened intently.

"Abe," said he, solemnly, "Douglas will answer yes, or equivocate, and that is all the assurance these Northern Democrats want to put Steve Douglas in the Senate. They'll snow you under."

"All right," answered Mr. Lincoln, quietly.

" '*All right*'?" asked Mr. Medill, reflecting the sheer astonishment of the others; "then why the devil are you wearing yourself out? And why are we spending our time and money on you?"

Mr. Lincoln laid his hand on Medill's sleeve.

"Joe," said he, "a rat in the larder is easier to catch than a rat that has the run of the cellar. You know where to set your trap in the larder. I'll tell you why I'm in this campaign: to catch Douglas now, and keep him out of the White House in 1860. To save this country of ours, Joe. She's sick."

There was a silence, broken by two exclamations.

"But see here, Abe," said Mr. Medill, as soon as ever he got his breath, "what have we got to show for it? Where do you come in?"

Mr. Lincoln smiled wearily.

"Nowhere, I reckon," he answered simply.

"Good Lord!" said Mr. Judd.

Mr. Medill gulped.

"You mean to say, as the candidate of the Republican party, you don't care whether you get to the Senate?"

"Not if I can send Steve Douglas there with his wings broken," was the calm reply.

"Suppose he does answer *yes*, that slavery can be excluded?" said Mr. Judd.

"Then," said Mr. Lincoln, "then Douglas loses the vote of the great slave-holders, the vote of the solid South, that he has been fostering ever since he has had the itch to be President. Without the solid South the Little Giant will never live in the White House. And unless I'm mightily mistaken, Steve Douglas has had his eye as far ahead as 1860 for some time."

Another silence followed these words. There was a stout man standing in the aisle, and he spat deftly out of the open window.

"You may wing Steve Douglas, Abe," said he, gloomily, "but the gun will kick you over the bluff."

"Don't worry about me, Ed," said Mr. Lincoln. "I'm not worth it."

In a wave of comprehension the significance of all this was revealed to Stephen Brice. The grim humor, the sagacious statesmanship, and (best of all) the superb self-sacrifice of it, struck him suddenly. I think it was in that hour that he realized the full extent of the wisdom he was near, which was like unto Solomon's.

Shame surged in Stephen's face that he should have misjudged him. He had come to patronize. He had remained to worship. And in after years, when he thought of this new vital force which became part of him that day, it was in the terms of Emerson: "Pythagoras was misunderstood, and Socrates, and Jesus, and Luther, and Copernicus, and Galileo, and Newton, and every pure and wise spirit that ever took flesh. To be great is to be misunderstood."

How many have conversed with Lincoln before and since, and knew him not!

If an outward and visible sign of Mr. Lincoln's greatness were needed, —he had chosen to speak to them in homely parables. The story of Farmer Bell was plain as day. Jim Rickets, who had life all his own way, was none other than Stephen A. Douglas, the easily successful. The ugly galoot, who dared to raise his eyes only to the pear, was Mr. Lincoln himself. And the pear was the Senatorship, which the galoot had denied himself to save Susan from being Mr. Rickets' bride.

Stephen could understand likewise the vehemence of the Republican leaders who crowded around their candidate and tried to get him to retract that Question. He listened quietly, he answered with a patient smile. Now and then he threw a story into the midst of this discussion which made them laugh in spite of themselves. The hopelessness of the case was quite plain to Mr. Hill, who smiled, and whispered in Stephen's ear:—

"He has made up his mind. They will not budge him an inch, and they know it."

Finally Mr. Lincoln took the scrap of paper, which was even more dirty and finger-marked by this time, and handed it to Mr. Hill. The train was slowing down for Freeport. In the distance, bands could be heard playing, and along the track, line upon line of men and women were cheering and waving. It was ten o'clock, raw and cold for that time of the year, and the sun was trying to come out.

"Bob," said Mr. Lincoln, "be sure you get that right in your notes. And, Steve, you stick close to me, and you'll see the show. Why, boys," he added, smiling, "there's the great man's private car, cannon and all."

All that Stephen saw was a regular day-car on a side-track. A brass cannon was on the tender hitched behind it.

CHAPTER V

THE CRISIS

STEPHEN A. DOUGLAS, called the Little Giant on account of his intellect, was a type of man of which our race has had some notable examples, although they are not characteristic. Capable of sacrifice to their country, personal ambition is, nevertheless, the mainspring of their actions. They must either be before the public, or else unhappy. This trait gives them a large theatrical strain, and sometimes brands them as adventurers. Their ability saves them from being demagogues.

In the case of Douglas, he had deliberately renewed some years before the agitation on the spread of slavery, by setting forth a doctrine of extreme cleverness. This doctrine, like many others of its kind, seemed at first sight to be the balm it pretended, instead of an irritant, as it really was. It was calculated to deceive all except thinking men, and to silence all save a merciless logician. And this merciless logician, who was heaven-sent in time of need, was Abraham Lincoln.

Mr. Douglas was a juggler, a political prestidigitateur. He did things before the eyes of the Senate and the nation. His balm for the healing of the nation's wounds was a patent medicine so cleverly concocted that experts alone could show what was in it. So abstruse and twisted were some of Mr. Douglas's doctrines that a genius alone might put them into simple words, for the common people.

The great panacea for the slavery trouble put forth by Mr. Douglas at that time was briefly this: that the people of the new territories should decide for themselves, subject to the Constitution, whether they should have slavery or not, and also decide for themselves all other questions under the Constitution. Unhappily for Mr. Douglas, there was the famous Dred Scott decision, which had set the South wild with joy the year before, and had cast a gloom over the North. The Chief Justice of the United States had declared that under the Constitution slaves were property,—and as such every American citizen owning slaves could carry them about with him wherever he went. Therefore the

124

territorial legislatures might pass laws until they were dumb, and yet
their settlers might bring with them all the slaves they pleased.

And yet we must love the Judge. He was a gentleman, a strong man,
and a patriot. He was magnanimous, and to his immortal honor be it
said that he, in the end, won the greatest of all struggles. He conquered
himself. He put down that mightiest thing that was in him,—his ambition for himself. And he set up, instead, his ambition for his country.
He bore no ill-will toward the man whose fate was so strangely linked
to his, and who finally came to that high seat of honor and of martyrdom
which he coveted. We shall love the Judge, and speak of him with
reverence, for that sublime act of kindness before the Capitol in 1861.

Abraham Lincoln might have prayed on that day of the Freeport
debate: "Forgive him, Lord. He knows not what he does." Lincoln
descried the danger afar, and threw his body into the breach.

That which passed before Stephen's eyes, and to which his ears listened at Freeport, was the Great Republic pressing westward to the
Pacific. He wondered whether some of his Eastern friends who pursed
their lips when the West was mentioned would have sneered or prayed.
A young English nobleman who was there that day did not sneer. He
was filled instead with something like awe at the vigor of this nation
which was sprung from the loins of his own. Crudeness he saw, vulgarity
he heard, but Force he felt, and marvelled.

America was in Freeport that day, the rush of her people and the
surprise of her climate. The rain had ceased, and quickly was come out
of the northwest a boisterous wind, chilled by the lakes and scented by
the hemlocks of the Minnesota forests. The sun smiled and frowned.
Clouds hurried in the sky, mocking the human hubbub below. Cheering
thousands pressed about the station as Mr. Lincoln's train arrived. They
hemmed him in his triumphal passage under the great arching trees to
the new Brewster House. The Chief Marshal and his aides, great men
before, were suddenly immortal. The county delegations fell into their
proper precedence like ministers at a state dinner. "*We have faith in
Abraham, Yet another County for the Rail-splitter, Abe the Giant-
killer,*"—so the banners read. Here, much bedecked, was the *Galena
Lincoln Club*, part of Joe Davies's shipment. Fifes skirled, and drums
throbbed, and the stars and stripes snapped in the breeze. And here was
a delegation headed by fifty sturdy ladies on horseback, at whom
Stephen gaped like a countryman. Then came carryalls of all ages and

degrees, wagons from this county and that county, giddily draped, drawn
by horses from one to six, or by mules, their inscriptions addressing their
senatorial candidate in all degrees of familiarity, but not contempt.
What they seemed proudest of was that he had been a rail-splitter, for
nearly all bore a fence-rail.

But stay, what is this wagon with the high sapling flagstaff in the
middle, and the leaves still on it?

>*"Westward the Star of Empire takes its way.*
>*The girls link on to Lincoln; their mothers were for Clay."*

Here was glory to blind you,—two and thirty maids in red sashes
and blue liberty caps with white stars. Each was a state of the Union,
and every one of them was for Abraham, who called them his "Basket
of Flowers." Behind them, most touching of all, sat a thirty-third
shackled in chains. That was Kansas. Alas, the mien of Kansas was far
from being as sorrowful as the part demanded,—in spite of her instructions she would smile at the boys. But the appealing inscription she
bore, "Set me free!" was greeted with storms of laughter, the boldest of
the young men shouting that she was too beautiful to be free, and some
of the old men, to their shame be it said, likewise shouted. No false embarrassment troubled Kansas. She was openly pleased. But the young
men who had brought their sweethearts to town, and were standing
hand in hand with them, for obvious reasons saw nothing. They scarcely
dared to look at Kansas, and those who did were so loudly rebuked that
they turned down the side streets.

During this part of the day these loving couples, whose devotion was
so patent to the whole world, were by far the most absorbing to Stephen.
He watched them having their fortunes told, the young women blushing
and crying, "Say!" and "Ain't he wicked?" and the young men getting
their ears boxed for certain remarks. He watched them standing open-
mouthed at the booths and side shows, with hands still locked, or again
they were chewing cream candy in unison. Or he glanced sidewise at
them, seated in the open places with the world so far below them that
even the insistent sound of the fifes and drums rose but faintly to their
ears.

And perhaps,—we shall not say positively,—perhaps Mr. Brice's
thoughts went something like this, "O that love were so simple a matter
to all!" But graven on his face was what is called the "Boston scorn."
And no scorn has been known like unto it since the days of Athens.

So Stephen made the best of his way to the Brewster House, the elegance and newness of which the citizens of Freeport openly boasted. Mr. Lincoln had preceded him, and was even then listening to a few remarks of burning praise by an honorable gentleman. Mr. Lincoln himself made a few remarks, which seemed so simple and rang so true, and were so free from political rococo and decoration generally, that even the young men forgot their sweethearts to listen. Then Mr. Lincoln went into the hotel, and the sun slipped under a black cloud.

The lobby was full, and rather dirty, since the supply of spittoons was so far behind the demand. Like the firmament, it was divided into little bodies which revolved about larger bodies. But there lacked not here supporters of the Little Giant, and discreet farmers of influence in their own counties who waited to hear the afternoon's debate before deciding. These and others did not hesitate to tell of the magnificence of the Little Giant's torchlight procession the previous evening. Every Dred-Scottite had carried a torch, and many transparencies, so that the very glory of it had turned night into day. The Chief Lictor had distributed these torches with an unheard-of liberality. But there lacked not detractors who swore that John Dibble and other Lincolnites had applied for torches for the mere pleasure of carrying them. Since dawn the delegations had been heralded from the house-tops, and wagered on while they were yet as worms far out on the prairie. All the morning these continued to come in, and form in line to march past their particular candidate. The second great event of the day was the event of the special over the Galena road, of sixteen cars and more than a thousand pairs of sovereign lungs. With military precision they repaired to the Brewster House, and ahead of them a banner was flung: *"Winnebago County for the Tall Sucker."* And the Tall Sucker was on the steps to receive them.

But Mr. Douglas, who had arrived the evening before to the booming of two and thirty guns, had his banners and his bunting, too. The neighborhood of Freeport was a stronghold of Northern Democrats, ardent supporters of the Little Giant if once they could believe that he did not intend to betray them.

Stephen felt in his bones the coming of a struggle, and was thrilled. Once he smiled at the thought that he had become an active partisan—nay, a worshipper—of the uncouth Lincoln. Terrible suspicion for a Bostonian,—had he been carried away? Was his hero, after all, a homespun demagogue? Had he been wise in deciding before he had caught a glimpse of the accomplished Douglas, whose name and fame filled the land? Stephen did not waver in his allegiance. But in his heart there lurked a fear of the sophisticated Judge and Senator and man of the world whom he had not yet seen. In his note-book he had made a copy of the Question, and young Mr. Hill discovered him pondering in a corner of the lobby at dinner-time. After dinner they went together to their candidate's room. They found the doors open and the place packed, and there was Mr. Lincoln's very tall hat towering above those of the other politicians pressed around him. Mr. Lincoln took three strides in Stephen's direction and seized him by the shoulder.

"Why, Steve," said he, "I thought you had got away again." Turning to a big burly man with a good-natured face, who was standing by, he added: "Jim, I want you to look out for this young man. Get him a seat on the stand, where he can hear."

Stephen stuck close to Jim. He never knew what the gentleman's last name was, or whether he had any. It was but a few minutes' walk to the grove where the speaking was to be. And as they made their way thither Mr. Lincoln passed them in a Conestoga wagon drawn by six milk-white horses. Jim informed Stephen that the Little Giant had had a six-horse coach. The grove was black with people. Hovering about the hem of the crowd were the sunburned young men in their Sunday best, still clinging fast to the hands of the young women. Bands blared "Columbia, Gem of the Ocean." Fakirs planted their stands in the way, selling pain-killers and ague cures, watermelons and lemonade. Jugglers juggled, and beggars begged. Jim said that there were sixteen thousand people in that grove. And he told the truth.

Stephen now trembled for his champion. He tried to think of himself as fifty years old, with the courage to address sixteen thousand people on such a day, and quailed. What a man of affairs it must take to do that! Sixteen thousand people, into each of whose breasts God had put different emotions and convictions! He had never even imagined such a crowd as this assembled merely to listen to a political debate. But then he remembered, as they dodged from in front of the horses, that it was not merely a political debate. The pulse of a nation was here, a great nation stricken with approaching fever. It was not now a case of excise, but of existence.

This son of toil who had driven his family thirty miles across the prairie, blanketed his tired horses and slept on the ground the night before, who was willing to stand all through the afternoon and listen with

pathetic eagerness to this debate, must be moved by a patriotism divine. In the breast of that farmer, in the breast of his tired wife who held
her child by the hand, had been instilled from birth that sublime fervor
which is part of their life who inherit the Declaration of Independence.
Instinctively these men who had fought and won the West had scented
the danger. With the spirit of their ancestors who had left their farms
to die on the bridge at Concord, or follow Ethan Allen into Ticonderoga,
these had come to Freeport. What were three days of bodily discomfort!
What even the loss of part of a cherished crop, if the nation's existence
were at stake and their votes might save it!

In the midst of that heaving human sea rose the bulwarks of a wooden
stand. But how to reach it? Jim was evidently a personage. The rough
farmers commonly squeezed a way for him. And when they did not, he
made it with his big body. As they drew near their haven, a great surging as of a tidal wave swept them off their feet. There was a deafening
shout, and the stand rocked on its foundations. Before Stephen could
collect his wits, a fierce battle was raging about him. Abolitionist and
Democrat, Free Soiler and Squatter Sov, defaced one another in a rush
for the platform. The committeemen and reporters on top of it rose to its
defence. Well for Stephen that his companion was along. Jim was recognized and hauled bodily into the fort, and Stephen after him. The pop-
ulace were driven off, and when the excitement died down again, he
found himself in the row behind the reporters. Young Mr. Hill paused
while sharpening his pencil to wave him a friendly greeting.

Stephen, craning in his seat, caught sight of Mr. Lincoln slouched
into one of his favorite attitudes, his chin resting in his hand.

But who is this, erect, compact, aggressive, searching with a confident eye the wilderness of upturned faces? A personage, truly, to be
questioned timidly, to be approached advisedly. Here indeed was a lion,
by the very look of him, master of himself and of others. By reason of
its regularity and masculine strength, a handsome face. A man of the
world to the cut of the coat across the broad shoulders. Here was one
to lift a youngster into the realm of emulation, like a character in a
play, to arouse dreams of Washington and its senators and great men.
For this was one to be consulted by the great alone. A figure of dignity
and power, with magnetism to compel moods. Since, when he smiled,
you warmed in spite of yourself, and when he frowned the world looked
grave.

The inevitable comparison was come, and Stephen's hero was shrunk once more. He drew a deep breath, searched for the word, and gulped. There was but the one word. How *country* Abraham Lincoln looked beside Stephen Arnold Douglas!

Had the Lord ever before made and set over against each other two such different men? Yes, for such are the ways of the Lord.

*   *   *   *   *   *   *   *   *

The preliminary speaking was in progress, but Stephen neither heard nor saw until he felt the heavy hand of his companion on his knee.

"There's something mighty strange, like fate, between them two," he was saying. "I recklect twenty-five years ago when they was first in the Legislatur' together. A man told me that they was both admitted to practice in the S'preme Court in '39, *on the same day, sir*. Then you know they was nip an' tuck after the same young lady. Abe got her. They've been in Congress together, the Little Giant in the Senate, and now, here they be in the greatest set of debates the people of this state ever heard. Young man, the hand of fate is in this here, mark my words—"

There was a hush, and the waves of that vast human sea were stilled. A man,—lean, angular, with coat-tails flapping—unfolded like a grotesque figure at a side-show. No confidence was there. Stooping forward, Abraham Lincoln began to speak, and Stephen Brice hung his head, and shuddered. Could this shrill falsetto be the same voice to which he had listened only that morning? Could this awkward, yellow man with his hands behind his back be he whom he had worshipped? Ripples of derisive laughter rose here and there, on the stand and from the crowd. Thrice distilled was the agony of those moments!

But what was this feeling that gradually crept over him? Surprise? Cautiously he raised his eyes. The hands were coming around to the front. Suddenly one of them was thrown sharply back, with a determined gesture, the head was raised,—and—and his shame was forgotten. In its stead wonder was come. But soon he lost even that, for his mind was gone on a journey. And when again he came to himself and looked upon Abraham Lincoln, this was a man transformed. The voice was no longer shrill. Nay, it was now a powerful instrument which played strangely on those who heard. Now it rose, and again it fell into tones so low as to start a stir which spread and spread, like a ripple in a pond, until it broke on the very edge of that vast audience.

"Can the people of a United States Territory, in any lawful way, against the wish of any citizen of the United States, exclude slavery from its limits prior to the formation of a State Constitution?"

It was out, at last, irrevocably writ in the recording book of History, for better, for worse. Beyond the reach of politician, committee, or caucus. But what man amongst those who heard and stirred might say that these minutes even now hasting into eternity held the Crisis of a nation that is the hope of the world? Not you, Judge Douglas, who sit there smiling. Consternation is a stranger in your heart,—but answer that Question if you can. Yes, your nimble wit has helped you out of many a tight corner. You do not feel the noose—as yet. You do not guess that your reply will make or mar the fortunes of your country. It is not you who can look ahead two short years and see the ship of Democracy splitting on the rocks at Charleston and at Baltimore, when the power of your name might have steered her safely.

But see! what is this man about whom you despise? One by one he is taking the screws out of the engine which you have invented to run your ship. Look, he holds them in his hands without mixing them, and shows the false construction of its secret parts.

For Abraham Lincoln dealt with abstruse questions in language so limpid that many a farmer, dulled by toil, heard and understood and marvelled. The simplicity of the Bible dwells in those speeches, and they are now classics in our literature. And the wonder in Stephen's mind was that this man who could be a buffoon, whose speech was coarse and whose person unkempt, could prove himself a tower of morality and truth. That has troubled many another, before and since the debate at Freeport.

That short hour came all too quickly to an end. And as the Moderator gave the signal for Mr. Lincoln, it was Stephen's big companion who snapped the strain, and voiced the sentiment of those about him.

"By Gosh!" he cried, "he baffles Steve. I didn't think Abe had it in him."

The Honorable Stephen A. Douglas, however, seemed anything but baffled as he rose to reply. As he waited for the cheers which greeted him to die out, his attitude was easy and indifferent, as a public man's should be. The Question seemed not to trouble him in the least. But for Stephen Brice the Judge stood there stripped of the glamour that made him, even as Abraham Lincoln had stripped his doctrine of its paint and colors, and left it punily naked.

Standing up, the very person of the Little Giant was contradictory, as was the man himself. His height was insignificant. But he had the head and shoulders of a lion, and even the lion's roar. What a contrast

the ring of his deep bass to the tentative falsetto of Mr. Lincoln's opening words! If Stephen expected the Judge to tremble, he was greatly
disappointed. Mr. Douglas was far from dismay. As if to show the people how lightly he held his opponent's warnings, he made them gape by
putting things down Mr. Lincoln's shirt-front and taking them out of
his mouth. But it appeared to Stephen, listening with all his might,
that the Judge was a trifle more on the defensive than his attitude might
lead one to expect. Was he not among his own Northern Democrats at
Freeport? And yet it seemed to give him a keen pleasure to call his
hearers "Black Republicans." "Not black," came from the crowd again
and again, and once a man shouted, "Couldn't you modify it and call it
brown?" "Not a whit!" cried the Judge, and dubbed them "Yankees,"
although himself a Vermonter by birth. He implied that most of these
Black Republicans desired negro wives.

But quick,—to the Question. How was the Little Giant, artful in
debate as he was, to get over that without offence to the great South?
Very skilfully the Judge disposed of the first of the interrogations. And
then, save for the gusts of wind rustling the trees, the grove might have
been empty of its thousands, such was the silence that fell. But tighter
and tighter they pressed against the stand, until it trembled.

Oh, Judge, the time of all artful men will come at length! How were
you to foresee a certain day under the White Dome of the Capitol? Had
your sight been long, you would have paused before your answer. Had
your sight been long, you would have seen this ugly Lincoln bareheaded
before the Nation, *and you are holding his hat.* Judge Douglas, this act
alone has redeemed your faults. It has given you a nobility of which we
did not suspect you. At the end God gave you strength to be humble,
and so you left the name of a patriot.

Judge, you thought there was a passage between Scylla and Charybdis
which your craftiness might overcome. "It matters not," you cried when
you answered the Question, "it matters not which way the Supreme
Court may hereafter decide as to the abstract question whether slavery
may or may not go into a territory under the Constitution. The people
have the lawful means to introduce or to exclude it as they please, for
the reason that slavery cannot exist a day or an hour anywhere unless it
is supported by local police regulations."

Judge Douglas, uneasy will you lie to-night, for you have uttered the
Freeport Heresy.

It only remains to be told how Stephen Brice, coming to the Brewster House after the debate, found Mr. Lincoln. On his knee, in transports of delight, was a small boy, and Mr. Lincoln was serenely playing on the child's Jew's-harp. Standing beside him was a proud father who had dragged his son across two counties in a farm wagon, and who was to return on the morrow to enter this event in the family Bible. In a corner of the room were several impatient gentlemen of influence who wished to talk about the Question.

But when he saw Stephen, Mr. Lincoln looked up with a smile of welcome that is still, and ever will be, remembered and cherished.

"Tell Judge Whipple that I have attended to that little matter, Steve," he said.

"Why, Mr. Lincoln," he exclaimed, "you have had no time."

"I have taken the time," Mr. Lincoln replied, "and I think that I am well repaid. Steve," said he, "unless I'm mightily mistaken, you know a little more than you did yesterday."

"Yes, sir; I do," said Stephen.

"Come, Steve," said Mr. Lincoln, "be honest. Didn't you feel sorry for me last night?"

Stephen flushed scarlet.

"I never shall again, sir," he said.

The wonderful smile, so ready to come and go, flickered and went out. In its stead on the strange face was ineffable sadness,—the sadness of the world's tragedies. Of Stephen stoned, of Christ crucified.

"Pray God that you may feel sorry for me again," he said.

Awed, the child on his lap was still. The politicians had left the room. Mr. Lincoln had kept Stephen's hand in his own.

"I have hopes of you, Stephen," he said. "Do not forget me."

Stephen Brice never has. Why was it that he walked to the station with a heavy heart? It was a sense of the man he had left, who had been and was to be. This Lincoln of the black loam, who built his neighbor's cabin and hoed his neighbor's corn, who had been storekeeper and postmaster and flat-boatman. Who had followed a rough judge dealing a rough justice around a rough circuit; who had rolled a local bully in the dirt; rescued women from insult; tended the bedside of many a sick coward who feared the Judgment; told coarse stories on barrels by candlelight (but these are pure beside the vice of great cities); who addressed political mobs in the raw, swooping down from the stump and flinging embroilers east and west. This physician who was one day to tend the sick-bed of the Nation in her agony; whose large hand was to be on her feeble pulse, and whose knowledge almost divine was to perform the miracle of her healing. So was it that the Physician Himself performed His cures, and when His work was done, died a Martyr.

Abraham Lincoln died in His name.

CHAPTER VI

GLENCOE

It was nearly noon when Stephen walked into the office the next day, dusty and travel-worn and perspiring. He had come straight from the ferry, without going home. And he had visions of a quiet dinner with Richter under the trees at the beer-garden, where he could talk about Abraham Lincoln. Had Richter ever heard of Lincoln?

But the young German met him at the top of the stairs, and his face was more serious than usual, although he showed his magnificent teeth in a smile of welcome.

"You are a little behind your time, my friend," said he. "What has happened to you?"

"Didn't the Judge get Mr. Lincoln's message?" asked Stephen, with anxiety.

The German shrugged his shoulders.

"Ah, I know not," he answered. "He has gone to Glencoe. The Judge is ill, Stephen. Doctor Polk says that he has worked all his life too hard. The Doctor and Colonel Carvel tried to get him to go to Glencoe. But he would not budge until Miss Carvel herself comes all the way from the country yesterday, and orders him. Ach!" exclaimed Richter, impulsively, "what wonderful women you have in America! I could lose my head when I think of Miss Carvel."

"Miss Carvel was here, you say?" Stephen repeated, in a tone of inquiry.

"*Donner!*" said Richter, disgusted, "you don't care."

Stephen laughed, in spite of himself.

"Why should I?" he answered. And becoming grave again, added: "Except on Judge Whipple's account. Have you heard from him to-day, Carl?"

"This morning one of Colonel Carvel's servants came for his letters. He must be feeling better. I—I pray that he is better," said Richter, his voice breaking. "He has been very good to me."

Stephen said nothing. But he had been conscious all at once of an affection for the Judge of which he had not suspected himself. That afternoon, on his way home, he stopped at Carvel & Company's to inquire. Mr. Whipple was better, so Mr. Hopper said, and added that he "presumed likely the Colonel would not be in for a week." It was then Saturday. Eliphalet was actually in the Colonel's sanctum behind the partition, giving orders to several clerks at the time. He was so prosperous and important that he could scarce spare a moment to answer Stephen, who went away wondering whether he had been wise to choose the law.

On Monday, when Stephen called at Carvel & Company's, Eliphalet was too busy to see him. But Ephum, who went out to Glencoe every night with orders, told him that the "Jedge was wuss, suh." On Wednesday, there being little change, Mrs. Brice ventured to despatch a jelly by Ephum. On Friday afternoon, when Stephen was deep in Whittlesey and the New Code, he became aware of Ephum standing beside him. In reply to his anxious question Ephum answered:—

"I reckon he better, suh. He an' de Colonel done commence wrastlin' 'bout a man name o' Linkum. De Colonel done wrote you dis note, suh."

It was a very polite note, containing the Colonel's compliments, asking Mr. Brice to Glencoe that afternoon with whatever papers or letters the Judge might wish to see. And since there was no convenient train in the evening, Colonel Carvel would feel honored if Mr. Brice would spend the night. The Colonel mentioned the train on which Mr. Brice was expected.

The Missouri side of the Mississippi is a very different country from the hot and treeless prairies of Illinois. As Stephen alighted at the little station at Glencoe and was driven away by Ned in the Colonel's buggy, he drew in deep breaths of the sweet air of the Meramec Valley. There had been a shower, and the sun glistened on the drops on grass and flowers, and the great trees hung heavy over the clay road. At last they came to a white gate in the picket fence, in sight of a rambling wooden house with a veranda in front covered with honeysuckle. And then he saw the Colonel, in white marseilles, smoking a cigar. This, indeed, was real country.

As Stephen trod the rough flags between the high grass which led toward the house, Colonel Carvel rose to his full height and greeted him.

"You are very welcome, sir," he said gravely. "The Judge is asleep now," he added. "I regret to say that we had a little argument this morning, and my daughter tells me it will be well not to excite him again to-day. Jinny is reading to him now, or she would be here to entertain you, Mr. Brice. Jackson!" cried Mr. Carvel, "show Mr. Brice to his room."

Jackson appeared hurriedly, seized Stephen's bag, and led the way upstairs through the cool and darkened house to a pretty little room on the south side, with matting, and roses on the simple dressing-table. After he had sat awhile staring at these, and at the wet flower-garden from between the slats of his shutters, he removed the signs of the railroad upon him, and descended. The Colonel was still on the porch, in his easy-chair. He had lighted another cigar, and on the stand beside him stood two tall glasses, green with the fresh mint. Colonel Carvel rose, and with his own hand offered one to Stephen.

"Your health, Mr. Brice," he said, "and I hope you will feel at home here, sir. Jackson will bring you anything you desire, and should you wish to drive, I shall be delighted to show you the country."

Stephen drank that julep with reverence, and then the Colonel gave him a cigar. He was quite overcome by this treatment of a penniless young Yankee. The Colonel did not talk politics—such was not his notion of hospitality to a stranger. He talked horse, and no great discernment on Stephen's part was needed to perceive that this was Mr. Carvel's hobby.

"I used to have a stable, Mr. Brice, before they ruined gentleman's sport with these trotters ten years ago. Yes, sir, we used to be at Lexington one week, and Louisville the next, and over here on the Ames track after that. Did you ever hear of Water Witch and Netty Boone?"

Yes, Stephen had, from Mr. Jack Brinsmade.

The Colonel's face beamed.

"Why, sir," he cried, "that very nigger, Ned, who drove you here from the cars—*he* used to ride Netty Boone. Would you believe that, Mr. Brice? He was the best jockey ever strode a horse on the Elleardsville track here. He wore my yellow and green, sir, until he got to weigh one hundred and a quarter. And I kept him down to that weight a whole year, Mr. Brice. Yes, sirree, a whole year."

"Kept him down!" said Stephen.

"Why, yes, sir. I had him wrapped in blankets and set in a chair with holes bored in the seat. Then we lighted a spirit lamp under him. Many a time I took off ten pounds that way. It needs fire to get flesh off a nigger, sir."

He didn't notice his guest's amazement.

"Then, sir," he continued, "they introduced these damned trotting races; trotting races are for white trash, Mr. Brice."

"Pa!"

The Colonel stopped short. Stephen was already on his feet. I wish you could have seen Miss Virginia Carvel as he saw her then. She wore a white lawn dress. A tea-tray was in her hand, and her head was tilted back, as women are apt to do when they carry a burden. It was so that these Southern families, who were so bitter against Abolitionists and Yankees, entertained them when they were poor, and nursed them when they were ill.

Stephen, for his life, could not utter a word. But Virginia turned to him with perfect self-possession.

"He has been boring you with his horses, Mr. Brice," she said. "Has he told you what a jockey Ned used to be before he weighed one hundred and a quarter?" (A laugh.) "Has he given you the points of Water Witch and Netty Boone?" (More laughter, increasing embarrassment for Stephen.) "Pa, I tell you once more that you will drive every guest from this house. Your jockey talk is intolerable."

O that you might have a notion of the way in which Virginia pronounced *intolerable*.

Mr. Carvel reached for another cigar. "My dear," he asked, "how is the Judge?"

"My dear," said Virginia, smiling, "he is asleep. Mammy Easter is with him, trying to make out what he is saying. He talks in his sleep, just as you do—"

"And what is he saying?" demanded the Colonel, interested.

Virginia set down the tray.

" 'A house divided against itself,' " said Miss Carvel, with a sweep of her arm, " 'cannot stand. I believe that this Government cannot endure permanently, half slave and half free. I do not expect the Union to dissolve—I do not expect the house to fall—but I *do* expect it will cease to be divided.' Would you like any more?" added Miss Virginia.

"No," cried the Colonel, and banged his fist down on the table. "Why," said he, thoughtfully, stroking the white goatee on his chin, "cuss me if that ain't from the speech that country bumpkin, Lincoln, made in June last before the Black Republican convention in Illinois."

Virginia broke again into laughter. And Stephen was very near it, for he loved the Colonel. That gentleman suddenly checked himself in his tirade, and turned to him.

"I beg your pardon, sir," he said; "I reckon that you have the same political sentiments as the Judge. Believe me, sir, I would not willingly offend a guest."

Stephen smiled. "I am not offended, sir," he said. A speech which caused Mr. Carvel to bestow a quick glance upon him. But Stephen did not see it. He was looking at Virginia.

The Colonel rose.

"You will pardon my absence for a while, sir," he said. "My daughter will entertain you."

In silence they watched him as he strode off under the trees through tall grass, a yellow setter at his heels. A strange peace was over Stephen. The shadows of the walnuts and hickories were growing long, and a rich country was giving up its scent to the evening air. From a cabin behind the house was wafted the melody of a plantation song. To the young man, after the burnt city, this was paradise. And then he remembered his mother as she must be sitting on the tiny porch in town, and sighed. Only two years ago she had been at their own place at Westbury.

He looked up, and saw the girl watching him. He dared not think that the expression he caught was one of sympathy, for it changed instantly.

"I am afraid you are the silent kind, Mr. Brice," said she; "I believe it is a Yankee trait."

Stephen laughed.

"I have known a great many who were not," said he. "When they are garrulous, they are very much so."

"I should prefer a garrulous one," said Virginia.

"I should think a Yankee were bad enough, but a noisy Yankee not to be put up with," he ventured.

Virginia did not deign a direct reply to this, save by the corners of her mouth.

"I wonder," said she, thoughtfully, "whether it is strength of mind or a lack of ideas that makes them silent."

"It is mostly prudence," said Mr. Brice. "Prudence is our dominant trait."

Virginia fidgeted. Usually she had an easier time.

"You have not always shown it," she said, with an innocence which in women is often charged with meaning.

Stephen started. Her antagonism was still there. He would have liked greatly to know whether she referred to his hasty purchase of Hester, or to his rashness in dancing with her at her party the winter before.

"We have something left to be thankful for," he answered. "We are still capable of action."

"On occasions it is violence," said Virginia, desperately. This man must not get ahead of her.

"It is just as violent," said he, "as the repressed feeling which prompts it."

This was a new kind of conversation to Virginia. Of all the young men she knew, not one had ever ventured into anything of the sort. They were either flippant, or sentimental, or both. She was at once flattered and annoyed. Flattered, because, as a woman, Stephen had conceded her a mind. Many of the young men she knew had minds, but deemed that these were wasted on women, whose language was generally supposed to be a kind of childish twaddle. Even Jack Brinsmade rarely risked his dignity and reputation at an intellectual tilt. This was one of Virginia's grievances. She often argued with her father, and, if the truth were told, had had more than one victory over Judge Whipple.

Virginia's annoyance came from the fact that she perceived in Stephen a natural and merciless logic,—a faculty for getting at the bottom of things. His brain did not seem to be thrown out of gear by local magnetic influences,—by beauty, for instance. He did not lose his head, as did some others she knew, at the approach of feminine charms. Here was a grand subject, then, to try the mettle of any woman. One with less mettle would have given it up. But Virginia thought it would be delightful to bring this particular Yankee to his knees, and—and leave him there.

"Mr. Brice," she said, "I have not spoken to you since the night of my party. I believe we danced together."

"Yes, we did," said he, "and I called, but was unfortunate."

"You called?"

Ah, Virginia!

"They did not tell you!" cried Stephen.

Now Miss Carvel was complacency itself.

"Jackson is so careless with cards," said she, "and very often I do not take the trouble to read them."

"I am sorry," said he, "as I wished for the opportunity to tell you how much I enjoyed myself. I have found everybody in St. Louis very kind to strangers."

Virginia was nearly disarmed. She remembered how she had opposed his coming. But honesty as well as something else prompted her to say:—

"It was my father who invited you."

Stephen did not reveal the shock his vanity had received.

"At least you were good enough to dance with me."

"I could scarcely refuse a guest," she replied.

He held up his head.

"Had I thought it would have given you annoyance," he said quietly, "I should not have asked you."

"Which would have been a lack of good manners," said Virginia, biting her lips.

Stephen answered nothing, but wished himself in St. Louis. He could not comprehend her cruelty. But, just then, the bell rang for supper, and the Colonel appeared around the end of the house.

It was one of those suppers for which the South is renowned. And when at length he could induce Stephen to eat no more, Colonel Carvel reached for his broad-brimmed felt hat, and sat smoking, with his feet against the mantel. Virginia, who had talked but little, disappeared with a tray on which she had placed with her own hands some dainties to tempt the Judge.

The Colonel regaled Stephen, when she was gone, with the pedigree and performance of every horse he had had in his stable. And this was a relief, as it gave him an opportunity to think without interruption upon Virginia's pronounced attitude of dislike. To him it was inconceivable that a young woman of such qualities as she appeared to have, should assail him so persistently for freeing a negress, and so depriving her of a maid she had set her heart upon. There were other New England young men in society. Mr. Weston and Mr. Carpenter, and more. They were not her particular friends, to be sure. But they called on her and danced with her, and she had shown them not the least antipathy. But it was to Stephen's credit that he did not analyze further.

He was reflecting on these things when he got to his room, when there came a knock at the door. It was Mammy Easter, in bright turban and apron,—was hospitality and comfort in the flesh.

"Is you got all you need, suh?" she inquired.

Stephen replied that he had. But Mammy showed no inclination to go, and he was too polite to shut the door.

"How you like Glencoe, Mistah Brice?"

He was charmed with it.

"We has some of de fust fam'lies out heah in de summer," said she. "But de Colonel, he ain't much on a gran' place laik in Kaintuck. Shucks, no, suh, dis ain't much of a 'stablishment! Young Massa won't have no lawns, no greenhouses, no nothin'. He say he laik it wil' and simple. He on'y come out fo' two months, mebbe. But Miss Jinny, she make it lively. Las' week, until the Jedge come we hab dis house chuck full, two—three young ladies in a room, an' five young gemmen on trunnle beds."

"Until the Judge came?" echoed Stephen.

"Yassuh. Den Miss Jinny low dey all hatter go. She say she ain't gwineter have 'em roun' 'sturbin' a sick man. De Colonel 'monstrated. He done give the Jedge his big room, and he say he and de young men gwine ober to Mistah Catherwood's. You ain't never seen Miss Jinny rise up, suh! She des swep' 'em all out" (Mammy emphasized this by rolling her hands) "an' declah she gwine ten' to the Jedge herself. She ain't never let me bring up one of his meals, suh." And so she left Stephen with some food for reflection.

Virginia was very gay at breakfast, and said that the Judge would see Stephen; so he and the Colonel, that gentleman with his hat on, went up to his room. The shutters were thrown open, and the morning sunlight filtered through the leaves and fell on the four-poster where the Judge sat up, gaunt and grizzled as ever. He smiled at his host, and then tried to destroy immediately the effect of the smile.

"Well, Judge," cried the Colonel, taking his hand, "I reckon we talked too much yesterday."

"No such thing, Carvel," said the Judge, forcibly. "If you hadn't left the room, your popular sovereignty would have been in rags in two minutes."

Stephen sat down in a corner, unobserved, in expectation of a renewal. But at this moment Miss Virginia swept into the room, very cool in a pink muslin.

"Colonel Carvel," said she, sternly, "I am the doctor's deputy here. I was told to keep the peace at any cost. And if you answer back, out you go, like that!" and she snapped her fingers.

The Colonel laughed. But the Judge, whose mind was on the argument, continued to mutter defiantly until his eye fell upon Stephen.

"Well, sir, well, sir," he said, "you've turned up at last, have you? I send you off with papers for a man, and I get back a piece of yellow paper saying that he's borrowed you. What did he do with you, Mr. Brice?"

"He took me to Freeport, sir, where I listened to the most remarkable speech I ever expect to hear."

"What!" cried the Judge, "so far from Boston?"

Stephen hesitated, uncertain whether to laugh, until he chanced to look at Virginia. She had pursed her lips.

"I was very much surprised, sir," he said.

"Humph!" grunted Mr. Whipple, "and what did you think of that ruffian, Lincoln?"

"He is the most remarkable man that I have ever met, sir," answered Stephen, with emphasis.

"Humph!"

It seemed as if the grunt this time had in it something of approval. Stephen had doubt as to the propriety of discussing Mr. Lincoln there, and he reddened. Virginia's expression bore a trace of defiance, and Mr. Carvel stood with his feet apart, thoughtfully stroking his goatee. But Mr. Whipple seemed to have no scruples.

"So you admired Lincoln, Mr. Brice?" he went on. "You must agree with that laudatory estimation of him which I read in the *Missouri Democrat*."

Stephen fidgeted.

"I do, sir, most decidedly," he answered.

"I should hardly expect a conservative Bostonian, of the class which respects property, to have said that. It might possibly be a good thing if more from your town could hear those debates."

"They will read them, sir; I feel confident of it."

At this point the Colonel could contain himself no longer.

"I reckon I might tell the man who wrote that *Democrat* article a few things, if I could find out who he is," said he.

"Pa!" said Virginia, warningly.

But Stephen had turned a fiery red.

"I wrote it, Colonel Carvel," he said.

For a dubious instant of silence Colonel Carvel stared. Then—then he slapped his knees, broke into a storm of laughter, and went out of the room. He left Stephen in a moist state of discomfiture.

The Judge had bolted upright from the pillows.

"You have been neglecting your law, sir," he cried.

"I wrote the article at night," said Stephen, indignantly.

"Then it must have been Sunday night, Mr. Brice."

At this point Virginia hid her face in her handkerchief, which trembled visibly. Being a woman, whose ways are unaccountable, the older man took no notice of her. But being a young woman, and a pretty one, Stephen was angry.

"I don't see what right you have to ask me that, sir," he said.

"The question is withdrawn, Mr. Brice," said the Judge. "Virginia, you may strike it from the records. And now, sir, tell me something about your trip."

Virginia departed.

An hour later Stephen descended to the veranda, and it was with apprehension that he discerned Mr. Carvel seated under the vines at the far end. Virginia was perched on the railing.

To Stephen's surprise the Colonel rose, and, coming toward him, laid a kindly hand on his shoulder.

"Stephen," said he, "there will be no law until Monday. You must stay with us until then. A little rest will do you good."

Stephen was greatly touched.

"Thank you, sir," he said. "I should like to very much. But I can't."

"Nonsense," said the Colonel. "I won't let the Judge interfere."

"It isn't that, sir. I shall have to go by the two o'clock train, I fear."

The Colonel turned to Virginia, who, meanwhile, had sat silently by.

"Jinny," he said, "we must contrive to keep him."

She slid off the railing.

"I'm afraid he is determined, Pa," she answered. "But perhaps Mr. Brice would like to see a little of the place before he goes. It is very primitive," she explained, "not much like yours in the East."

Stephen thanked her, and bowed to the Colonel. And so she led him past the low, crooked outbuildings at the back, where he saw old Uncle Ben busy over the preparation of his dinner, and frisky Rosetta, his daughter, playing with one of the Colonel's setters. Then Virginia took a well-worn path, on each side of which the high grass bent with its load of seed, which entered the wood. Oaks and hickories and walnuts and persimmons spread out in a glade, and the wild grape twisted fantastically around the trunks. All this beauty seemed but a fit setting to the strong girlish figure in the pink frock before him. So absorbed was he in contemplation of this, and in wondering whether indeed she were to marry her cousin, Clarence Colfax, that he did not see the wonders of view unrolling in front of him. She stopped at length beside a great patch of wild rose bushes. They were on the edge of the bluff, and in front of them a little rustic summer-house, with seats on its five sides. Here Virginia sat down. But Stephen, going to the edge, stood and marvelled. Far, far below him, down the wooded steep, shot the crystal Meramec, chafing over the shallow gravel beds and tearing headlong at the deep passes.

Beyond, the dimpled green hills rose and fell, and the stream ran indigo and silver. A hawk soared over the water, the only living creature in all that wilderness.

The glory of the place stirred his blood. And when at length he turned, he saw that the girl was watching him.

"It is very beautiful," he said.

Virginia had taken other young men here, and they had looked only upon her. And yet she was not offended. This sincerity now was as new to her as that with which he had surprised her in the Judge's room.

And she was not quite at her ease. A reply to those simple words of his was impossible. At honest Tom Catherwood in the same situation she would have laughed. Clarence never so much as glanced at scenery. Her replies to him were either flippant, or else maternal, as to a child.

A breeze laden with the sweet abundance of that valley stirred her hair. And with that womanly gesture which has been the same through the ages she put up her hand, deftly tucking in the stray wisp behind.

She glanced at the New Englander, against whom she had been in strange rebellion since she had first seen him. His face, thinned by the summer in town, was of the sternness of the Puritan. Stephen's features were sharply marked for his age. The will to conquer was there. Yet justice was in the mouth, and greatness of heart. Conscience was graven on the broad forehead. The eyes were the blue gray of the flint, kindly yet imperishable. The face was not handsome.

Struggling, then yielding to the impulse, Virginia let herself be led on into the years. Sanity was the word that best described him. She saw him trusted of men, honored of women, feared by the false. She saw him in high places, simple, reserved, poised evenly as he was now.

"Why do you go in this afternoon?" she asked abruptly.

He started at the change in her tone.

"I wish that I might stay," he said regretfully. "But I cannot, Miss Carvel."

He gave no reason. And she was too proud to ask it. Never before had she stooped to urge young men to stay. The difficulty had always been to get them to go. It was natural, perhaps, that her vanity was wounded. But it hurt her to think that she had made the overture, had tried to conquer whatever it was that set her against him, and had failed through him.

"You must find the city attractive. Perhaps," she added, with a little laugh, "perhaps it is Bellefontaine Road."

"No," he answered, smiling.

"Then" (with a touch of derision), "then it is because you cannot miss an afternoon's work. You are that kind."

"I was not always that kind," he answered. "I did not work at Harvard. But now I have to or—or starve," he said.

For the second time his complete simplicity had disarmed her. He had not appealed to her sympathy, nor had he hinted at the luxury in which he was brought up. She would have liked to question Stephen on this former life. But she changed the subject suddenly.

"What did you really think of Mr. Lincoln?" she asked.

"I thought him the ugliest man I ever saw, and the handsomest as well."

"But you admired him?"

"Yes," said Stephen, gravely.

"You believe with him that this government cannot exist half slave and half free. Then a day will come, Mr. Brice, when you and I shall be foreigners one to the other."

"You have forgotten," he said eagerly, "you have forgotten the rest of the quotation. 'I do not expect the Union to be dissolved—I do not expect the house to fall—but cease to be divided.' It will become all one thing or all the other."

Virginia laughed. "That seemed to me very equivocal," said she. "Your rail-splitter is well named."

"Will you read the rest of that speech?" he asked.

"Judge Whipple is very clever. He has made a convert of you," she answered.

"The Judge has had nothing to do with it," cried Stephen. "He is not given to discussion with me, and until I went to Springfield he had never mentioned Mr. Lincoln's name to me."

Glancing at her, he surprised a sparkle of amusement in her eyes. Then she laughed openly.

"Why do you suppose that you were sent to Springfield?" she asked.

"With an important communication for Mr. Lincoln," he answered.

"And that most important communication was—yourself. There, now, I have told you," said Virginia.

"Was myself? I don't understand."

Virginia puckered her lips.

"Then you haven't the sense I thought you had," she replied impatiently. "Do you know what was in that note? No? Well, a year ago

last June this Black Republican lawyer whom you are all talking of made
a speech before a convention in Illinois. Judge Whipple has been crazy
on the subject ever since—he talks of Lincoln in his sleep; he went to
Springfield and spent two days with him, and now he can't rest until *you*
have seen and known and heard him. So he writes a note to Lincoln and
asks him to take you to the debate—"

She paused again to laugh at his amazement.

"But he told me to go to Springfield!" he exclaimed.

"He told you to find Lincoln. He knew that you would obey his orders,
I suppose."

"But I didn't know—" Stephen began, trying to compass within an
instant the memory of his year's experience with Mr. Whipple.

"You didn't know that he thought anything about you," said Virginia.
"That is his way, Mr. Brice. He has more private charities on his list
than any man in the city except Mr. Brinsmade. Very few know it. He
thinks a great deal of you. But there," she added, suddenly blushing crimson, "I am sorry I told you."

"Why?" he asked.

She did not answer, but sat tapping the seat with her fingers. And
when she ventured to look at him, he had fallen into thought.

"I think it must be time for dinner," said Virginia, "if you really wish
to catch the train."

The coldness in her voice, rather than her words, aroused him. He rose,
took one lingering look at the river, and followed her to the house.

At dinner, when not talking about his mare, the Colonel was trying to
persuade Stephen to remain. Virginia did not join in this, and her father
thought the young man's refusal sprang from her lack of cordiality.
Colonel Carvel himself drove to the station.

When he returned, he found his daughter sitting idly on the porch.

"I like that young man, if he is a Yankee," he declared.

"I don't," said Virginia, promptly.

"My dear," said her father, voicing the hospitality of the Carvels, "I
am surprised at you. One should never show one's feelings toward a guest.
As mistress of this house it was your duty to press him to stay."

"He did not want to stay."

"Do you know why he went, my dear?" asked the Colonel.

"No," said Virginia.

"I asked him," said the Colonel.

"Pa! I did not think it of you!" she cried. And then, "What was it?" she demanded.

"He said that his mother was alone in town, and needed him."

Virginia got up without a word, and went into Judge Whipple's room. And there the Colonel found her some hours later, reading aloud from a scrap-book certain speeches of Mr. Lincoln's which Judge Whipple had cut from newspapers. And the Judge, lying back with his eyes half closed, was listening in pure delight. Little did he guess at Virginia's penance!

CHAPTER VII

AN EXCURSION

I AM going ahead two years. Two years during which a nation struggled in agony with sickness, and even the great strength with which she was endowed at birth was not equal to the task of throwing it off. In 1620 a Dutch ship had brought from Guinea to his Majesty's Colony of Virginia the germs of that disease for which the Nation's blood was to be let so freely. During these years signs of dissolution, of death, were not wanting.

In the city by the Father of Waters where the races met, men and women were born into the world, who were to die in ancient Cuba, who were to be left fatherless in the struggle soon to come, who were to live to see new monsters rise to gnaw at the vitals of the Republic, and to hear again the cynical laugh of Europe. But they were also to see their country a power in the world, perchance the greatest power. While Europe had wrangled, the child of the West had grown into manhood and taken a seat among the highest, to share with them the responsibilities of manhood.

Meanwhile, Stephen Brice had been given permission to practise law in the sovereign state of Missouri. Stephen understood Judge Whipple better. It cannot be said that he was intimate with that rather formidable personage, although the Judge, being a man of habits, had formed that of taking tea at least once a week with Mrs. Brice. Stephen had learned to love the Judge, and he had never ceased to be grateful to him for a knowledge of that man who had had the most influence upon his life,—Abraham Lincoln.

For the seed, sowed in wisdom and self-denial, was bearing fruit. The sound of gathering conventions was in the land, and the Freeport Heresy was not forgotten.

We shall not mention the number of clients thronging to Mr. Whipple's office to consult Mr. Brice. These things are humiliating. Some of Stephen's income came from articles in the newspapers of that day. What funny newspapers they were, the size of a blanket! No startling head-

149

lines such as we see now, but a continued novel among the advertise-
ments on the front page and verses from some gifted lady of the town,
signed *Electra*. And often a story of pure love, but more frequently of
ghosts or other eerie phenomena taken from a magazine, or an anecdote
of a cat or a chicken. There were letters from citizens who had the mania
of print, bulletins of different ages from all parts of the Union, clippings
out of day-before-yesterday's newspaper of Chicago or Cincinnati to
three-weeks letters from San Francisco, come by the pony post to Lexington and then down the swift Missouri. Of course, there was news by
telegraph, but that was precious as fine gold,—not to be lightly read and
cast aside.

In the autumn of '59, through the kindness of Mr. Brinsmade, Stephen
had gone on a steamboat up the river to a great convention in Iowa. On
this excursion was much of St. Louis's bluest blood. He widened his circle
of acquaintances, and spent much of his time walking the guards between Miss Anne Brinsmade and Miss Puss Russell. Perhaps it is unfair
to these young ladies to repeat what they said about Stephen in the
privacy of their staterooms, gentle Anne remonstrating that they should
not gossip, and listening eagerly the while, and laughing at Miss Puss,
whose mimicry of Stephen's severe ways brought tears to her eyes.

Mr. Clarence Colfax was likewise on the boat, and passing Stephen on
the guards, bowed distantly. But once, on the return trip, when Stephen
had a writing pad on his knee, the young Southerner came up to him in
his frankest manner and with an expression of the gray eyes which was
not to be withstood.

"Making a case, Brice?" he said. "I hear you are the kind that cannot
be idle even on a holiday."

"Not as bad as all that," replied Stephen, smiling at him.

"Reckon you keep a diary, then," said Clarence, leaning against the
rail. He made a remarkably graceful figure, Stephen thought. He was tall,
and his movements had what might be called a commanding indolence.
Stephen, while he smiled, could not but admire the tone and gesture with
which Colfax bade a passing negro to get him a handkerchief from his
cabin. The alacrity of the black to do the errand was amusing enough.
Stephen well knew it had not been such if *he* wanted a handkerchief.

Stephen said it was not a diary. Mr. Colfax was too well bred to inquire further; so he never found out that Mr. Brice was writing an account of the Convention and the speechmaking for the *Missouri Democrat*.

"Brice," said the Southerner, "I want to apologize for things I've done to you and said about you. I hated you for a long time after you beat me out of Hester, and—" he hesitated.

Stephen looked up. For the first time he actually liked Colfax. He had been long enough among Colfax's people to understand how difficult it was for him to say the thing he wished.

"You may remember a night at my uncle's, Colonel Carvel's, on the occasion of my cousin's birthday?"

"Yes," said Stephen, in surprise.

"Well," blurted Clarence, boyishly, "I was rude to you in my uncle's house, and I have since been sorry."

He held out his hand, and Stephen took it warmly.

"I was younger then, Mr. Colfax," he said, "and I didn't understand your point of view as well as I do now. Not that I have changed my ideas," he added quickly, "but the notion of the girl's going South angered me. I was bidding against the dealer rather than against you. Had I then known Miss Carvel—" he stopped abruptly.

The winning expression died from the face of the other. He turned away, and leaning across the rail, stared at the high bluffs, red-bronzed by the autumn sun. A score of miles beyond that precipice was a long low building of stone, surrounded by spreading trees,—the school for young ladies, celebrated throughout the West, where our mothers and grandmothers were taught,—Monticello. Thither Miss Virginia Carvel had gone, some thirty days since, for her second winter.

Perhaps Stephen guessed the thought in the mind of his companion, for he stared also. The music in the cabin came to an abrupt pause, and only the tumbling of waters through the planks of the great wheels broke the silence. They were both startled by laughter at their shoulders. There stood Miss Russell, the picture of merriment, her arm locked in Anne Brinsmade's.

"It is the hour when all devout worshippers turn towards the East," she said. "The goddess is enshrined at Monticello."

Both young men, as they got to their feet, were crimson. Whereupon Miss Russell laughed again. Anne, however, blushed for them. But this was not the first time Miss Russell had gone too far. Young Mr. Colfax, with the excess of manner which was his at such times, excused himself and left abruptly. This to the further embarrassment of Stephen and Anne, and the keener enjoyment of Miss Russell.

"Was I not right, Mr. Brice?" she demanded. "Why, you are even writing verses to her!"

"I scarcely know Miss Carvel," he said, recovering. "And as for writing verse—"

"You never did such a thing in your life! I can well believe it."

Miss Russell made a face in the direction Colfax had taken.

"He always acts like that when you mention her," she said.

"But you are so cruel, Puss," said Anne. "You can't blame him."

"Hairpins!" said Miss Russell.

"Isn't she to marry him?" said Stephen, in his natural voice.

He remembered his pronouns too late.

"That has been the way of the world ever since Adam and Eve," remarked Puss. "I suppose you meant to ask, Mr. Brice, whether Clarence is to marry Virginia Carvel."

Anne nudged her.

"My dear, what will Mr. Brice think of us?"

"Listen, Mr. Brice," Puss continued, undaunted. "I shall tell you some gossip. Virginia was sent to Monticello, and went with her father to Kentucky and Pennsylvania this summer, that she might be away from Clarence Colfax."

"Oh, Puss!" cried Anne.

Miss Russell paid not the slightest heed.

"Colonel Carvel is right," she went on. "I should do the same thing. They are first cousins, and the Colonel doesn't like that. I am fond of Clarence. But he isn't good for anything in the world except horse racing and—and fighting. He wanted to help drive the Black Republican emigrants out of Kansas, and his mother had to put a collar and chain on him. He wanted to go filibustering with Walker, and she had to get down on her knees. And yet," she cried, "if you Yankees push us as far as war, Mr. Brice, just look out for him."

"But—" Anne interposed.

"Oh, I know what you are going to say,—that Clarence has money."

"Puss!" cried Anne, outraged. "How dare you!"

Miss Russell slipped an arm around her waist.

"Come, Anne," she said, "we mustn't interrupt the Senator any longer. He is preparing his maiden speech."

That was the way in which Stephen got his nickname. It is scarcely necessary to add that he wrote no more until he reached his little room in the house on Olive Street.

They had passed Alton, and the black cloud that hung in the still autumn air over the city was in sight. It was dusk when the *Jackson* pushed her nose into the levee, and the song of the negro stevedores rose from below as they pulled the gang-plank on to the landing-stage. Stephen stood apart on the hurricane deck, gazing at the dark line of sooty warehouses. How many young men with their way to make have felt the same as he did after some pleasant excursion. The presence of a tall form beside him shook him from his revery, and he looked up to recognize the benevolent face of Mr. Brinsmade.

"Mrs. Brice may be anxious, Stephen, at the late hour," said he. "My carriage is here, and it will give me great pleasure to convey you to your door."

Dear Mr. Brinsmade! He is in heaven now, and knows at last the good he wrought upon earth. Of the many thoughtful charities which Stephen received from him, this one sticks firmest in his remembrance: A stranger, tired and lonely, and apart from the gay young men and women who stepped from the boat, he had been sought out by this gentleman, to whom had been given the divine gift of forgetting none.

"Oh, Puss," cried Anne, that evening, for Miss Russell had come to spend the night, "how could you have talked to him so? He scarcely spoke on the way up in the carriage. You have offended him."

"Why should I set him upon a pedestal?" said Puss, with a thread in her mouth; "why should you all set him upon a pedestal? He is only a Yankee," said Puss, tossing her head, "and not so very wonderful."

"I did not say he was wonderful," replied Anne, with dignity.

"But you girls think him so. Emily and Eugénie and Maude. He had better marry Belle Cluyme. A great man, he may give some decision to that family. Anne!"

"Yes."

"Shall I tell you a secret?"

"Yes," said Anne. She was human, and she was feminine.

"Then—Virginia Carvel is in love with him."

"With Mr. Brice!" cried astonished Anne. "She *hates* him!"

"She thinks she hates him," said Miss Russell, calmly.

Anne looked up at her companion admiringly. Her two heroines were Puss and Virginia. Both had the same kind of daring, but in Puss the trait had developed into a somewhat disagreeable outspokenness which made many people dislike her. Her judgments were usually well founded, and her prophecies had so often come to pass that Anne often believed in them for no other reason.

"How do you know?" said Anne, incredulously.

"Do you remember that September, a year ago, when we were all out at Glencoe, and Judge Whipple was ill, and Virginia sent us all away and nursed him herself?"

"Yes," said Anne.

"And did you know that Mr. Brice had gone out, with letters, when the Judge was better?"

"Yes," said Anne, breathless.

"It was a Saturday afternoon that he left, although they had begged him to stay over Sunday. Virginia had written for me to come back, and I arrived in the evening. I asked Easter where Jinny was, and I found her—"

"You found her—?" said Anne.

"Sitting alone in the summer-house over the river. Easter said she had been there for two hours. And I have never known Jinny to be such miserable company as she was that night."

"Did she mention Stephen?" asked Anne.

"No."

"But you did," said Anne, with conviction.

Miss Russell's reply was not as direct as usual.

"You know Virginia never confides unless she wants to," she said.

Anne considered.

"Virginia has scarcely seen him since then," she said. "You know that I was her room-mate at Monticello last year, and I think I should have discovered it."

"Did she speak of him?" demanded Miss Russell.

"Only when the subject was mentioned. I heard her repeat once what Judge Whipple told her father of him,—that he had a fine legal mind. He was often in my letters from home, because they have taken Pa's house next door, and because Pa likes them. I used to read those letters to Jinny," said Anne, "but she never expressed any desire to hear them."

"I, too, used to write Jinny about him," confessed Puss.

"Did she answer your letter?"

"No," replied Miss Puss, "but that was just before the holidays, you remember. And then the Colonel hurried her off to see her Pennsylvania relatives, and I believe they went to Annapolis, too, where the Carvels come from."

Stephen, sitting in the next house, writing out his account, little dreamed that he was the subject of a conference in the third story front of the Brinsmades'. Later, when the young ladies were asleep, he carried his manuscript to the *Democrat* office, and delivered it into the hands of his friend, the night editor, who was awaiting it.

Toward the end of that week, Miss Virginia Carvel was sitting with her back to one of the great trees at Monticello reading a letter. Every once in a while she tucked it under her cloak and glanced hastily around. It was from Miss Anne Brinsmade.

"I have told you all about the excursion, my dear, and how we missed you. You may remember" (ah, Anne, the guile there is in the best of us), "you may remember Mr. Stephen Brice, whom we used to speak of. Pa and Ma take a great interest in him, and Pa had him invited on the excursion. He is more serious than ever, since he has become a full-fledged lawyer. But he has a dry humor which comes out when you know him well, of which I did not suspect him. His mother is the dearest lady I have ever known, so quiet, so dignified, and so well bred. They come in to supper very often. And the other night Mr. Brice told Pa so many things about the people south of Market Street, the Germans, which he did not know, that Pa was astonished. He told all about German history, and how they were persecuted at home and why they came here. Pa was surprised to hear that many of them were University men, and that they were already organizing to defend the Union. I heard Pa say, 'That is what Mr. Blair meant when he assured me that we need not fear for the city.'

"Jinny dear, I ought not to have written you this, because you are for Secession, and in your heart you think Pa a traitor, because he comes from a slave state and has slaves of his own. But I shall not tear it up.

"It is sad to think how rich Mrs. Brice was when she lived in Boston, and what she has had to come to. One servant and a little house, and no place to go to in the summer, when they used to have such a large one. I often go in to sew with her, but she has never once mentioned her past to me.

"Your father has no doubt sent you the *Democrat* with the account of the Convention. It is the fullest published, by far, and was so much admired that Pa asked the editor who wrote it. Who do you think, but Stephen Brice! So now Pa knows why Mr. Brice hesitated when Pa asked him to go up the river, and then consented. This is not the end. Yesterday, when I went in to see Mrs. Brice, a new black silk was on her bed, and as long as I live I shall never forget how sweet was her voice when she said, 'It is a surprise from my son, my dear. I did not expect ever to have another.' Jinny, I just *know* he bought it with the money he got for the article. That was what he was writing on the boat when Clarence Colfax interrupted him. Puss accused him of writing verses to you."

At this point Miss Virginia Carvel stopped reading. Whether she had read that part before, who shall say? But she took Anne's letter between her fingers and tore it into bits and flung the bits into the wind, so that they were tossed about and lost among the dead leaves under the great trees. And when she reached her room, there was the hated *Missouri Democrat* lying, still open, on her table. A little later a great black piece of it came tossing out of the chimney above, to the affright of little Miss Brown, teacher of Literature, who was walking in the grounds, and who ran to the principal's room with the story that the chimney was afire.

CHAPTER VIII

THE COLONEL IS WARNED

It is difficult to refrain from mention of the leave-taking of Miss Virginia Carvel from the Monticello "Female Seminary," so called in the *Democrat*. Most young ladies did not graduate in those days. There were exercises. Stephen chanced to read in the *Republican* about these ceremonies, which mentioned that Miss Virginia Carvel, "Daughter of Colonel Comyn Carvel, was without doubt the beauty of the day. She wore—" but why destroy the picture? I have the costumes under my hand. The words are meaningless to all males, and young women might laugh at a critical time. Miss Emily Russell performed upon "that most superb of all musical instruments, the human voice." Was it *Auld Robin Gray* that she sang? I am sure it was Miss Maude Catherwood who recited *To My Mother*, with such effect. Miss Carvel, so Stephen learned with alarm, was to read a poem by Mrs. Browning, but was "unavoidably prevented." The truth was, as he heard afterward from Miss Puss Russell, that Miss Jinny had refused point blank. So the Lady Principal, to save her reputation for discipline, had been forced to deceive the press.

There was another who read the account of the exercises with intense interest, a gentleman of whom we have lately forborne to speak. This is Mr. Eliphalet Hopper. Eliphalet has prospered. It is to be doubted if that somewhat easy-going gentleman, Colonel Carvel, realized the full importance of Eliphalet to Carvel & Company. Mr. Hood had been superseded. Ephum still opened the store in the mornings, but Mr. Hopper was within the ground-glass office before the place was warm, and through warerooms and shipping rooms, rubbing his hands, to see if any were late. Many of the old force were missed, and a new and greater force were come in. These feared Eliphalet as they did the devil, and worked the harder to please him, because Eliphalet had hired that kind. To them the Colonel was lifted high above the sordid affairs of the world. He was at the store every day in the winter, and Mr. Hopper always followed him obsequiously into the ground-glass office, called in the book-keeper, and showed him the books and the increased earnings.

157

The Colonel thought of Mr. Hood and his slovenly management, and sighed, in spite of his doubled income. Mr. Hopper had added to the Company's list of customers whole districts in the growing Southwest, and yet the honest Colonel did not like him. Mr. Hopper, by a gradual process, had taken upon his own shoulders, and consequently off the Colonel's, responsibility after responsibility. There were some painful scenes, of course, such as the departure of Mr. Hood, which never would have occurred had not Eliphalet proved without question the incapacity of the ancient manager. Mr. Hopper only narrowed his lids when the Colonel pensioned Mr. Hood. But the Colonel had a will before which, when roused, even Mr. Hopper trembled. So that Eliphalet was always polite to Ephum, and careful never to say anything in the darkey's presence against incompetent clerks or favorite customers, who, by the charity of the Colonel, remained on his books.

One spring day, after the sober home-coming of Colonel Carvel from the Democratic Convention at Charleston, Ephum accosted his master as he came into the store of a morning. Ephum's face was working with excitement.

"What's the matter with you, Ephum?" asked the Colonel, kindly. "You haven't been yourself lately."

"No, Marsa, I ain't 'zactly."

Ephum put down the duster, peered out of the door of the private office, and closed it softly.

"Marse Comyn?"

"Yes?"

"Marse Comyn, I ain't got no use fo' dat Misteh Hoppa'. I'se kinder sup'stitious 'bout him, Marsa."

The Colonel put down his newspaper.

"Has he treated you badly, Ephum?" he asked quietly.

The faithful negro saw another question in his master's face. He well knew that Colonel Carvel would not descend to ask an inferior concerning the conduct of a superior.

"Oh no, suh. And I ain't sayin' nuthin' gin his honesty. He straight, but he powerful sharp, Marse Comyn. An' he jus' mussiless down to a cent."

The Colonel sighed. He realized that which was beyond the grasp of the negro's mind. New and thriftier methods of trade from New England were fast replacing the old open-handedness of the large houses.

Competition had begun, and competition is cruel. Edwards, James, & Company had taken a Yankee into the firm. They were now Edwards, James, & Doddington, and Mr. Edwards's coolness towards the Colonel was manifest since the rise of Eliphalet. They were rivals now instead of friends. But Colonel Carvel did not know until after years that Mr. Hopper had been offered the place which Mr. Doddington filled later.

As for Mr. Hopper, increase of salary had not changed him. He still lived in the same humble way, in a single room in Miss Crane's boarding-house, and he paid very little more for his board than he had that first week in which he swept out Colonel Carvel's store. He was superintendent, now, of Mr. Davitt's Sunday School, and a church officer. At night, when he came home from business, he would read the widow's evening paper, and the Colonel's morning paper at the office. Of true Puritan abstemiousness, his only indulgence was chewing tobacco. It was as early as 1859 that the teller of the Boatman's Bank began to point out Mr. Hopper's back to casual customers, and he was more than once seen to enter the president's room, which had carpet on the floor.

Eliphalet's suavity with certain delinquent customers from the South-west was according to Scripture. When they were profane, and invited him into the street, he reminded them that the city had a police force and a jail. While still a young man, he had a manner of folding his hands and smiling which is peculiar to capitalists, and he knew the laws concerning mortgages in several different states.

But Eliphalet was content still to remain in the sphere in which Providence had placed him, and so to be an example for many of us. He did not buy, or even hire, an evening suit. He was pleased to superintend some of the details for a dance at Christmas-time before Virginia left Monticello, but he sat as usual on the stair-landing. There Mr. Jacob Cluyme (who had been that day in conversation with the teller of the Boatman's Bank) chanced upon him. Mr. Cluyme was so charmed at the facility with which Eliphalet recounted the rise and fall of sugar and cotton and wheat that he invited Mr. Hopper to dinner. And from this meal may be reckoned the first appearance of the family of which Eliphalet Hopper was the head into polite society. If the Cluyme household was not polite, it was nothing. Eliphalet sat next to Miss Belle, and heard the private history of many old families, which he cherished for future use. Mrs. Cluyme apologized for the dinner, which (if the truth were told) needed an apology. All of which is significant, but sordid and uninteresting. Jacob Cluyme usually bought stocks before a rise.

There was only one person who really bothered Eliphalet as he rose into prominence, and that person was Captain Elijah Brent. If, upon entering the ground-glass office, he found Eliphalet without the Colonel, Captain Lige would walk out again just as if the office were empty. The inquiries he made were addressed always to Ephum. Once, when Mr. Hopper had bidden him good morning and pushed a chair toward him, the honest Captain had turned his back and marched straight to the house on Tenth Street, where he found the Colonel alone at breakfast. The Captain sat down opposite.

"Colonel," said he, without an introduction, "I don't *like* this here business of letting Hopper run your store. He's a fish, I tell you."

The Colonel drank his coffee in silence.

"Lige," he said gently, "he's nearly doubled my income. It isn't the old times, when we all went our own way and kept our old customers year in and year out. You know that."

The Captain took a deep draught of the coffee which Jackson had laid before him.

"Colonel Carvel," he said emphatically, "the fellow's a damned rascal, and will ruin you yet if you don't take advice."

The Colonel shifted uneasily.

"The books show that he's honest, Lige."

"Yes," cried Lige, with his fist on the table. "Honest to a mill. But if that fellow ever gets on *top* of you, or any one else, he'll grind you into *dust*."

"He isn't likely to get on top of me, Lige. I know the business, and keep watch. And now that Jinny's coming home from Monticello, I feel that I can pay more attention to her—kind of take her mother's place," said the Colonel, putting on his felt hat and tipping his chair. "Lige, I want that girl to have every advantage. She ought to go to Europe and see the world. That trip East last summer did her a heap of good. When we were at Calvert House, Dan read her something that my grandfather had written about London, and she was regularly fired. First I must take her to the Eastern Shore to see Carvel Hall. Dan still owns it. Now it's London and Paris."

The Captain walked over to the window, and said nothing. He did not see the searching gray eyes of his old friend upon him.

"Lige!" said the Colonel.

The Captain turned.

"Lige, why don't you give up steamboating and come along to Europe? You're not forty yet, and you have a heap of money laid by."

The Captain shook his head with the vigor that characterized him.

"This ain't no time for me to leave," he said. "Colonel, I tell you there's a storm *comin'.*"

The Colonel pulled his goatee uneasily. Here, at last, was a man in whom there was no guile.

"Lige," he said, "isn't it about time you got married?"

Upon which the Captain shook his head again, even with more vigor. He could not trust himself to speak. After the Christmas holidays he had driven Virginia across the frozen river, all the way to Monticello, in a sleigh. It was night when they had reached the school, the light of its many windows casting long streaks on the snow under the trees. He had helped her out, and had taken her hand as she stood on the step.

"Be good, Jinny," he had said. "Remember what a short time it will be until June. And your Pa will come over to see you."

She had seized him by the buttons of his great coat, and said tearfully:—

"O Captain Lige! I shall be so lonely when you are away. Aren't you going to kiss me?"

He had put his lips to her forehead, driven madly back to Alton, and spent the night. The first thing he did the next day when he reached St. Louis was to go straight to the Colonel and tell him bluntly of the circumstance.

"Lige, I'd hate to give her up," Mr. Carvel said; "but I'd rather you'd marry her than any man I can think of."

CHAPTER IX

SIGNS OF THE TIMES

In that spring of 1860 the time was come for the South to make her final stand. And as the noise of gathering conventions shook the ground, Stephen Brice was not the only one who thought of the Question at Freeport. The hour was now at hand for it to bear fruit.

Meanwhile, his hero, the hewer of rails and forger of homely speech, Abraham Lincoln, had made a little tour eastward the year before, and had startled Cooper Union with a new logic and a new eloquence. They were the same logic and the same eloquence which had startled Stephen.

Even as he predicted who had given it birth, the Question destroyed the great Democratic Party. Colonel Carvel travelled to the convention in historic Charleston soberly and fearing God, as many another Southern gentleman. In old Saint Michael's they knelt to pray for harmony, for peace; for a front bold and undismayed toward those who wronged them. All through the week chosen orators wrestled in vain. Judge Douglas, you flattered yourself that you had evaded the Question. Do you see the Southern delegates rising in their seats? Alabama leaves the hall, followed by her sister states. The South has not forgotten your Freeport Heresy. Once she loved you, now she will have none of you.

Gloomily, indeed, did Colonel Carvel return home. He loved the Union and the flag for which his grandfather Richard had fought so bravely. That flag was his inheritance. So the Judge, laying his hand upon the knee of his friend, reminded him gravely. But the Colonel shook his head. The very calmness of their argument had been portentous.

"No, Whipple," said he. "You are a straightforward man. You can't disguise it. You of the North are bent upon taking away from us the rights we had when our fathers formed the Constitution. However the nigger got to this country, sir, in your Bristol and Newport traders, as well as in our Virginia and Maryland ships, he is here, and he was here when the Constitution was written. He is happier in slavery than are your factory hands in New England; and he is no more fit to exercise the solemn rights of citizenship, I say, than the halfbreeds in the South American states."

The Judge attempted to interrupt, but Mr. Carvel stopped him.

"Suppose you deprive me of my few slaves, you do not ruin me. Yet you do me as great a wrong as you do my friend Samuels, of Louisiana, who depends on the labor of five hundred. Shall I stand by selfishly and see him ruined, and thousands of others like him?"

Profoundly depressed, Colonel Carvel did not attend the adjourned Convention at Baltimore, which split once more on Mason and Dixon's line. The Democrats of the young Northwest stood for Douglas and Johnson, and the solid South, in another hall, nominated Breckenridge and Lane. This, of course, became the Colonel's ticket.

What a Babel of voices was raised that summer! Each with its cure for existing ills. Between the extremes of the Black Republican Negro Worshippers and the Southern Rights party of Breckenridge, your conservative had the choice of two candidates,—of Judge Douglas or Senator Bell. A most respectable but practically extinct body of gentlemen in ruffled shirts, the Old Line Whigs, had likewise met in Baltimore. A new name being necessary, they called themselves Constitutional Unionists. Senator Bell was their candidate, and they proposed to give the Nation soothing-syrup. So said Judge Whipple, with a grunt of contempt, to Mr. Cluyme, who was then a prominent Constitutional Unionist. Other and most estimable gentlemen were also Constitutional Unionists, notably Mr. Calvin Brinsmade. Far be it from any one to cast disrespect upon the reputable members of this party, whose broad wings sheltered likewise so many weak brethren.

One Sunday evening in May, the Judge was taking tea with Mrs. Brice. The occasion was memorable for more than one event—which was that he addressed Stephen by his first name for the first time.

"You're an admirer of Abraham Lincoln," he had said.

Stephen, used to Mr. Whipple's ways, smiled quietly at his mother. He had never dared mention to the Judge his suspicions concerning his journey to Springfield and Freeport.

"Stephen," said the Judge (here the surprise came in), "Stephen, what do you think of Mr. Lincoln's chances for the Republican nomination?"

"We hear of no name but Seward's, sir," said Stephen, when he had recovered.

The Judge grunted.

"Do you think that Lincoln would make a good President?" he added.

"I have thought so, sir, ever since you were good enough to give me the opportunity of knowing him."

It was a bold speech—the Judge drew his great eyebrows together, but he spoke to Mrs. Brice.

"I'm not as strong as I was once, ma'am," said he. "And yet I am going to that Chicago convention."

Mrs. Brice remonstrated mildly, to the effect that he had done his share of political work. He scarcely waited for her to finish.

"I shall take a younger man with me, in case anything happens. In fact, ma'am, I had thought of taking your son, if you can spare him."

And so it was that Stephen went to that most dramatic of political gatherings,—in the historic Wigwam. It was so that his eyes were opened to the view of the monster which maims the vitality of the Republic,—the political machine. Mr. Seward had brought his machine from New York,—a legion prepared to fill the Wigwam with their bodies, and to drown with their cries all names save that of their master.

Stephen indeed had his eyes opened. Through the kindness of Judge Whipple he heard many quiet talks between that gentleman and delegates from other states—Pennsylvania and Illinois and Indiana and elsewhere. He perceived that the Judge was no nonentity in this new party. Mr. Whipple sat in his own room, and the delegates came and ranged themselves along the bed. Late one night, when the delegates were gone, Stephen ventured to speak what was in his mind.

"Mr. Lincoln did not strike me as the kind of man, sir, who would permit a bargain."

"Mr. Lincoln's at home playing barn-ball," said the Judge, curtly. "He doesn't expect the nomination."

"Then," said Stephen, rather hotly, "I think you are unfair to him."

You are expecting the Judge to thunder. Sometimes he liked this kind of speech.

"Stephen, I hope that politics may be a little cleaner when you become a delegate," he answered, with just the suspicion of a smile. "Supposing you are convinced that Abraham Lincoln is the only man who can save the Union, and supposing that the one way to get him nominated is to meet Seward's gang with their own methods, what would you do, sir? I want a practical proposition, sir," said Mr. Whipple, "one that we can use to-night. It is now one o'clock."

As Stephen was silent, the Judge advised him to go to bed. And the next morning, while Mr. Seward's henchmen, confident and uproarious, were parading the streets of Chicago with their bands and their bunting, the vast Wigwam was quietly filling up with bony Westerners whose ally was none other than the state of Pennsylvania. These gentlemen possessed wind which they had not wasted in processions. And the Lord delivered Seward and all that was his into their hands.

How the light of Mr. Seward's hope went out after the first ballot, and how some of the gentlemen attached to his person wept; and how the voices shook the Wigwam, and the thunder of the guns rolled over the tossing waters of the lake, many now living remember. That day a name was delivered to the world through the mouths of political schemers which was destined to enter history as that of the saviour of the Nation.

Down in little Springfield, on a vacant lot near the station, a tall man in his shirt sleeves was playing barn-ball with some boys. The game finished, he had put on his black coat and was starting homeward under the trees,—when a fleet youngster darted after him with a telegram. The tall man read it, and continued on his way, his head bent and his feet taking long strides. Later in the day he was met by a friend.

"Abe," said the friend, "I'm almighty glad there's somebody in this town's got *notorious* at last."

In the early morning of their return from Chicago, Judge Whipple and Stephen were standing in the front of a ferry-boat crossing the Mississippi. The sun was behind them. The Judge had taken off his hat, and his gray hair was stirred by the river breeze. Illness had set a yellow seal on the face, but the younger man remarked it not. For Stephen, staring at the black blur of the city's outline, was filled with a strange exaltation which might have belonged to his Puritan forefathers. Now at length was come his chance to be of use in life,—to dedicate the labor of his hands and of his brains to Abraham Lincoln, uncouth prophet of the West. With all his might he would work to save the city for the man who was the hope of the Union.

The bell rang. The great paddles scattered the brown waters with white foam, and the Judge voiced his thoughts.

"Stephen," said he, "I guess we'll have to put our shoulders to the wheel this summer. If Lincoln is not elected, I have lived my sixty-five years for nothing."

As he descended the plank, he laid a hand on Stephen's arm, and tottered. The big *Louisiana,* Captain Brent's boat, just in from New Orleans, was blowing off her steam as with slow steps they climbed the levee and the steep pitch of the street beyond it. The clatter of hooves and the crack of whips reached their ears, and, like many others before them and since, they stepped into Carvel & Company's. On the inside of the glass partition of the private office, a voice of great suavity was heard. It was Eliphalet Hopper's.

"If you will give me the numbers of the bales, Captain Brent, I'll send a dray down to your boat and get them."

It was a very decisive voice that answered.

"No, sir, I prefer to do business with my *friend,* Colonel Carvel. I guess I can *wait.*"

"I could sell the goods to Texas buyers who are here in the store right now."

"Until I get instructions from one of the *concern,*" vowed Captain Lige, "I shall do as I always have done, sir. What is your position here, Mr. Hopper?"

"I am manager, I callate."

The Captain's fist was heard to come down on the desk.

"You don't manage me," he said, "and I reckon you don't manage the Colonel."

Mr. Hopper's face was not pleasant to see as he emerged. But at sight of Judge Whipple on the steps his suavity returned.

"The Colonel will be in any minute, sir," said he.

But the Judge walked past him without reply, and into the office. Captain Brent, seeing him, sprang to his feet.

"Well, well, Judge," said he, heartily, "you fellows *have* done it now, *sure.* I'll say this for you, you've picked a *smart* man."

"Better vote for him, Lige," said the Judge, sitting down.

The Captain smiled at Stephen.

"A man's got a lot of choice this year," said he. "Two governments, thirty-three governments, one government patched up for a year or two."

"Or no government," finished the Judge. "Lige, you're not such a fool as to vote against the Union?"

"Judge," said the Captain, instantly, "I'm not the only one in this town who will have to decide whether my *sympathies* are wrong. My *sympathies* are with the South."

"It's not a question of sympathy, Captain," answered the Judge, wryly. "Abraham Lincoln himself was born in Kentucky."

They had not heard a step without.

"Gentlemen, mark my words. If Abraham Lincoln is elected, the South leaves this Union."

The Judge started, and looked up. The speaker was Colonel Carvel himself.

"Then, sir," Mr. Whipple cried hotly, "then you will be chastised and brought back. For at last we have chosen a man who is strong enough,— who does not fear your fire-eaters,—whose electors depend on Northern votes alone."

Stephen rose apprehensively. So did Captain Lige. The Colonel had taken a step forward, and a fire was quick to kindle in his gray eyes. It was as quick to die. Judge Whipple, deathly pale, staggered and fell into Stephen's arms. But it was the Colonel who laid him on the horse-hair sofa.

"Silas!" he said, "Silas!"

Nor could the two who listened sound the depth of the pathos the Colonel put into those two words.

But the Judge had not fainted. And the brusqueness in his weakened voice was even more pathetic—

"Tut, tut," said he. "A little heat, and no breakfast."

The Colonel already had a bottle of the famous Bourbon in his hand, and Captain Lige brought a glass of muddy iced water. Mr. Carvel made an injudicious mixture of the two, and held it to the lips of his friend. He was pushed away.

"Come, Silas," he said.

"No!" cried the Judge, and with this effort he slipped back again. Those who stood there thought that the stamp of death was already on Judge Whipple's face. But the lips were firmly closed, bidding defiance, as ever, to the world. The Colonel, stroking his goatee, regarded him curiously.

"Silas," he said slowly, "if you won't drink it for me, perhaps you will drink it—for—Abraham—Lincoln."

The two who watched that scene have never forgotten it. Outside, in the great cool store, the rattle of the trucks was heard, and Mr. Hopper giving commands. Within was silence. The straight figure of the Colonel towered above the sofa while he waited. A full minute passed. Once Judge Whipple's bony hand opened and shut, and once his features worked. Then, without warning, he sat up.

"Colonel," said he, "I reckon I wouldn't be much use to Abe if I took that. But if you'll send Ephum after a cup of coffee——"

Mr. Carvel set the glass down. In two strides he had reached the door and given the order. Then he came back and seated himself on the sofa.

Stephen found his mother at breakfast. He had forgotten the convention. He told her what had happened at Mr. Carvel's store, and how the Colonel had tried to persuade Judge Whipple to take the Glencoe house while he was in Europe, and how the Judge had refused. Tears were in the widow's eyes when Stephen finished.

"And he means to stay here in the heat and go through the campaign?" she asked.

"He says that he will not stir."

"It will kill him, Stephen," Mrs. Brice faltered.

"So the Colonel told him. And he said that he would die willingly— after Abraham Lincoln was elected. He had nothing to live for but to fight for that. He had never understood the world, and had quarrelled with it all his life."

"He said that to Colonel Carvel?"

"Yes."

"Stephen!"

He didn't dare to look at his mother, nor she at him. And when he reached the office, half an hour later, Mr. Whipple was seated in his chair, defiant and unapproachable. Stephen sighed as he settled down to his work. The thought of one who might have accomplished what her father could not was in his head. She was at Monticello.

Some three weeks later Mr. Brinsmade's buggy drew up at Mrs. Brice's door. The Brinsmade family had been for some time in the country. And frequently, when that gentleman was detained in town by business, he would stop at the little home for tea. The secret of the good man's visit came out as he sat with them on the front steps afterward.

"I fear that it will be a hot summer, ma'am," he had said to Mrs. Brice. "You should go to the country."

"The heat agrees with me remarkably, Mr. Brinsmade," said the lady, smiling.

"I have heard that Colonel Carvel wishes to rent his house at Glen-

coe," Mr. Brinsmade continued. "The figure is not high." He mentioned it. And it was, indeed, nominal. "It struck me that a change of
air would do you good, Mrs. Brice, and Stephen. Knowing that you
shared in our uneasiness concerning Judge Whipple, I thought—"

He stopped, and looked at her. It was a hard task even for that best
and most tactful of gentlemen, Mr. Brinsmade. He too had misjudged
this calm woman.

"I understand you, Mr. Brinsmade," she said. She saw, as did Stephen,
the kindness behind the offer—Colonel Carvel's kindness and his own.
The gentleman's benevolent face brightened.

"And, my dear Madam, do not let the thought of this little house
trouble you. It was never my expectation to have it occupied in the
summer. If we could induce the Judge to go to Glencoe with you for the
summer, I am sure it would be a relief for us all."

He did not press the matter, but begged Stephen to call in on him in
a day or two, at the bank.

"What do you think, Stephen?" asked his mother, when Mr. Brinsmade was gone.

Stephen did not reply at once. What, indeed, could he say? The vision
of that proud figure of Miss Virginia was before him, and he revolted.
What was kindness from Colonel Carvel and Mr. Brinsmade was charity
from her. He could not bear the thought of living in a house haunted by
her. And yet why should he let his pride and his feelings stand in the
way of the health—perhaps of the life—of Judge Whipple?

It was characteristic of his mother's strength of mind not to mention
the subject again that evening. Stephen did not sleep in the hot night.
But when he rose in the morning he had made up his mind. After breakfast he went straight to the Colonel's store, and fortunately found Mr.
Carvel at his desk, winding up his affairs.

The next morning, when the train for the East pulled out of Illinois-
town, Miss Jinny Carvel stood on the platform tearfully waving good-
bye to a knot of friends. She was leaving for Europe. Presently she went
into the sleeping-car to join the Colonel, who wore a gray linen duster.
For a long time she sat gazing at the young corn waving on the prairie,
fingering the bunch of June roses on her lap. Clarence had picked them
only a few hours ago, in the dew at Bellegarde. She saw her cousin standing disconsolate under the train sheds, just as she had left him. She pictured him riding out the Bellefontaine Road that afternoon, alone.

Now that the ocean was to be between them, was it love that she felt for Clarence at last? She glanced at her father. Once or twice she had suspected him of wishing to separate them. Her Aunt Lillian, indeed, had said as much, and Virginia had silenced her. But when she had asked the Colonel to take Clarence to Europe, he had refused. And yet she knew that he had begged Captain Lige to go.

Virginia had been at home but a week. She had seen the change in Clarence and exulted. The very first day she had surprised him on the porch at Bellegarde with "Hardee's tactics." From a boy, Clarence had suddenly become a man with a Purpose,—and that was the Purpose of the South.

"They have dared to nominate that dirty Lincoln," he said. "Do you think that we will submit to nigger equality rule? Never! never!" he cried. "If they elect him, I will stand and fight them until my legs are shot from under me, and then I will shoot down the Yankees from the ground."

Virginia's heart had leaped within her at the words, and into her eyes had flashed once more the look for which the boy had waited and hoped in vain. He had the carriage of a soldier, the animation and endurance of the thoroughbred when roused. He was of the stuff that made the resistance of the South the marvel of the world. And well we know, whatever the sound of it, that his speech was not heroics. Nor was it love for his cousin that inspired it, save in this: he had apotheosized Virginia. To him she was the inspired goddess of the South,—his country. His admiration and affection had of late been laid upon an altar. Her ambition for him he felt was likewise the South's ambition for him.

His mother, Virginia's aunt, felt this too, and strove against it with her feeble might. She never had had power over her son; nor over any man, save the temporal power of beauty. And to her mortification she found herself actually in fear of this girl who might have been her daughter. So in Virginia's presence she became more trivial and petty than ever. It was her one defence.

It had of course been a foregone conclusion that Clarence should join Company A. Few young men of family did not. And now he ran to his room to don for Virginia that glorious but useless full dress,—the high bearskin hat, the red pigeon-tailed coat, the light blue trousers, and the gorgeous, priceless shackle. Indeed, the boy looked stunning. He held his big rifle like a veteran, and his face was set with a high resolve there was no mistaking. The high color of her pride was on the cheek of the girl as he brought his piece to the salute of her, his mistress. And yet, when he was gone, and she sat alone amid the roses awaiting him, came wilfully before her another face that was relentless determination,—the face of Stephen Brice, as he had stood before her in the summer-house at Glencoe. Strive as she might against the thought, deny it to herself and others, to Virginia Carvel his was become the face of the North. Her patriotism and all that was in her of race rebelled. To conquer that face she would have given her own soul, and Clarence's. Angrily she had arisen and paced the garden walks, and cried out aloud that it was not inflexible.

And now, by the car window, looking out over the endless roll of the prairie, the memory of this was bitter within her.

Suddenly she turned to her father.

"Did you rent our house at Glencoe?" she asked.

"No, Jinny."

"I suppose Mr. Brice was too proud to accept it at your charitable rent, even to save Mr. Whipple's life."

The Colonel turned to his daughter in mild surprise. She was leaning back on the seat, her eyes half closed.

"Once you dislike a person, Jinny, you never get over it. I always had a fancy for the young man, and now I have a better opinion of him than ever before. It was I who insulted them by naming that rent."

"What did he do?" Virginia demanded.

"He came to my office yesterday morning. 'Colonel Carvel,' said he, 'I hear you wish to rent your house.' I said yes. 'You rented it once before, sir,' said he. 'Yes,' said I. 'May I ask you what price you got for it?' said he."

"And what did you say?" she asked, leaning forward.

"I told him," said the Colonel, smiling. "But I explained that I could not expect to command that price now on short notice. He replied that they would pay it, or not consider the place."

Virginia turned her head away and stared out over the fields.

"How could they afford it!" she murmured.

"Mr. Brinsmade tells me that young Brice won rather a remarkable case last winter, and since then has had some practice. And that he writes for the newspapers. I believe he declined some sort of an editorial position, preferring to remain at the law."

"And so they are going into the house?" she asked presently.

"No," said the Colonel. "Whipple refused point-blank to go to the country. He said that he would be shirking the only work of his life likely to be worth anything. So the Brices remain in town."

Colonel Carvel sighed. But Virginia said nothing.

CHAPTER X

RICHTER'S SCAR

This was the summer when Mr. Stephen Brice began to make his appearance in public. The very first was rather encouraging than otherwise, although they were not all so. It was at a little town on the outskirts of the city where those who had come to scoff and jeer remained to listen.

In writing that speech Stephen had striven to bear in mind a piece of advice which Mr. Lincoln had given him: "Speak so that the lowest may understand, and the rest will have no trouble." And it had worked. At the halting lameness of the beginning an egg was thrown,—fortunately wide of the mark. After this incident Stephen fairly astonished his audience,—especially an elderly gentleman who sat on a cracker-box in the rear, out of sight of the stand. This may have been Judge Whipple, although we have no proof of the fact.

Stephen himself would not have claimed originality for that speech. He laughs now when it is spoken of, and calls it a boyish effort, which it was. I have no doubt that many of the master's phrases slipped in, as young Mr. Brice could repeat most of the Debates, and the Cooper Union speech by heart. He had caught more than the phrasing, however. So imbued was he with the spirit of Abraham Lincoln that his hearers caught it; and that was the end of the rotten eggs and the cabbages. The event is to be especially noted because they crowded around him afterward to ask questions. For one thing, he had not mentioned abolition. Wasn't it true, then, that this Lincoln wished to tear the negro from his master, give him a vote and a subsidy, and set him up as the equal of the man that owned him? "Slavery may stay where it is," cried the young orator. "If it is content there, so are we content. What we say is that it shall not go one step farther. No, not one inch into a northern territory."

On the next occasion Mr. Brice was one of the orators at a much larger meeting in a garden in South St. Louis. The audience was mostly German. And this was even a happier event, inasmuch as Mr. Brice

173

was able to trace with some skill the history of the Fatherland from the Napoleonic wars to its Revolution. Incidentally he told them why they had emigrated to this great and free country. And when in an inspired moment he coupled the names of Abraham Lincoln and Father Jahn, the very leaves of the trees above them trembled at their cheers.

And afterwards there was a long-remembered supper in the moonlit grove with Richter and a party of his college friends from Jena. There was Herr Tiefel with the little Dresden-blue eyes, red and round and jolly; and Hauptmann, long and thin and sallow; and Körner, red-bearded and ponderous; and König, a little clean-cut man with a blond mustache that pointed upward. They clattered their steins on the table and sang wonderful Jena songs, while Stephen was lifted up and his soul carried off to far-away Saxony,—to the clean little University town with its towers and crooked streets. And when they sang the *Volksmelodie*, *"Bemooster Bursche zieh' ich aus,—Ade!"* a big tear rolled down the scar on Richter's cheek.

> *"Fahrt wohl, ihr Strassen grad und krumm!*
> *Ich zieh' nicht mehr in euch herum,*
> *Durchtön euch nicht mehr mit Gesang,*
> *Mit Larm nicht mehr und Sporenklang."*

As the deep tones died away, the soft night was steeped in the sadness of that farewell song. It was Richter who brought the full force of it home to Stephen.

"Do you recall the day you left your Harvard, and your Boston, my friend?" he asked.

Stephen only nodded. He had never spoken of the bitterness of that, even to his mother. And here was the difference between the Saxon and the Anglo-Saxon.

Richter smoked his pipe 'mid dreamy silence, the tears still wet upon his face.

"Tiefel and I were at the University together," he said at length. "He remembers the day I left Jena for good and all. Ah, Stephen, that is the most pathetic thing in life, next to leaving the Fatherland. We dine with our student club for the last time at the *Burg Keller*, a dingy little tavern under a grim old house, but very dear to us. We swear for the last time to be clean and honorable and patriotic, and to die for the Fatherland, if God so wills. And then we march at the head of a slow procession out

of the old West Gate, two and two, old members first, then the fox major and the foxes."

"The foxes?" Stephen interrupted.

"The youngsters—the freshmen, you call them," answered Richter,
smiling.

"And after the foxes," said Herr Tiefel, taking up the story, "after
the foxes comes the empty carriage, with its gay postilion and four. It
is like a long funeral. And every man is chanting that song. And so we
go slowly until we come to the Oil Mill Tavern, where we have had
many a *Schläger-bout* with the aristocrats. And the president of our society makes his farewell speech under the vines, and we drink to you
with all the honors. And we drank to you, Carl, renowned swordsman!"
And Herr Tiefel, carried away by the recollection, rose to his feet.

The others caught fire, and stood up with their mugs high in the air,
shouting:—

"*Lebe wohl, Carl! Lebe wohl! Salamander, salamander, salamander!
Ein ist ein, zwei ist zwei, drei ist drei! Lebe wohl!*"

And so they toasted every man present, even Stephen himself, whom
they complimented on his speech. And he soon learned to cry *Salamander,* and to rub his mug on the table, German fashion. He was not long
in discovering that Richter was not merely a prime favorite with his
companions, but likewise a person of some political importance in South
St. Louis. In the very midst of their merriment an elderly man whom
Stephen recognized as one of the German leaders (he afterwards became
a United States general) came and stood smiling by the table and
joined in the singing. But presently he carried Richter away with him.

"What a patriot he would have made, had our country been spared
to us!" exclaimed Herr König. "I think he was the best man with the
Schläger that Jena ever saw. Even Körner likes not to stand against
him in mask and fencing hat, all padded. Eh, Rudolph?"

Herr Körner gave a good-natured growl of assent.

"I have still a welt that he gave me a month since," he said. "He has
left his mark on many an aristocrat."

"And why did you always fight the aristocrats?" Stephen asked.

They all tried to tell him at once, but Tiefel prevailed.

"Because they were for making our country Austrian, my friend," he
cried. "Because they were overbearing, and ground the poor. Because the
most of them were immoral like the French, and we knew that it must
be by morality and pure living that our *Vaterland* was to be rescued.

And so we formed our guilds in opposition to theirs. We swore to live by the standards of the great Jahn, of whom you spoke. We swore to strive for the freedom of Germany with manly courage. And when we were not duelling with the nobles, we had *Schläger-bouts* among ourselves."

"Broadswords?" exclaimed Stephen, in amazement.

"*Ja wohl*," answered Körner, puffing heavily. The slit in his nose was plain even in the moonlight. "To keep our hands in, as you would say. You Americans are a brave people—without the *Schläger*. But we fought that we might not become effete."

It was then that Stephen ventured to ask a question that had been long burning within him.

"See here, Mr. Körner," said he, "how did Richter come by that scar? He always gets red when I mention it. He will never tell me."

"Ah, I can well believe that," answered Körner. "I will recount that matter,—if you do not tell Carl, *lieber Freund*. He would not forgive me. I was there in Berlin at the time. It was a famous time. Tiefel will bear me out."

"*Ja, ja!*" said Tiefel, eagerly.

"Mr. Brice," Herr Körner continued, "has never heard of the Count von Kalbach. No, of course. We at Jena had, and all Germany. Many of us of the *Burschenschaft* will bear to the grave the marks of his *Schläger*. Von Kalbach went to Bonn, that university of the aristocrats, where he was worshipped. When he came to Berlin with his sister, crowds would gather to look at them. They were like Wodan and Freya. *Donner!*" exclaimed Herr Körner, "there is something in blood, when all is said. He was as straight and strong as an oak of the Black Forest, and she as fair as a poplar. It is so with the Pomeranians.

"It was in the year '47, when Carl Richter was gone home to Berlin before his last *semester*, to see his father. One fine morning von Kalbach rode in at the Brandenburg gate on a great black stallion. He boasted openly that day that none of the despised *Burschenschaft* dare stand before him. And Carl Richter took up the challenge. Before night all Berlin had heard of the temerity of the young Liberal of the Jena *Burschenschaft*. To our shame be it said, we who knew and loved Carl likewise feared for him.

"Carl chose for his second Ebhardt, a man of our own Germanian Club at Jena, since killed in the *Breite Strasse*. And if you will believe me, my friend, I tell you that Richter came to the glade at daybreak *smoking his pipe*. The place was filled, the nobles on one side and the *Burschenschaft* on the other, and the sun coming up over the trees. Richter would not listen to any of us, not even the surgeon. He would not have the silk wound on his arm, nor the padded breeches, nor the neck covering. Nothing! So Ebhardt put on his gauntlets and peaked cap, and his apron with the device of the Germanians.

"There stood the Count in his white shirt in the pose of a statue. And when it was seen that Richter likewise had no protection, but was calmly smoking the little short pipe with a charred bowl, a hush fell upon all. At the sight of the pipe von Kalbach ground his heel in the turf, and when the word was given he rushed at Richter like a wild beast. You, my friend, who have never heard the whistle of sharp *Schläger* cannot know the song which a skilled arm draws from the blade. It was music that morning. You should have seen the noble's mighty strokes—*Prim und Second und Terz und Quart*. You would have marked how Richter met him at every blow. Von Kalbach never once took his eyes from the blue smoke from the bowl. He was terrible in his fury, and I shiver now to think how we of the *Burschenschaft* trembled when we saw that our champion was driven back a step, and then another. You must know that it is a lasting disgrace to be forced over one's own line. It seemed as if we could not bear the agony. And then, while we counted out the last seconds of the half, came a snap like that of a whip's lash,—and the bowl of Richter's pipe lay smouldering on the grass. The noble had cut the stem as clean as it were a sapling twig, and there stood Richter with the piece still clenched in his teeth, his eyes ablaze, and his cheek running blood. He pushed the surgeon away when he came forward with his needles. The Count was smiling as he put up his sword, his friends crowding around him, when Ebhardt cried out that his man could fight the second *Mensur*,—though the wound was three needles long. Then Kalbach cried aloud that he would kill him. But he had not seen Carl's eyes. Something was in them that made us think as we washed the cut. But when we spoke to him he said nothing. Nor could we force the pipe stem from his teeth.

"*Donner Schock!*" exclaimed Herr Körner, but reverently, "if I live to be a hundred I never hope to see such a sight as that *Mensur*. The word was given. The *Schläger* flew so fast that we only saw the light and heard the ring alone. Before we of the *Burschenschaft* knew what had happened the Count von Kalbach was over his line and had flung his *Schläger* into a great tree, and was striding from the place with his head hung and the tears streaming down his face."

Amid a silence, Herr Körner lifted his great mug and emptied it slowly. A wind was rising, bearing with it song and laughter from distant groups,—Teutonic song and laughter. The moonlight trembled through the shifting leaves. And Stephen was filled with a sense of the marvelous. It was as if this fierce duel, so full of national significance to a German, had been fought in another existence. It was incredible to him that the unassuming lawyer he knew, so wholly Americanized, had been the hero of it. Strange, indeed, that the striving life of these leaders of a European Revolution had been suddenly cut off in its vigor. There came to Stephen a flash of that world-comprehension which marks great statesmen. Was it not with a divine purpose that this measureless force of patriotism and high ideal had been given to this youngest of the nations, that its high mission might be fulfilled?

Miss Russell heard of Stephen's speeches. She and her brothers and Jack Brinsmade used to banter him when he came a-visiting in Bellefontaine Road. The time was not yet come when neighbor stared coldly upon neighbor, when friends of long standing passed each other with averted looks. It was not even a wild dream that white-trash Lincoln would be elected. And so Mr. Jack, who made speeches for Breckenridge in the face of Mr. Brinsmade's Union leanings, laughed at Stephen when he came to spend the night. He joined forces with Puss in making clever fun of the booby Dutch, which Stephen was wise enough to take good-naturedly. But once or twice when he met Clarence Colfax at these houses he was aware of a decided change in the attitude of that young gentleman. This troubled him more than he cared to admit. For he liked Clarence, who reminded him of Virginia—at once a pleasure and a pain.

It is no harm to admit (for the benefit of the Society for Psychical Research) that Stephen still dreamed of her. He would go about his work absently all the morning with the dream still in his head, and the girl so vividly near him that he could not believe her to be travelling in England, as Miss Russell said. Puss and Anne were careful to keep him informed as to her whereabouts. Stephen set this down as a most natural supposition on their part that all young men must have an interest in Virginia Carvel.

How needless to add that Virginia in her correspondence never mentioned Stephen, although Puss in her letters took pains to record the fact every time that he addressed a Black Republican meeting. Miss Carvel paid no attention to this part of the communications. Her concern for Judge Whipple Virginia did not hide. Anne wrote of him. How he stood the rigors of that campaign were a mystery to friend and foe alike.

CHAPTER XI

HOW A PRINCE CAME

W<small>HO</small> has not heard of the St. Louis Agricultural Fair. And what memories of its October days the mere mention of it brings back to us who knew that hallowed place as children. There was the vast wooden amphitheatre where mad trotting races were run; where stolid cattle walked past the Chinese pagoda in the middle circle, and shook the blue ribbons on their horns. But it was underneath the tiers of seats (the whole way around the ring) that the chief attractions lay hid. These were the church booths, where fried oysters and sandwiches and cake and white candy and ice-cream were sold by your mothers and sisters for charity. These ladies wore white aprons as they waited on the burly farmers. And toward the close of the day for which they had volunteered they became distracted. Christ Church had a booth, and St. George's and Dr. Thayer's, Unitarian, where Mrs. Brice might be found; and Mr. Davitt's, conducted by Mr. Eliphalet Hopper on strictly business principles; and the Roman Catholic Cathedral, where Miss Rénault and other young ladies of French descent presided; and Dr. Posthelwaite's, Presbyterian, which we shall come to presently. And others, the whole way around the ring.

There is one Fair which old St. Louisans still delight to recall,—that of the autumn of 1860. Think for a minute. You will remember that Virginia Carvel came back from Europe, and made quite a stir in a town where all who were worth knowing were intimates. Stephen caught a glimpse of her on the street, received a distant bow, and dreamed of her that night. Mr. Eliphalet Hopper, in his Sunday suit, was at the ferry to pay his respects to the Colonel, to offer his services, and to tell him how the business fared. His was the first St. Louis face that Virginia saw (Captain Lige being in New Orleans), and if she conversed with Eliphalet on the ferry with more warmth than ever before, there is nothing strange in that. Mr. Hopper rode home with them in the carriage, and walked to Miss Crane's with his heart thumping against his breast, and wild thoughts whirling in his head.

The next morning, in Virginia's sunny front room, tears and laughter mingled. There was a present for Eugénie and Anne and Emily and Puss and Maude, and a hearty kiss from the Colonel for each. And more tears and laughter and sighs as Mammy Easter and Rosetta unpacked the English trunks, and with trembling hands and rolling eyes laid each Parisian gown upon the bed.

But the Fair, the Fair!

At the thought of that glorious year my pen fails me. Why mention the dread possibility of the negro-worshipper Lincoln being elected the very next month? Why listen to the rumblings in the South? Pompeii had chariot-races to the mutterings of Vesuvius. St. Louis was in gala garb to greet a Prince.

That was the year that Miss Virginia Carvel was given charge of the booth in Dr. Posthelwaite's church,—the booth next one of the great arches through which prancing horses and lowing cattle came.

Now who do you think stopped at the booth for a chat with Miss Jinny? Who made her blush as pink as her Paris gown? Who slipped into her hand the contribution for the church, and refused to take the cream candy she laughingly offered him as an equivalent?

None other than Albert Edward, Prince of Wales, Duke of Saxony, Duke of Cornwall and Rothesay, Earl of Chester and Carrick, Baron Renfrew, and Lord of the Isles. Out of compliment to the Republic which he visited, he bore the simple title of Lord Renfrew.

Bitter tears of envy, so it was said, were shed in the other booths. Belle Cluyme made a remark which is best suppressed. Eliphalet Hopper, in Mr. Davitt's booth, stared until his eyes watered. A great throng peered into the covered way, kept clear for his Royal Highness and suite, and for the prominent gentlemen who accompanied them. And when the Prince was seen to turn to His Grace, the Duke of Newcastle, and the subscription was forthcoming, a great cheer shook the building, while Virginia and the young ladies with her bowed and blushed and smiled. Colonel Carvel, who was a Director, laid his hand paternally on the blue coat of the young Prince. Reversing all precedent, he *presented* his Royal Highness to his daughter and to the other young ladies. It was done with the easy grace of a Southern gentleman. Whereupon Lord Renfrew bowed and smiled too, and stroked his mustache, which was a habit he had, and so fell naturally into the ways of Democracy.

Miss Puss Russell, who has another name, and whose hair is now white, will tell you how Virginia carried off the occasion with credit to her country.

It is safe to say that the Prince forgot "Silver Heels" and "Royal Oak," although they had been trotted past the Pagoda only that morning for his delectation. He had forgotten his Honor the Mayor, who had held fast to the young man's arm as the four coal-black horses had pranced through the crowds all the way from Barnum's Hotel to the Fair Grounds. His Royal Highness forgot himself still further, and had at length withdrawn his hands from the pockets of his ample pantaloons and thrust his thumbs into his yellow waistcoat. And who shall blame him if Miss Virginia's replies to his sallies enchained him?

Not the least impressive of those who stood by, smiling, was the figure of the tall Colonel, his hat off for once, and pride written on his face. Oh, that his dear wife might have lived to see this!

What was said in that historic interview with a future Sovereign of England, far from his royal palaces, on Democratic sawdust, with an American Beauty across a board counter, was immediately recorded by the Colonel, together with an exact description of his Royal Highness's blue coat, and light, flowing pantaloons, and yellow waistcoat, and colored kids; even the Prince's habit of stroking his mustache did not escape the watchful eye. It is said that his Grace of Newcastle smiled twice at Miss Virginia's retorts, and Lord Lyons, the British Minister, has more than two to his credit. But suddenly a strange thing happened. Miss Virginia in the very midst of a sentence paused, and then stopped. Her eyes had strayed from the Royal Countenance, and were fixed upon a point in the row of heads outside the promenade. Her sentence was completed—with some confusion. Perhaps it is no wonder that my Lord Renfrew, whose intuitions are quick, remarked that he had already remained too long, thus depriving the booth of the custom it otherwise should have had. This was a graceful speech, and a kingly. Followed by his retinue and the prominent citizens, he moved on. And it was remarked by keen observers that his Honor the Mayor had taken hold once more of the Prince's elbow, who divided his talk with Colonel Carvel.

Dear Colonel Carvel! What a true American of the old type you were. You, nor the Mayor, nor the rest of the grave and elderly gentlemen were not blinded by the light of a royal Presence. You saw in him only an amiable and lovable young man, who was to succeed the most virtuous and lovable of sovereigns, Victoria. You, Colonel Carvel, were not one to

cringe to royalty. Out of respect for the just and lenient Sovereign, his
mother, you did honor to the Prince. But you did not remind him, as you
might have, that your ancestors fought for the King at Marston Moor,
and that your grandfather was once an intimate of Charles James Fox.
But what shall we say of Mr. Cluyme, and of a few others whose wealth
alone enabled them to be Directors of the Fair? Miss Isabel Cluyme was
duly presented, in proper form, to his Royal Highness. Her father owned
a "peerage," and had been abroad likewise. *He* made no such bull as the
Colonel. And while the celebrated conversation of which we have spoken
was in progress, Mr. Cluyme stood back and blushed for his countryman,
and smiled apologetically at the few gentlemen of the royal suite who
glanced his way.

His Royal Highness then proceeded to luncheon, which is described
by a most amiable Canadian correspondent who sent to his newspaper
an account of it that I cannot forbear to copy. You may believe what he
says, or not, just as you choose: "So interested was his Royal Highness
in the proceedings that he stayed in the ring three and a half hours wit-
nessing these trotting matches. He was invited to take lunch in a little
wooden shanty prepared for the Directors, to which he accordingly repaired, but whether he got anything to eat or not, I cannot tell. After
much trouble he forced his way to the table, which he found surrounded
by a lot of ravenous animals. And upon some half dozen huge dishes were
piled slices of beef, mutton, and buffalo tongue; beside them were great
jugs of lager beer, rolls of bread, and plates of a sort of cabbage cut into
thin shreds, raw, and mixed with vinegar. There were neither salt spoons
nor mustard spoons, the knives the gentlemen were eating with serving
in their stead; and, by the aid of nature's forks, the slices of beef and
mutton were transferred to the plates of those who desired to eat. While
your correspondent stood looking at the spectacle, the Duke of Newcastle came in, and he sat looking too. He was evidently trying to look
democratic, but could not manage it. By his side stood a man urging him
to try the lager beer, and cabbage also, I suppose. Henceforth, let the
New York Aldermen who gave to the Turkish Ambassador ham sandwiches and bad sherry rest in peace."

Even that great man whose memory we love and revere, Charles Dickens, was not overkind to us, and saw our faults rather than our virtues.
We were a nation of grasshoppers, and spat tobacco from early morning
until late at night. This some of us undoubtedly did, to our shame be it
said. And when Mr. Dickens went down the Ohio, early in the '40's, he

complained of the men and women he met; who, bent with care, bolted
through silent meals, and retired within their cabins. Mr. Dickens saw
our ancestors bowed in a task that had been too great for other blood,—
the task of bringing into civilization in the compass of a century a wilderness three thousand miles in breadth. And when his Royal Highness came
to St. Louis and beheld one hundred thousand people at the Fair, we are
sure that he knew how recently the ground he stood upon had been conquered from the forest.

A strange thing had happened, indeed. For, while the Prince lingered
in front of the booth of Dr. Posthelwaite's church and chatted with Virginia, a crowd had gathered without. They stood peering over the barri-
cade into the covered way, proud of the self-possession of their young
countrywoman. And here, by a twist of fate, Mr. Stephen Brice found
himself perched on a barrel beside his friend Richter. It was Richter who
discovered her first.

"Himmel! It is Miss Carvel herself, Stephen," he cried, impatient at
the impassive face of his companion. "Look, Stephen, look there."

"Yes," said Stephen, "I see."

"Ach!" exclaimed the disgusted German, "will nothing move you? I
have seen German princesses that are peasant women beside her. How
she carries it off! See, the Prince is laughing!"

Stephen saw, and horror held him in a tremor. His one thought was of
escape. What if she should raise her eyes, and amid those vulgar stares
discern his own? And yet that was within him which told him that she
would look up. It was only a question of moments, and then,—and then
she would in truth despise him! Wedged tightly between the people, to
move was to be betrayed. He groaned.

Suddenly he rallied, ashamed of his own false shame. This was because
of one whom he had known for the short space of a day—whom he was
to remember for a lifetime. The man he worshipped, and she detested.
Abraham Lincoln would not have blushed between honest clerks and
farmers. Why should Stephen Brice? And what, after all, was this girl
to him? He could not tell. Almost the first day he had come to St. Louis
the wires of their lives had crossed, and since then had crossed many
times again, always with a spark. By the might of generations she was
one thing, and he another. They were separated by a vast and ever-
widening breach only to be closed by the blood and bodies of a million of
their countrymen. And yet he dreamed of her.

Gradually, charmed like the simple people about him, Stephen became lost in the fascination of the scene. Suddenly confronted at a booth in a public fair with the heir to the English throne, who but one of her own kind might have carried it off so well, have been so complete a mistress of herself? Since, save for a heightened color, Virginia gave no sign of excitement. Undismayed, forgetful of the admiring crowd, unconscious of their stares until—until the very strength of his gaze had compelled her own. Such had been the prophecy within him. Nor did he wonder because, in that multitude of faces, her eyes had flown so straightly homeward to his.

With a rough effort that made an angry stir, Stephen flung the people aside and escaped, the astonished Richter following in his wake. Nor could the honest German dissuade him from going back to the office for the rest of the day, or discover what had happened.

But all through the afternoon that scene was painted on the pages of Stephen's books. The crude booth in the darkened way. The free pose of the girl standing in front of her companions, a blue wisp of autumn sunlight falling at her feet. The young Prince laughing at her sallies, and the elderly gentleman smiling with benevolence upon the pair.

CHAPTER XII

INTO WHICH A POTENTATE COMES

VIRGINIA danced with the Prince, "by Special Appointment," at the ball that evening. So did her aunt, Mrs. Addison Colfax. So likewise was Miss Belle Cluyme among those honored and approved. But Virginia wore the most beautiful of her Paris gowns, and seemed a princess to one watching from the gallery. Stephen was sure that his Royal Highness made that particular dance longer than the others. It was decidedly longer than the one he had with Miss Cluyme, although that young lady had declared she was in heaven.

Alas, that princes cannot abide with us forever! His Royal Highness bade farewell to St. Louis, and presently that same *City of Alton* which bore him northward came back again in like royal state, and this time it was in honor of a Democrat potentate. He is an old friend now, Senator and Judge and Presidential Candidate,—Stephen Arnold Douglas,— father of the doctrine of Local Sovereignty, which he has come to preach. So goes the world. We are no sooner rid of one hero than we are ready for another.

Blow, you bandsmen on the hurricane deck, let the shores echo with your national airs! Let the gay bunting wave in the river breeze! Uniforms flash upon the guards, for no campaign is complete without the military. Here are brave companies of the Douglas Guards, the Hickory Sprouts, and the Little Giants to do honor to the person of their hero. Cannon are booming as he steps into his open carriage that evening on the levee, where the piles of river freight are covered with people. Transparencies are dodging in the darkness. A fresh band strikes up "Hail Columbia," and the four horses prance away, followed closely by the "Independent Broom Rangers." "The shouts for Douglas," remarked a keen observer who was present, "must have penetrated Abraham's bosom at Springfield."

Mr. Jacob Cluyme, who had been a Bell and Everett man until that day, was not the only person of prominence converted. After the speech he assured the Judge that he was now undergoing the greatest pleasure of his life in meeting the popular orator, the true representative man of the Great West, the matured statesman, and the able advocate of national principles. And although Mr. Douglas looked as if he had heard something of the kind before, he pressed Mr. Cluyme's hand warmly.

So was the author of Popular Sovereignty, "the great Bulwark of American Independence," escorted to the Court House steps, past houses of his stanch supporters, which were illuminated in his honor. Stephen, wedged among the people, remarked that the Judge had lost none of his self-confidence since that day at Freeport. Who, seeing the Democratic candidate smiling and bowing to the audience that blocked the wide square, would guess that the Question troubled him at all, or that he missed the votes of the solid South? How gravely the Judge listened to the eulogy of the prominent citizen, who reminded him that his work was not yet finished, and that he still was harnessed to the cause of the people! And how happy was the choice of that word *harnessed!*

The Judge had heard (so he said) with deep emotion the remarks of the chairman. Then followed one of those masterful speeches which wove a spell about those who listened,—which, like the most popular of novels, moved to laughter and to tears, to anger and to pity. Mr. Brice and Mr. Richter were not the only Black Republicans who were depressed that night. And they trudged homeward with a wild enthusiasm still ringing in their ears, heavy with the thought that the long, hot campaign of their own Wide-Awakes might be in vain.

They had a grim reproof from Judge Whipple in the morning.

"So you too, gentlemen, took opium last night," was all he said.

The dreaded possibility of Mr. Lincoln's election did not interfere with the gayeties. The week after the Fair Mr. Clarence Colfax gave a great dance at Bellegarde, in honor of his cousin, Virginia, to which Mr. Stephen Brice was not invited. A majority of Company A was there. Virginia would have liked to have had them in uniform.

It was at this time that Anne Brinsmade took the notion of having a ball in costume. Virginia, on hearing the news, rode over from Bellegarde, and flinging her reins to Nicodemus ran up to Anne's little dressing-room.

"Whom have you invited, Anne?" she demanded.

Anne ran over the long list of their acquaintance, but there was one name she omitted.

"Are you sure that that is all?" asked Virginia, searchingly, when she had finished.

Anne looked mystified.

"I have invited Stephen Brice, Jinny," she said. "But—"

"*But!*" cried Virginia. "I knew it. Am I to be confronted with that Yankee everywhere I go? It is always 'Stephen Brice,' and he is ushered in with a *but*."

Anne was quite overcome by this outburst. She had dignity, however, and plenty of it. And she was a loyal friend.

"You have no right to criticise my guests, Virginia."

Virginia, seated on the arm of a chair, tapped her foot on the floor.

"Why couldn't things remain as they were?" she said. "We were so happy before these Yankees came. And they are not content in trying to deprive us of our rights. They must spoil our pleasure, too."

"Stephen Brice is a gentleman," answered Anne. "He spoils no one's pleasure, and goes no place that he is not asked."

"He has not behaved according to *my* idea of a gentleman, the few times that I have been unfortunate enough to encounter him," Virginia retorted.

"You are the only one who says so, then." Here the feminine got the better of Anne's prudence, and she added, "I saw you waltz with him once, Jinny Carvel, and I am sure you never enjoyed a dance as much in your life."

Virginia blushed purple.

"Anne Brinsmade!" she cried. "You may have your ball, and your Yankees, all of them you want. But I shan't come. How I wish I had never seen that horrid Stephen Brice! Then you would never have insulted me."

Virginia rose and snatched her riding-whip. This was too much for Anne. She threw her arms around her friend without more ado.

"Don't quarrel with me, Jinny," she said tearfully. "I couldn't bear it. He—Mr. Brice is not coming, I am sure."

Virginia disengaged herself.

"He is not coming?"

"No," said Anne. "You asked me if he was invited. And I was going on to tell you that he could not come."

She stopped, and stared at Virginia in bewilderment. That young lady, instead of beaming, had turned her back. She stood flicking her whip at the window, gazing out over the trees, down the slope to the river. Miss Russell might have interpreted these things. Simple Anne!

"Why isn't he coming?" said Virginia, at last.

"Because he is to be one of the speakers at a big meeting that night. Have you seen him since you got home, Jinny? He is thinner than he was. We are much worried about him, because he has worked so hard this summer."

"A Black Republican meeting!" exclaimed Virginia, scornfully ignoring the rest of what was said. "Then I'll come, Anne dear," she cried, tripping the length of the room. "I'll come as Titania. Who will you be?"

She cantered off down the drive and out of the gate, leaving a very puzzled young woman watching her from the window. But when Virginia reached the forest at the bend of the road, she pulled her horse down to a walk. She bethought herself of the gown which her Uncle Daniel had sent her from Calvert House, and of the pearls. And she determined to go as her great-grandmother, Dorothy Carvel.

Shades of romance! How many readers will smile before the rest of this true incident is told?

What had happened was this. Miss Anne Brinsmade had driven to town in her mother's *Jenny Lind* a day or two before, and had stopped (as she often did) to pay a call on Mrs. Brice. This lady, as may be guessed, was not given to discussion of her husband's ancestors, nor of her own. But on the walls of the little dining-room hung a Copley and two Stuarts. One of the Stuarts was a full length of an officer in the buff and blue of the Continental Army. And it was this picture which caught Anne's eye that day.

"How like Stephen!" she exclaimed. And added: "Only the face is much older. Who is it, Mrs. Brice?"

"Colonel Wilton Brice, Stephen's grandfather. There is a marked look about all the Brices. He was only twenty years of age when the Revolution began. That picture was painted much later in life, after Stuart came back to America, when the Colonel was nearly forty. He had kept his uniform, and his wife persuaded him to be painted in it."

"If Stephen would only come as Colonel Wilton Brice!" she cried. "Do you think he would, Mrs. Brice?"

Mrs. Brice laughed, and shook her head.

"I am afraid not, Anne," she said. "I have a part of the uniform upstairs, but I could never induce him even to try it on."

As she drove from shop to shop that day, Anne reflected that it certainly would not be like Stephen to wear his grandfather's uniform to a ball. But she meant to ask him, at any rate. And she had driven home immediately to write her invitations. It was with keen disappointment that she read his note of regret.

However, on the very day of the ball, Anne chanced to be in town again, and caught sight of Stephen pushing his way among the people on Fourth Street. She waved her hand to him, and called to Nicodemus to pull up at the sidewalk.

"We are all so sorry that you are not coming," said she impulsively. And there she stopped short. For Anne was a sincere person, and remembered Virginia. "That is, I am so sorry," she added, a little hastily. "Stephen, I saw the portrait of your grandfather, and I wanted you to come in his costume."

Stephen, smiling down on her, said nothing. And poor Anne, in her fear that he had perceived the shade in her meaning, made another unfortunate remark.

"If you were not a—a Republican—" she said.

"A Black Republican," he answered, and laughed at her discomfiture. "What then?"

Anne was very red.

"I only meant that if you were not a Republican, there would be no meeting to address that night."

"It does not make any difference to you what my politics are, does it?" he asked, a little earnestly.

"Oh, Stephen!" she exclaimed, in gentle reproof.

"Some people *have* discarded me," he said, striving to smile.

She wondered whether he meant Virginia, and whether he cared. Still further embarrassed, she said something which she regretted immediately.

"Couldn't you contrive to come?"

He considered.

"I will come, after the meeting, if it is not too late," he said at length. "But you must not tell any one."

He lifted his hat, and hurried on, leaving Anne in a quandary. She wanted him. But what was she to say to Virginia? Virginia was coming on the condition that he was not to be there. And Anne was scrupulous.

Stephen, too, was almost instantly sorry that he had promised. The little costumer's shop (the only one in the city at that time) had been ransacked for the occasion, and nothing was left to fit him. But when he reached home there was a strong smell of camphor in his mother's room.

Colonel Brice's cocked hat and sword and spurs lay on the bed, and presently Hester brought in the blue coat and buff waistcoat from the kitchen, where she had been pressing them. Stephen must needs yield to his mother's persuasions and try them on—they were more than a passable fit. But there were the breeches and cavalry boots to be thought of, and the ruffled shirt and the powdered wig. So before tea he hurried down to the costumer's again, not quite sure that he was not making a fool of himself, and yet at last sufficiently entered into the spirit of the thing. The coat was mended and freshened. And when after tea he dressed in the character, his appearance was so striking that his mother could not refrain from some little admiration. As for Hester, she was in transports. Stephen was human, and young. But still the frivolity of it all troubled him. He had inherited from Colonel Wilton Brice, the Puritan, other things beside clothes. And he felt in his heart as he walked soberly to the hall that this was no time for fancy dress balls. All intention of going was banished by the time his turn had come to speak.

But mark how certain matters are beyond us. Not caring to sit out the meeting on the platform, he made his way down the side of the crowded hall, and ran into (of all people) big Tom Catherwood. As the Southern Rights politics of the Catherwood family were a matter of note in the city, Stephen did not attempt to conceal his astonishment. Tom himself was visibly embarrassed. He congratulated Stephen on his speech, and volunteered the news that he had come in a spirit of fairness to hear what the intelligent leaders of the Republican party, such as Judge Whipple, had to say. After that he fidgeted. But the sight of him started in Stephen a train of thought that closed his ears for once to the Judge's words. He had had before a huge liking for Tom. Now he admired him, for it was no light courage that took one of his position there. And Stephen remembered that Tom was not risking merely the displeasure of his family and his friends, but likewise something of greater value than either. From childhood Tom had been the devoted slave of Virginia Carvel, with as little chance of marrying her as a man ever had. And now he was endangering even that little chance.

And so Stephen began to think of Virginia, and to wonder what she would wear at Anne's party; and to speculate how she would have treated him if he had gone. To speak truth, this last matter had no little weight in his decision to stay away. But we had best leave motives to those whose business and equipment it is to weigh to a grain. Since that agonizing moment when her eyes had met his own among the curiously vulgar at the Fair, Stephen's fear of meeting Virginia had grown to the proportions of a terror. And yet there she was in his mind, to take possession of it on the slightest occasion.

When Judge Whipple had finished, Tom rose. He awoke Mr. Brice from a trance.

"Stephen," said he, "of course you're going to the Brinsmade's."

Stephen shook his head.

"Why not?" said Tom, in surprise. "Haven't you a costume?"

"Yes," he answered dubiously.

"Why, then, you've got to come with me," says Tom, heartily. "It isn't too late, and they'll want you. I've a buggy, and I'm going to the Russells' to change my clothes. Come along!"

Stephen went.

CHAPTER XIII

AT MR. BRINSMADE'S GATE

THE eastern side of the Brinsmade house is almost wholly taken up by the big drawing-room where Anne gave her fancy-dress ball. From the windows might be seen, through the trees in the grounds, the Father of Waters below. But the room is gloomy now, that once was gay, and a heavy coat of soot is spread on the porch at the back, where the apple blossoms still fall thinly in the spring. The huge black town has coiled about the place. The garden still struggles on, but the giants of the forest are dying and dead. Bellefontaine Road itself, once the drive of fashion, is no more. Trucks and cars crowd the streets which follow its once rural windings, and gone forever are those comely wooded hills and green pastures,—save in the memory of those who have been spared to dream.

Still the old house stands, begrimed but stately, rebuking the sordid life around it. Still come into it the Brinsmades to marriage and to death. Five and sixty years are gone since Mr. Calvin Brinsmade took his bride there. They sat on the porch in the morning light, harking to the whistle of the quail in the corn, and watching the frightened deer scamper across the open. Do you see the bride in her high-waisted gown, and Mr. Calvin in his stock and his blue tail-coat and brass buttons?

Old people will tell you of the royal hospitality then, of the famous men and women who promenaded under those chandeliers, and sat down to the game-laden table. In 1835 General Atkinson and his officers thought nothing of the twenty miles from Jefferson Barracks below, nor of dancing all night with the Louisville belles, who were Mrs. Brinsmade's guests. Thither came Miss Todd of Kentucky, long before she thought of taking for a husband that rude man of the people, Abraham Lincoln. Foreigners of distinction fell in love with the place, with its open-hearted master and mistress, and wrote of it in their journals. Would that many of our countrymen, who think of the West as rough, might have known the quality of the Brinsmades and their neighbors!

An era of charity, of golden simplicity, was passing on that October night of Anne Brinsmade's ball. Those who made merry there were soon to be driven and scattered before the winds of war; to die at Wilson's Creek, or Shiloh, or to be spared for heroes of the Wilderness. Some were to eke out a life of widowhood in poverty. All were to live soberly, chastened by what they had seen. A fear knocked at Colonel Carvel's heart as he stood watching the bright figures.

"Brinsmade," he said, "do you remember this room in May, '46?"

Mr. Brinsmade, startled, turned upon him quickly.

"Why, Colonel, you have read my very thoughts," he said. "Some of those who were here then are—are still in Mexico."

"And some who came home, Brinsmade, blamed God because they had not fallen," said the Colonel.

"Hush, Comyn, His will be done," he answered: "He has left a daughter to comfort you."

Unconsciously their eyes sought Virginia. In her gown of faded primrose and blue with its quaint stays and short sleeves, she seemed to have caught the very air of the decorous century to which it belonged. She was standing against one of the pilasters at the side of the room, laughing demurely at the antics of Becky Sharp and Sir John Falstaff,—Miss Puss Russell and Mr. Jack Brinsmade, respectively.

Mr. Tennyson's "Idylls" having appeared but the year before, Anne was dressed as Elaine, a part which suited her very well. It was strange indeed to see her waltzing with Daniel Boone (Mr. Clarence Colfax) in his Indian buckskins. Eugénie went as Marie Antoinette. Tall Maude Catherwood was most imposing as Rebecca and her brother George made a towering Friar Tuck. Even little fifteen-year-old Spencer Catherwood, the contradiction of the family, was there. He went as the lieutenant Napoleon, walking about with his hands behind his back and his brows thoughtfully contracted.

The Indian summer night was mild. It was at the very height of the festivities that Dorothy Carvel and Mr. Daniel Boone were making their way together to the porch when the giant gate-keeper of Kenilworth Castle came stalking up the steps out of the darkness, brandishing his club in their faces. Dorothy screamed, and even the doughty Daniel gave back a step.

"Tom Catherwood! How dare you? You frightened me nearly to death."

"I'm sorry, Jinny, indeed I am," said the giant, repentant, and holding her hand in his.

"Where have you been?" demanded Virginia, a little mollified. "What makes you so late?"

"I've been to a Lincoln meeting," said honest Tom, "where I heard a very fine speech from a friend of yours."

Virginia tossed her head.

"You might have been better employed," said she, and added, with dignity, "I have no friends who speak at Black Republican meetings."

"How about Judge Whipple?" said Tom.

She stopped. "Did you mean the Judge?" she asked, over her shoulder.

"No," said Tom, "I meant—"

He got no further. Virginia slipped her arm through Clarence's, and they went off together to the end of the veranda. Poor Tom! He passed on into the gay drawing-room, but the zest had been taken out of his antics for that night.

"Whom did he mean, Jinny?" said Clarence, when they were on the seat under the vines.

"He meant that Yankee, Stephen Brice," answered Virginia, languidly. "I am so tired of hearing about him."

"So am I," said Clarence, with a fervor by no means false. "By George, I think he will make a Black Republican out of Tom, if he keeps on. Puss and Jack have been talking about him all summer, until I am out of patience. I reckon he has brains. But suppose he has addressed fifty Lincoln meetings, as they say, is that any reason for making much of him? I should not have him at Bellegarde. I am surprised that Mr. Russell allows him in his house. I can see why Anne likes him."

"Why?"

"He is on the Brinsmade charity list."

"He is not on their charity list, nor on any other," said Virginia, quickly. "Stephen Brice is the last person who would submit to charity."

"And you are the last person who I supposed would stand up for him," cried her cousin, surprised and nettled.

There was an instant's silence.

"I want to be fair, Max," she said quietly. "Pa offered them our Glencoe House last summer at a low price, and they insisted on paying what Mr. Edwards gave five years ago,—or nothing. You know that I detest a Yankee as much as you do," she continued, indignation growing in her voice. "I did not come out here with you to be insulted."

With her hand on the rail, she made as if to rise. Clarence was perforce mollified.

"Don't go, Jinny," he said beseechingly. "I didn't mean to make you angry—"

"I can't see why you should always be dragging in this Mr. Brice," she said, almost tearfully. (It will not do to pause now and inquire into Virginia's logic.) "I came out to hear what you had to tell me."

"Jinny, I have been made second lieutenant of Company A."

"Oh, Max, I am so glad! I am so proud of you!"

"I suppose that you have heard the result of the October elections, Jinny."

"Pa said something about them to-night," she answered, "why?"

"It looks now as if there were a chance of the Republicans winning," he answered. But it was elation that caught his voice, not gloom.

"You mean that this white trash Lincoln may be President?" she exclaimed, seizing his arm.

"Never!" he cried. "The South will not submit to that until every man who can bear arms is shot down." He paused. The strains of a waltz mingled with talk and laughter floated out of the open window. His voice dropped to a low intensity. "We are getting ready in Company A," he said; "the traitors will be dropped. We are getting ready to fight for Missouri and for the South."

The girl felt his excitement, his exaltation.

"And if you were not, Max, I should disown you," she whispered.

He leaned forward until his face was close to hers.

"And now?" he said.

"I am ready to work, to starve, to go to prison, to help—"

He sank back heavily into the corner.

"Is that all, Jinny?"

"All?" she repeated. "Oh, if a woman could only do more!"

"And is there nothing—for me?"

Virginia straightened.

"Are you doing this for a reward?" she demanded.

"No," he answered passionately. "You know that I am not. Do you remember when you told me that I was good for nothing, that I lacked purpose?"

"Yes, Max."

"I have thought it over since," he went on rapidly; "you were right. I cannot work—it is not in me. But I have always felt that I could make a name for myself—for you—in the army. I am sure that I could command a regiment. And now the time is coming."

She did not answer him, but absently twisted the fringe of his buckskins in her fingers.

"Ever since I have known what love is I have loved you, Jinny. It was so when we climbed the cherry trees at Bellegarde. And you loved me then—I know you did. You loved me when I went East to school at the Military Institute. But it has not been the same of late," he faltered. "Something has happened. I felt it first on that day you rode out to Bellegarde when you said that my life was of no use. Jinny, I don't ask much. I am content to prove myself. War is coming, and we shall have to free ourselves from Yankee insolence. It is what we have both wished for. When I am a general, will you marry me?"

For a wavering instant she might have thrown herself into his outstretched arms. Why not, and have done with sickening doubts? Perhaps her hesitation hung on the very boyishness of his proposal. Perhaps the revelation that she did not then fathom was that he had not developed since those childish days. But even while she held back, came the beat of hoofs on the gravel below them, and one of the Bellegarde servants rode into the light pouring through the open door. He called for his master.

Clarence muttered his dismay as he followed his cousin to the steps.

"What is it?" asked Virginia, alarmed.

"Nothing; I forgot to sign the deed to the Elleardsville property, and Worington wants it to-night." Cutting short Sambo's explanations, Clarence vaulted on the horse. Virginia was at his stirrup. Leaning over in the saddle, he whispered: "I'll be back in a quarter of an hour. Will you wait?"

"Yes," she said, so that he barely heard.

"Here?"

She nodded.

He was away at a gallop, leaving Virginia standing bareheaded to the night, alone. A spring of pity, of affection for Clarence suddenly welled up within her. There came again something of her old admiration for a boy, impetuous and lovable, who had tormented and defended her with the same hand.

Patriotism, stronger in Virginia than many of us now can conceive, was on Clarence's side. Ambition was strong in her likewise. Now was she all afire with the thought that she, a woman, might by a single word give the South a leader. That word would steady him, for there was no question of her influence. She trembled at the reckless lengths he might go in his dejection, and a memory returned to her of a day at Glencoe, before he had gone off to school, when she had refused to drive with him. Colonel Carvel had been away from home. She had pretended not to care. In spite of Ned's beseechings Clarence had ridden off on a wild thoroughbred colt and had left her to an afternoon of agony. Vividly she recalled his home-coming in the twilight, his coat torn and muddy, a bleeding cut on his forehead, and the colt quivering tame.

In those days she had thought of herself unreservedly as meant for him. Dash and courage and generosity had been the beacon lights on her horizon. But now? Were there not other qualities? Yes, and Clarence should have these, too. She would put them into him. She also had been at fault, and perhaps it was because of her wavering loyalty to him that he had not gained them.

Her name spoken within the hall startled Virginia from her reverie, and she began to walk rapidly down the winding drive. A fragment of the air to which they were dancing brought her to a stop. It was the Jenny Lind waltz. And with it came clear and persistent the image she had sought to shut out and failed. As if to escape it now, she fairly ran all the way to the light at the entrance and hid in the magnolias clustered beside the gateway. It was her cousin's name she whispered over and over to herself as she waited, vibrant with a strange excitement. It was as though the very elements might thwart her will. Clarence would be delayed, or they would miss her at the house, and search. It seemed an eternity before she heard the muffled thud of a horse cantering on the clay road.

Virginia stood out in the light fairly between the gateposts. Too late she saw the horse rear as the rider flew back in his seat, for she had seized the bridle. The beams from the lamp fell upon a Revolutionary horseman, with cocked hat and sword and high riding-boots. For her his profile was in silhouette, and the bold nose and chin belonged to but one man she knew. He was Stephen Brice. She gave a cry of astonishment and dropped the rein in dismay. Hot shame was surging in her face. Her impulse was to fly, nor could she tell what force it was that stayed her feet.

As for Stephen, he stood high in his stirrups and stared down at the girl. She was standing full in the light,—her lashes fallen, her face crimson. But no sound of surprise escaped him because it was she, nor did he wonder at her gown of a gone-by century. Her words came first, and they were low. She did not address him by name.

"I—I thought that you were my cousin," she said. "What must you think of me!"

Stephen was calm.

"I expected it," he answered.

She gave a step backward, and raised her frightened eyes to his.

"You expected it?" she faltered.

"I can't say why," he said quickly, "but it seems to me as if this had happened before. I know that I am talking nonsense—"

Virginia was trembling now. And her answer was not of her own choosing.

"It has happened before," she cried. "But where? And when?"

"It may have been in a dream," he answered her, "that I saw you as you stand there by my bridle. I even know the gown you wear."

She put her hand to her forehead. Had it been a dream? And what mystery was it that sent him here this night of all nights? She could not even have said that it was her own voice making reply.

"And I—I have seen you, with the sword, and the powdered hair, and the blue coat and the buff waistcoat. It is a buff waistcoat like that my great-grandfather wears in his pictures."

"It is a buff waistcoat," he said, all sense of strangeness gone.

The roses she held dropped on the gravel, and she put out her hand against his horse's flank. In an instant he had leaped from his saddle, and his arm was holding her. She did not resist, marvelling rather at his own steadiness, nor did she then resent a tenderness in his voice.

"I hope you will forgive me—Virginia," he said. "I should not have mentioned this. And yet I could not help it."

She looked up at him rather wildly.

"It was I who stopped you," she said; "I was waiting for—"

"For whom?"

The interruption brought remembrance.

"For my cousin, Mr. Colfax," she answered, in another tone. And as she spoke she drew away from him, up the driveway. But she had scarcely taken five steps when she turned again, her face burning defiance. "They told me you were not coming," she said almost fiercely. "Why did you come?"

It was a mad joy that Stephen felt.

"You did not wish me to come?" he demanded.

"Oh, why do you ask that?" she cried. "You know I would not have been here had I thought you were coming. Anne promised me that you would not come."

What would she not have given for those words back again!

Stephen took a stride toward her, and to the girl that stride betokened a thousand things that went to the man's character. Within its compass the comparison in her mind was all complete. He was master of himself when he spoke.

"You dislike me, Miss Carvel," he said steadily. "I do not blame you. Nor do I flatter myself that it is only because you believe one thing, and I another. But I assure you that it is my misfortune rather than my fault that I have not pleased you,—that I have met you only to anger you."

He paused, for she did not seem to hear him. She was gazing at the distant lights moving on the river. Had he come one step farther?—but he did not. Presently she knew that he was speaking again, in the same measured tone.

"Had Miss Brinsmade told me that my presence here would cause you annoyance, I should have stayed away. I hope that you will think nothing of the—the mistake at the gate. You may be sure that I shall not mention it. Good night, Miss Carvel."

He lifted his hat, mounted his horse, and was gone. She had not even known that he could ride—that was strangely the first thought. The second discovered herself intent upon the rhythm of his canter as it died southward upon the road. There was shame in this, mingled with a thankfulness that he would not meet Clarence. She hurried a few steps toward the house, and stopped again. What should she say to Clarence now? What could she say to him?

But Clarence was not in her head. Ringing there was her talk with Stephen Brice, as though it were still rapidly going on. His questions and her replies—over and over again. Each trivial incident of an encounter real and yet unreal! His transformation in the uniform, which had seemed so natural. Though she strove to make it so, nothing of all this was unbearable now, nor the remembrance of the firm touch of his arm about her; nor yet again his calling her by her name.

Absently she took her way again up the drive, now pausing, now going on, forgetful. First it was alarm she felt when her cousin leaped down at her side,—then dread.

"I thought I should never get back," he cried breathlessly, as he threw his reins to Sambo. "I ought not to have asked you to wait outside. Did it seem long, Jinny?"

She answered something. There was a seat near by under the trees. To lead her to it he seized her hand, but it was limp and cold, and a sudden fear came into his voice.

"Jinny!"

"Yes."

She resisted, and he dropped her fingers. She remembered long how he stood in the scattered light from the bright windows, a tall, black figure of dismay. She felt the yearning in his eyes. But her own response, warm half an hour since, was lifeless.

"Jinny," he said, "what is the matter?"

"Nothing, Max. Only I was very foolish to say I would wait for you."

"Then—then you won't marry me?"

"Oh, Max," she cried, "it is no time to talk of that now. I feel to-night as if something dreadful were to happen."

"Do you mean war?" he asked.

"Yes," she said. "Yes."

"But war is what we want," he cried, "what we have prayed for, what we have both been longing for to-night, Jinny. War alone will give us our rights—"

He stopped short. Virginia had bowed her head in her hands, and he saw her shoulders shaken by a sob. Clarence bent over her in bewilderment and anxiety.

"You are not well, Jinny," he said.

"I am not well," she answered. "Take me into the house."

But when they went in at the door, he saw that her eyes were dry.

Those were the days when a dozen young ladies were in the habit of staying all night after a dance in the country; of long whispered talks (nay, not always whispered) until early morning. And of late breakfasts. Miss Russell had not been the only one who remarked Virginia's long absence with her cousin; but Puss found her friend in one of those moods which even she dared not disturb. Accordingly Miss Russell stayed all night with Anne. And the two spent most of the dark hours remaining in unprofitable discussion as to whether Virginia were at last engaged to her cousin, and in vain queried over another unsolved mystery. This mystery was taken up at the breakfast table the next morning, when Miss Carvel surprised Mrs. Brinsmade and the male household by appearing at half-past seven.

"Why, Jinny," cried Mr. Brinsmade, "what does this mean? I always thought that young ladies did not get up after a ball until noon."

Virginia smiled a little nervously.

"I am going to ask you to take me to town when you go, Mr. Brinsmade."

"Why, certainly, my dear," he said. "But I understood that your aunt was to send for you this afternoon from Bellegarde."

Virginia shook her head. "There is something I wish to do in town."

"I'll drive her in, Pa," said Jack. "You're too old. Will you go with me, Jinny?"

"Of course, Jack."

"But you must eat some breakfast, Jinny," said Mrs. Brinsmade, glancing anxiously at the girl.

Mr. Brinsmade put down his newspaper.

"Where was Stephen Brice last night, Jack?" he asked. "I understood Anne to say that he had spoken of coming late."

"Why, sir," said Jack, "that's what we can't make out. Tom Catherwood, who is always doing queer things, you know, went to a Black Republican meeting last night, and met Stephen there. They came out in Tom's buggy to the Russells', and Tom got into his clothes first and rode over. Stephen was to have followed on Puss Russell's horse. But he never got here. At least I can find no one who saw him. Did you, Jinny?"

But Virginia did not raise her eyes from her plate. A miraculous intervention came through Mrs. Brinsmade.

"There might have been an accident, Jack," said that lady, with concern. "Send Nicodemus over to Mrs. Russell's at once to inquire. You know that Mr. Brice is a Northerner, and may not be able to ride."

Jack laughed.

"He rides like a dragoon, mother," said he. "I don't know where he picked it up."

"The reason I mentioned him," said Mr. Brinsmade, lifting the blanket sheet and adjusting his spectacles, "was because his name caught my eye in this paper. His speech last night at the Library Hall is one of the *few* sensible Republican speeches I have read. I think it very remarkable for a man as young as he." Mr. Brinsmade began to read: " 'While waiting for the speaker of the evening, who was half an hour late, Mr. Tiefel rose in the audience and called loudly for Mr. Brice. Many citizens in the hall were astonished at the cheering which followed the mention of this name. Mr. Brice is a young lawyer with a quiet manner and a determined face, who has sacrificed much to the Party's cause this summer. He was introduced by Judge Whipple, in whose office he is. He had hardly begun to speak before he had the ear of every one in the house. Mr. Brice's personality is prepossessing, his words are spoken sharply, and he has a singular emphasis at times which seems to drive his arguments into the minds of his hearers. We venture to say that if party orators here and elsewhere were as logical and temperate as Mr. Brice; if, like him, they appealed to reason rather than to passion, those bitter and lamentable differences which threaten our country's peace might be amicably adjusted.' Let me read what he said."

But he was interrupted by the rising of Virginia. A high color was on the girl's face as she said:—

"Please excuse me, Mrs. Brinsmade, I must go and get ready."

"But you've eaten nothing, my dear."

Virginia did not reply. She was already on the stairs.

"You ought not have read that, Pa," Mr. Jack remonstrated: "you know that she detests Yankees."

CHAPTER XIV

THE BREACH BECOMES TOO WIDE

ABRAHAM LINCOLN!

At the foot of Breed's Hill in Charlestown an American had been born into the world, by the might of whose genius that fateful name was sped to the uttermost parts of the nation. Abraham Lincoln was elected President of the United States. And the moan of the storm gathering in the South grew suddenly loud and louder.

Stephen Brice read the news in the black headlines and laid down the newspaper, a sense of the miraculous upon him. There again was the angled, low-ceiled room of the country tavern, reeking with food and lamps and perspiration; for a central figure the man of surpassing homeliness,—coatless, tieless, and vestless,—telling a story in the vernacular. He reflected that it might well seem strange—yea, and intolerable—to many that this comedian of the country store, this crude lawyer and politician, should inherit the seat dignified by Washington and the Adamses.

And yet Stephen believed. For to him had been vouchsafed the glimpse beyond.

That was a dark winter that followed, the darkest in our history. Gloom and despondency came fast upon the heels of Republican exultation. Men rose early for tidings from Charleston, the storm centre. The Union was cracking here and there. Would it crumble in pieces before Abraham Lincoln got to Washington?

One smoky morning early in December Stephen arrived late at the office to find Richter sitting idle on his stool, concern graven on his face.

"The Judge has had no breakfast, Stephen," he whispered. "Listen! Shadrach tells me he has been doing that since six this morning, when he got his newspaper."

Stephen listened, and he heard the Judge pacing and pacing in his room. Presently the door was flung open, and they saw Mr. Whipple standing in the threshold, stern and dishevelled. Astonishment did not

204

pause here. He came out and sat down in Stephen's chair, striking the newspaper in his hand, and they feared at first that his mind had wandered.

"Propitiate!" he cried, "propitiate, propitiate, and again propitiate. How long, O Lord?" Suddenly he turned upon Stephen, who was frightened. But now his voice was natural, and he thrust the paper into the young man's lap. "Have you read the President's message to Congress, sir? God help me that I am spared to call that wobbling Buchanan President. Read it. Read it, sir. You have a legal brain. Perhaps you can tell me why, if a man admits that it is wrong for a state to abandon this Union, he cannot call upon Congress for men and money to bring her back. No, this weakling lets Floyd stock the Southern arsenals. He pays tribute to Barbary. He is for bribing them not to be angry. Take Cuba from Spain, says he, and steal the rest of Mexico that the maw of slavery may be filled, and the demon propitiated."

They dared not answer him. And so he went back into his room, shutting the door. That day no clients saw him, not even those poor ones dependent on his charity whom he had never before denied. Richter and Stephen took counsel together, and sent Shadrach out for his dinner.

Three weeks passed. There arrived a sparkling Sunday, brought down the valley of the Missouri from the frozen northwest. The Saturday had been soggy and warm. Thursday had seen South Carolina leave that Union into which she was born, amid prayers and the ringing of bells. Tuesday was to be Christmas day. A young lady, who had listened to a solemn sermon of Dr. Posthelwaite's, slipped out of Church before the prayers were ended, and hurried into that deserted portion of the town about the Court House where on week days business held its sway. She stopped once at the bottom of the grimy flight of steps leading to Judge Whipple's office. At the top she paused again, and for a short space stood alert, her glance resting on the little table in the corner, on top of which a few thumbed law books lay neatly piled. Once she made a hesitating step in this direction. Then, as if by a resolution quickly taken, she turned her back and softly opened the door of the Judge's room. He was sitting upright in his chair. A book was open in his lap, but it did not seem to Virginia that he was reading it.

"Uncle Silas," she said, "aren't you coming to dinner any more?"

He looked up swiftly from under his shaggy brows. The book fell to the floor.

"Uncle Silas," said Virginia, bravely, "I came to get you to-day."

Never before had she known him to turn away from man or woman, but now Judge Whipple drew his handkerchief from his pocket and blew his nose violently. A woman's intuition told her that locked tight in his heart was what he longed to say, and could not. The shiny black overcoat he wore was on the bed. Virginia picked it up and held it out to him, an appeal in her eyes.

He got into it. Then she handed him his hat. Many people walking home from church that morning marvelled as they saw these two on Locust Street together, the young girl supporting the elderly man over the slippery places at the crossings. For neighbor had begun to look coldly upon neighbor.

Colonel Carvel beheld them from his armchair by the sitting-room window, and leaned forward with a start. His lips moved as he closed his Bible reverently and marked his place. At the foot of the stairs he surprised Jackson by waving him aside, for the Colonel himself flung open the door and held out his hand to his friend. The Judge released Virginia's arm, and his own trembled as he gave it.

"Silas," said the Colonel, "Silas, we've missed you."

Virginia stood by, smiling, but her breath came deeply. Had she done right? Could any good come of it all? Judge Whipple did not go in at the door. He stood uncompromisingly planted on the threshold, his head flung back, and actual fierceness in his stare.

"Do you guess we can keep off the subject, Comyn?" he demanded.

Even Mr. Carvel, so used to the Judge's ways, was a bit taken aback by this question. It set him tugging at his goatee, and his voice was not quite steady as he answered:—

"God knows, Silas. We are human, and we can only try."

Then Mr. Whipple marched in. It lacked a quarter of an hour of dinner,—a crucial period to tax the resources of any woman. Virginia led the talk, but oh, the pathetic lameness of it. Her own mind was wandering when it should not, and recollections she had tried to strangle had sprung up once more. Only that morning in church she had lived over again the scene by Mr. Brinsmade's gate, and it was then that a wayward but resistless impulse to go to the Judge's office had seized her. The thought of the old man lonely and bitter in his room decided her. On her knees she prayed that she might save the bond between him and her father. For the Colonel had been morose on Sundays, and had taken to reading the Bible, a custom he had not had since she was a child.

In the dining-room Jackson, bowing and smiling, pulled out the Judge's chair, and got his customary curt nod as a reward. Virginia carved.

"Oh, Uncle Silas," she cried, "I am so glad that we have a wild turkey. And you shall have your side-bone." The girl carved deftly, feverishly, talking the while, aided by that most kind and accomplished of hosts, her father. In the corner the dreaded skeleton of the subject grinned sardonically. Were they going to be able to keep it off? There was to be no help from Judge Whipple, who sat in grim silence. A man who feels his soul burning is not given to small talk. Virginia alone had ever possessed the power to make him forget.

"Uncle Silas, I am sure there are some things about our trip that we never told you. How we saw Napoleon and his beautiful Empress driving in the Bois, and how Eugénie smiled and bowed at the people. I never saw such enthusiasm in my life. And oh, I learned such a lot of French history. All about Francis the First, and Pa took me to see his chateaus along the Loire. Very few tourists go there. You really ought to have gone with us."

Take care, Virginia!

"I had other work to do, Jinny," said the Judge.

Virginia rattled on.

"I told you that we stayed with a real lord in England, didn't I?" said she. "He wasn't half as nice as the Prince. But he had a beautiful house in Surrey, all windows, which was built in Elizabeth's time. They called the architecture Tudor, didn't they, Pa?"

"Yes, dear," said the Colonel, smiling.

"The Countess was nice to me," continued the girl, "and took me to garden parties. But Lord Jermyn was always talking politics."

The Colonel was stroking his goatee.

"Tell Silas about the house, Jinny. Jackson, help the Judge again."

"No," said Virginia, drawing a breath. "I'm going to tell him about that queer club where my great-grandfather used to bet with Charles Fox. We saw a great many places where Richard Carvel had been in England. That was before the Revolution. Uncle Daniel read me some of his memoirs when we were at Calvert House. I know that you would be interested in them, Uncle Silas. He sailed under Paul Jones."

"And fought for his country and for his flag, Virginia," said the Judge, who had scarcely spoken until then. "No, I could not bear to read them now, when those who should love that country are leaving it in passion."

There was a heavy silence. Virginia did not dare to look at her father. But the Colonel said, gently:—

"Not in passion, Silas, but in sorrow."

The Judge tightened his lips. But the effort was beyond him, and the flood within him broke loose.

"Colonel Carvel," he cried, "South Carolina is mad! She is departing in sin, in order that a fiendish practice may be perpetuated. If her people stopped to think they would know that slavery cannot exist except by means of this Union. But let this milksop of a President do his worst. We have chosen a man who has the strength to say, 'You *shall* not go!' "

It was an awful moment. The saving grace of it was that respect and love for her father filled Virginia's heart. In his just anger Colonel Carvel remembered that he was the host, and strove to think only of his affection for his old friend.

"To invade a sovereign state, sir, is a crime against the sacred spirit of this government," he said.

"There is no such thing as a sovereign state, sir," exclaimed the Judge, hotly. "I am an American, and not a Missourian."

"When the time comes, sir," said the Colonel, with dignity, "Missouri will join with her sister sovereign states against oppression."

"Missouri will not secede, sir."

"Why not, sir?" demanded the Colonel.

"Because, sir, when the worst comes, the Soothing Syrup men will rally for the Union. And there are enough loyal people here to keep her straight."

"Dutchmen, sir! Hessians! Foreign Republican hirelings, sir," exclaimed the Colonel, standing up. "We shall drive them like sheep if they oppose us. You are drilling them now that they may murder your own blood when you think the time is ripe."

The Colonel did not hear Virginia leave the room, so softly had she gone. He made a grand figure of a man as he stood up, straight and tall, those gray eyes a-kindle at last. But the fire died as quickly as it had flared. Pity had come and quenched it,—pity that an unselfish life of suffering and loneliness should be crowned with these. The Colonel longed then to clasp his friend in his arms. Quarrels they had had by the hundreds, never yet a misunderstanding. God had given to Silas Whipple a nature stern and harsh that repelled all save the charitable few whose gift it was to see below the surface, and Colonel Carvel had been the chief of them. But now the Judge's vision was clouded.

Steadying himself by his chair, he had risen glaring, the loose skin twitching on his sallow face. He began firmly but his voice shook ere he had finished.

"Colonel Carvel," said he, "I expect that the day has come when you go your way and I go mine. It will be better if—we do not meet again, sir."

And so he turned from the man whose friendship had stayed him for the score of years he had battled with his enemies, from that house which had been for so long his only home. For the last time Jackson came forward to help him with his coat. The Judge did not see him, nor did he see the tearful face of a young girl leaning over the banisters above. Ice was on the stones. And Mr. Whipple, blinded by a moisture strange to his eyes, clung to the iron railing as he felt his way down the steps. Before he reached the bottom a stronger arm had seized his own, and was helping him.

The Judge brushed his eyes with his sleeve, and turned a defiant face upon Captain Elijah Brent—then his voice broke. His anger was suddenly gone, and his thoughts had flown back to the Colonel's thousand charities.

"Lige," he said, "Lige, it has come."

In answer the Captain pressed the Judge's hand, nodding vigorously to hide his rising emotion. There was a pause.

"And you, Lige?" said Mr. Whipple, presently.

"My God!" cried the Captain, "I wish I knew."

"Lige," said the Judge, gravely, "you're too good a man to be for Soothing Syrup."

The Captain choked.

"You're too smart to be fooled, Lige," he said, with a note near to pleading. "The time has come when you Bell people and the Douglas people have got to decide. Never in my life did I know it to be good to dodge a question. We've got to be white or black, Lige. Nobody's got much use for the grays. And don't let yourself be fooled with Constitutional Union Meetings and Conditional Union Meetings, and compromises. The time is almost here, Lige, when it will take a rascal to steer a middle course."

Captain Lige listened, and he shifted from one foot to the othe:, and rubbed his hands, which were red. Some odd trick of the mind had put into his head two people—Eliphalet Hopper and Jacob Cluyme. Was he like them?

"Lige, you've got to decide. Do you love your country, sir? Can you

look on while our own states defy us, and not lift a hand? Can you sit
still while the Governor and all the secessionists in this state are plotting
to take Missouri, too, out of the Union? The militia is riddled with rebels,
and the rest are forming companies of minute men."

"And you Black Republicans," the Captain cried, "have organized
your Dutch Wideawakes, and are arming them to resist Americans born."

"They are Americans by our Constitution, sir, which the South pre-
tends to revere," cried the Judge. "And they are showing themselves better Americans than many who have been on the soil for generations."

"My sympathies are with the South," said the Captain, doggedly,
"and my love is for the South."

"And your conscience?" said the Judge.

There was no answer. Both men raised their eyes to the house of him
whose loving hospitality had been a light in the lives of both. When at
last the Captain spoke, his voice was rent with feeling.

"Judge," he began, "when I was a poor young man on the old *Vicksburg,* second officer under old Stetson, Colonel Carvel used to take me
up to his house on Fourth Street to dinner. And he gave me the clothes
on my back, so that I might not be ashamed before the fashion which
came there. He treated me like a son, sir. One day the sheriff sold the
Vicksburg. You remember it. That left me high and dry in the mud.
Who bought her, sir? Colonel Carvel. And he says to me, 'Lige, you're
captain now, the youngest captain on the river. And she's your boat.
You can pay me principal and interest when you get ready.' Judge
Whipple, I never had any other home than right in this house. I never
had any other pleasure than bringing Jinny presents, and tryin' to show
'em gratitude. He took me into his house and cared for me at a time
when I wanted to go to the devil along with the stevedores—when I was
a wanderer he kept me out of the streets, and out of temptation. Judge,
I'd a heap rather go down and jump off the stern of my boat than step
in here and tell him I'd fight for the North."

The Judge steadied himself on his hickory stick and walked off without a word. For a while Captain Lige stood staring after him. Then he
slowly climbed the steps and disappeared.

CHAPTER XV

MUTTERINGS

EARLY in the next year, 1861,—that red year in the Calendar of our history,—several gentlemen met secretly in the dingy counting-room of a prominent citizen to consider how the state of Missouri might be saved to the Union. One of these gentlemen was Judge Whipple; another, Mr. Brinsmade; and another a masterly and fearless lawyer who afterward became a general, and who shall be mentioned in these pages as the Leader. By his dash and boldness and statesmanlike grasp of a black situation St. Louis was snatched from the very bosom of secession.

Alas, that chronicles may not stretch so as to embrace all great men of a time. There is Captain Nathaniel Lyon,—name with the fateful ring. Nathaniel Lyon, with the wild red hair and blue eye, born and bred a soldier, ordered to St. Louis, and become subordinate to a wavering officer of ordnance. Lyon was one who brooked no trifling. He had the face of a man who knows his mind and intention; the quick speech and action which go with this. Red tape made by the reel to bind him, he broke. Courts-martial had no terrors for him. He proved the ablest of lieutenants to the strong civilian who was the Leader. Both were the men of the occasion. If God had willed that the South should win, there would have been no occasion.

Even as Judge Whipple had said, the time was come for all men to decide. Out of the way, all hopes of compromises that benumbed Washington. No Constitutional Unionists, no Douglas Democrats, no Republicans now.

All must work to save the ship. The speech-making was not done with yet. Partisanship must be overcome, and patriotism instilled in its place. One day Stephen Brice saw the Leader go into Judge Whipple's room, and presently he was sent for. After that he was heard of in various out-of-the-way neighborhoods, exhorting all men to forget their quarrels and uphold the flag.

The Leader himself knew not night from day in his toil,—organizing, conciliating, compelling when necessary. Letters passed between him

and Springfield. And, after that solemn inauguration, between him and
Washington. It was an open secret that the Governor of Missouri held
out his arms to Jefferson Davis, just elected President of the new Southern Confederacy. It soon became plain to the feeblest brain what the
Leader and his friends had perceived long before, that the Governor
intended to use the militia (purged of Yankee sympathizers) to save
the state for the South.

The Government Arsenal, with its stores of arms and ammunition, was
the prize. This building and its grounds lay to the south of the City,
overlooking the river. It was in command of a doubting major of ordnance; the corps of officers of Jefferson Barracks hard by was mottled
with secession. Trade was still. The Mississippi below was practically
closed. In all the South, Pickens and Sumter alone stood stanch to the
flag. A general, wearing the uniform of the army of the United States,
surrendered the whole state of Texas.

The St. Louis Arsenal was next in succession, and the little band of
regulars at the Barracks was powerless to save it. What could the
Leader and Captain Lyon do without troops? That was the question
that rang in Stephen's head, and in the heads of many others. For, if
President Lincoln sent troops to St. Louis, that would precipitate the
trouble. And the President had other uses for the handful in the army.

There came a rain-sodden night when a mysterious message arrived
at the little house in Olive Street. Both anxiety and pride were in Mrs.
Brice's eyes as they followed her son out of the door. At Twelfth Street
two men were lounging on the corners, each of whom glanced at him
listlessly as he passed. He went up a dark and narrow stair into a lighted
hall with shrouded windows. Men with sober faces were forming line
on the sawdust of the floors. The Leader was there giving military orders in a low voice. That marked the beginning of the aggressive Union
movement.

Stephen, standing apart at the entrance, remarked that many of the
men were Germans. Indeed, he spied his friend Tiefel there, and presently Richter came from the ranks to greet him.

"My friend," he said, "you are made second lieutenant of our company, the *Black Jaegers*."

"But I have never drilled in my life," said Stephen.

"Never mind. Come and see the Leader."

The Leader, smiling a little, put a vigorous stop to his protestations, and told him to buy a tactics. The next man Stephen saw was big Tom Catherwood, who blushed to the line of his hair as he returned Stephen's grip.

"Tom, what does this mean?" he asked.

"Well," said Tom, embarrassed, "a fellow has got to do what he think's right."

"And your family?" asked Stephen.

A spasm crossed Tom's face.

"I reckon they'll disown me, Stephen, when they find it out."

Richter walked home as far as Stephen's house. He was to take the Fifth Street car for South St. Louis. And they talked of Tom's courage, and of the broad and secret military organization the Leader had planned that night. But Stephen did not sleep till the dawn. Was he doing right? Could he afford to risk his life in the war that was coming, and leave his mother dependent upon charity?

It was shortly after this that Stephen paid his last visit for many a long day upon Miss Puss Russell. It was a Sunday afternoon, and Puss was entertaining, as usual, a whole parlor-full of young men, whose leanings and sympathies Stephen divined while taking off his coat in the hall. Then he heard Miss Russell cry:—

"I believe that they are drilling those nasty Dutch hirelings in secret."

"I am sure they are," said George Catherwood. "One of the halls is on Twelfth Street, and they have sentries posted out so that you can't get near them. Pa has an idea that Tom goes there. And he told him that if he ever got evidence of it, he'd show him the door."

"Do you really think that Tom is with the Yankees?" asked Jack Brinsmade.

"Tom's a fool," said George, with emphasis, "but he isn't a coward. He'd just as soon tell Pa to-morrow that he was drilling if the Yankee leaders wished it known."

"Virginia will never speak to him again," said Eugénie, in an awed voice.

"Pooh!" said Puss, "Tom never had a chance with Jinny. Did he, George? Clarence is in high favor now. Did you ever know any one to change so, since this military business has begun? He acts like a colonel. I hear that they are thinking of making him captain of a company of dragoons."

"They are," George answered. "And that is the company I intend to join."

"Well," began Puss, with her usual recklessness, "it's a good thing for Clarence that all this is happening. I know somebody else—"

Poor Stephen in the hall knew not whether to stay or fly. An accident decided the question. Emily Russell came down the stairs at that instant and spoke to him. As the two entered the parlor, there was a hush pregnant with many things unsaid. Puss's face was scarlet, but her hand was cold as she held it out to him. For the first time in that house he felt like an intruder. Jack Brinsmade bowed with great ceremony, and took his departure. There was scarcely a distant cordiality in the greeting of the other young men. And Puss, whose tongue was loosed again, talked rapidly of entertainments to which Stephen either had not been invited, or from which he had stayed away. The rest of the company were almost moodily silent.

Profoundly depressed, Stephen sat straight in the velvet chair, awaiting a seasonable time to bring his visit to a close. This was to be the last, then, of his intercourse with a warm-hearted and lovable people. This was to be the end of his friendship with this impetuous and generous girl who had done so much to brighten his life since he had come to St. Louis. Henceforth this house would be shut to him, and all others save Mr. Brinsmade's.

Presently, in one of the intervals of Miss Russell's feverish talk, he rose to go. Dusk was gathering, and a deep and ominous silence penetrated like the shadows into the tall room. No words came to him. Impulsively, almost tearfully, Puss put her hand in his. Then she pressed it unexpectedly, so that he had to gulp down a lump that was in his throat. Just then a loud cry was heard from without, the men jumped from their chairs, and something heavy dropped on the carpet.

Some ran to the window, others to the door. Directly across the street was the house of Mr. Harmsworth, a noted Union man. One of the third story windows was open, and out of it was pouring a mass of gray wood smoke. George Catherwood was the first to speak.

"I hope it will burn down," he cried.

Stephen picked up the object on the floor, which had dropped from his pocket, and handed it to him.

It was a revolver.

CHAPTER XVI

THE GUNS OF SUMTER

WINTER had vanished. Spring was come with a hush. Toward a little island set in the blue waters of Charleston harbor anxious eyes were strained.

Was the flag still there?

God alone may count the wives and mothers who listened in the still hours of the night for the guns of Sumter. One sultry night in April Stephen's mother awoke with fear in her heart, for she had heard them. Hark! that is the roar now, faint but sullen. That is the red flash far across the black Southern sky. For in our beds are the terrors and cruelties of life revealed to us. There is a demon to be faced, and fought alone.

Mrs. Brice was a brave woman. She walked that night with God.

Stephen, too, awoke. The lightning revealed her as she bent over him. On the wings of memory he flew back to his childhood in the great Boston house with the rounded front, and he saw the nursery with its high windows looking out across the Common. Often in the dark had she come to him thus, her gentle hand passing over him to feel if he were covered.

"What is it, mother?" he said.

She said: "Stephen, I am afraid that the war has come."

He sat up, blindly. Even he did not guess the agony in her heart.

"You will have to go, Stephen."

It was long before his answer came.

"You know that I cannot, mother. We have nothing left but the little I earn. And if I were—" He did not finish the sentence, for he felt her trembling. But she said again, with that courage which seems woman's alone:—

"Remember Wilton Brice. Stephen—I can get along. I can sew."

It was the hour he had dreaded, stolen suddenly upon him out of the night. How many times had he rehearsed this scene to himself! He,

Stephen Brice, who had preached and slaved and drilled for the Union, a renegade to be shunned by friend and foe alike! He had talked for his country, but he would not risk his life for it. He heard them repeating the charge. He saw them passing him silently on the street. Shamefully he remembered the time, five months agone, when he had worn the very uniform of his Revolutionary ancestor. And high above the tier of his accusers he saw one face, and the look of it stung to the very quick of his soul.

Before the storm he had fallen asleep in sheer weariness of the struggle, that face shining through the black veil of the darkness. If he were to march away in the blue of his country (alas, not of hers!) she would respect him for risking life for conviction. If he stayed at home, she would not understand. It was his plain duty to his mother. And yet he knew that Virginia Carvel and the women like her were ready to follow with bare feet the march of the soldiers of the South.

The rain was come now, in a flood. Stephen's mother could not see in the blackness the bitterness on his face. Above the roar of the waters she listened for his voice.

"I will not go, mother," he said. "If at length every man is needed, that will be different."

"It is for you to decide, my son," she answered. "There are many ways in which you can serve your country here. But remember that you may have to face hard things."

"I have had to do that before, mother," he replied calmly. "I cannot leave you dependent upon charity."

She went back into her room to pray, for she knew that he had laid his ambition at her feet.

It was not until a week later that the dreaded news came. All through the Friday shells had rained on the little fort while Charleston looked on. No surrender yet. Through a wide land was that numbness which precedes action. Force of habit sent men to their places of business, to sit idle. A prayerful Sunday intervened. Sumter had fallen. South Carolina had shot to bits the flag she had once revered.

On the Monday came the call of President Lincoln for volunteers. Missouri was asked for her quota. The outraged reply of her governor went back,—never would she furnish troops to invade her sister states. Little did Governor Jackson foresee that Missouri was to stand fifth of all the Union in the number of men she was to give. To her was credited in the end even more men than stanch Massachusetts.

The noise of preparation was in the city—in the land. On the Monday morning, when Stephen went wearily to the office, he was met by Richter at the top of the stairs, who seized his shoulders and looked into his face. The light of the zealot was on Richter's own.

"We shall drill every night now, my friend, until further orders. It is the Leader's word. Until we go to the front, Stephen, to put down rebellion." Stephen sank into a chair, and bowed his head. What would he think,—this man who had fought and suffered and renounced his native land for his convictions? Who in this nobler allegiance was ready to die for them? How was he to confess to Richter, of all men?

"Carl," he said at length, "I—I cannot go."

"You—you cannot go? You who have done so much already! And why?"

Stephen did not answer. But Richter, suddenly divining, laid his hands impulsively on Stephen's shoulders.

"*Ach*, I see," he said. "Stephen, I have saved some money. It shall be for your mother while you are away."

At first Stephen was too surprised for speech. Then, in spite of his feelings, he stared at the German with a new appreciation of his character. Then he could merely shake his head.

"Is it not for the Union?" implored Richter. "I would give a fortune, if I had it. Ah, my friend, that would please me so. And I do not need the money now. I have—nobody."

Spring was in the air; the first faint smell of verdure wafted across the river on the wind. Stephen turned to the open window, tears of intense agony in his eyes. In that instant he saw the regiment marching, and the flag flying at its head.

"It is my duty to stay here, Carl," he said brokenly.

Richter took an appealing step toward him and stopped. He realized that with this young New Englander a decision once made was unalterable. In all his knowledge of Stephen he never remembered him to change. With the demonstrative sympathy of his race, he yearned to comfort him, and knew not how. Two hundred years of Puritanism had barriers not to be broken down.

At the end of the office the stern figure of the Judge appeared.

"Mr. Brice!" he said sharply.

Stephen followed him into the littered room behind the ground-glass door, scarce knowing what to expect,—and scarce caring, as on that first day he had gone in there. Mr. Whipple himself closed the door, and then the transom. Stephen felt those keen eyes searching him from their hiding-place.

"Mr. Brice," he said at last, "the President has called for seventy-five thousand volunteers to crush this rebellion. They will go, and be swallowed up, and more will go to fill their places. Mr. Brice, people will tell you that the war will be over in ninety days. But I tell you, sir, that it will not be over in seven times ninety days." He brought down his fist heavily upon the table. "This, sir, will be a war to the death. One side or the other will fight until their blood is all let, and until their homes are all ruins." He darted at Stephen one look from under those fierce eyebrows. "Do you intend to go, sir?"

Stephen met the look squarely. "No, sir," he answered, steadily, "not now."

"Humph," said the Judge. Then he began what seemed a never-ending search among the papers on his desk. At length he drew out a letter, put on his spectacles and read it, and finally put it down again.

"Stephen," said Mr. Whipple, "you are doing a courageous thing. But if we elect to follow our conscience in this world, we must not expect to escape persecution, sir. Two weeks ago," he continued slowly, "two weeks ago I had a letter from Mr. Lincoln about matters here. He mentions you."

"He remembers me!" cried Stephen.

The Judge smiled a little. "Mr. Lincoln never forgets any one," said he. "He wishes me to extend to you his thanks for your services to the Republican party, and sends you his kindest regards."

This was the first and only time that Mr. Whipple spoke to him of his labors. Stephen has often laughed at this since, and said that he would not have heard of them at all had not the Judge's sense of duty compelled him to convey the message. And it was with a lighter heart than he had felt for many a day that he went out of the door.

Some weeks later, five regiments were mustered into the service of the United States. The Leader was in command of one. And in response to his appeals, despite the presence of officers of higher rank, the President had given Captain Nathaniel Lyon supreme command in Missouri.

Stephen stood among the angry, jeering crowd that lined the streets as the regiments marched past. Here were the *Black Jaegers*. No wonder the crowd laughed. Their step was not as steady, nor their files as straight, as Company A. There was Richter, his head high, his blue eyes defiant. And there was little Tiefel marching in that place of sec-

ond lieutenant that Stephen himself should have filled. Here was another company, and at the end of the first four, big Tom Catherwood.
His father had disowned him the day before. His two brothers, George
and little Spencer, were in a house not far away,—a house from which
a strange flag drooped.

Clouds were lowering over the city, and big drops falling, as Stephen
threaded his way homeward, the damp and gloom of the weather in his
very soul. He went past the house where the strange flag hung against
its staff. In that big city it flaunted all unchallenged. The house was
thrown wide open that day, and in its windows lounged young men
of honored families. And while they joked of German boorishness and
Yankee cowardice they held rifles across their knees to avenge any
insult to the strange banner that they had set up. In the hall, through
the open doorway, the mouth of a shotted field gun could be seen. The
guardians were the *Minute Men,* organized to maintain the honor and
dignity of the state of Missouri.

Across the street from the house was gathered a knot of curious people, and among these Stephen paused. Two young men were standing
on the steps, and one was Clarence Colfax. His hands were in his pockets,
and a careless, scornful smile was on his face when he glanced down
into the street. Stephen caught that smile. Anger swept over him in a
hot flame, as at the slave auction years agone. That was the unquench-
able fire of the war. The blood throbbed in his temples as his feet obeyed,
—and yet he stopped.

What right had he to pull down that flag, to die on the pavement before that house?

CHAPTER XVII

CAMP JACKSON

WHAT enthusiasm on that gusty Monday morning, the Sixth of May, 1861! Twelfth Street to the north of the Market House is full three hundred feet across, and the militia of the Sovereign State of Missouri is gathering there. Thence by order of her Governor they are to march to Camp Jackson for a week of drill and instruction.

Half a mile nearer the river, on the house of the Minute Men, the strange flag leaps wildly in the wind this day.

On Twelfth Street the sun is shining, drums are beating, and bands are playing, and bright aides dashing hither and thither on spirited chargers. One by one the companies are marching up, and taking place in line; the city companies in natty gray fatigue, the country companies often in their Sunday clothes. But they walk with heads erect and chests out, and the ladies wave their gay parasols and cheer them. Here are the aristocratic St. Louis Grays, Company A; there come the Washington Guards and Washington Blues, and Laclede Guards and Missouri Guards and *Davis* Guards. Yes, this is Secession Day, this Monday. And the colors are the Stars and Stripes and the Arms of Missouri crossed.

What are they waiting for? Why don't they move? Hark! A clatter and a cloud of dust by the market place, an ecstasy of cheers running in waves the length of the crowd. Make way for the dragoons! Here they come at last, four and four, the horses prancing and dancing and pointing quivering ears at the tossing sea of hats and parasols and ribbons. Maude Catherwood squeezes Virginia's arm. There, riding in front, erect and firm in the saddle, is Captain Clarence Colfax. Virginia is red and white and red again,—true colors of the Confederacy. How proud she was of him now! How ashamed that she ever doubted him! Oh, that was his true calling, a soldier's life. In that moment she saw him at the head of armies from the South, driving the Yankee hordes northward and still northward until the roar of the lakes warns them of annihilation. She saw his chivalry sparing them. Yes, this is Secession Monday.

Down to a trot they slow, Clarence's black thoroughbred arching his

220

long neck, proud as his master of the squadron which follows, four and four. The square young man of bone and sinew in the first four, whose horse is built like a Crusader's, is George Catherwood. And Eugénie gives a cry and points to the rear where Maurice is riding.

Whose will be the Arsenal now? Can the Yankee regiments with their slouchy Dutchmen hope to capture it? If there are any Yankees in Twelfth Street that day, they are silent. Yes, there are some. And there are some—even in the ranks of this Militia—who will fight for the Union. These are sad indeed.

There is another wait, the companies standing at ease. Some of the dragoons dismount, but not the handsome young captain, who rides straight to the bright group which has caught his eye. Colonel Carvel wrings his gauntleted hand.

"Clarence, we are proud of you, sir," he says.

And Virginia repeats his words, her eyes sparkling, her fingers caressing the silken curve of Jefferson's neck. "Clarence, you will drive Captain Lyon and his Hessians into the river."

"Hush, Jinny," he answered, "we are merely going into camp to learn to drill, that we may be ready to defend the state when the time comes."

Virginia laughed. "I had forgotten," she said.

"You will have your cousin court-martialed, my dear," said the Colonel.

Just then the call is sounded. But he must needs press Virginia's hand first, and allow admiring Maude and Eugénie to press his. Then he goes off at a slow canter to join his dragoons, waving his glove at them, and turning to give the sharp order, "Attention!" to his squadron.

Virginia is deliriously happy. Once more she has swept from her heart every vestige of doubt. Now is Clarence the man she can admire. Chosen unanimously captain of the Squadron but a few days since, Clarence had taken command like a veteran. George Catherwood and Maurice had told the story.

And now at last the city is to shake off the dust of the North. "On to Camp Jackson!" was the cry. The bands are started, the general and staff begin to move, and the column swings into the Olive Street road, followed by a concourse of citizens awheel and afoot, the horse cars crowded. Virginia and Maude and the Colonel in the Carvel carriage, and behind Ned, on the box, is their luncheon in a hamper. Standing up, the girls can just see the nodding plumes of the dragoons far to the front.

Olive Street, now paved with hot granite and disfigured by trolley wires, was a country road then. Green trees took the place of crowded

rows of houses and stores, and little "bob-tail" yellow cars were drawn by
plodding mules to an inclosure in a timbered valley, surrounded by a
board fence, known as Lindell Grove. It was then a resort, a picnic
ground, what is now covered by close residences which have long shown
the wear of time.

Into Lindell Grove flocked the crowd, the rich and the poor, the proprietor and the salesmen, to watch the soldiers pitch their tents under
the spreading trees. The galiant dragoons were off to the west, across a
little stream which trickled through the grounds. By the side of it Virginia and Maude, enchanted, beheld Captain Colfax shouting his orders
while his troopers dragged the canvas from the wagons, and staggered
under it to the line. Alas! that the girls were there! The Captain lost his
temper, his troopers, perspiring over Gordian knots in the ropes, uttered
strange soldier oaths, while the mad wind which blew that day played
a hundred pranks.

To the discomfiture of the young ladies, Colonel Carvel pulled his
goatee and guffawed. Virginia was for moving away.

"How mean, Pa," she said indignantly. "How can you expect them to
do it right the first day, and in this wind?"

"Oh, Jinny, look at Maurice!" exclaimed Maude, giggling. "He is
pulled over on his head."

The Colonel roared. And the gentlemen and ladies who were standing
by laughed, too. Virginia did not laugh. It was all too serious for her.

"You will see that they can fight," she said. "They can beat the Yankees and Dutch."

This speech made the Colonel glance around him. Then he smiled,—
in response to other smiles.

"My dear," he said, "you must remember that this is a peaceable camp
of instruction of the state militia. There fly the Stars and Stripes from
the general's tent. Do you see that they are above the state flag? Jinny,
you forget yourself."

Jinny stamped her foot.

"Oh, I hate dissimulation," she cried. "Why can't we say outright that
we are going to run that detestable Captain Lyon and his Yankees and
Hessians out of the Arsenal?"

"Why not, Colonel Carvel?" cried Maude. She had forgotten that one
of her brothers was with the Yankees and Hessians.

"Why aren't women made generals and governors?" said the Colonel.

"If we were," answered Virginia, "something might be accomplished."

"Isn't Clarence enough of a fire-eater to suit you?" asked her father.

But the tents were pitched, and at that moment the young Captain was seen to hand over his horse to an orderly, and to come toward them. He was followed by George Catherwood.

"Come, Jinny," cried her cousin, "let us go over to the main camp."

"And walk on Davis Avenue," said Virginia, flushing with pride. "Isn't there a Davis Avenue?"

"Yes, and a Lee Avenue, and a Beauregard Avenue," said George, taking his sister's arm.

"We shall walk in them all," said Virginia.

What a scene of animation it was! The rustling trees, and the young grass of early May, and the two hundred and forty tents in lines of military precision. Up and down the grassy streets flowed the promenade, proud fathers and mothers, and sweethearts and sisters and wives in gala dress. Wear your bright gowns now, you devoted women. The day is coming when you will make them over and over again, or tear them to lint, to stanch the blood of these young men who wear their new gray so well.

Every afternoon Virginia drove with her father and her aunt to Camp Jackson. All the fashion and beauty of the city were there. The bands played, the black coachmen flecked the backs of their shining horses, and walking in the avenues or seated under the trees were natty young gentlemen in white trousers and brass-buttoned jackets. All was not soldier fare at the regimental messes. Cakes and jellies and even ices and more substantial dainties were laid beneath those tents. Dress parade was one long sigh of delight. Better not to have been born than to have been a young man in St. Louis, early in Camp Jackson week, and not be a militiaman.

One young man whom we know, however, had little of pomp and vanity about him,—none other than the young manager (some whispered "silent partner") of Carvel & Company. If Mr. Eliphalet had had political ambition, or political leanings, during the half-year which had just passed, he had not shown them. Mr. Cluyme (no mean business man himself) had pronounced Eliphalet a conservative young gentleman who attended to his own affairs and let the mad country take care of itself. This is precisely the wise course Mr. Hopper chose. Seeing a regiment of Missouri Volunteers slouching down Fifth Street in citizens' clothes, he had been remarked to smile cynically. But he kept his opinions so close that he was supposed not to have any.

On Thursday of Camp Jackson week, an event occurred in Mr. Carvel's store which excited a buzz of comment. Mr. Hopper announced to Mr. Barbo, the book-keeper, that he should not be there after four o'clock. To be sure, times were more than dull. The Colonel that morning had read over some two dozen letters from Texas and the Southwest, telling of the impossibility of meeting certain obligations in the present state of the country. The Colonel had gone home to dinner with his brow furrowed. On the other hand, Mr. Hopper's equanimity was spoken of at the widow's table.

At four o'clock, Mr. Hopper took an Olive Street car, tucking himself into the far corner where he would not be disturbed by any ladies who might enter. In the course of an hour or so, he alighted at the western gate of the camp on the Olive Street road. Refreshing himself with a little tobacco, he let himself be carried leisurely by the crowd between the rows of tents. A philosophy of his own (which many men before and since have adopted) permitted him to stare with a superior good nature at the open love-making around him. He imagined his own figure,—which was already growing a little stout,—in a light gray jacket and duck trousers, and laughed. Eliphalet was not burdened with illusions of that kind. These heroes might have their hero-worship. Life held something dearer for him.

As he was sauntering toward a deserted seat at the foot of a tree, it so chanced that he was overtaken by Mr. Cluyme and his daughter Belle. Only that morning, this gentleman, in glancing through the real estate column of his newspaper, had fallen upon a deed of sale which made him wink. He reminded his wife that Mr. Hopper had not been to supper of late. So now Mr. Cluyme held out his hand with more than common cordiality. When Mr. Hopper took it, the fingers did not close any too tightly over his own. But it may be well to remark that Mr. Hopper himself did not do any squeezing. He took off his hat grudgingly to Miss Belle. He had never liked the custom.

"I hope you will take pot luck with us soon again, Mr. Hopper," said the elder gentleman. "We only have plain and simple things, but they are wholesome, sir. Dainties are poor things to work on. I told that to his Royal Highness when he was here last fall. He was speaking to me on the merits of roast beef—"

"It's a fine day," said Mr. Hopper.

"So it is," Mr. Cluyme assented. Letting his gaze wander over the camp, he added casually: "I see that they have got a few mortars and howitzers since yesterday. I suppose that is the stuff we heard so much about, which came on the *Swan* marked 'marble.' They say Jeff Davis sent the stuff to 'em from the Government arsenal the Secesh captured at Baton Rouge. They're pretty near ready to move on *our* arsenal now."

Mr. Hopper listened with composure. He was not greatly interested in this matter which had stirred the city to the quick. Neither had Mr. Cluyme spoken as one who was deeply moved. Just then, as if to spare the pains of a reply, a "Jenny Lind" passed them. Miss Belle recognized the carriage immediately as belonging to an elderly lady who was well known in St. Louis. Every day she drove out, dressed in black bomba-zine, and heavily veiled. But she was blind. As the mother-in-law of the stalwart Union leader of the city, Miss Belle's comment about her appearance in Camp Jackson was not out of place.

"Well!" she exclaimed, "I'd like to know what she's doing here!"

Mr. Hopper's answer revealed a keenness which, in the course of a few days, engendered in Mr. Cluyme as lusty a respect as he was capable of.

"I don't know," said Eliphalet; "but I cal'late she's got stouter."

"What do you mean by that?" Miss Belle demanded.

"That Union principles must be healthy," said he, and laughed.

Miss Cluyme was prevented from following up this enigma. The appearance of two people on Davis Avenue drove the veiled lady from her mind. Eliphalet, too, had seen them. One was the tall young Captain of Dragoons, in cavalry boots, and the other a young lady with dark brown hair, in a lawn dress.

"Just look at them!" cried Miss Belle. "They think they are alone in the garden of Eden. Virginia didn't use to care for him. But since he's a captain, and has got a uniform, she's come round pretty quick. I'm thankful I never had any silly notions about uniforms."

She glanced at Eliphalet, to find that his eyes were fixed on the approaching couple.

"Clarence is handsome, but worthless," she continued in her sprightly way. "I believe Jinny will be fool enough to marry him. Do you think she's so *very* pretty, Mr. Hopper?"

Mr. Hopper lied.

"Neither do I," Miss Belle assented. And upon that, greatly to the astonishment of Eliphalet, she left him and ran towards them. "Virginia!" she cried; "Jinny, I have something so interesting to tell you!"

Virginia turned impatiently. The look she bestowed upon Miss Cluyme was not one of welcome, but Belle was not sensitive. Putting her arm through Virginia's, she sauntered off with the pair toward the parade grounds, Clarence maintaining now a distance of three feet, and not caring to hide his annoyance.

Eliphalet's eyes smouldered, following the three until they were lost in the crowd. That expression of Virginia's had reminded him of a time, years gone, when she had come into the store on her return from Kentucky, and had ordered him to tell her father of her arrival. He had smarted then. And Eliphalet was not the sort to get over smarts.

"A beautiful young lady," remarked Mr. Cluyme. "And a deserving one, Mr. Hopper. Now, she is my notion of quality. She has wealth, and manners, and looks. And her father is a good man. Too bad he holds such views on secession. I have always thought, sir, that you were singularly fortunate in your connection with him."

There was a point of light now in each of Mr. Hopper's green eyes. But Mr. Cluyme continued:—

"What a pity, I say, that he should run the risk of crippling himself by his opinions. Times are getting hard."

"Yes," said Mr. Hopper.

"And southwestern notes are not worth the paper they are written on—"

But Mr. Cluyme has misjudged his man. If he had come to Eliphalet for information of Colonel Carvel's affairs, or of any one else's affairs, he was not likely to get it. It is not meet to repeat here the long business conversation which followed. Suffice it to say that Mr. Cluyme, who was in dry goods himself, was as ignorant when he left Eliphalet as when he met him. But he had a greater respect than ever for the shrewdness of the business manager of Carvel & Company.

* * * * * * *

That same Thursday, when the first families of the city were whispering jubilantly in each other's ears of the safe arrival of the artillery and stands of arms at Camp Jackson, something of significance was happening within the green inclosure of the walls of the United States arsenal, far to the southward.

The days had become alike in sadness to Stephen. Richter gone, and the Judge often away in mysterious conference, he was left for hours at a spell the sole tenant of the office. Fortunately there was work of Richter's and of Mr. Whipple's left undone that kept him busy. This

Thursday morning, however, he found the Judge getting into that best black coat which he wore on occasions. His manner had recently lost much of its gruffness.

"Stephen," said he, "they are serving out cartridges and uniforms to the regiments at the arsenal. Would you like to go down with me?"

"Does that mean Camp Jackson?" asked Stephen, when they had reached the street.

"Captain Lyon is not the man to sit still and let the Governor take the first trick, sir," said the Judge.

As they got on the Fifth Street car, Stephen's attention was at once attracted to a gentleman who sat in a corner, with his children about him. He was lean, and he had a face of great keenness and animation. He had no sooner spied Judge Whipple than he beckoned to him with a kind of military abruptness.

"That is Major William T. Sherman," said the Judge to Stephen. "He used to be in the army, and fought in the Mexican War. He came here two months ago to be the President of this Fifth Street car line."

They crossed over to him, the Judge introducing Stephen to Major Sherman, who looked at him very hard, and then decided to bestow on him a vigorous nod.

"Well, Whipple," he said, "this nation is going to the devil, eh?"

Stephen could not resist a smile. For it was a bold man who expressed radical opinions (provided they were not Southern opinions) in a St. Louis street car early in '61.

The Judge shook his head. "We may pull out," he said.

"Pull out!" exclaimed Mr. Sherman. "Who's man enough in Washington to shake his fist in a rebel's face? Our leniency—our timidity—has paralyzed us, sir."

By this time those in the car began to manifest considerable interest in the conversation. Major Sherman paid them no attention, and the Judge, once launched in an argument, forgot his surroundings.

"I have faith in Mr. Lincoln. He is calling out volunteers."

"Seventy-five thousand for three months!" said the Major, vehemently, "a bucketful on a conflagration! I tell you, Whipple, we'll need all the water we've got in the North."

The Judge expressed his belief in this, and also that Mr. Lincoln would draw all the water before he got through.

"Upon my soul," said Mr. Sherman, "I'm disgusted. Now's the time to stop 'em. The longer we let 'em rear and kick, the harder to break 'em.

You don't catch me going back to the army for three months. If they want me, they've got to guarantee me three years. That's more like it." Turning to Stephen, he added: "Don't you sign any three months' contract, young man."

Stephen grew red. By this time the car was full, and silent. No one had offered to quarrel with the Major. Nor did it seem likely that any one would.

"I'm afraid I can't go, sir."

"Why not?" demanded Mr. Sherman.

"Because, sir," said the Judge, bluntly, "his mother's a widow, and they have no money. He was a lieutenant in one of Blair's companies before the call came."

The Major looked at Stephen, and his expression changed.

"Find it pretty hard?" he asked.

Stephen's expression must have satisfied him, but he nodded again, more vigorously than before.

"Just you *wait*, Mr. Brice," he said. "It won't hurt you any."

Stephen was grateful. But he hoped to fall out of the talk. Much to his discomfiture, the Major gave him another of those queer looks. His whole manner, and even his appearance, reminded Stephen strangely of Captain Elijah Brent.

"Aren't you the young man who made the Union speech in Mercantile Library Hall?"

"Yes, sir," said the Judge. "He is."

At that the Major put out his hand impulsively, and gripped Stephen's.

"Well, sir," he said, "I have yet to read a more sensible speech, except some of Abraham Lincoln's. Brinsmade gave it to me to read. Whipple, that speech reminded me of Lincoln. It was his style. Where did you get it, Mr. Brice?" he demanded.

"I heard Mr. Lincoln's debate with Judge Douglas at Freeport," said Stephen, beginning to be amused.

The Major laughed.

"I admire your frankness, sir," he said. "I meant to say that its logic rather than its substance reminded me of Lincoln."

"I tried to learn what *I* could from him, Major Sherman."

At length the car stopped, and they passed into the Arsenal grounds. Drawn up in lines on the green grass were four regiments, all at last in the blue of their country's service. Old soldiers with baskets of cartridges were stepping from file to file, giving handfuls to the recruits. Many of these thrust them in their pockets, for there were not enough belts to go around. The men were standing at ease, and as Stephen saw them laughing and joking lightheartedly his depression returned. It was driven away again by Major Sherman's vivacious comments. For suddenly Captain Lyon, the man of the hour, came into view.

"Look at him!" cried the Major, "he's a man after my own heart. Just look at him running about with his hair flying in the wind, and the papers bulging from his pockets. Not dignified, eh, Whipple? But this isn't the time to be dignified. If there were some like Lyon in Washington, our troops would be halfway to New Orleans by this time. Don't talk to me of Washington! Just look at him!"

The gallant Captain was a sight, indeed, and vividly described by Major Sherman's picturesque words as he raced from regiment to regiment, and from company to company, with his sandy hair awry, pointing, gesticulating, commanding. In him Stephen recognized the force that had swept aside stubborn army veterans of wavering faith, that snapped the tape with which they had tied him.

Would he be duped by the Governor's ruse of establishing a State Camp at this time? Stephen, as he gazed at him, was sure that he would not. This man could see to the bottom, through every specious argument. Little matters of law and precedence did not trouble him. Nor did he believe elderly men in authority when they told him gravely that the state troops were there for peace.

After the ranks were broken, Major Sherman and the Judge went to talk to Captain Lyon and the Union Leader, who was now a Colonel of one of the Volunteer regiments. Stephen sought Richter, who told him that the regiments were to assemble the morning of the morrow, prepared to march.

"To Camp Jackson?" asked Stephen.

Richter shrugged his shoulders.

"We are not consulted, my friend," he said. "Will you come into my quarters and have a bottle of beer with Tiefel?"

Stephen went. It was not their fault that his sense of their comradeship was gone. To him it was as if the ties that had bound him to them were asunder, and he was become an outcast.

CHAPTER XVIII

THE STONE THAT IS REJECTED

THAT Friday morning Stephen awoke betimes with a sense that something was to happen. For a few moments he lay still in the half comprehension which comes after sleep, when suddenly he remembered yesterday's incidents at the Arsenal, and leaped out of bed.

"I think that Lyon is going to attack Camp Jackson to-day," he said to his mother after breakfast, when Hester had left the room.

Mrs. Brice dropped her knitting in her lap.

"Why, Stephen?"

"I went down to the Arsenal with the Judge yesterday and saw them finishing the equipment of the new regiments. Something was in the wind. Any one could see that from the way Lyon was flying about. I think he must have proof that the Camp Jackson people have received supplies from the South."

Mrs. Brice looked fixedly at her son, and then smiled in spite of the apprehension she felt.

"Is that why you were working over that map of the city last night?" she asked.

"I was trying to see how Lyon would dispose his troops. I meant to tell you about a gentleman we met in the street car, a Major Sherman who used to be in the army. Mr. Brinsmade knows him, and Judge Whipple, and many other prominent men here. He came to St. Louis some months ago to take the position of president of the Fifth Street Line. He is the keenest, the most original man I have ever met. As long as I live I shall never forget his description of Lyon."

"Is the Major going back into the army?" said Mrs. Brice. Stephen did not remark the little falter in her voice. He laughed over the recollection of the conversation in the street car.

"Not unless matters in Washington change to suit him," he said. "He thinks that things have been very badly managed, and does not scruple to say so anywhere. I could not have believed it possible that two men could have talked in public as he and Judge Whipple did yesterday and not be shot down. I thought that it was as much as a man's life is worth to mention allegiance to the Union here in a crowd. And the way Mr. Sherman pitched into the 'Rebels' in that car full of people was enough to make your hair stand on end."

"He must be a bold man," murmured Mrs. Brice. "Does he think that the—the Rebellion can be put down?"

"Not with seventy-five thousand men, nor with ten times that number."

Mrs. Brice sighed, and furtively wiped her eyes with her handkerchief.

"I am afraid we shall see great misery, Stephen," she said.

He was silent. From that peaceful little room war and its horrors seemed very far away. The morning sun poured in through the south windows and was scattered by the silver on the sideboard. From above, on the wall, Colonel Wilton Brice gazed soberly down. Stephen's eyes lighted on the portrait, and his thoughts flew back to the boyhood days when he used to ply his father with questions about it. Then the picture had suggested only the glory and honor which illumines the page of history. Something worthy to look back upon, to keep one's head high. The hatred and the suffering and the tears, the heartrending, tearing apart for all time of loving ones who have grown together,—these were not upon that canvas. Will war ever be painted with a wart?

The sound of feet was heard on the pavement. Stephen rose, glancing at his mother. Her face was still upon her knitting.

"I am going to the Arsenal," he said. "I must see what is happening."

To her, as has been said, was given wisdom beyond most women. She did not try to prevent him as he kissed her good-bye. But when the door had shut behind him, a little cry escaped her, and she ran to the window to strain her eyes after him until he had turned the corner below.

His steps led him irresistibly past the house of the strange flag, ominously quiet at that early hour. At sight of it anger made him hot again. The car for South St. Louis stood at the end of the line, fast filling with curious people who had read in their papers that morning of the equipment of the new troops. There was little talk among them, and that little guarded.

It was a May morning to rouse a sluggard; the night air tingled into life at the touch of the sunshine, the trees in the flitting glory of their first green. Stephen found the shaded street in front of the Arsenal already filled with an expectant crowd. Sharp commands broke the silence, and he saw the blue regiment forming on the lawn inside the wall. Truly, events were in the air,—great events in which he had no part.

As he stood leaning against a tree-box by the curb, dragged down once more by that dreaded feeling of detachment, he heard familiar voices close beside him. Leaning forward, he saw Eliphalet Hopper and Mr. Cluyme. It was Mr. Cluyme who was speaking.

"Well, Mr. Hopper," he said, "in spite of what you say, I expect you are just as eager as I am to see what is going on. You've taken an early start this morning for sight-seeing."

Eliphalet's equanimity was far from shaken.

"I don't cal'late to take a great deal of stock in the military," he answered. "But business is business. And a man must keep an eye on what is moving."

Mr. Cluyme ran his hand through his chop whiskers, and lowered his voice.

"You're right, Hopper," he assented. "And if this city is going to be Union, we ought to know it right away."

Stephen, listening with growing indignation to this talk, was unaware of a man who stood on the other side of the tree, and who now came forward before Mr. Hopper. He presented a somewhat uncompromising front. Mr. Cluyme instantly melted away.

"My friend," said the stranger, quietly, "I think we have met before, when your actions were not greatly to your credit. I do not forget a face, even when I see it in the dark. Now I hear you utter words which are a disgrace to a citizen of the United States. I have some respect for a rebel. I have none for you, sir."

As soon as Stephen recovered from the shock of his surprise, he saw that Eliphalet had changed countenance. The manner of an important man of affairs, which he had so assiduously cultivated, fell away from him. He took a step backward, and his eyes made an ugly shift. Stephen rejoiced to see the stranger turn his back on the manager of Carvel & Company before that dignitary had time to depart, and stand unconcernedly there as if nothing had occurred.

Then Stephen stared at him.

He was not a man you would look at twice, ordinarily. He was smoking a great El Sol cigar. He wore clothes that were anything but new, a slouch hat, and coarse-grained, square-toed boots. His trousers were creased at the knees. His head fell forward a little from his square shoulders, and leaned a bit to one side, as if meditatively. He had a light brown beard that was reddish in the sun, and he was rather short than otherwise.

This was all that Stephen saw. And yet the very plainness of the man's appearance only added to his curiosity. Who was this stranger? His words, his action, too, had been remarkable. The art of administering a rebuke like that was not given to many men. It was perfectly quiet, perfectly final. And then, when it was over, he had turned his back and dismissed it.

Next Stephen began to wonder what he could know about Hopper. Stephen had suspected Eliphalet of subordinating principles to business gain, and hence the conversation with Mr. Cluyme had given him no shock in the way of a revelation. But if Hopper were a rogue, ought not Colonel Carvel to hear it? Ought not he, Stephen Brice, to ask this man with the cigar what he knew, and tell Judge Whipple? The sudden rattle of drums gave him a start, and cruelly reminded him of the gulf of prejudice and hatred fast widening between the friends.

All this time the stranger stood impassively chewing his cigar, his hand against the tree-box. A regiment in column came out of the Arsenal gate, the Union leader, in his colonel's uniform, on horseback at its head. He pulled up in the street opposite to Stephen, and sat in his saddle, chatting with other officers around him.

Then the stranger stepped across the limestone gutter and walked up to the Colonel's horse. He was still smoking. This move, too, was surprising enough. It argued even more assurance. Stephen listened intently.

"Colonel Blair, my name is Grant," he said briefly.

The Colonel faced quickly about, and held out his gloved hand cordially.

"Captain Ulysses Grant," said he, "of the old army?"

Mr. Grant nodded.

"I wanted to wish you luck," he said.

"Thank you, Grant," answered the Colonel. "But you? Where are you living now?"

"I moved to Illinois after I left here," replied Mr. Grant, as quietly as before, "and have been in Galena, in the leather business there. I went down to Springfield with the company they organized in Galena, to be of any help I could. They made me a clerk in the adjutant general's office of the state. I ruled blanks, and made out forms for a while." He paused, as if to let the humble character of this position sink into the Colonel's comprehension. "Then they found out that I'd been quartermaster and commissary, and knew something about military orders. Now I'm a state mustering officer. I came down to Belleville to muster in a regiment, which wasn't ready. And so I ran over here to see what you fellows were doing."

If this humble account had been delivered volubly, and in another tone, it is probable that the citizen-colonel would not have listened, since the events of that day were to crown his work of a winter. But Mr. Grant possessed a manner of holding attention. It was very evident, however, that Colonel Blair had other things to think of. Nevertheless he said kindly:—

"Aren't you going in, Grant?"

"I can't afford to go in as a captain of volunteers," was the calm reply. "I served nine years in the regular army, and I think I can command a regiment."

The Colonel, whose attention was called away at that moment, did not reply. Mr. Grant moved off up the street. Some of the younger officers who were there, laughed as they followed his retreating figure.

"Command a regiment!" cried one, a lieutenant whom Stephen recognized as having been a book-keeper at Edwards, James, & Doddington's, and whose stiff blue uniform coat creased awkwardly. "I guess I'm about as fit to command a regiment as Grant is."

"That man's forty years old, if he's a day," put in another. "I remember when he came here to St. Louis in '54, played out. He'd resigned from the army on the Pacific Coast. He put up a log cabin down on the Gravois Road, and there he lived in the hardest luck of any man I ever saw until last year. You remember him, Joe."

"Yep," said Joe. "I spotted him by the El Sol cigar. He used to bring a load of wood to the city once in a while, and then he'd go over to the Planters' House, or somewhere else, and smoke one of these long fellows, and sit against the wall as silent as a wooden Indian. After that he came up to the city without his family and went into real estate one winter. But he didn't make it go. Curious, it is just a year ago this month that he went over to Illinois. He's an honest fellow, and hard working enough, but he don't know how. He's just a dead failure."

"Command a regiment!" laughed the first, again, as if this in particular had struck his sense of humor. "I guess he won't get a regiment in a hurry. There's lots of those military carpet-baggers hanging around for good jobs now."

"He might fool you fellows yet," said the one called Joe, though his tone was not one of conviction. "I understand he had a first-rate record in the Mexican War."

Just then an aide rode up, and the Colonel gave a sharp command which put an end to this desultory talk. As the First Regiment took up the march, the words "Camp Jackson" ran from mouth to mouth on the sidewalks. Catching fire, Stephen ran with the crowd, and leaping on a passing street car, was borne cityward with the drums of the coming hosts beating in his ears.

In the city, shutters were going up on the stores. The streets were filled with restless citizens seeking news, and drays were halted here and there on the corners, the white eyes and frenzied calls of the negro drivers betraying their excitement. While Stephen related to his mother the events of the morning, Hester burned the dinner. It lay, still untouched, on the table when the throbbing of drums sent them to the front steps. Sigel's regiment had swung into the street, drawing in its wake a seething crowd.

Three persons came out of the big house next door. One was Anne Brinsmade; and there was her father, his white hairs uncovered. The third was Jack. His sister was clinging to him appealingly, and he struggling in her grasp. Out of his coat pocket hung the curved butt of a big pepper-box revolver.

"Let me go, Anne!" he cried. "Do you think I can stay here while my people are shot down by a lot of damned Dutchmen?"

"John," said Mr. Brinsmade, sternly, "I cannot let you join a mob. I cannot let you shoot at men who carry the Union flag."

"You cannot prevent me, sir," shouted the young man, in a frenzy. "When foreigners take our flag for their own, it is time for us to shoot them down."

Wrenching himself free, he ran down the steps and up the street ahead of the regiment. Then the soldiers and the noisy crowd were upon them; and while these were passing, the two stood there as in a dream. After that a silence fell upon the street, and Mr. Brinsmade turned and went back into the house, his head bowed as in prayer. Stephen and his mother drew back, but Anne saw them.

"He is a rebel," she faltered. "It will break my father's heart."

She looked at Stephen appealingly, unashamed of the tears in her eyes. Then she, too, went in.

"I cannot stay here, mother," he said.

As he slammed the gate, Anne ran down the steps, calling his name. He paused, and she caught his sleeve.

"I knew you would go," she said. "I knew you would go. Oh, Stephen, you have a cool head. Try to keep Jack—out of mischief."

He left her standing on the pavement. But when he reached the corner and looked back he saw that she had gone in at his own little gate to meet his mother. Then he walked rapidly westward. Now and again he was stopped by feverish questions, but at length he reached the top of the second ridge from the river, along which crowded Eighteenth Street now runs. There stood the new double mansion Mr. Spencer Catherwood had built two years before on the outskirts of the town, with the wall at the side, and the brick stable and stable yard. As Stephen approached it, the thought came to him how little this world's goods avail in times of trouble. One of the big Catherwood boys was in the blue marching regiments that day, and had been told by his father never again to darken his doors. Another was in Clarence Colfax's company of dragoons, and still another had fled southward the night after Sumter.

Stephen stopped at the crest of the hill, in the white dust of the new-turned street, to gaze westward. Clouds were gathering in the sky, but the sun still shone brightly. Halfway up the rise two blue lines had crawled, followed by black splotches, and at the southwest was the glint of the sun on rifle barrels. Directed by a genius in the art of war, the regiments were closing about Camp Jackson.

As he stood there meditating, and paying no attention to those who hurried past, a few familiar notes were struck on a piano. They came through the wide-shuttered window above his head. Then a girl's voice rose above the notes, in tones that were exultant:—

> "Away down South in de fields of cotton,
> Cinnamon seed and sandy bottom,
> Look away, look away,
> Look away, look away.
> Den I wish I was in Dixie's Land,
> Oh, oh! oh, oh!
> In Dixie's Land I'll take my stand,
> And live and die in Dixie's Land.
> Away, away, away.
> Away down South in Dixie."

The song ceased amid peals of girlish laughter. Stephen was rooted to the spot.

"Jinny! Jinny Carvel, how dare you!" came through the shutters. "We shall have a whole regiment of Hessians in here."

Old Uncle Ben, the Catherwoods' coachman, came out of the stable yard. The whites of his eyes were rolling, half in amusement, half in terror. Seeing Stephen standing there, he exclaimed:—

"Mistah Brice, if de Dutch take Camp Jackson, is we niggers gwinter be free?"

Stephen did not answer, for the piano had started again.

> "If ever I consent to be married,—
> And who could refuse a good mate?—
> The man whom I give my hand to,
> Must believe in the Rights of the State."

More laughter. Then the blinds were flung aside, and a young lady in a dress of white trimmed with crimson stood in the window, smiling. Suddenly she perceived Stephen in the road. Her smile faded. For an instant she stared at him, and then turned to the girls crowding behind her. What she said, he did not wait to hear. He was striding down the hill.

CHAPTER XIX

THE TENTH OF MAY

WOULD the sons of the first families surrender! "Never!" cried a young lady who sat behind the blinds in Mrs. Catherwood's parlor. It seemed to her when she stopped to listen for the first guns of the coming battle that the tumult in her heart would drown their roar.

"But, Jinny," ventured that Miss Puss Russell who never feared to speak her mind, "it would be folly for them to fight. The Dutch and Yankees outnumber them ten to one, and they haven't any powder and bullets."

"And Camp Jackson is down in a hollow," said Maude Catherwood, dejectedly. And yet hopefully, too, for at the thought of bloodshed she was near to fainting.

"Oh," exclaimed Virginia, passionately, "I believe you want them to surrender. I should rather see Clarence dead than giving his sword to a Yankee."

At that the other two were silent again, and sat on through an endless afternoon of uncertainty and hope and dread in the darkened room. Now and anon Mr. Catherwood's heavy step was heard as he paced the hall. From time to time they glanced at Virginia, as if to fathom her thought. She and Puss Russell had come that day to dine with Maude. Mr. Catherwood's Ben, reeking of the stable, had brought the rumor of the marching on the camp into the dining-room, and close upon the heels of this the rumble of the drums and the passing of Sigel's regiment. It was Virginia who had the presence of mind to slam the blinds in the faces of the troops, and the crowd had cheered her. It was Virginia who flew to the piano to play Dixie ere they could get by, to the awe and admiration of the girls and the delight of Mr. Catherwood, who applauded her spirit despite the trouble which weighed upon him. Once more the crowd had cheered,—and hesitated. But the Dutch regiment slouched on, impassive, and the people followed.

Virginia remained at the piano, her mood exalted patriotism, uplifted in spirit by that grand song. At first she had played it with all

238

her might. Then she sang it. She laughed in very scorn of the booby soldiers she had seen. A million of these, with all the firearms in the world, could not prevail against the flower of the South. Then she had begun whimsically to sing a verse of a song she had heard the week before, and suddenly her exaltation was fled, and her fingers left the keys. Gaining the window, trembling, half-expectant, she flung open a blind. The troops, the people, were gone, and there alone in the road stood— Stephen Brice. The others close behind her saw him, too, and Puss cried out in her surprise. The impression, when the room was dark once more, was of sternness and sadness,—and of strength. Effaced was the picture of the plodding recruits with their coarse and ill-fitting uniforms of blue.

Virginia shut the blinds. Not a word escaped her, nor could they tell why they did not dare to question her then. An hour passed, perhaps two, before the shrill voice of a boy was heard in the street below:—

"Camp Jackson has surrendered!"

They heard the patter of his bare feet on the pavement, and the cry repeated:—

"Camp Jackson has surrendered!"

And so the war began for Virginia. Bitter before, now was she on fire. Close her lips as tightly as she might, the tears forced themselves to her eyes. The ignominy of it!

How hard it is for us of this age to understand that feeling.

"I do not believe it!" she cried. "I cannot believe it!"

The girls gathered around her, pale and frightened and anxious. Suddenly courage returned to her, the courage which made Spartans of Southern women. She ran to the front door. Mr. Catherwood was on the sidewalk, talking to a breathless man. That man was Mr. Barbo, Colonel Carvel's book-keeper.

"Yes," he was saying, "they—they surrendered. There was nothing else for them to do. They were surrounded and overpowered."

Mr. Catherwood uttered an oath. But it did not shock Virginia.

"And not a shot fired?" he said.

"And not a shot fired?" Virginia repeated, mechanically.

Both men turned. Mr. Barbo took off his hat.

"No ma'am."

"Oh, how could they!" exclaimed Virginia.

Her words seemed to arouse Mr. Catherwood from a kind of stupor. He turned, and took her hand.

"Virginia, we shall make them smart for this yet. My God!" he cried, "what have I done that my son should be a traitor, in arms against his own brother fighting for his people? To think that a Catherwood should be with the Yankees! You, Ben," he shouted, suddenly perceiving an object for his anger. "What do you mean by coming out of the yard? By G—d, I'll have you whipped. I'll show you niggers whether you're to be free or not."

And Mr. Catherwood was a good man, who treated his servants well. Suddenly he dropped Virginia's hand and ran westward down the hill. Well that she could not see beyond the second rise!

Let us go there—to the camp. Let us stand on the little mound at the northeast of it, on the Olive Street Road, whence Captain Lyon's artillery commands it. What a change from yesterday! Davis Avenue is no longer a fashionable promenade, flashing with bright dresses. Those quiet men in blue, who are standing beside the arms of the state troops, stacked and surrendered, are United States regulars. They have been in Kansas, and are used to scenes of this sort.

The five Hessian regiments have surrounded the camp. Each commander has obeyed the master mind of his chief, who has calculated the time of marching with precision. Here, at the western gate, Colonel Blair's regiment is in open order. See the prisoners taking their places between the ranks, some smiling, as if to say all is not over yet; some with heads hung down, in sulky shame. Still others, who are true to the Union, openly relieved. But who is this officer breaking his sword to bits against the fence, rather than surrender it to a Yankee? Listen to the crowd as they cheer him. Listen to the epithets and vile names which they hurl at the stolid blue line of the victors. "Mudsills!" "Negro Worshippers!"

Yes, the crowd is there, seething with conflicting passions. Men with brows bent and fists clenched, yelling excitedly. Others pushing, and eager to see,—there in curiosity only. And, alas! women and children by the score, as if what they looked upon were not war, but a parade, a spectacle. As the gray uniforms file out of the gate, the crowd has become a mob, now flowing back into the fields on each side of the road, now pressing forward vindictively until stopped by the sergeants and corporals. Listen to them calling to sons, and brothers, and husbands in gray! See, there is a woman who spits in a soldier's face!

Throughout it all, the officers sit their horses, unmoved. A man on the bank above draws a pistol and aims at a captain. A German private steps from the ranks, forgetful of discipline, and points at the man, who is cursing the captain's name. The captain, imperturbable, orders his man back to his place. And the man does not shoot—yet.

Now are the prisoners of that regiment all in place between the two files of it. A band (one of those which played lightsome music on the birthday of the camp) is marched around to the head of the column. The regiment with its freight moves on to make place for a battalion of regulars, amid imprecations and cries of "Hurrah for Jeff Davis!" and "Damn the Dutch!" "Kill the Hessians!"

Stephen Brice stood among the people in Lindell's Grove, looking up at the troops on the road, which was on an embankment. Through the rows of faces he had searched in vain for one. His motive he did not attempt to fathom—in truth, he was not conscious at the time of any motive. He heard the name shouted at the gate.

"Here they are,—the dragoons! Three cheers for Colfax! Down with the Yankees!"

A storm of cheers and hisses followed. Dismounted, at the head of his small following, the young Captain walked erect. He did not seem to hear the cheers. His face was set, and he held his gloved hand over the place where his sword had been, as if over a wound. On his features, in his attitude, was stamped the undying determination of the South. How those thoroughbreds of the Cavaliers showed it! Pain they took lightly. The fire of humiliation burned, but could not destroy their indomitable spirit. They were the first of their people in the field, and the last to leave it. Historians may say that the classes of the South caused the war; they cannot say that they did not take upon themselves the greatest burden of the suffering.

Twice that day was the future revealed to Stephen. Once as he stood on the hill-crest, when he had seen a girl in crimson and white in a window,—in her face. And now again he read it in the face of her cousin. It was as if he had seen unrolled the years of suffering that were to come.

In that moment of deep bitterness his reason wavered. What if the South should win? Surely there was no such feeling in the North as these people betrayed. That most dangerous of gifts, the seeing of two sides of a quarrel, had been given him. He saw the Southern view. He sympathized with the Southern people. They had befriended him in his poverty. Why had he not been born, like Clarence Colfax, the owner of a large plantation, the believer in the divine right of his race to rule? Then this girl who haunted his thoughts! Would that his path had been as straight, his duty as easy, as that of the handsome young Captain! Presently these thoughts were distracted by the sight of a back strangely familiar. The back belonged to a gentleman who was energetically climbing the embankment in front of him, on the top of which Major Saxton, a regular army officer, sat his horse. The gentleman was pulling a small boy after him by one hand, and held a newspaper tightly rolled in the other. Stephen smiled to himself when it came over him that this gentleman was none other than that Mr. William T. Sherman he had met in the street car the day before. Somehow Stephen was fascinated by the decision and energy of Mr. Sherman's slightest movements. He gave Major Saxton a salute, quick and genial. Then, almost with one motion he unrolled the newspaper, pointed to a paragraph, and handed it to the officer. Major Saxton was still reading when a drunken ruffian clambered up the bank behind them and attempted to pass through the lines. The column began to move forward. Mr. Sherman slid down the bank with his boy into the grove beside Stephen.

Suddenly there was a struggle. A corporal pitched the drunkard backwards over the bank, and he rolled at Mr. Sherman's feet. With a curse, he picked himself up, fumbling in his pocket. There was a flash, and as the smoke rolled from before his eyes, Stephen saw a man of a German regiment stagger and fall.

It was the signal for a rattle of shots. Stones and bricks filled the air, and were heard striking steel and flesh in the ranks. The regiment quivered,—then halted at the loud command of the officers, and the ranks faced out with level guns. Stephen reached for Mr. Sherman's boy, but a gentleman had already thrown him and was covering his body. He contrived to throw down a woman standing beside him before the minié balls swished over their heads, and the leaves and branches began to fall. Between the popping of the shots sounded the shrieks of wounded women and children, the groans and curses of men, and the stampeding of hundreds.

"Lie down, Brice! For God's sake lie down!" Mr. Sherman cried.

He was about to obey when a young man, small and agile, ran past him from behind, heedless of the panic. Stopping at the foot of the bank he dropped on one knee, resting his revolver in the hollow of his left arm. It was Jack Brinsmade. At the same time two of the soldiers above lowered their barrels to cover him. Then smoke hid the scene. When it rolled away, Brinsmade lay on the ground. He staggered to his feet with an oath, and confronted a young man who was hatless, and upon whose forehead was burned a black powder mark.

"Curse you!" he cried, reaching out wildly; "curse you, you d—d Yankee. I'll teach you to fight!"

Maddened, he made a rush at Stephen's throat. But Stephen seized his hands and bent them down, and held them firmly while he kicked and struggled.

"Curse you!" he panted; "curse you, you let me go and I'll kill you,—you Yankee upstart!"

But Stephen held on. Brinsmade became more and more frantic. One of the officers, seeing the struggle, started down the bank, was reviled, and hesitated. At that moment Major Sherman came between them.

"Let him go, Brice," he said, in a tone of command.

Stephen did as he was bid. Whereupon Brinsmade made a dash for his pistol on the ground. Mr. Sherman was before him.

"Now see here, Jack," he said, picking it up, "I don't want to shoot you, but I may have to. That young man saved your life at the risk of his own. If that fool Dutchman had had a ball in his gun instead of a wad, Mr. Brice would have been killed."

A strange thing happened. Brinsmade took one long look at Stephen, turned on his heel, and walked off rapidly through the grove. And it may be added that for some years after he was not seen in St. Louis.

For a moment the other two stood staring after him. Then Mr. Sherman took his boy by the hand.

"Mr. Brice," he said, "I've seen a few things done in my life, but nothing better than this. Perhaps the day may come when you and I may meet in the army. They don't seem to think much of us now," he added, smiling, "but we may be of use to 'em later. If ever I can serve you, Mr. Brice, I beg you to call on me."

Stephen stammered his acknowledgments. And Mr. Sherman, nodding his head vigorously, went away southward through the grove, toward Market Street.

The column was moving on. The dead were being laid in carriages, and the wounded tended by such physicians as chanced to be on the spot. Stephen, dazed at what had happened, took up the march to town. He strode faster than the regiments with their load of prisoners, and presently he found himself abreast of the little file of dragoons who were guarded by some of Blair's men. It was then that he discovered that the prisoners' band in front was playing "Dixie."

They are climbing the second hill, and are coming now to the fringe of new residences which the rich citizens have built. Some of them are closed and dark. In the windows and on the steps of others women are crying or waving handkerchiefs and calling out to the prisoners, some of whom are gay, and others sullen. A distracted father tries to break through the ranks and rescue his son. Ah, here is the Catherwood house. That is open. Mrs. Catherwood, with her hand on her husband's arm, with red eyes, is scanning those faces for the sight of George. Will he ever come back to her? Will the Yankees murder him for treason, or send him North to languish the rest of his life? No, she will not go inside. She must see him. She will not faint, though Mrs. James has, across the street, and is even now being carried into the house. Few of us can see into the hearts of those women that day, and speak of the suffering there.

Near the head of Mr. Blair's regiment is Tom. His face is cast down as he passes the house from which he is banished. Nor do father, or mother, or sister in their agony make any sound or sign. George is coming. The welcome and the mourning and the tears are all for him.

The band is playing "Dixie" once more. George is coming, and some one else. The girls are standing in a knot behind the old people, dry-eyed, their handkerchiefs in their hands. Some of the prisoners take off their hats and smile at the young lady with chiselled features and brown hair, who wears the red and white of the South as if she were born to them. Her eyes are searching. Ah, at last she sees him, walking erect at the head of his dragoons. He gives her one look of entreaty, and that smile which should have won her heart long ago. As if by common consent the heads of the troopers are uncovered before her.

How bravely she waves at them until they are gone down the street! Then only do her eyes fill with tears, and she passes into the house.

Had she waited, she might have seen a solitary figure leaving the line of march and striding across to Pine Street.

That night the sluices of the heavens were opened, and the blood was washed from the grass in Lindell Grove. The rain descended in floods on the distracted city, and the great river rose and flung brush from Minnesota forests high up on the stones of the levee. Down in the long barracks weary recruits, who had stood and marched all the day long, went supperless to their hard pallets. Government fare was hard. Many a boy, prisoner or volunteer, sobbed himself to sleep in the darkness.

All were prisoners alike, prisoners of war. Sobbed themselves to sleep, to dream of the dear homes that were here within sight and sound of them, and to which they were powerless to go. Sisters, and mothers, and wives were there, beyond the rain, holding out arms to them.

Is war a thing to stir the blood? Ay, while the day lasts. But what of the long nights when husband and wife have lain side by side? What of the children who ask piteously where their father is going, and who are gathered by a sobbing mother to her breast? Where is the picture of that last breakfast at home? So in the midst of the cheer which is saddest in life comes the thought that, just one year ago, he who is the staff of the house was wont to sit down just so merrily to his morning meal, before going to work in the office. Why had they not thanked God on their knees for peace while they had it?

See the brave little wife waiting on the porch of her home for him to go by. The sun shines, and the grass is green on the little plot, and the geraniums red. Last spring she was sewing here with a song on her lips, watching for him to turn the corner as he came back to dinner. But now! Hark! Was that the beat of the drums? Or was it thunder? Her good neighbors, the doctor and his wife, come in at the little gate to cheer her. She does not hear them. Why does God mock her with sunlight and with friends?

Tramp, tramp, tramp! They are here. Now the band is blaring. *That* is his company. And that is his dear face, the second from the end. Will she ever see it again? Look, he is smiling bravely, as if to say a thousand tender things. "Will, are the flannels in your knapsack? You have not forgotten that medicine for your cough?" What courage sublime is that which lets her wave at him? Well for you, little woman, that you cannot see the faces of the good doctor and his wife behind you. Oh, those guns of Sumter, how they roar in your head! Ay, and will roar again, through forty years of widowhood!

Mrs. Brice was in the little parlor that Friday night, listening to the cry of the rain outside. Some thoughts such as these distracted her. Why should she be happy, and other mothers miserable? The day of reckoning for her happiness must surely come, when she must kiss Stephen a brave farewell and give him to his country. For the sins of the fathers are visited on the children, unto the third and fourth generation of them that hate Him who is the Ruler of all things.

The bell rang, and Stephen went to the door. He was startled to see

Mr. Brinsmade. That gentleman was suddenly aged, and his clothes were wet and spattered with mud. He sank into a chair, but refused the spirits and water which Mrs. Brice offered him in her alarm.

"Stephen," he said, "I have been searching the city for John. Did you see him at Camp Jackson—was he hurt?"

"I think not, sir," Stephen answered, with clear eyes. "I saw him walking southward after the firing was all over."

"Thank God," exclaimed Mr. Brinsmade, fervently. "If you will excuse me, madam, I shall hurry to tell my wife and daughter. I have been able to find no one who saw him."

As he went out he glanced at Stephen's forehead. But for once in his life, Mr. Brinsmade was too much agitated to inquire about the pain of another.

"Stephen, you did not tell me that you saw John," said his mother, when the door was closed.

CHAPTER XX

IN THE ARSENAL

THERE was a dismal tea at Colonel Carvel's house in Locust Street that evening. Virginia did not touch a mouthful, and the Colonel merely made a pretence of eating. About six o'clock Mrs. Addison Colfax had driven in from Bellegarde, nor could it rain fast enough or hard enough to wash the foam from her panting horses. She did not wait for Jackson to come out with an umbrella, but rushed through the wet from the carriage to the door in her haste to urge the Colonel to go to the Arsenal and demand Clarence's release. It was in vain that Mr. Carvel assured her it would do no good; in vain that he told her of a more important matter that claimed him. Could there be a more important matter than his own nephew kept in durance, and in danger of being murdered by Dutch butchers in the frenzy of their victory? Mrs. Colfax shut herself up in her room, and through the door Virginia heard her sobs as she went down to tea.

The Colonel made no secret of his uneasiness. With his hat on his head, and his hands in his pockets, he paced up and down the room. He let his cigar go out,—a more serious sign still. Finally he stood with his face to the black window, against which the big drops were beating in a fury.

Virginia sat expressionless at the head of the table, still in that gown of white and crimson, which she had worn in honor of the defenders of the state. Expressionless, save for a glance of solicitation at her father's back. If resolve were feminine, Virginia might have sat for that portrait. There was a light in her dark blue eyes. Underneath there were traces of the day's fatigue. When she spoke, there was little life in her voice.

"Aren't you going to the Planters' House, Pa?"

The Colonel turned, and tried to smile.

"I reckon not to-night, Jinny. Why?"

"To find out what they are going to do with Clarence," she said indignantly.

"I reckon they don't know at the Planters' House," he said.

"Then—" began Virginia, and stopped.

"Then what?" he asked, stroking her hair.

"Then why not go to the Barracks? Order the carriage, and I will go with you."

His smile faded. He stood looking down at her fixedly, as was sometimes his habit. Grave tenderness was in his tone.

"Jinny," he said slowly, "Jinny, do you mean to marry Clarence?"

The suddenness of the question took her breath. But she answered steadily:—

"Yes."

"Do you love him?"

"Yes," she answered. But her lashes fell.

Still he stood, and it seemed to her that her father's gaze pierced to her secret soul.

"Come here, my dear," he said.

He held out his arms, and she fluttered into them. The tears were come at last. It was not the first time she had cried out her troubles against that great heart which had ever been her strong refuge. From childhood she had been comforted there. Had she broken her doll, had Mammy Easter been cross, had lessons gone wrong at school, was she ill, or weary with that heaviness of spirit which is woman's inevitable lot,— this was her sanctuary. But now! This burden God Himself had sent, and none save her Heavenly Father might cure it. Through his great love for her it was given to Colonel Carvel to divine it—only vaguely.

Many times he strove to speak, and could not. But presently, as if ashamed of her tears, she drew back from him and took her old seat on the arm of his chair.

By the light of his intuition, the Colonel chose his words well. What he had to speak of was another sorrow, yet a healing one.

"You must not think of marriage now, my dear, when the bread we eat may fail us. Jinny, we are not as rich as we used to be. Our trade was in the South and West, and now the South and West cannot pay. I had a conference with Mr. Hopper yesterday, and he tells me that we must be prepared."

She laid her hand upon his.

"And did you think I would care, dear?" she asked gently. "I can bear with poverty and rags, to win this war."

His own eyes were dim, but pride shone in them. Jackson came in on tiptoe, and hesitated. At the Colonel's motion he took away the china and the silver, and removed the white cloth, and turned low the lights in the chandelier. He went out softly, and closed the door.

"Pa," said Virginia, presently, "do you trust Mr. Hopper?"

The Colonel gave a start.

"Why, yes, Jinny. He improved the business greatly before this trouble came. And even now we are not in such straits as some other houses."

"Captain Lige doesn't like him."

"Lige has prejudices."

"So have I," said Virginia. "Eliphalet Hopper will serve you so long as he serves himself. No longer."

"I think you do him an injustice, my dear," answered the Colonel. But uneasiness was in his voice. "Hopper is hard working, scrupulous to a cent. He owns two slaves now who are running the river. He keeps out of politics, and he has none of the Yankee faults."

"I wish he had," said Virginia.

The Colonel made no answer to this. Getting up, he went over to the bell-cord at the door and pulled it. Jackson came in hurriedly.

"Is my bag packed?"

"Yes, Marsa."

"Where are you going?" cried Virginia, in alarm.

"To Jefferson City, dear, to see the Governor. I got word this afternoon."

"In the rain?"

He smiled, and stooped to kiss her.

"Yes," he answered, "in the rain as far as the depot. I can trust you, Jinny. And Lige's boat will be back from New Orleans to-morrow or Sunday."

The next morning the city awoke benumbed, her heart beating but feebly. Her commerce had nearly ceased to flow. A long line of boats lay idle, with noses to the levee. Men stood on the street corners in the rain, reading of the capture of Camp Jackson, and of the riot, and thousands lifted up their voices to execrate the Foreign City below Market Street. A vague terror, maliciously born, subtly spread. The Dutch had broken up the camp, a peaceable state institution, they had shot down innocent women and children. What might they not do to the defenceless city under their victorious hand, whose citizens were nobly loyal to the South? Sack it? Yes, and burn, and loot it. Ladies who ventured out that day crossed the street to avoid Union gentlemen of their acquaintance.

It was early when Mammy Easter brought the newspaper to her mistress. Virginia read the news, and ran joyfully to her aunt's room. Three times she knocked, and then she heard a cry within. Then the key was turned and the bolt cautiously withdrawn, and a crack of six inches disclosed her aunt.

"Oh, how you frightened me, Jinny!" she cried. "I thought it was the Dutch coming to murder us all. What have they done to Clarence?"

"We shall see him to-day, Aunt Lillian," was the joyful answer. "The newspaper says that all the Camp Jackson prisoners are to be set free to-day, on parole. Oh, I knew they would not dare to hold them. The whole state would have risen to their rescue."

Mrs. Colfax did not receive these tidings with transports. She permitted her niece to come into her room, and then sank into a chair before the mirror of her dressing-table, and scanned her face there.

"I could not sleep a wink, Jinny, all night long. I look wretchedly. I am afraid I am going to have another of my attacks. How it is raining! What does the newspaper say?"

"I'll get it for you," said Virginia, used to her aunt's vagaries.

"No, no, tell me. I am much too nervous to read it."

"It says that they will be paroled to-day, and that they passed a comfortable night."

"It must be a Yankee lie," said the lady. "Oh, what a night! I saw them torturing him in a thousand ways—the barbarians! I know he had to sleep on a dirty floor with low-down trash."

"But we shall have him here to-night, Aunt Lillian!" cried Virginia. "Mammy, tell Uncle Ben that Mr. Clarence will be here for tea. We must have a feast for him. Pa said that they could not hold them."

"Where is Comyn?" inquired Mrs. Colfax. "Has he gone down to see Clarence?"

"He went to Jefferson City last night," replied Virginia. "The Governor sent for him."

Mrs. Colfax exclaimed in horror at this news.

"Do you mean that he has deserted us?" she cried. "That he has left us here defenceless,—at the mercy of the Dutch, that they may wreak their vengeance upon us women? How can you sit still, Virginia? If I were your age and able to drag myself to the street, I should be at the

Arsenal now. I should be on my knees before that detestable Captain Lyon, even if he is a Yankee."

Virginia kept her temper.

"I do not go on my knees to any man," she said. "Rosetta, tell Ned I wish the carriage at once."

Her aunt seized her convulsively by the arm.

"Where are you going, Jinny?" she demanded. "Your Pa would never forgive me if anything happened to you."

A smile, half pity, crossed the girl's anxious face.

"I am afraid that I must risk adding to your misfortune, Aunt Lillian," she said, and left the room.

Virginia drove to Mr. Brinsmade's. His was one of the Union houses which she might visit and not lose her self-respect. Like many Southerners, when it became a question of go or stay, Mr. Brinsmade's unfaltering love for the Union had kept him in. He had voted for Mr. Bell, and later had presided at Crittenden Compromise meetings. In short, as a man of peace, he would have been willing to sacrifice much for peace. And now that it was to be war, and he had taken his stand uncompromisingly with the Union, the neighbors whom he had befriended for so many years could not bring themselves to regard him as an enemy. He never hurt their feelings; and almost as soon as the war began he set about that work which has been done by self-denying Christians of all ages,—the relief of suffering. He visited with comfort the widow and the fatherless, and many a night in the hospital he sat through beside the dying, Yankee and Rebel alike, and wrote their last letters home.

And Yankee and Rebel alike sought his help and counsel in time of perplexity or trouble, rather than hot-headed advice from their own leaders.

Mr. Brinsmade's own carriage was drawn up at his door, and that gentleman himself standing on the threshold. He came down his steps bareheaded in the wet to hand Virginia from her carriage.

Courteous and kind as ever, he asked for her father and her aunt as he led her into the house. However such men may try to hide their own trials under a cheerful mien, they do not succeed with spirits of a kindred nature. With the others, who are less generous, it matters not. Virginia was not so thoughtless nor so selfish that she could not perceive that a trouble had come to this good man. Absorbed as she was in her own affairs, she forgot some of them in his presence. The fire left her tongue, and to him she could not have spoken harshly even of an enemy.

Such was her state of mind, when she was led into the drawing-room. From the corner of it Anne arose and came forward to throw her arms around her friend.

"Jinny, it was so good of you to come. You don't hate me?"

"Hate you, Anne dear!"

"Because we are Union," said honest Anne, wishing to have no shadow of doubt.

Virginia was touched. "Anne," she cried, "if you were *German,* I believe I should love you."

"How good of you to come. I should not have dared go to your house, because I know that you feel so deeply. You—you heard?"

"Heard what?" asked Virginia, alarmed.

"That Jack has run away—has gone South, we think. Perhaps," she cried, "perhaps he may be dead." And tears came into the girl's eyes.

It was then that Virginia forgot Clarence. She drew Anne to the sofa and kissed her.

"No, he is not dead," she said gently, but with a confidence in her voice of rare quality. "He is not dead, Anne dear, or you would have heard."

Had she glanced up, she would have seen Mr. Brinsmade's eye upon her. He looked kindly at all people, but this expression he reserved for those whom he honored. A life of service to others had made him guess that, in the absence of her father, this girl had come to him for help of some kind.

"Virginia is right, Anne," he said. "John has gone to fight for his principles, as every gentleman who is free should; we must remember that this is his home, and that we must not quarrel with him, because we think differently." He paused, and came over to Virginia. "There is something I can do for you, my dear?" said he.

She rose. "Oh, no, Mr. Brinsmade," she cried. And yet her honesty was as great as Anne's. She would not have it thought that she came for other reasons. "My aunt is in such a state of worry over Clarence that I came to ask you if you thought the news true, that the prisoners are to be paroled. She thinks it is a—" Virginia flushed, and bit a rebellious tongue. "She does not believe it."

Even good Mr. Brinsmade smiled at the slip she had nearly made. He understood the girl, and admired her. He also understood Mrs. Colfax.

"I will drive to the Arsenal with you, Jinny," he answered. "I know Captain Lyon, and we shall find out certainly."

"You will do nothing of the kind, sir," said Virginia, with emphasis. "Had I known this—about John, I should not have come."

He checked her with a gesture. What a gentleman of the old school he was, with his white ruffled shirt and his black stock and his eye kindling with charity.

"My dear," he answered, "Nicodemus is waiting. I was just going myself to ask Captain Lyon about John."

Virginia's further objections were cut short by the violent clanging of the door-bell, and the entrance of a tall, energetic gentleman, whom Virginia had introduced to her as Major Sherman, late of the army, and now president of the Fifth Street Railroad. The Major bowed and shook hands. He then proceeded, as was evidently his habit, directly to the business on which he was come.

"Mr. Brinsmade," he said, "I heard, accidentally, half an hour ago that you were seeking news of your son. I regret to say, sir, that the news I have will not lead to a knowledge of his whereabouts. But in justice to a young gentleman of this city I think I ought to tell you what happened at Camp Jackson."

"I shall be most grateful, Major. Sit down, sir."

But the Major did not sit down. He stood in the middle of the room. With some gesticulation which added greatly to the force of the story, he gave a most terse and vivid account of Mr. John's arrival at the embankment by the grove—of his charging a whole regiment of Union volunteers. Here was honesty again. Mr. Sherman did not believe in mincing matters even to a father and sister.

"And, sir," said he, "you may thank the young man who lives next door to you—Mr. Brice, I believe—for saving your son's life."

"Stephen Brice!" exclaimed Mr. Brinsmade, in astonishment.

Virginia felt Anne's hand tighten. But her own was limp. A hot wave swept over her. Was she never to hear the end of this man?

"Yes, sir, Stephen Brice," answered Mr. Sherman. "And I never in my life saw a finer thing done, in the Mexican War or out of it."

Mr. Brinsmade grew a little excited.

"Are you sure that you know him?"

"As sure as I know you," said the Major, with excessive conviction.

"But," said Mr. Brinsmade, "I was in there last night. I knew the young man had been at the camp. I asked him if he had seen Jack. He told me that he had, by the embankment. But he never mentioned a word about saving his life."

"He didn't!" cried the Major. "By glory, but he's even better than I thought him. Did you see a black powder mark on his face?"

"Why, yes, sir, I saw a bad burn of some kind on his forehead."

"Well, sir, if one of the Dutchmen who shot at Jack had known enough to put a ball in his musket, he would have killed Mr. Brice, who was only ten feet away, standing before your son."

Anne gave a little cry—Virginia was silent. Her lips were parted. Though she realized it not, she was thirsting to hear the whole of the story.

The Major told it, soldier fashion, but well. How John rushed up to the line; how he (Mr. Sherman) had seen Brice throw the woman down and had cried to him to lie down himself; how the fire was darting down the regiment, and how men and women were falling all about them; and how Stephen had flung Jack and covered him with his body.

It was all vividly before Virginia's eyes. Had she any right to treat such a man with contempt? She remembered how he had looked at her when he stood on the corner by the Catherwoods' house. And, worst of all, she remembered many spiteful remarks she had made, even to Anne, the gist of which had been that Mr. Brice was better at preaching than at fighting. She knew now—and she had known in her heart before— that this was the greatest injustice she could have done him.

"But Jack? What did Jack do?"

It was Anne who tremblingly asked the Major. But Mr. Sherman, apparently, was not the man to say that Jack would have shot Stephen had he not interfered. That was the ugly part of the story. John would have shot the man who saved his life. To the day of his death neither Mr. Brinsmade nor his wife knew this. But while Mr. Brinsmade and Anne had gone upstairs to the sick-bed, these were the tidings the Major told Virginia, who kept it in her heart. The reason he told her was because she had guessed a part of it.

Nevertheless Mr. Brinsmade drove to the Arsenal with her that Saturday, in his own carriage. Forgetful of his own grief, long habit came to him to talk cheerily with her. He told her many little anecdotes of his travel, but not one of them did she hear. Again, at the moment when she thought her belief in Clarence and her love for him at last secure, she found herself drawing searching comparisons between him and the quieter young Bostonian. In spite of herself she had to admit that Stephen's deed was splendid. Was this disloyal? She flushed at the thought. Clarence had been capable of the deed,—even to the rescue of an enemy. But—alas, that she should carry it out to a remorseless end—would Clarence have been equal to keeping silence when Mr. Brinsmade came to him? Stephen Brice had not even told his mother, so Mr. Brinsmade believed.

As if to aggravate her torture, Mr. Brinsmade's talk drifted to the subject of young Mr. Brice. This was but natural. He told her of the brave struggle Stephen had made, and how he had earned luxuries, and often necessities, for his mother by writing for the newspapers.

"Often," said Mr. Brinsmade, "often I have been unable to sleep, and have seen the light in Stephen's room until the small hours of the morning."

"Oh, Mr. Brinsmade," cried Virginia. "Can't you tell me something bad about him? Just once."

The good gentleman started, and looked searchingly at the girl by his side, flushed and confused. Perhaps he thought—but how can we tell what he thought? How can we guess that our teachers laugh at our pranks after they have caned us for them? We do not remember that our parents have once been young themselves, and that some word or look of our own brings a part of their past vividly before them. Mr. Brinsmade was silent, but he looked out of the carriage window, away from Virginia. And presently, as they splashed through the mud near the Arsenal, they met a knot of gentlemen in state uniforms on their way to the city. Nicodemus stopped at his master's signal. Here was George Catherwood, and his father was with him.

"They have released us on parole," said George. "Yes, we had a fearful night of it. They could not have kept us—they had no quarters."

How changed he was from the gay trooper of yesterday! His bright uniform was creased and soiled and muddy, his face unshaven, and dark rings of weariness under his eyes.

"Do you know if Clarence Colfax has gone home?" Mr. Brinsmade inquired.

"Clarence is an idiot," cried George, ill-naturedly. "Mr. Brinsmade, of all the prisoners here, he refused to take the parole, or the oath of allegiance. He swears he will remain a prisoner *until he is exchanged.*"

"The young man is Quixotic," declared the elder Catherwood, who was not himself in the best of humors.

"Sir," said Mr. Brinsmade, with as much severity as he was ever known to use, "sir, I honor that young man for this more than I can tell you. Nicodemus, you may drive on." And he slammed the door.

Perhaps George had caught sight of a face in the depths of the carriage, for he turned purple, and stood staring on the pavement after his choleric parent had gone on.

It was done. Of all the thousand and more young men who had upheld the honor of their state that week, there was but the one who chose to remain in durance vile within the Arsenal wall—Captain Clarence Colfax, late of the Dragoons.

Mr. Brinsmade was rapidly admitted to the Arsenal, and treated with the respect which his long service to the city deserved. He and Virginia were shown into the bare military room of the commanding officer, and thither presently came Captain Lyon himself. Virginia tingled with antagonism when she saw this man who had made the city tremble, who had set an iron heel on the flaming brand of her Cause. He, too, showed the marks of his Herculean labors, but only on his clothes and person. His long red hair was unbrushed, his boots covered with black mud, and his coat unbuttoned. His face was ruddy and his eye as clear as though he had arisen from twelve hours' sleep. He bowed to Virginia (not too politely, to be sure). Her own nod of bare recognition did not seem to trouble him.

"Yes, sir," he said incisively, in response to Mr. Brinsmade's question, "we are forced to retain Captain Colfax. He prefers to remain a prisoner until he is exchanged. He refuses to take the oath of allegiance to the United States."

"And why should he be made to, Captain Lyon? In what way has he opposed the United States troops?"

It was Virginia who spoke. Both looked at her in astonishment.

"You will pardon me, Miss Carvel," said Captain Lyon, gravely, "if I refuse to discuss that question with you."

Virginia bit her tongue.

"I understand that Mr. Colfax is a near relative of yours, Miss Carvel," the Captain continued. "His friends may come here to see him during the day. And I believe it is not out of place for me to express my admiration of the Captain's conduct. You may care to see him now—"

"Thank you," said Virginia, curtly.

"Orderly, my respects to Captain Colfax, and ask him if he will be kind enough to come in here. Mr. Brinsmade," said the Captain, "I should like a few words with you, sir."

And so, thanks to the Captain's delicacy, when Clarence arrived he found Virginia alone. She was much agitated. She ran toward him as he entered the door, calling his name.

"Max, you are going to stay here?"

"Yes, until I am exchanged."

Aglow with admiration, she threw herself into his arms. Now, indeed, was she proud of him. Of all the thousand defenders of the state, he alone was true to his principles—to the South. Within sight of home, he alone had chosen privation.

She looked up into his face, which showed marks of excitement and fatigue. But above all, excitement. She knew that he could live on excitement. The thought came to her—was it that which sustained him now? She put it away as treason. Surely the touch of this experience would transform the boy into the man. This was the weak point in the armor which she wore so bravely for her cousin. He had grown up to idleness. He had known neither care nor responsibility. His one longing from a child had been that love of fighting and adventure which is born in the race. Until this gloomy day in the Arsenal, Virginia had never characterized it as a love of excitement—as anything which contained a selfish element. She looked up into his face, I say, and saw that which it is given to a woman only to see. His eyes burned with a light that was far away. Even with his arms around her he seemed to have forgotten her presence, and that she had come all the way to the Arsenal to see him. Her hands dropped limply from his shoulders. She drew away, as he did not seem to notice.

So it is with men. Above and beyond the sacrifice of a woman's life, the joy of possessing her soul and affection, is something more desirable still—fame and glory—personal fame and glory. The woman may share them, of course, and be content with the radiance. When the Governor is making his inauguration speech, does he always think of the help the little wife has given him? And so, in moments of excitement, when we see far ahead into a glorious future, we do not feel the arms about us, or value the sweets which, in more humdrum days, we labored so hard to attain.

Virginia drew away, and the one searching glance she gave him he did not see. He was staring far beyond. Tears started in her eyes, and she turned from him to look out over the Arsenal grounds, still wet and heavy with the night's storm. The day itself was dark and damp. She thought of the supper cooking at home. It would not be eaten now.

And yet, in that moment of bitterness Virginia loved him. Such are the ways of women, even of the proudest, who love their country too. It was but right that he should not think of her when the honor of the South was at stake; and the anger that rose within her was against those nine hundred and ninety-nine who had weakly accepted the parole.

"Why did Uncle Comyn not come?" asked Clarence.

"He has gone to Jefferson City, to see the Governor."

"And you came alone?"

"No, Mr. Brinsmade brought me."

"And mother?"

She was waiting for that question. What a relief that it should have come among the first.

"Aunt Lillian feels very badly. She was in her room when I left. She was afraid" (Virginia had to smile), "she was afraid the Yankees would kill you."

"They have behaved very well for Yankees," replied he. "No luxury, and they will not hear of my having a servant. They are used to doing their own work. But they have treated me much better since I refused to take their abominable oath."

"And you will be honored for it when the news reaches town."

"Do you think so, Jinny?" Clarence asked eagerly. "I reckon they will think me a fool."

"I should like to hear any one say so," she flashed out. "No," said Virginia, "our friends will force them to release you. I do not know much about law. But you have done nothing to be imprisoned for."

Clarence did not answer at once. Finally he said:—

"I do not want to be released."

"You do not want to be released!" she repeated.

"No," he said. "They can exchange me. If I remain a prisoner, it will have a greater effect—for the South."

She smiled again, this time at the boyish touch of heroics. Experience, responsibility, and he would get over that. She remembered once, long ago, when his mother had shut him up in his room for a punishment, and he had tortured her by remaining there for two whole days.

It was well on in the afternoon when she drove back to the city with Mr. Brinsmade. Neither of them had eaten since morning, nor had they even thought of hunger. Mr. Brinsmade was silent, leaning back in the corner of the carriage, and Virginia absorbed in her own thoughts. Drawing near the city, that dreaded sound, the rumble of drums, roused them. A shot rang out, and they were jerked violently by the starting of the horses. As they dashed across Walnut at Seventh came the fusillade. Virginia leaned out of the window. Down the vista of the street was a mass of blue uniforms, and a film of white smoke hanging about the columns of the old Presbyterian Church. Mr. Brinsmade quietly drew her back into the carriage.

The shots ceased, giving place to an angry roar that struck terror to her heart that wet and lowering afternoon. The powerful black horses galloped on, Nicodemus tugging at the reins, and great splotches of mud flying in at the windows. The roar of the crowd died to an ominous moaning behind them. Then she knew that Mr. Brinsmade was speaking:—

"From battle and murder, and from sudden death—from all sedition, privy conspiracy, and rebellion,—Good Lord, deliver us."

He was repeating the Litany—that Litany which had come down through the ages. They had chanted it in Cromwell's time, when homes were ruined and laid waste, and innocents slaughtered. They had chanted it on the dark, barricaded stairways of mediæval Paris, through St. Bartholomew's night, when the narrow and twisted streets ran with blood. They had chanted it in ancient India, and now it was heard again in the New World and the New Republic of Peace and Good Will.

Rebellion! The girl flinched at the word which the good gentleman had uttered in his prayers. Was she a traitor to that flag for which her people had fought in three wars? *Rebellion!* She burned to blot it forever from the book. Oh, the bitterness of that day, which was a prophecy of the bitterness to come.

Rain was dropping as Mr. Brinsmade escorted her up her own steps. He held her hand a little at parting, and bade her be of good cheer. Perhaps he guessed something of the trial she was to go through that night alone with her aunt, Clarence's mother. Mr. Brinsmade did not go directly home. He went first to the little house next door to his. Mrs. Brice and Judge Whipple were in the parlor. What passed between them there has not been told, but presently the Judge and Mr. Brinsmade came out together and stood a long time in the yard, conversing, heedless of the rain.

CHAPTER XXI

THE STAMPEDE

SUNDAY dawned, and the people flocked to the churches. But even in the house of God were dissension and strife. From the Carvel pew at Dr. Posthelwaite's Virginia saw men and women rise from their knees and walk out—their faces pale with anger. At St. Mark's the prayer for the President of the United States was omitted. Mr. Russell and Mr. Catherwood nodded approvingly over the sermon in which the South was justified, and the sanction of Holy Writ laid upon her Institution. With not indifferent elation these gentlemen watched the departure of brethren with whom they had labored for many years, save only when Mr. Brinsmade walked down the aisle never to return. So it is that war, like a devastating flood, creeps insistent into the most sacred places, and will not be denied. Mr. Davitt, at least, preached that day to an united congregation,—which is to say that none of them went out. Mr. Hopper, who now shared a pew with Miss Crane, listened as usual with a most reverent attention.

The clouds were low and the streets wet as people walked home to dinner, to discuss, many in passion and some in sorrow, the doings of the morning. A certain clergyman had prayed to be delivered from the Irish, the Dutch, and the Devil. Was it he who started the old rumor which made such havoc that afternoon? Those barbarians of the foreign city to the south, drunk with power, were to sack and loot the city. How it flew across street and alley, from yard to yard, and from house to house! Privileged Ned ran into the dining-room where Virginia and her aunt were sitting, his eyes rolling and his face ashen with terror, crying out that the Dutch were marching on the city, firebrands in hand and murder in their hearts.

"De Gen'ral done gib out er procl'mation, Miss Jinny," he cried. "De Gen'ral done say in dat procl'mation dat he ain't got no control ober de Dutch soldiers."

Mrs. Colfax fainted.

"Oh Miss Jinny, ain't you gwineter Glencoe? Ain't you gwineter flee

away? Every fambly on dis here street's gwine away—is packin' up fo'
de country. Doan't you hear 'em, Miss Jinny? What'll your pa say to
Ned ef he ain't make you clear out! Doan't you hear de carridges
a-rattlin' off to de country?"

Virginia rose in agitation, yet trying to be calm, and to remember that
the safety of the household depended upon her alone. That was her
thought,—bred into her by generations,—the safety of the household,
of the humblest slave whose happiness and welfare depended upon her
father's bounty. How she longed in that instant for her father or Captain Lige, for some man's strength, to depend upon. Would there be
wisdom in flight?

"Do you want to go, Ned?" she asked. She has seen her aunt swoon before, and her maid Susan knows well what to do. "Do you want to go,
Ned?"

"Laws Mussy, no, Miss Jinny. One nigger laik me doan't make no
difference. My Marsa he say: 'Whaffor you leave ma house to be ram-
sacked by de Dutch?' What I gwineter answer? Oh Miss Jinny, you an'
Miss Lill an' Mammy Easter an' Susan's gwine with Jackson, an' de
othah niggahs can walk. Ephum an' me'll jes' put up de shutters an'
load de Colonel's gun."

By this time the room was filled with excited negroes, some crying,
and some laughing hysterically. Uncle Ben had come in from the
kitchen; Jackson was there, and the women were a wailing bunch in the
corner by the sideboard. Old Ephum, impassive, and Ned stood together. Virginia's eye rested upon them, and the light of love and affection was in it. She went to the window. Yes, carriages were indeed rattling outside, though a sharp shower was falling. Across the street Alphonse, M. Rénault's butler, was depositing bags and bundles on the
steps. M. Rénault himself bustled out into the rain, gesticulating excitedly. Spying her at the window, he put his hands to his mouth, cried
out something, and ran in again. Virginia flung open the sash and
listened for the dreaded sound of drums. Then she crossed quickly over
to where her aunt was lying on the lounge.

"O Jinny," murmured that lady, who had revived, "can't you do
something? Haven't you done anything? They will be here any moment
to burn us, to murder us—to—oh, my poor boy! Why isn't he here to
protect his mother! Why was Comyn so senseless, so thoughtless, as to
leave us at such a time!"

"I don't think there is any need to be frightened," said Virginia, with a calmness that made her aunt tremble with anger. "It is probably only a rumor. Ned, run to Mr. Brinsmade's and ask him about it."

However loath to go, Ned departed at once. All honor to those old-time negroes who are now memories, whose devotion to their masters was next to their love of God. A great fear was in Ned's heart, but he went. And he believed devoutly that he would never see his young mistress any more.

And while Ned is running to Mr. Brinsmade's, Mrs. Colfax is summoning that courage which comes to persons of her character at such times. She gathers her jewels into a bag, and her fine dresses into her trunk, with trembling hands, although she is well enough now. The picture of Clarence in the diamond frame she puts inside the waist of her gown. No, she will not go to Bellegarde. That is too near the city. With frantic haste she closes the trunk, which Ephum and Jackson carry downstairs and place between the seats of the carriage. Ned had had the horses in it since church time. It is not safe outside. But where to go? To Glencoe? It is three in the afternoon, and Jackson explains that, with the load, they would not reach there until midnight, if at all. To Kirkwood or Webster? Yes; many of the first families live there, and would take them in for the night. Equipages of all sorts are passing,—private carriages and public, and corner-stand hacks. The black drivers are cracking whips over galloping horses. Pedestrians are hurrying by with bundles under their arms, some running east, and some west, and some stopping to discuss excitedly the chances of each direction. From the river comes the hoarse whistle of the boats breaking the Sabbath stillness there. It is a panic to be remembered.

Virginia leaned against the iron railing of the steps, watching the scene, and waiting for Ned to return from Mr. Brinsmade's. Her face was troubled, as well it might be. The most alarming reports were cried up to her from the street, and she looked every moment for the black smoke of destruction to appear to the southward. Around her were gathered the Carvel servants, most of them crying, and imploring her not to leave them. And when Mrs. Colfax's trunk was brought down and placed in the carriage where three of them might have ridden to safety, a groan of despair and entreaty rose from the faithful group that went to her heart.

"Miss Jinny, you ain't gwineter leave yo' ol' mammy?"

"Hush, Mammy," she said. "No, you shall all go, if I have to stay myself. Ephum, go to the livery stable and get another carriage."

She went up into her own deserted room to gather the few things she would take with her—the little jewellery case with the necklace of pearls which her great-grandmother had worn at her wedding. Rosetta and Mammy Easter were of no use, and she had sent them downstairs again. With a flutter she opened her wardrobe door, to take one last look at the gowns there. You will pardon her. They were part of happier days gone by. She fell down on her knees and opened the great drawer at the bottom, and there on the top lay the dainty gown which had belonged to Dorothy Manners. A tear fell upon one of the flowers of the stays. Irresistibly pressed into her mind the memory of Anne's fancy dress ball,—of the episode by the gate, upon which she had thought so often with burning face.

The voices below grow louder, but she does not hear. She is folding the gown hurriedly into a little package. It was her great-grandmother's; her chief heirloom after the pearls. Silk and satin from Paris are left behind. With one glance at the bed in which she had slept since childhood, and at the picture over it which had been her mother's she hurries downstairs. And Dorothy Manners's gown is under her arm. On the landing she stops to brush her eyes with her handkerchief. If only her father were here!

Ah, here is Ned back again. Has Mr. Brinsmade come? What did he say? Ned simply pointed out a young man standing on the steps behind the negroes. Crimson stains were on Virginia's cheeks, and the package she carried under her arm was like lead. The young man, although he showed no signs of excitement, reddened too as he came forward and took off his hat. But the sight of him had a curious effect upon Virginia, of which she was at first unconscious. A sense of security came upon her as she looked at his face and listened to his voice.

"Mr. Brinsmade has gone to the hospital, Miss Carvel," he said. "Mrs. Brinsmade asked me to come here with your man in the hope that I might persuade you to stay where you are."

"Then the Germans are not moving on the city?" she said.

In spite of himself, Stephen smiled. It was that smile that angered her, that made her rebel against the advice he had to offer; that made her forget the insult he had risked at her hands by coming there. For she believed him utterly, without reservation. The moment he had spoken she was convinced that the panic was a silly scare which would be food for merriment in future years. And yet—was not that smile in derision of herself—of her friends who were running away? Was it not an assumption of Northern superiority, to be resented?

"It is only a malicious rumor, Miss Carvel," he answered.

"You have been told so upon good authority, I suppose," she said dryly. And at the change in her tone she saw his face fall.

"I have not," he replied honestly, "but I will submit it to your own judgment. Yesterday General Harney superseded Captain Lyon in command in St. Louis. Some citizens of prominence begged the General to send the troops away, to avoid further ill-feeling and perhaps—bloodshed." (They both winced at the word.) "Colonel Blair represented to the General that the troops could not be sent away, as they had been enlisted to serve only in St. Louis; whereupon the General in his proclamation states that he has no control over these Home Guards. That sentence has been twisted by some rascal into a confession that the Home Guards are not to be controlled. I can assure you, Miss Carvel," added Stephen, speaking with a force which made her start and thrill, "I can assure you from a personal knowledge of the German troops that they are not a riotous lot, and that they are under perfect control. If they were not, there are enough regulars in the city to repress them."

He paused. And she was silent, forgetful of the hub-bub around her. It was then that her aunt called out to her, with distressing shrillness, from the carriage:—

"Jinny, Jinny, how can you stand there talking to young men when our lives are in danger?"

She glanced hurriedly at Stephen, who said gently:—

"I do not wish to delay you, Miss Carvel, if you are bent upon going."

She wavered. His tone was not resentful, simply quiet. Ephum turned the corner of the street, the perspiration running on his black face.

"Miss Jinny, dey ain't no carridges to be had in this town. No'm, not for fifty dollars."

This was the occasion for another groan from the negroes, and they began once more to beseech her not to leave them. In the midst of their cries she heard her aunt calling from the carriage, where, beside the trunk, there was just room for her to squeeze in.

"Jinny," cried that lady, frantically, "are you to go or stay? The Hessians will be here at any moment. Oh, I cannot stay here to be murdered!"

Unconsciously the girl glanced again at Stephen. He had not gone, but was still standing in the rain on the steps, the one figure of strength and coolness she had seen this afternoon. Distracted, she blamed the fate which had made this man an enemy. How willingly would she have leaned upon such as he, and submitted to his guidance.

Unluckily at that moment came down the street a group which had been ludicrous on any other day, and was, in truth, ludicrous to Stephen then. At the head of it was a little gentleman with red mutton-chop whiskers, hatless, in spite of the rain beginning to fall. His face was the very caricature of terror. His clothes, usually neat, were awry, and his arms were full of various things, not the least conspicuous of which was a magnificent bronze clock. It was this object that caught Virginia's eye. But years passed before she laughed over it. Behind Mr. Cluyme (for it was he) trotted his family. Mrs. Cluyme, in a pink wrapper, carried an armful of the family silver; then came Belle with certain articles of feminine apparel which need not be enumerated, and the three small Cluymes of various ages brought up the rear.

Mr. Cluyme, at the top of his speed, was come opposite to the carriage when the lady occupant got out of it. Clutching at his sleeve, she demanded where he was going. The bronze clock had a narrow escape.

"To the river," he gasped. "To the river, madam!" His wife coming after him had a narrower escape still. Mrs. Colfax retained a handful of lace from the wrapper, the owner of which emitted a shriek of fright.

"Virginia, I am going to the river," said Mrs. Colfax. "You may go where you choose. I shall send the carriage back for you. Ned, to the levee!"

Ned did not lift a rein.

"What, you black rascal! You won't obey me!"

Ned swung on his seat. "No, indeedy, Miss Lilly, I ain't a-gwine 'thout young Miss. The Dutch kin cotch me an' hang me, but I ain't a-gwine 'thout Miss Jinny."

Mrs. Colfax drew her shawl about her shoulders with dignity.

"Very well, Virginia," she said. "Ill as I am, I shall walk. Bear witness that I have spent a precious hour trying to save you. If I live to see your father again, I shall tell him that you preferred to stay here and carry on disgracefully with a *Yankee,* that you let your own aunt risk her life alone in the rain. Come, Susan!"

Virginia was very pale. She did not run down the steps, but she caught her aunt by the arm ere that lady had taken six paces. The girl's face frightened Mrs. Colfax into submission, and she let herself be led back into the carriage beside the trunk. Those words of Mrs.

Colfax's stung Stephen to righteous anger and resentment—for Virginia. As to himself, he had looked for insult. He turned to go that he might not look upon her confusion; and hanging on the resolution, swung on his heel again, his eyes blazing. He saw in hers the deep blue light of the skies after an evening's storm. She was calm, and save for a little quiver of the voice, mistress of herself as she spoke to the group of cowering servants.

"Mammy," she said, "get up on the box with Ned. And, Ned, walk the horses to the levee, so that the rest may follow. Ephum, you stay here with the house, and I will send Ned back to keep you company."

With these words, clasping tightly the precious little bundle under her arm, she stepped into the carriage.

Heedless of the risk he ran, sheer admiration sent Stephen to the carriage door.

"If I can be of any service, Miss Carvel," he said, "I shall be happy."

She glanced at him wildly.

"No," she cried, "no. Drive on, Ned!"

And as the horses slipped and started she slammed the door in his face.

Down on the levee wheels rattled over the white stones washed clean by the driving rain. The drops pelted the chocolate water into froth, and a blue veil hid the distant bluffs beyond the Illinois bottom-lands. Down on the levee rich and poor battled for places on the landing-stages, and would have thrown themselves into the flood had there been no boats to save them from the dreaded Dutch. Attila and his Huns were not more feared. Oh, the mystery of that foreign city! What might not its Barbarians do when roused? The rich and poor struggled together; but money was a power that day, and many were pitilessly turned off because they did not have the high price to carry them—who knew where?

Boats which screamed, and boats which had a dragon's roar were backing out of the close ranks where they had stood wheel-house to wheel-house, and were dodging and bumping in the channel. See, their guards are black with people! Mrs. Colfax, when they are come out of the narrow street into the great open space, remarks this with alarm. All the boats will be gone before they can get near one. But Virginia does not answer. She is thinking of other things than the steamboats, and wondering whether it had not been preferable to be killed by Hessians.

Ned spies the *Barbara Lane*. He knows that her captain, Mr. Vance, is a friend of the family. What a mighty contempt did Ned and his kind have for foot-passengers! Laying about him with his whip, and shouting at the top of his voice to make himself heard, he sent the Colonel's Kentucky bays through the crowd down to the *Barbara's* landing stage, the people scampering to the right and left, and the Carvel servants, headed by Uncle Ben, hanging on to the carriage springs, trailing behind. Here was a triumph for Ned, indeed! He will tell you to this day how Mr. Catherwood's carriage was pocketed by drays and bales, and how Mr. James's horses were seized by the bridles and turned back. Ned had a head on his shoulders, and eyes in his head. He spied Captain Vance himself on the stage, and bade Uncle Ben hold to the horses while he shouldered his way to that gentleman. The result was that the Captain came bowing to the carriage door, and offered his own cabin to the ladies. But the niggers—he would take no niggers except a maid for each; and he begged Mrs. Colfax's pardon—he could not carry her trunk.

So Virginia chose Mammy Easter, whose red and yellow turban was awry from fear lest she be left behind; and Ned was instructed to drive the rest with all haste to Bellegarde. Captain Vance gave Mrs. Colfax his arm, and Virginia his eyes. He escorted the ladies to quarters in the texas, and presently was heard swearing prodigiously as the boat was cast off. It was said of him that he could turn an oath better than any man on the river, which was no mean reputation.

Mrs. Colfax was assisted to bed by Susan. Virginia stood by the little window of the cabin, and as the *Barbara* paddled and floated down the river she looked anxiously for signals of a conflagration. Nay, in that hour she wished that the city might burn. So it is that the best of us may at times desire misery to thousands that our own malice may be fed. Virginia longed to see the yellow flame creep along the wet, gray clouds. Passionate tears came to her eyes at the thought of the humiliation she had suffered,—and before *him*, of all men. Could she ever live with her aunt after what she had said? "Carrying on with that Yankee!" The horrible injustice of it!

Her anger, too, was still against Stephen. Once more he had been sent by circumstances to mock her and her people. If the city would only burn, that his cocksure judgment might for once be mistaken, his calmness for once broken!

The rain ceased, the clouds parted, and the sun turned the muddy river to gold. The bluffs shone May-green in the western flood of light.

and a haze hung over the bottom-lands. Not a sound disturbed the quiet of the city receding to the northward, and the rain had washed the pall of smoke from over it. On the boat excited voices died down to natural tones; men smoked on the guards and promenaded on the hurricane deck, as if this were some pleasant excursion. Women waved to the other boats flocking after. Laughter was heard, and joking. Mrs. Colfax stirred in her berth and began to talk.

"Virginia, where are we going?"

Virginia did not move.

"Jinny!"

She turned. In that hour she remembered that great good-natured man, her mother's brother, and for his sake Colonel Carvel had put up with much from his wife's sister-in-law. She could pass over, but never forgive what her aunt had said to her that afternoon. Mrs. Colfax had often been cruel before, and inconsiderate. But as the girl thought of the speech, staring out on the waters, it suddenly occurred to her that no lady would have uttered it. In all her life she had never realized till now that her aunt was not a lady. From that time forth Virginia's attitude toward her aunt was changed.

She controlled herself, however, and answered something, and went out listlessly to find the Captain and inquire the destination of the boat. Not that this mattered much to her. At the foot of the companionway leading to the saloon deck she saw, of all people, Mr. Eliphalet Hopper leaning on the rail, and pensively expectorating on the roof of the wheelhouse. In another mood Virginia would have laughed, for at sight of her he straightened convulsively, thrust his quid into his cheek, and removed his hat with more zeal than the grudging deference he usually accorded to the sex. Clearly Eliphalet would not have chosen the situation.

"I cal'late we didn't get out any too soon, Miss Carvel," he remarked, with a sad attempt at jocoseness. "There won't be a great deal in that town when the Dutch get through with it."

"I think that there are enough men left in it to save it," said Virginia.

Apparently Mr. Hopper found no suitable answer to this, for he made none. He continued to glance at her uneasily. There was an impudent tribute in his look which she resented strongly.

"Where is the Captain?" she demanded.

"He's down below—ma'am," he replied. "Can—can I do anything?"

"Yes," she said, with abrupt maliciousness, "you may tell me where you are going."

"I cal'late, up the Cumberland River. That's where she's bound for, if she don't stop before she gets there. Guess there ain't many of 'em inquired where she was goin', or cared much," he added, with a ghastly effort to be genial.

"Do you care?" she demanded, curiously.

Eliphalet grinned.

"Not a great deal," he said. Then he felt called upon to defend himself. "I didn't see any use in gettin' murdered, when I couldn't do anything."

She left him. He stared after her up the companionway, bit off a generous piece of tobacco, and ruminated. If to be a genius is to possess an infinite stock of patience, Mr. Hopper was a genius. There was patience in his smile. But it was not a pleasant smile to look upon.

Virginia did not see it. She had told her aunt the news, and stood in the breeze on the hurricane deck looking southward, with her hand shading her eyes. The *Barbara Lane* happened to be a boat with a record, and her name was often in the papers. She had already caught up with and distanced others which had had half an hour's start of her, and was near the head of the procession.

Virginia presently became aware that people were gathering around her in knots, gazing at a boat coming toward them. Others had been met which, on learning the dread news, turned back. But this one kept her bow steadily up the current, although she had passed within a biscuit-toss of the leader of the line of refugees. It was then that Captain Vance's hairy head appeared above the deck.

"Dang me!" he said, "if here ain't pig-headed Brent steaming the *Jewanita* straight to destruction."

"Oh, are you sure it's Captain Brent?" cried Virginia.

The Captain looked around in surprise.

"If that there was Shreve's old *Enterprise* come to life again, I'd lay cotton to sawdust that Brent had her. Danged if he wouldn't take her right into the jaws of the Dutch."

The Captain's words spread, and caused considerable excitement. On board the *Barbara Lane* were many gentlemen who had begun to be shamefaced over their panic, and these went in a body to the Captain and asked him to communicate with the *Juanita*. Whereupon a certain number of whistles were sounded, and the *Barbara's* bows headed for the the other side of the channel.

As the *Juanita* drew near, Virginia saw the square figure and clean, smooth-shaven face of Captain Lige standing in front of his wheelhouse. Peace crept back into her soul, and she tingled with joy as the bells clanged and the bucket-planks churned, and the great New Orleans packet crept slowly to the *Barbara's* side.

"You ain't goin' in, Brent?" shouted the *Barbara's* captain.

"Why not?" responded Mr. Brent. At the sound of his voice Virginia could have wept.

"The Dutch are sacking the city," said Vance. "Didn't they tell you?"

"The Dutch—hell!" said Mr. Brent, calmly. "Who's afraid of the Dutch?"

A general titter went along the guards, and Virginia blushed. Why could not the Captain see her?

"I'm on my reg'lar trip, of course," said Vance. Out there on the sunlit river the situation seemed to call for an apology.

"Seems to be a little more *loaded* than common," remarked Captain Lige, dryly, at which there was another general laugh.

"If you're really goin' up," said Captain Vance, "I reckon there's a few here would like to be massacred, if you'll take 'em."

"Certainly," answered Mr. Brent; "I'm bound for the *barbecue*." And he gave a command.

While the two great boats were manœuvring, and slashing with one wheel and the other, the gongs sounding, Virginia ran into the cabin.

"Oh, Aunt Lillian," she exclaimed, "here is Captain Lige and the *Juanita,* and he is going to take us back with him. He says there is no danger."

It 's unnecessary here to repeat the moral persuasion which Virginia used to get her aunt up and dressed. That lady, when she had heard the whistle and the gongs, had let her imagination loose. Turning her face to the wall, she was in the act of repeating her prayers as her niece entered.

A big stevedore carried her down two decks to where the gang-plank was thrown across. Captain Lige himself was at the other end. His face lighted. Pushing the people aside, he rushed across, snatched the lady from the negro's arms, crying:—

"Jinny! Jinny Carvel! Well, if this ain't *fortunate!*"

The stevedore's services were required for Mammy Easter. And behind the burly shield thus formed, a stoutish gentleman slipped over, all unnoticed, with a carpet-bag in his hand. It bore the initials *E. H.*

The plank was drawn in. The great wheels began to turn and hiss, the *Barbara's* passengers waved good-by to the foolhardy lunatics who had elected to go back into the jaws of destruction. Mrs. Colfax was put into a cabin; and Virginia, in a glow, climbed with Captain Lige to the hurricane deck. There they stood for a while in silence, watching the broad stern of the *Barbara* growing smaller.

"Just to think," Miss Carvel remarked, with a little hysterical sigh, "just to think that some of those people brought bronze clocks instead of tooth-brushes."

"And what did you bring, my girl?" asked the Captain, glancing at the parcel she held so tightly under her arm.

He never knew why she blushed so furiously.

CHAPTER XXII

THE STRAINING OF ANOTHER FRIENDSHIP

CAPTAIN LIGE asked but two questions: where was the Colonel, and was it true that Clarence had refused to be paroled? Though not possessing over-fine susceptibilities, the Captain knew a mud-drum from a lady's watch, as he himself said. In his solicitude for Virginia, he saw that she was in no state of mind to talk of the occurrences of the last few days. So he helped her to climb the little stair that winds to the top of the texas,—that sanctified roof where the pilot-house squats. The girl clung to her bonnet. Will you like her any the less when you know that it was a shovel bonnet, with long red ribbons that tied under her chin? It became her wonderfully. "Captain Lige," she said, almost tearfully, as she took his arm, "how I thank heaven that you came up the river this afternoon!"

"Jinny," said the Captain, "did you ever know why cabins are called *staterooms?*"

"Why, no," answered she, puzzled.

"There was an old fellow named Shreve who ran steamboats before Jackson fought the redcoats at New Orleans. In Shreve's time the cabins were curtained off, just like these new-fangled sleeping-car berths. The old man built wooden rooms, and he named them after the different states, Kentucky, and Illinois, and Pennsylvania. So that when a fellow came aboard he'd say: 'What *state* am I in, Cap?' And from this river has the name spread all over the world—*stateroom*. That's mighty interesting," said Captain Lige.

"Yes," said Virginia; "why didn't you tell me long ago?"

"And I'll bet you can't say," the Captain continued, "why this house we're standing on is called the texas."

"Because it is annexed to the states," she replied, quick as a flash.

"Well, you're *bright*," said he. "Old Tufts got that notion, when Texas came in. Like to see Bill Jenks?"

"Of course," said Virginia.

Bill Jenks was Captain Brent's senior pilot. His skin hung on his face

272

in folds, like that of a rhinoceros. It was very much the same color. His grizzled hair was all lengths, like a worn-out mop; his hand reminded one of an eagle's claw, and his teeth were a pine yellow. He greeted only such people as he deemed worthy of notice, but he had held Virginia in his arms.

"William," said the young lady, roguishly, "how is the eye, location, and memory?"

William abandoned himself to a laugh. When this happened it was put in the *Juanita's* log.

"So the Cap'n be still harpin' on that?" he said. "Miss Jinny, he's just plumb crazy on a pilot's qualifications."

"He says that you are the best pilot on the river, but I don't believe it," said Virginia.

William cackled again. He made a place for her on the leather-padded seat at the back of the pilot house, where for a long time she sat staring at the flag trembling on the jackstaff between the great sombre pipes. The sun fell down, but his light lingered in the air above as the big boat forged abreast the foreign city of South St. Louis. There was the arsenal, grim despite its dress of green, where Clarence was confined alone.

Captain Lige came in from his duties below. "Well, Jinny, we'll soon be at home," he said. "We've made a quick trip against the rains."

"And—and do you think the city is safe?"

"Safe!" he cried. "As safe as London!" He checked himself. "Jinny, would you like to blow the whistle?"

"I should just love to," said Virginia. And following Mr. Jenks's directions she put her toe on the tread, and shrank back when the monster responded with a snort and a roar. River men along the levee heard that signal and laughed. The joke was certainly not on sturdy Elijah Brent.

An hour later, Virginia and her aunt and the Captain, followed by Mammy Easter and Rosetta and Susan, were walking through the streets of the stillest city in the Union. All that they met was a provost's guard, for St. Louis was under Martial Law. Once in a while they saw the light of some contemptuous citizen of the residence district who had stayed to laugh. Out in the suburbs, at the country houses of the first families, people of distinction slept five and six in a room—many with only a quilt between body and matting. Little wonder that these dreamed of Hessians and destruction. In town they slept with their doors open, those who remained and had faith. Martial law means passes and explanations, and walking generally in the light of day. Martial law means that the Commander-in-chief, if he be an artist in well doing, may use his boot freely on politicians bland or beetle-browed. No police force ever gave the sense of security inspired by a provost guard.

Captain Lige sat on the steps of Colonel Carvel's house that night, long after the ladies were gone to bed. The only sounds breaking the silence of the city were the beat of the feet of the marching squads and the call of the corporal's relief. But the Captain smoked in agony until the clouds of two days slipped away from under the stars, for he was trying to decide a Question. Then he went up to a room in the house which had been known as his since the rafters were put down on that floor.

The next morning, as the Captain and Virginia sit at breakfast together with only Mammy Easter to cook and Rosetta to wait on them, the Colonel bursts in. He is dusty and travel-stained from his night on the train, but his gray eyes light with affection as he sees his friend beside his daughter.

"Jinny," he cries as he kisses her, "Jinny, I'm proud of you, my girl! You didn't let the Yankees frighten you. But where is Jackson?"

And so the whole miserable tale has to be told over again, between laughter and tears on Virginia's part, and laughter and strong language on Colonel Carvel's. What a blessing that Lige met them, else the Colonel might now be starting for the Cumberland River in search of his daughter. The Captain does not take much part in the conversation, and he refuses the cigar which is offered him. Mr. Carvel draws back in surprise.

"Lige," he says, "this is the first time to my knowledge."

"I smoked too many last night," says the Captain.

The Colonel sat down, with his feet against the mantel, too full of affairs to take much notice of Mr. Brent's apathy.

"The Yanks have taken the first trick—that's sure," he said. "But I think we'll laugh last, Jinny. Jefferson City isn't precisely quiet. The state has got more militia, or will have more militia in a day or two. We won't miss the thousand they stole in Camp Jackson. They're organizing up there. And I've got a few commissions right here," and he tapped his pocket.

"Pa," said Virginia, "did you volunteer?"

The Colonel laughed.

"The Governor wouldn't have me," he answered. "He said I was more good here in St. Louis. I'll go later. What's this I hear about Clarence?"

Virginia related the occurrences of Saturday. The Colonel listened with many exclamations, slapping his knee from time to time as she proceeded.

"By gum!" he cried, when she had finished, "the boy has it in him, after all! They can't hold him a day—can they, Lige?" (No answer from the Captain, who is eating his breakfast in silence.) "All that we have to do is to go for Worington and get a *habeas corpus* from the United States District Court. Come on, Lige."

The Captain got up excitedly, his face purple.

"I reckon you'll have to excuse me, Colonel," he said. "There's a cargo on my boat which has *got* to come off."

And without more ado he left the room. In consternation they heard the front door close behind him. And yet, neither father nor daughter dared in that hour add to the trial of the other by speaking out the dread that was in their hearts. The Colonel smoked for a while, not a word escaping him, and then he patted Virginia's cheek.

"I reckon I'll run over and see Russell, Jinny," he said, striving to be cheerful. "We must get the boy out. I'll see a lawyer." He stopped abruptly in the hall and pressed his hand to his forehead. "My God," he whispered to himself, "if I could only go to Silas!"

The good Colonel got Mr. Russell, and they went to Mr. Worington, Mrs. Colfax's lawyer, of whose politics it is not necessary to speak. There was plenty of excitement around the Government building where his Honor issued the writ. There lacked not gentlemen of influence who went with Mr. Russell and Colonel Carvel and the lawyer and the Commissioner to the Arsenal. They were admitted to the presence of the indomitable Lyon, who informed them that Captain Colfax was a prisoner of war, and, since the arsenal was Government property, *not in the state*. The Commissioner thereupon attested the affidavit to Colonel Carvel, and thus the application for the writ was made legal.

These things the Colonel reported to Virginia; and to Mrs. Colfax, who received them with red eyes and a thousand queries as to whether that Yankee ruffian would pay any attention to the Sovereign law which he pretended to uphold; whether the Marshal would not be cast over the Arsenal wall by the slack of his raiment when he went to serve the writ. This was not the language, but the purport, of the lady's questions. Colonel Carvel had made but a light breakfast: he had had no dinner and little rest on the train. But he answered his sister-in-law with unfailing courtesy. He was too honest to express a hope which he did not feel. He had returned that evening to a dreary household. During the day the servants had straggled in from Bellegarde, and Virginia had had prepared those dishes which her father loved. Mrs. Colfax chose to keep her room, for which the two were silently thankful. Jackson announced supper. The Colonel was humming a tune as he went down the stairs, but Virginia was not deceived. He would not see the yearning in her eyes as he took his chair; he would not glance at Captain Lige's empty seat. It was because he did not dare. She caught her breath when she saw that the food on his plate lay untouched.

"Pa, are you ill?" she faltered.

He pushed his chair away, such suffering in his look as she had never seen.

"Jinny," he said, "I reckon Lige is for the Yankees."

"I have known it all along," she said, but faintly.

"Did he tell you?" her father demanded.

"No."

"My God," cried the Colonel, in agony, "to think that he kept it from me! to think that Lige kept it from me!"

"It is because he loves you, Pa," answered the girl, gently, "it is because he loves us."

He said nothing to that. Virginia got up, and went softly around the table. She leaned over his shoulder.

"Pa!"

"Yes," he said, his voice lifeless.

But her courage was not to be lightly shaken.

"Pa, will you forbid him to come here—now?"

A long while she waited for his answer, while the big clock ticked out the slow seconds in the hall, and her heart beat wildly.

"No," said the Colonel. "As long as I have a roof, Lige may come under it."

He rose abruptly and seized his hat. She did not ask him where he was going, but ordered Jackson to keep the supper warm, and went into the drawing-room. The lights were out, then, but the great piano that was her mother's lay open. Her fingers fell upon the keys. That wondrous hymn which Judge Whipple loved, which for years has been the comfort of those in distress, floated softly with the night air out of the open window. It was "Lead, Kindly Light." Colonel Carvel heard it, and paused.

Shall we follow him?

He did not stop again until he reached the narrow street at the top of the levee bank, where the quaint stone houses of the old French residents were being loaded with wares. He took a few steps back—up the hill. Then he wheeled about, walked swiftly down the levee, and on to the landing-stage beside which the big *Juanita* loomed in the night. On her bows was set, fantastically, a yellow street-car.

The Colonel stopped mechanically. Its unexpected appearance there had served to break the current of his meditations. He stood staring at it, while the roustabouts passed and repassed, noisily carrying great logs of wood on shoulders padded by their woollen caps.

"That'll be the first street-car used in the city of New Orleans, if it ever gets there, Colonel."

The Colonel jumped. Captain Lige was standing beside him.

"Lige, is that you? We waited supper for you."

"Reckon I'll have to stay here and boss the cargo all night. Want to get in as many trips as I can before—navigation closes," the Captain concluded significantly.

Colonel Carvel shook his head. "You were never too busy to come for supper, Lige. I reckon the cargo isn't all."

Captain Lige shot at him a swift look. He gulped.

"Come out here on the levee," said the Colonel, sternly.

They walked out together, and for some distance in silence.

"Lige," said the elder gentleman, striking his stick on the stones, "if there ever was a straight goer, that's you. You've always dealt squarely with me, and now I'm going to ask you a plain question. Are you North or South?"

"I'm North, I reckon," answered the Captain, bluntly.

The Colonel bowed his head. It was a long time before he spoke again. The Captain waited like a man who expects and deserves the severest verdict. But there was no anger in Mr. Carvel's voice—only reproach.

"And you wouldn't tell me, Lige? You kept it from me."

"My God, Colonel," exclaimed the other, passionately, "how could I? I owe what I have to your charity. But for you and—and Jinny I should have gone to the devil. If you and she are taken away, what have I left in life? I was a coward, sir, not to tell you. You must have guessed it. And yet,—God help me,—I can't stand by and see the nation go to *pieces*. Your nation as well as mine, Colonel. Your fathers fought that we Americans might inherit the earth—" He stopped abruptly. Then he continued haltingly, "Colonel, I know you're a man of strong feelings

and *convictions*. All I ask is that you and Jinny will think of me as a
friend—"

He choked, and turned away, not heeding the direction of his feet.
The Colonel, his stick raised, stood looking after him. He was folded in
the near darkness before he called his name.

"Lige!"

"Yes, Colonel."

He came back, wondering, across the rough stones until he stood beside the tall figure. Below them, the lights glided along the dark water.

"Lige, didn't I raise you? Haven't I taught you that my house was
your home? Come back, Lige. But—but never speak to me again of this
night! Jinny is waiting for us."

Not a word passed between them as they went up the quiet street.
At the sound of their feet in the entry the door was flung open, and
Virginia, with her hands outstretched, stood under the hall light.

"Oh, Pa, I knew you would bring him back," she said.

CHAPTER XXIII

OF CLARENCE

CAPTAIN CLARENCE COLFAX, late of the State Dragoons, awoke on Sunday morning the chief of the many topics of the conversation of a big city. His conduct drew forth enthusiastic praise from the gentlemen and ladies who had thronged Beauregard and Davis avenues, and honest admiration from the party which had broken up the camp. The boy had behaved well. There were many doting parents, like Mr. Catherwood, whose boys had accepted the parole, whose praise was a trifle lukewarm, to be sure. But popular opinion, when once aroused, will draw a grunt from the most grudging.

We are not permitted, alas, to go behind these stern walls and discover how Captain Colfax passed that eventful Sunday of the Exodus. We know that, in his loneliness, he hoped for a visit from his cousin, and took to pacing his room in the afternoon, when a smarting sense of injustice crept upon him. Clarence was young. And how was he to guess, as he looked out in astonishment upon the frightened flock of white boats swimming southward, that his mother and his sweetheart were there?

On Monday, while the Colonel and many prominent citizens were busying themselves about procuring the legal writ which was at once to release Mr. Colfax, and so cleanse the whole body of Camp Jackson's defenders from any veiled intentions toward the Government, many well-known carriages drew up before the Carvel House in Locust Street to congratulate the widow and the Colonel upon the possession of such a son and nephew. There were some who slyly congratulated Virginia, whose martyrdom it was to sit up with people all the day long. For Mrs. Colfax kept her room, and admitted only a few of her bosom friends to cry with her. When the last of the callers was gone, Virginia was admitted to her aunt's presence.

"Aunt Lillian, to-morrow morning Pa and I are going to the Arsenal with a basket for Max. Pa seems to think there is a chance that he may come back with us. You will go, of course."

The lady smiled wearily at the proposal, and raised her hands in pro-

279

test, the lace on the sleeves of her dressing-gown falling away from her white arms.

"Go, my dear?" she exclaimed, "when I can't walk to my bureau after that terrible Sunday. You are crazy, Jinny. No," she added, with conviction, "I never again expect to see him alive. Comyn says they may release him, does he? Is he turning Yankee, too?"

The girl went away, not in anger or impatience, but in sadness. Brought up to reverence her elders, she had ignored the shallowness of her aunt's character in happier days. But now Mrs. Colfax's conduct carried a prophecy with it. Virginia sat down on the landing to ponder on the years to come,—on the pain they were likely to bring with them from this source—Clarence gone to the war; her father gone (for she felt that he would go in the end), Virginia foresaw the lonely days of trial in company with this vain woman whom accident made her cousin's mother. Ay, and more, fate had made her the mother of the man she was to marry. The girl could scarcely bear the thought—through the hurry and swing of the events of two days she had kept it from her mind. But now—Clarence was to be released. To-morrow he would be coming home to her joyfully for his reward, and she did not love him. She was bound to face that again and again. She had cheated herself again and again with other feelings. She had set up intense love of country in the shrine where it did not belong, and it had answered— for a while. She saw Clarence in a hero's light—until a fatal intimate knowledge made her shudder and draw back. And yet her resolution should not be water. She would carry it through.

Captain Lige's cheery voice roused her from below—and her father's laugh. And as she went down to them she thanked God that this friend had been spared to him. Never had the Captain's river yarns been better told than at the table that evening. Virginia did not see him glance at the Colonel when at last he had brought a smile to her face.

"I'm going to leave Jinny with you, Lige," said Mr. Carvel, presently. "Worington has some notion that the Marshal may go to the Arsenal to-night with the writ. I mustn't neglect the boy."

Virginia stood in front of him.

"Won't you let me go?" she pleaded.

The Colonel was taken aback. He stood looking down at her, stroking his goatee, and marveling at the ways of woman.

"The horses have been out all day, Jinny," he said, "I am going in the cars."

"I can go in the cars, too."

The Colonel looked at Captain Lige.

"There is only a chance that we shall see Clarence," he went on, uneasily.

"It is better than sitting still," cried Virginia, as she ran away to get the bonnet with the red strings.

"Lige," said the Colonel, as the two stood awaiting her in the hall, "I can't make her out. Can you?"

The Captain did not answer.

It was a long journey, in a bumping car with bad springs that rattled unceasingly, past the string of provost guards. The Colonel sat in the corner, with his head bent down over his stick. At length, cramped and weary, they got out, and made their way along the Arsenal wall, past the sentries to the entrance. The sergeant brought his rifle to a "port."

"Commandant's orders, sir. No one admitted," he said.

"Is Captain Colfax here?" asked Mr. Carvel.

"Captain Colfax was taken to Illinois in a skiff, quarter of an hour since."

Captain Lige gave vent to a long, low whistle.

"A skiff!" he exclaimed, "and the river this high! A skiff!"

Virginia clasped his arm in terror.

"Is there danger?"

Before he could answer came the noise of steps from the direction of the river, and a number of people hurried up excitedly. Colonel Carvel recognized Mr. Worington, the lawyer, and caught him by the sleeve.

"Anything happened?" he demanded.

Worington glanced at the sentry, and pulled the Colonel past the entrance and into the street. Virginia and Captain Lige followed.

"They have started across with him in a light skiff—four men and a captain. The young fool! We had him rescued."

"Rescued!"

"Yes. There were but five in the guard. And a lot of us, who suspected what they were up to, were standing around. When we saw 'em come down, we made a rush and had the guard overpowered. But Colfax called out to stand back."

"Well, sir."

"Cuss me if I understand him," said Mr. Worington. "He told us to disperse, and that he proposed to remain a prisoner and go where they sent him."

There was a silence. Then—

"Move on please, gentlemen," said the sentry, and they started to walk toward the car line, the lawyer and the Colonel together. Virginia put her hand through the Captain's arm. In the darkness he laid his big one over it.

"Don't you be frightened, Jinny, at what I said. I reckon they'll fetch up in Illinois all right, if I know *Lyon*. There, there," said Captain Lige, soothingly. Virginia was crying softly. She had endured more in the past few days than often falls to the lot of one-and-twenty. "There, there, Jinny." He felt like crying himself. He thought of the many, many times he had taken her on his knee and kissed her tears. He might do that no more, now. There was the young Captain, a prisoner on the great black river, who had a better right. Elijah Brent wondered, as they waited in the silent street for the lonely car, if Clarence loved her as well as he.

It was very late when they reached home, and Virginia went silently up to her room. Colonel Carvel stared grimly after her, then glanced at his friend as he turned down the lights. The eyes of the two met, as of old, in true understanding.

The sun was still slanting over the tops of the houses the next morning when Virginia, a ghostly figure, crept down the stairs and withdrew the lock and bolt on the front door. The street was still, save for the twittering of birds and the distant rumble of a cart in its early rounds. The chill air of the morning made her shiver as she scanned the entry for the newspaper. Dismayed, she turned to the clock in the hall. Its hands were at quarter past five.

She sat long behind the curtains in her father's little library, the thoughts whirling in her brain as she watched the growing life of another day. What would it bring forth? Once she stole softly back to the entry, self-indulgent and ashamed, to rehearse again the bitter and the sweet of that scene of the Sunday before. She summoned up the image of the young man who had stood on these steps in front of the frightened servants. She seemed to feel again the calm power and earnestness of his face, to hear again the clear-cut tones of his voice as he advised her. Then she drew back, frightened, into the sombre library, conscience-stricken that she should have yielded to this temptation then, when Clarence—She dared not follow the thought, but she saw the light skiff at the mercy of the angry river and the dark night. This had haunted her. If he were spared, she prayed for strength to consecrate herself to him. A book lay on the table, and Virginia took refuge in it. And her eyes, glancing over the pages, rested on this verse:

> "Thy voice is heard thro' rolling drums,
> That beat to battle where he stands;
> Thy face across his fancy comes,
> And gives the battle to his hands."

The paper brought no news, nor mentioned the ruse to which Captain Lyon had resorted to elude the writ by transporting his prisoner to Illinois. Newspapers were not as alert then as now. Colonel Carvel was off early to the Arsenal in search of tidings. He would not hear of Virginia's going with him. Captain Lige, with a surer instinct, went to the river. What a morning of suspense! Twice Virginia was summoned to her aunt, and twice she made excuse. It was the Captain who returned first, and she met him at the door.

"Oh, what have you heard?" she cried.

"He is alive," said the Captain, tremulously, "alive and well, and escaped South."

She took a step toward him, and swayed. The Captain caught her. For a brief instant he held her in his arms, and then he led her to the great armchair that was the Colonel's.

"Lige," she said, "are you sure that this is not—a kindness?"

"No, Jinny," he answered quickly, "but things were mighty *close*. I was afraid last night. The river was roarin'. They struck out straight across, but they drifted and drifted like log-wood. And then she began to fill, and all five of 'em to bail. Then—then she went down. The five soldiers came up on that bit of an island below the Arsenal. They hunted all night, but they didn't find Clarence. And they got taken off to the Arsenal this morning."

"And how do you know?" she faltered.

"I knew that much this morning," he continued, "and so did your pa. But the *Andrew Jackson* is just in from Memphis, and the Captain tells me that he spoke the Memphis packet off Cape Girardeau, and that Clarence was aboard. She picked him up by a miracle, after he had just missed a round *trip* through her wheel-house."

BOOK III

CHAPTER I

INTRODUCING A CAPITALIST

A CORDON of blue regiments surrounded the city at first from Carondelet to North St. Louis, like an open fan. The crowds liked best to go to Compton Heights, where the tents of the German citizen-soldiers were spread out like so many slices of white cake on the green beside the city's reservoir. Thence the eye stretched across the town, catching the dome of the Court House and the spire of St. John's. Away to the west, on the line of the Pacific railroad that led halfway across the state, was another camp. Then another, and another, on the circle of the fan, until the river was reached to the northward, far above the bend. Within was a peace that passed understanding,—the peace of martial law.

Without the city, in the great state beyond, an irate governor had gathered his forces from the east and from the west. Letters came and went between Jefferson City and Jefferson Davis, their purport being that the Governor was to work out his own salvation, for a while at least. Young men of St. Louis, struck in a night by the fever of militarism, arose and went to Glencoe. Prying sergeants and commissioned officers, mostly of hated German extraction, thundered at the door of Colonel Carvel's house, and other houses, there—for Glencoe was a border town. They searched the place more than once from garret to cellar, muttered guttural oaths, and smelled of beer and sauerkraut. The haughty appearance of Miss Carvel did not awe them—they were blind to all manly sensations. The Colonel's house, alas, was one of many in Glencoe written down in red ink in a book at headquarters as a place toward which the feet of the young men strayed. Good evidence was handed in time and time again that the young men had come and gone, and red-faced commanding officers cursed indignant subalterns, and implied that Beauty had had a hand in it. Councils of war were held over the advisability of seizing Mr. Carvel's house at Glencoe, but proof was lacking until one rainy night in June a captain and ten men spurred up the drive and swung into a big circle around the house. The Captain took off his cavalry gauntlet and knocked at the door, more gently than usual. Miss Virginia was home, so Jackson said. The Captain was given an audience more formal than one with the queen of Prussia could have been. Miss Carvel was infinitely more haughty than her Majesty. Was not the Captain hired to do a degrading service? Indeed, he thought so as he followed her about the house, and he felt like the lowest of criminals as he opened a closet door or looked under a bed. He was a beast of the field, of the mire. How Virginia shrank from him if he had occasion to pass her! Her gown would have been defiled by his touch. And yet the Captain did not smell of beer, nor of sauerkraut; nor did he swear in any language. He did his duty apologetically, but he did it. He pulled a man (aged seventeen) out from under a great hoop skirt in a little closet, and the man had a pistol that refused its duty when snapped in the Captain's face. This was little Spencer Catherwood, just home from a military academy.

Spencer was taken through the rain by the chagrined Captain to the headquarters, where he caused a little embarrassment. No damning evidence was discovered on his person, for the pistol had long since ceased to be a firearm. And so after a stiff lecture from the Colonel he was finally given back into the custody of his father.

Despite the pickets, the young men filtered through daily,—or rather nightly. Presently some of them began to come back, gaunt and worn and tattered, among the grim cargoes that were landed by the thousands and tens of thousands on the levee. And they took them (oh, the pity of it!) they took them to Mr. Lynch's slave pen, turned into a Union prison of detention, where their fathers and grandfathers had been wont to send their disorderly and insubordinate niggers. They were packed away, as the miserable slaves had been, to taste something of the bitterness of the negro's lot. So came Bert Russell to welter in a low room whose walls gave out the stench of years. How you cooked for them, and schemed for them, and cried for them, you devoted women of the South! You spent the long hot summer in town, and every day you went with your baskets to Gratiot Street, where the infected old house stands, until—until one morning a lady walked out past the guard, and down the street. She was civilly detained at the corner, because she wore army boots. After that permits were issued. If you were a young lady of the proper principles in those days, you climbed a steep pair of stairs in the heat, and stood in line until it became your turn to be catechised by an indifferent young officer in blue who sat behind a table and smoked a horrid cigar. He had little time to be courteous. He was not to be dazzled by a bright gown or a pretty face; he was indifferent to a smile which would have won a savage. His duty was to look down into your heart, and extract therefrom the nefarious scheme you had made to set free the man you loved ere he could be sent north to Alton or Columbus. My dear, you wish to rescue him, to disguise him, send him south by way of Colonel Carvel's house at Glencoe. Then he will be killed. At least, he will have died for the South.

First politics, and then war, and then more politics, in this our country. Your masterful politician obtains a regiment, and goes to war, sword in hand. He fights well, but he is still the politician. It was not a case merely of fighting for the Union, but first of getting permission to fight. Camp Jackson taken, and the prisoners exchanged south, Captain Lyon, who moved like a whirlwind, who loved the Union beyond his own life, was thrust down again. A mutual agreement was entered into between the Governor and the old Indian fighter in command of the Western Department, to respect each other. A trick for the Rebels. How Lyon chafed, and paced the Arsenal walks while he might have saved the state. Then two gentlemen went to Washington, and the next thing that happened was Brigadier General Lyon, Commander of the Department of the West.

Would General Lyon confer with the Governor of Missouri? Yes, the General would give the Governor a safe-conduct into St. Louis, but his Excellency must come to the General. His Excellency came, and the General deigned to go with the Union leader to the Planters' House. Conference, five hours; result, a safe-conduct for the Governor back. And this is how General Lyon ended the talk. His words, generously preserved, by a Confederate colonel who accompanied his Excellency, deserve to be writ in gold on the National Annals.

"Rather than concede to the state of Missouri the right to demand that my Government shall not enlist troops within her limits, or bring troops into the state whenever it pleases; or move its troops at its own will into, out of, or through, the state; rather than concede to the state of Missouri for one single instant the right to dictate to my Government in any matter, however unimportant, I would" (rising and pointing in turn to every one in the room) "see you, and you, and you, and you, and every man, woman, and child in this state, dead and buried." Then, turning to the Governor, he continued, "This means war. In an hour one of my officers will call for you and conduct you out of my lines."

And thus, without another word, without an inclination of the head, he turned upon his heel and strode out of the room, rattling his spurs and clanking his sabre.

It did mean war. In less than two months that indomitable leader was lying dead beside Wilson's Creek, among the oaks on Bloody Hill. What he would have been to this Union, had God spared him, we shall never know. He saved Missouri, and won respect and love from the brave men who fought against him.

Those first fierce battles in the state! What prayers rose to heaven, and curses sank to hell, when the news of them came to the city by the river! Flags were made by loving fingers, and shirts and bandages. Trembling young ladies of Union sympathies presented colors to regiments on the Arsenal Green, or at Jefferson Barracks, or at Camp Benton to the northwest near the Fair Grounds. And then the regiments marched through the streets with bands playing that march to which the words of the Battle Hymn were set, and those bright ensigns snapping at the front; bright now, and new, and crimson. But soon to be stained a darker red, and rent into tatters, and finally brought back and talked over and cried over; and tenderly laid above an inscription in a glass case, to be revered by generations of Americans to come. What can stir the soul more than the sight of those old flags, standing in ranks like the veterans they are, whose duty has been nobly done? The blood of the color-sergeant is there, black now with age. But where are the tears of the sad women who stitched the red and the white and the blue together?

The regiments marched through the streets and aboard the boats, and pushed off before a levee of waving handkerchiefs and flags. Then heart-breaking suspense. Later—much later, black headlines, and grim lists three columns long,—three columns of a blanket sheet! "The *City of Alton* has arrived with the following Union dead and wounded, and the following Confederate wounded (prisoners)." Why does the type run together?

In a never-ceasing procession they steamed up the river; those calm boats which had been wont to carry the white cargoes of Commerce now bearing the red cargoes of war. And they bore away to new battle-fields thousands of fresh-faced boys from Wisconsin and Michigan and

Minnesota, gathered at Camp Benton. Some came back with their color gone and their red cheeks sallow and bearded and sunken. Others came not back at all.

Stephen Brice, with a pain over his heart and a lump in his throat, walked on the pavement beside his old company, but his look avoided their faces. He wrung Richter's hand on the landing-stage. Richter was now a captain. The good German's eyes were filled as he said good-by.

"You will come, too, my friend, when the country needs you," he said. "Now" (and he shrugged his shoulders), "now have we many with no cares to go. I have not even a father—" And he turned to Judge Whipple, who was standing by, holding out a bony hand.

"God bless you, Carl," said the Judge. And Carl could scarce believe his ears. He got aboard the boat, her decks already blue with troops, and as she backed out with her whistle screaming, the last objects he saw were the gaunt old man and the broad-shouldered young man side by side on the edge of the landing.

Stephen's chest heaved, and as he walked back to the office with the Judge, he could not trust himself to speak. Back to the silent office where the shelves mocked them. The Judge closed the ground-glass door behind him, and Stephen sat until five o'clock over a book. No, it was not Whittlesey, but Hardee's "Tactics." He shut it with a slam, and went to Verandah Hall to drill recruits on a dusty floor,—narrow-chested citizens in suspenders, who knew not the first motion in *right about face*. For Stephen was an adjutant in the Home Guards—what was left of them.

One we know of regarded the going of the troops and the coming of the wounded with an equanimity truly philosophical. When the regiments passed Carvel & Company on their way riverward to embark, Mr. Hopper did not often take the trouble to rise from his chair, nor was he ever known to go to the door to bid them God-speed. This was all very well, because they were Union regiments. But Mr. Hopper did not contribute a horse, nor even a saddle-blanket, to the young men who went away secretly in the night, without fathers or mothers or sisters to wave at them. Mr. Hopper had better use for his money.

One scorching afternoon in July Colonel Carvel came into the office, too hurried to remark the pain in honest Ephum's face as he watched his master. The sure signs of a harassed man were on the Colonel. Since May he had neglected his business affairs for others which he deemed public, and which were so mysterious that even Mr. Hopper could not get wind of them. These matters had taken the Colonel out of town. But now the necessity of a pass made that awkward, and he went no farther than Glencoe, where he spent an occasional Sunday. To-day Mr. Hopper rose from his chair when Mr. Carvel entered,—a most unprecedented action. The Colonel cleared his throat. Sitting down at his desk, he drummed upon it uneasily.

"Mr. Hopper!" he said at length.

Eliphalet crossed the room quickly, and something that was very near a smile was on his face. He sat down close to Mr. Carvel's chair with a semi-confidential air,—one wholly new, had the Colonel given it a thought. He did not, but began to finger some printed slips of paper which had indorsements on their backs. His fine lips were tightly closed, as if in pain.

"Mr. Hopper," he said, "these Eastern notes are due this week, are they not?"

"Yes, sir."

The Colonel glanced up swiftly.

"There is no use mincing matters, Hopper. You know as well as I that there is no money to pay them," said he, with a certain pompous attempt at severity which characterized his kind nature. "You have served me well. You have brought this business up to a modern footing, and made it as prosperous as any in the town. I am sorry, sir, that those contemptible Yankees should have forced us to the use of arms, and cut short many promising business careers such as yours, sir. But we have to face the music. We have to suffer for our principles. These notes cannot be met, Mr. Hopper." And the good gentleman looked out of the window. He was thinking of a day, before the Mexican War, when his young wife had sat in the very chair filled by Mr. Hopper now. "These notes cannot be met," he repeated, and his voice was near to breaking.

The flies droning in the hot office made the only sound. Outside the partition, among the bales, was silence.

"Colonel," said Mr. Hopper, with a remarkable ease, "I cal'late these notes can be met."

The Colonel jumped as if he had heard a shot, and one of the notes fell to the floor. Eliphalet picked it up tenderly, and held it.

"What do you mean, sir?" Mr. Carvel cried. "There isn't a bank in town that will lend me money. I—I haven't a friend—a friend I may ask who can spare it, sir."

Mr. Hopper lifted up his hand. It was a fat hand. Suavity was come upon it like a new glove and changed the man. He was no longer cring-

ing. Now he had poise, such poise as we in these days are accustomed to
see in leather and mahogany offices. The Colonel glared at him uncom-
fortably.

"I will take up those notes myself, sir."

"*You!*" cried the Colonel, incredulously, "*You?*"

We must do Eliphalet justice. There was not a deal of hypocrisy in his
nature, and now he did not attempt the part of Samaritan. He did not
beam upon the Colonel and remind him of the day on which, homeless
and friendless, he had been frightened into his store by a drove of mules.
No. But his day,—the day toward which he had striven unknown and
unnoticed for so many years—the day when he would laugh at the
pride of those who had ignored and insulted him, was dawning at last.
When we are thoughtless of our words, we do not reckon with that spark
in little bosoms that may burst into flame and burn us. Not that Colonel
Carvel had ever been aught but courteous and kind to all. His station in
life had been his offence to Eliphalet, who strove now to hide an exultation that made him tremble.

"What do you mean, sir?" demanded the Colonel again.

"I cal'late that I can gather together enough to meet the notes,
Colonel. Just a little friendly transaction."

Here followed an interval of sheer astonishment for Mr. Carvel.

"You have this money?" he said at length.

Mr. Hopper nodded.

"And you will take my note for the amount?"

"Yes, sir."

The Colonel pulled his goatee, and sat back in his chair, trying to face
the new light in which he saw his manager. He knew well enough that the
man was not doing this out of charity, or even gratitude. He reviewed
his whole career, from that first morning when he had carried bales to
the shipping room, to his replacement of Mr. Hood, and there was nothing with which to accuse him. He remembered the warnings of Captain
Lige and Virginia. He could not in honor ask a cent from the Captain
now. He would not ask his sister-in-law, Mrs. Colfax, to let him touch
the money he had so ably invested for her; that little which Virginia's
mother had left the girl was sacred.

Night after night Mr. Carvel had lain awake with the agony of those
Eastern debts. Not to pay was to tarnish the name of a Southern gentleman. He could not sell the business. His house would bring nothing in
these times. He rose and began to pace the floor, tugging at his chin.

Twice he paused to stare at Mr. Hopper, who sat calmly on, and the third time stopped abruptly before him.

"See here," he cried. "Where the devil did you get this money, sir?"

Mr. Hopper did not rise.

"I haven't been extravagant, Colonel, since I've worked for you," he said. "It don't cost me much to live. I've been fortunate in investments."

The furrows in the Colonel's brow deepened.

"You offer to lend me five times more than I have ever paid you, Mr. Hopper. Tell me how you have made this money before I accept it."

Eliphalet had never been able to meet that eye since he had known it. He did not meet it now. But he went to his desk, and drew a long sheet of paper from a pigeon-hole.

"These be some of my investments," he answered, with just a tinge of surliness. "I cal'late they'll stand inspection. I ain't forcing you to take the money, sir," he flared up, all at once. "I'd like to save the business."

Mr. Carvel was disarmed. He went unsteadily to his desk, and none save God knew the shock that his pride received that day. To rescue a name which had stood untarnished since he had brought it into the world, he drew forth some blank notes, and filled them out. But before he signed them he spoke:—

"You are a business man, Mr. Hopper," said he. "And as a business man you must know that these notes will not legally hold. It is martial law. The courts are abolished, and all transactions here in St. Louis are invalid."

Eliphalet was about to speak.

"One moment, sir," cried the Colonel, standing up and towering to his full height. "Law or no law, you shall have the money and interest, or your security, which is this business. I need not tell you, sir, that my word is sacred, and binding forever upon me and mine."

"I'm not afraid, Colonel," answered Mr. Hopper, with a feeble attempt at geniality. He was, in truth, awed at last.

"You need not be, sir!" said the Colonel, with equal force. "If you were—this instant you should leave this place." He sat down, and continued more calmly: "It will not be long before a Southern Army marches into St. Louis, and the Yankee Government submits." He leaned forward. "Do you reckon we can hold the business together until then, Mr. Hopper?"

God forbid that we should smile at the Colonel's simple faith. And if Eliphalet Hopper had done so, his history would have ended here.

"Leave that to me, Colonel," he said soberly.

Then came the reaction. The good Colonel sighed as he signed away that business which had been an honor to the city where it was founded. I thank heaven that we are not concerned with the details of their talk that day. Why should we wish to know the rate of interest on those notes, or the time? It was war-time.

Mr. Hopper filled out his check, and presently departed. It was the signal for the little force which remained to leave. Outside, in the store, Ephum paced uneasily, wondering why his master did not come out. Presently he crept to the door of the office, pushed it open, and beheld Mr. Carvel with his head bowed down in his hands.

"Marse Comyn!" he cried, "Marse Comyn!"

The Colonel looked up. His face was haggard.

"Marse Comyn, you know what I done promise young Miss long time ago, befo'—befo' she done left us?"

"Yes, Ephum."

He saw the faithful old negro but dimly. Faintly he heard the pleading voice.

"Marse Comyn, won' you give Ephum a pass down river, ter fotch Cap'n Lige?"

"Ephum," said the Colonel, sadly, "I had a letter from the Captain yesterday. He is at Cairo. His boat is a Federal transport, and he is in Yankee pay."

Ephum took a step forward, appealingly. "But de Cap'n's yo' friend, Marse Comyn. He ain't never fo'get what you done fo' him, Marse Comyn. He ain't in de army, suh."

"And I am the Captain's friend, Ephum," answered the Colonel, quietly. "But I will not ask aid from any man employed by the Yankee Government. No—not from my own brother, who is in a Pennsylvania regiment."

Ephum shuffled out, and his heart was lead as he closed the store that night.

Mr. Hopper has boarded a Fifth Street car, which jangles on with many halts until it comes to Bremen, a German settlement in the north of the city. At Bremen great droves of mules fill the street, and crowd the entrances of the sale stables there. Whips are cracking like pistol shots. Gentlemen with the yellow cavalry stripe of the United States Army are pushing to and fro among the drivers and the owners, and fingering the frightened animals. A herd breaks from the confusion and is driven like a whirlwind down the street, dividing at the Market House. They are going to board the Government transport—to die on the battlefields of Kentucky and Missouri.

Mr. Hopper alights from the car with complacency. He stands for a while on a corner, against the hot building, surveying the busy scene, unnoticed. Mules! Was it not a prophecy,—that drove which sent him into Mr. Carvel's store?

Presently a man with a gnawed yellow mustache and a shifty eye walks out of one of the offices, and perceives our friend.

"Howdy, Mr. Hopper?" says he.

Eliphalet extends a hand to be squeezed and returned.

"Got them vouchers?" he asks. He is less careful of his English here.

"Wal, I jest reckon," is the answer. The fellow was interrupted by the appearance of a smart young man in a smart uniform, who wore an air of genteel importance. He could not have been more than two and twenty, and his face and manners were those of a clerk. The tan of field service was lacking on his cheek, and he was black under the eyes.

"Hullo, Ford," he said, jocularly.

"Howdy, Cap," retorted the other. "Wal, suh, that last lot was an *extry,* fo' sure. As clean a lot as ever I seed. Not a lump on 'em. Gov'ment ain't cheated much on them there at one-eighty a head, I reckon."

Mr. Ford said this with such an air of conviction and such a sober face that the Captain smiled. And at the same time he glanced down nervously at the new line of buttons on his chest.

"I guess I know a mule from a Newfoundland dog by this time," said he.

"Wal, I jest reckon," asserted Mr. Ford, with a loud laugh. "Cap'n Wentworth, allow me to make you acquainted with Mr. Hopper. Mr. Hopper, Cap'n Wentworth."

The Captain squeezed Mr. Hopper's hand with fervor.

"*You* interested in mules, Mr. Hopper?" asked the military man.

"I don't cal'late to be," said Mr. Hopper. Let us hope that our worthy has not been presented as being wholly without a sense of humor. He grinned as he looked upon this lamb in the uniform of Mars, and added, "I'm just naturally patriotic, I guess. Cap'n, 'll you have a drink?"

"And a segar," added Mr. Ford.

"Just one," says the Captain. "It's d—d tiresome lookin' at mules all day in the sun."

Well for Mr. Davitt that his mission work does not extend to Bremen, that the good man's charity keeps him at the improvised hospital down town. Mr. Hopper has resigned the superintendency of his Sunday School, it is true, but he is still a pillar of the church.

The young officer leans against the bar, and listens to stories by Mr. Ford, which it behooves no church members to hear. He smokes Mr. Hopper's cigar and drinks his whiskey. And Eliphalet understands that the good Lord put some fools into the world in order to give the smart people a chance to practise their talents. Mr. Hopper neither drinks nor smokes, but he uses the spittoon with more freedom in this atmosphere.

When at length the Captain has marched out, with a conscious but manly air, Mr. Hopper turns to Ford—

"Don't lose no time in presenting them vouchers at headquarters," says he. "Money is worth something now. And there's grumbling about this Department in the Eastern papers. If we have an investigation, we'll whistle. How much to-day?"

"Three thousand," says Mr. Ford. He tosses off a pony of Bourbon, but his face is not a delight to look upon. "Hopper, you'll be a d—d rich man some day."

"I cal'late to."

"I do the dirty work. And because I ain't got no capital, I only get four per cent."

"Don't one-twenty a day suit you?"

"You get blasted near a thousand. And you've got horse contracts, and blanket contracts besides. I know you. What's to prevent my goin' south when the vouchers is cashed?" he cried. "Ain't it possible?"

"I presume likely," said Mr. Hopper, quietly. "Then your mother'll have to move out of her little place."

CHAPTER II

NEWS FROM CLARENCE

"THE epithet *aristocrat* may become odious and fatal on the banks of the Mississippi as it was on the banks of the Seine. Let no man deceive himself! These are fearful times. Thousands of our population, by the sudden stoppage of business, are thrown out of employment. When gaunt famine intrudes upon their household, it is but natural that they should inquire the cause. Hunger began the French Revolution."

Virginia did not read this editorial, because it appeared in that abhorred organ of the Mudsills, the *Missouri Democrat.* The wheels of fortune were turning rapidly that first hot summer of the war time. Let us be thankful that our flesh and blood are incapable of the fury of the guillotine. But when we think calmly of those days, can we escape without a little pity for the aristocrats? Do you think that many of them did not know hunger and want long before that cruel war was over?

How bravely they met the grim spectre which crept so insidiously into their homes!

"Virginia, child," said Mrs. Colfax, peevishly, one morning as they sat at breakfast, "why do you persist in wearing that old gown? It has gotten on my nerves, my dear. You really must have something new made, even if there are no men here to dress for."

"Aunt Lillian, you must not say such things. I do not think that I ever dressed to please men."

"Tut, tut, my dear, we all do. I did, even after I married your uncle. It is natural. We must not go shabby in such times as these, or be out of fashion. Did you know that Prince Napoleon was actually coming here for a visit this autumn? We must be ready for him. I am having a fitting at Miss Elder's to-day."

Virginia was learning patience. She did not reply as she poured out her aunt's coffee.

"Jinny," said that lady, "come with me to Elder's, and I will give you some gowns. If Comyn had been as careful of his own money as of mine, you could dress decently."

"I think I do dress decently, Aunt Lillian," answered the girl. "I do not need the gowns. Give me the money you intend to pay for them, and I can use it for a better purpose."

Mrs. Colfax arranged her lace pettishly.

"I am sick and tired of this superiority, Jinny." And in the same breath. "What would you do with it?"

Virginia lowered her voice. "Hodges goes through the lines to-morrow night. I should send it to Clarence."

"But you have no idea where Clarence is."

"Hodges can find him."

"Pshaw!" exclaimed her aunt, "I would not trust him. How do you know that he will get through the Dutch pickets to Price's army? Wasn't Souther captured last week, and that rash letter of Puss Russell's to Jack Brinsmade published in the *Democrat?*" She laughed at the recollection, and Virginia was fain to laugh too. "Puss hasn't been around much since. I hope that will cure her of saying what she thinks of people."

"It won't," said Virginia.

"I'll save my money until Price drives the Yankees from the state, and Clarence marches into the city at the head of a regiment," Mrs. Colfax went on. "It won't be long now."

Virginia's eyes flashed.

"Oh, you can't have read the papers! And don't you remember the letter Maude had from George? They need the bare necessities of life, Aunt Lillian. And half of Price's men have no arms at all."

"Jackson," said Mrs. Colfax, "bring me a newspaper. Is there any news to-day?"

"No," answered Virginia, quickly. "All we know is that Lyon has left Springfield to meet our troops, and that a great battle is coming. Perhaps—perhaps it is being fought to-day."

Mrs. Colfax burst into tears.

"Oh, Jinny," she cried, "how can you be so cruel!"

That very evening a man, tall and lean, but with the shrewd and kindly eye of a scout, came into the sitting-room with the Colonel and handed a letter to Mrs. Colfax. In the hall he slipped into Virginia's hand another, in a "Jefferson Davis" envelope, and she thrust it in her gown—the girl was on fire as he whispered in her ear that he had seen Clarence, and that he was well. In two days an answer might be left at Mr. Russell's house. But she must be careful what she wrote, as the Yankee scouts were active.

Clarence, indeed, had proven himself a man. Glory and uniform became him well, but danger and deprivation better. The words he had written, careless and frank and boyish, made Virginia's heart leap with pride. Mrs. Colfax's letter began with the adventure below the Arsenal, when the frail skiff had sunk near the island. He told how he had heard the captain of his escort sing out to him in the darkness, and how he had floated down the current instead, until, chilled and weary, he had contrived to seize the branches of a huge tree floating by. And how by a miracle the moon had risen. When the great Memphis packet bore down upon him, he had been seen from her guards, and rescued and made much of; and set ashore at the next landing, for fear her captain would get into trouble. In the morning he had walked into the country, first providing himself with butternuts and rawhide boots and a bowie-knife. Virginia would never have recognized her dashing captain of dragoons in this guise.

The letter was long for Clarence, and written under great difficulties from date to date. For nearly a month he had tramped over mountains and across river bottoms, waiting for news of an organized force of resistance in Missouri. Begging his way from cabin to cabin, and living on greasy bacon and corn pone, at length he crossed the swift Gasconade (so named by the French settlers because of its brawling ways) where the bridge of the Pacific railroad had been blown up by the Governor's orders. Then he learned that the untiring Lyon had steamed up the Missouri and had taken possession of Jefferson City without a blow, and that the ragged rebel force had fought and lost at Booneville. Footsore, but undaunted, he pushed on to join the army, which he heard was retreating southward along the western tier of counties of the state.

On the banks of the Osage he fell in with two other young men in as bad a plight as himself. They travelled together, until one day some rough farmers with shotguns leaped out of a bunch of willows on the borders of a creek and arrested all three for Union spies. And they laughed when Mr. Clarence tried to explain that he had not long since been the dapper captain of the State Dragoons.

His Excellency, the Governor of Missouri (so acknowledged by all good Southerners), likewise laughed when Mr. Colfax and the two others were brought before him. His Excellency sat in a cabin surrounded by a camp which had caused the dogs of war to howl for very shame.

"Colfax!" cried the Governor. "A Colfax of St. Louis in butternuts and rawhide boots?"

"Give me a razor," demanded Clarence, with indignation, "a razor and a suit of clothes, and I will prove it."

The Governor laughed once more.

"A razor, young man! A suit of clothes! You know not what you ask."

"Are there any gentlemen from St. Louis here?"

George Catherwood was brought in,—or rather what had once been George. Now he was a big frontiersman with a huge blond beard, and a bowie knife stuck into his trousers in place of a sword. He recognized his young captain of dragoons; the Governor apologized, and Clarence slept that night in the cabin. The next day he was given a horse, and a bright new rifle which the Governor's soldiers had taken from the Dutch at Cole Camp on the way south. And presently they made a junction with three thousand more who were their images. This was Price's army, but Price had gone ahead into Kansas to beg the great McCulloch and his Confederates to come to their aid and save the state.

"Dear mother, I wish that you and Jinny and Uncle Comyn could have seen this country rabble. How you would have laughed, and cried, because we are just like them. In the combined army two thousand have only bowie-knives or clubs. Some have long rifles of Daniel Boone's time, not fired for thirty years. And the impedimenta are a sight. Open wagons and conestogas and carryalls and buggies, and even barouches, weighted down with frying-pans and chairs and *feather beds*. But we've got spirit, and we can whip Lyon's Dutchmen and Yankees just as we are. Spirit is what counts, and the Yankees haven't got it. I was made to-day a Captain of Cavalry under Colonel Rives. I ride a great, raw-boned horse like an elephant. He jolts me until I am sore,—not quite as easy as my thoroughbred, Jefferson. Tell Jinny to care for him, and have him ready when we march into St. Louis."

"COWSKIN PRAIRIE, 9th July.

"We have whipped Sigel on the prairie by Coon Creek and killed—we don't know how many. Tell Maude that George distinguished himself in the fight. We cavalry did not get a chance.

"We have at last met McCulloch and his *real soldiers*. We cheered until we cried when we saw their ranks of gray, with the gold buttons and the gold braid and the gold stars. General McCulloch has taken me on his staff, and promised me a uniform. But how to clothe and feed and arm our men! We have only a few poor cattle, and no money. But our men don't complain. We shall whip the Yankees before we starve."

For many days Mrs. Colfax did not cease to bewail the hardship which her dear boy was forced to endure. He, who was used to linen sheets and eider down, was without a rough blanket or shelter; who was used to the best table in the state, was reduced to husks.

"But, Aunt Lillian," cried Virginia, "he is fighting for the South. If he were fed and clothed like the Yankees, we should not be half so proud of him."

Why set down for colder gaze the burning words that Clarence wrote to Virginia. How she pored over that letter, and folded it so that even the candle-droppings would not be creased and fall away! He was happy, though wretched because he could not see her. It was the life he had longed for. At last (and most pathetic!) he was proving his usefulness in this world. He was no longer the mere idler whom she had chidden.

"Jinny, do you remember saying so many years ago that our ruin would come of our not being able to work? How I wish you could see us felling trees to make bullet-moulds, and forging slugs for canister, and making cartridges at night with our bayonets as candlesticks. Jinny dear, I know that *you* will keep up your courage. I can see you sewing for us, I can hear you praying for us."

It was, in truth, how Virginia learned to sew. She had always detested it. Her fingers were pricked and sore weeks after she began. Sad to relate, her bandages, shirts, and havelocks never reached the front,—those havelocks, to withstand the heat of the tropic sun, which were made in thousands by devoted Union women that first summer of the war, to be ridiculed as nightcaps by the soldiers. "Why should not *our* soldiers have them, too?" said Virginia to the Russell girls. They were never so happy as when sewing on them against the arrival of the Army of Liberation, which never came.

The long, long days of heat dragged slowly, with little to cheer those families separated from their dear ones by a great army. Clarence might die, and a month—perhaps a year—pass without news, unless he were brought a prisoner to St. Louis. How Virginia envied Maude because the Union lists of dead and wounded would give her tidings of her brother Tom, at least! How she coveted the many Union families, whose sons and brothers were at the front, this privilege!

We were speaking of the French Revolution, when, as Balzac remarked, to be a spy was to be a patriot. Heads are not so cheap in our Anglo-Saxon countries; passions not so fierce and uncontrollable. Com-

pare, with a prominent historian, our Boston Massacre and St. Bartholomew. They are both massacres. Compare Camp Jackson, or Baltimore,
where a few people were shot, with some Paris street scenes after the
Bastille. Feelings in each instance never ran higher. Our own provost
marshal was hissed in the street, and called "Robespierre," and yet he
did not fear the assassin's knife. Our own Southern aristocrats were
hemmed in in a Union city (their own city). No women were thrown
into prison, it is true. Yet one was not permitted to shout for Jeff Davis
on the street corner before the provost's guard. Once in a while a detachment of the Home Guards, commanded by a lieutenant, would march
swiftly into a street and stop before a house, whose occupants would run
to the rear, only to encounter another detachment in the alley.

One day, in great excitement, Eugénie Rénault rang the bell of the
Carvel house, and ran past the astounded Jackson up the stairs to Virginia's room, the door of which she burst open.

"Oh, Jinny!" she cried, "Puss Russell's house is surrounded by Yankees, and Puss and Emily and all the family are prisoners!"

"Prisoners! What for?" said Virginia, dropping in her excitement her
last year's bonnet, which she was trimming with red, white, and red.

"Because," said Eugénie, sputtering with indignation, "because they
waved at some of our poor fellows who were being taken to the slave
pen. They were being marched past Mr. Russell's house under guard—
Puss had a small—"

"Confederate flag," put in Virginia, smiling in spite of herself.

"And she waved it between the shutters," Eugénie continued. "And
some one told the provost marshal. He has had the house surrounded,
and the family have to stay there."

"But if the food gives out?"

"Then," said Miss Rénault, in a voice of awe, "then each one of the
family is to have just a *common army ration*. They are to be treated as
prisoners."

"Oh, those Yankees are detestable!" exclaimed Virginia. "But they
shall pay for it. As soon as our army is organized and equipped, they
shall pay for it ten times over." She tried on the bonnet, conspicuous
with its red and white ribbons, before the glass. Then she ran to the
closet and drew forth the white gown with its red trimmings. "Wait for
me, Génie," she said, "and we'll go down to Puss's house together. It may
cheer her to see us."

"But not in that dress," said Eugénie, aghast. "They will arrest you."

"Oh, how I wish they would!" cried Virginia. And her eyes flashed so that Eugénie was frightened. "How I wish they would!"

Miss Rénault regarded her friend with something of adoration from beneath her black lashes. It was about five in the afternoon when they started out together under Virginia's white parasol, Eugénie's slimmer courage upheld by her friend's bearing. We must remember that Virginia was young, and that her feelings were akin to those our great-grandmothers experienced when the British held New York. It was as if she had been born to wear the red and white of the South. Elderly gentlemen of Northern persuasion paused in their homeward walk to smile in admiration,—some sadly, as Mr. Brinsmade. Young gentlemen found an excuse to retrace their steps a block or two. But Virginia walked on air, and saw nothing. She was between fierce anger and exaltation. She did not deign to drop her eyes as low as the citizen sergeant and guard in front of Puss Russell's house (these men were only human, after all); she did not so much as glance at the curious people standing on the corner, who could not resist a murmur of delight. The citizen sergeant only smiled, and made no move to arrest the young lady in red and white. Nor did Puss fling open the blinds and wave at her.

"I suppose it's because Mr. Russell won't let her," said Virginia, disconsolately. "Génie, let's go to headquarters, and show this Yankee General Frémont that we are not afraid of him."

Eugénie's breath was taken away by the very boldness of this proposition. She looked up timidly into Virginia's face, and hero-worship got the better of prudence.

The house which General Frémont appropriated for his use when he came back from Europe to assume command in the West was not a modest one. It still stands, a large mansion of brick with a stone front, very tall and very wide, with an elaborate cornice and plate-glass windows, both tall and broad, and a high basement. Two stately stone porches capped by elaborate iron railings adorn it in front and on the side. The chimneys are generous and proportional. In short, the house is of that type built by many wealthy gentlemen in the middle of the century, which has best stood the test of time,—the only type which, if repeated to-day, would not clash with the architectural education which we are receiving. A spacious yard well above the pavement surrounds it, sustained by a wall of dressed stones, capped by an iron fence. The whole expressed wealth, security, solidity, conservatism.

Alas, that the coal deposits under the black mud of our Western states should, at length, have driven the owners of these houses out of them! They are now blackened, almost buried in soot; empty, or half-tenanted by boarders. Descendants of the old families pass them on their way to business or to the theatre with a sigh. The sons of those who owned them have built westward, and westward again, until now they are six miles from the river.

On that summer evening forty years ago, when Virginia and Eugénie came in sight of the house, a scene of great animation was before them. Talk was rife over the commanding general's pomp and circumstance. He had just returned from Europe, where pomp and circumstance and the military were wedded. Foreign officers should come to America to teach our army dress and manners. A dashing Hungarian commanded the general's body-guard, which honorable corps was even then drawn up in the street before the house, surrounded at a respectable distance by a crowd that feared to jest. They felt like it save when they caught the stern military eye of the Hungarian captain. Virginia gazed at the glittering uniforms, resplendent in the sun, and at the sleek and well-fed horses, and scalding tears came as she thought of the half-starved rabble of Southern patriots on the burning prairies. Just then a sharp command escaped in broken English from the Hungarian. The people in the yard of the mansion parted, and the General himself walked proudly out of the gate to the curb, where his charger was pawing the gutter. As he put foot to the stirrup, the eye of the great man (once candidate, and again to be, for President) caught the glint of red and white on the corner. For an instant he stood transfixed to the spot, with one leg in the air. Then he took it down again and spoke to a young officer of his staff, who smiled and began to walk toward them. Little Eugénie's knees trembled. She seized Virginia's arm, and whispered in agony:—

"Oh, Jinny, you are to be arrested, after all. Oh, I wish you hadn't been so bold!"

"Hush!" said Virginia, as she prepared to slay the young officer with a look. She felt like flying at his throat, and choking him for the insolence of that smile. How dare he march undaunted to within six paces of those eyes? The crowd drew back. But did Miss Carvel retreat? Not a step. "Oh, I hope he will arrest me," she said passionately, to Eugénie. "He will start a conflagration beyond the power of any Yankee to quell."

But hush! he was speaking. "You are my prisoners?" No, those were not the words, surely. The lieutenant had taken off his cap. He bowed very low and said: "Ladies, the General's compliments, and he begs that this much of the sidewalk may be kept clear for a few moments."

What was left for them, after that, save a retreat? But it was not precipitate. Miss Virginia crossed the street with a dignity and bearing which drew even the eyes of the body-guard to one side. And there she stood haughtily until the guard and the General had thundered away.

A crowd of black-coated civilians, and quartermasters and other officers in uniform, poured out of the basement of the house into the yard. One civilian, a youngish man a little inclined to stoutness, stopped at the gate, stared, then thrust some papers in his pocket and hurried down the side street. Three blocks thence he appeared abreast of Miss Carvel. More remarkable still, he lifted his hat clear of his head. Virginia drew back. Mr. Hopper, with his newly acquired equanimity and poise, startled her.

"May I have the pleasure," said that gentleman, "of accompanying you home?"

Eugénie giggled. Virginia was more annoyed than she showed.

"You must not come out of your way," she said. Then she added: "I am sure you must go back to the store. It is only six o'clock."

Had Virginia but known, this occasional tartness in her speech gave Eliphalet an infinite delight, even while it hurt him. His was a nature which liked to gloat over a goal on the horizon. He cared not a whit for sweet girls; they cloyed. But a real lady was something to attain. He had revised his vocabulary for just such an occasion, and thrown out some of the vernacular.

"Business is not so pressing nowadays, Miss Carvel," he answered, with a shade of meaning.

"Then existence must be rather heavy for you," she said. She made no attempt to introduce him to Eugénie.

"If we should have any more victories like Bull Run, prosperity will come back with a rush," said the son of Massachusetts. "Southern Confederacy, with Missouri one of its stars—industrial development of the South—fortunes in cotton."

Virginia turned quickly. "Oh, how dare you?" she cried. "How dare you speak flippantly of such things?"

His suavity was far from overthrown.

"Flippantly, Miss Carvel?" said he. "I assure you that I want to see the South win." What he did not know was that words seldom convince

women. But he added something which reduced her incredulity for the
time. "Do you cal'late," said he, "that I could work for your father, and
wish ruin to his country?"

"But you are a Yankee born," she exclaimed.

"There be a few sane Yankees," replied Mr. Hopper, dryly. A remark
which made Eugénie laugh outright, and Virginia could not refrain from
a smile.

But much against her will he walked home with her. She was indignant
by the time she reached Locust Street. He had never dared do such a
thing before. What had got into the man? Was it because he had become
a manager, and governed the business during her father's frequent
absences? No matter what Mr. Hopper's politics, he would always be to
her a low-born Yankee, a person wholly unworthy of notice.

At the corner of Olive Street, a young man walking with long strides
almost bumped into them. He paused, looked back, and bowed as if uncertain of an acknowledgment. Virginia barely returned his bow. He had
been very close to her, and she had had time to notice that his coat was
threadbare. When she looked again, he had covered half the block. Why
should she care if Stephen Brice had seen her in company with Mr.
Hopper?

Eliphalet, too, had seen Stephen, and this had added zest to his enjoyment. It was part of the fruits of his reward. He wished in that short walk
that he might meet Mr. Cluyme and Belle, and every man and woman
and child in the city whom he knew. From time to time he glanced at the
severe profile of the aristocrat beside him (he had to look up a bit, likewise), and that look set him down among the beasts of prey. For she was
his rightful prey, and he meant not to lose one tittle of enjoyment in the
progress of the game. Many and many a night in the bare little back
room at Miss Crane's Eliphalet had gloated over the very event which
was now come to pass. Not a step of the way but what he had lived
through before. The future is laid open to such men as he. Since he had
first seen the black cloud of war rolling up from the South, a hundred
times had he rehearsed the scene with Colonel Carvel which had actually
taken place a week before. A hundred times had he prepared his speech
and manner for this first appearance in public with Virginia after he had
forced the right to walk in her company. The words he had prepared—
commonplace, to be sure, but carefully chosen—flowed from his lips in
a continual nasal stream. The girl answered absently, her feminine instinct groping after a reason for it all. She brightened when she saw her

father at the door; and, saying good-by to Eugénie, tripped up the steps, bowing to Eliphalet coldly.

"Why, bless us, Jinny," said the Colonel, "you haven't been parading the town in that costume! You'll have us in Lynch's slave pen by to-morrow night. My land!" laughed he, patting her under the chin, "there's no doubt about your sentiments, anyhow."

"I've been over to Puss Russell's house," said she, breathless. "They've closed it up, you know—" (He nodded.) "And then we went—Eugénie and I, to headquarters, just to see what the Yankees would do."

The Colonel's smile faded. He looked grave. "You must take care, honey," he said, lowering his voice. "They suspect me now of communicating with the Governor and McCulloch. Jinny, it's all very well to be brave, and to stand by your colors. But this sort of thing," said he, stroking the gown, "this sort of thing doesn't help the South, my dear, and only sets spies upon us. Ned tells me that there was a man in plain clothes standing in the alley last night for three hours."

"Oh, Pa," cried the girl, "I'm so sorry." Suddenly searching his face with a swift instinct, she perceived that these months had made it yellow and lined. "Pa, dear, you must come to Glencoe to-morrow and rest. You must not go off on any more trips."

The Colonel shook his head sadly.

"It isn't the trips, Jinny. There are duties, my dear, pleasant duties—Jinny—"

"Yes?"

The Colonel's eye had suddenly fallen on Mr. Hopper, who was still standing at the bottom of the steps. He checked himself abruptly as Eliphalet pulled off his hat.

"Howdy, Colonel?" he said.

Virginia was motionless, with her back to the intruder. She was frozen by a presentiment. As she saw her father start down the steps, she yearned to throw herself in front of him—to warn him of something, she knew not what. Then she heard the Colonel's voice, courteous and kindly as ever. And yet it broke a little as he greeted his visitor.

"Won't—won't you come in, Mr. Hopper?"

Virginia started.

"I don't know but what I will, thank you, Colonel," he answered, easily. "I took the liberty of walking home with your daughter."

Virginia fairly flew into the house and up the stairs. Gaining her room, she shut the door and turned the key, as though he might pursue her there. The man's face had all at once become a terror. She threw herself on the lounge and buried her face in her hands, and she saw it still leering at her with a new confidence. Presently she grew calmer; rising, she put on the plainest of her scanty wardrobe, and went down the stairs, all in a strange trepidation new to her. She had never been in fear of a man before. She harkened over the banisters for his voice, heard it, and summoned all her courage. How cowardly she had been to leave her father alone with him!

Eliphalet stayed to tea. It mattered little to him that Mrs. Colfax ignored him as completely as if his chair had been vacant. He glanced at that lady once, and smiled, for he was tasting the sweets of victory. It was Virginia who entertained him, and even the Colonel never guessed what it cost her. Eliphalet himself marvelled at her change of manner, and gloated over that likewise. Not a turn or a quiver of the victim's pain is missed by your beast of prey. The Colonel was gravely polite, but preoccupied. Had he wished it, he could not have been rude to a guest. He offered Mr. Hopper a cigar with the same air that he would have given it to a governor.

"Thank'ee, Colonel, I don't smoke," he said, waving the box away.

Mrs. Colfax flung herself out of the room.

It was ten o'clock when Eliphalet reached Miss Crane's, and picked his way up the front steps where the boarders were gathered.

"The war doesn't seem to make any difference in your business, Mr. Hopper," his landlady remarked; "where have you been so late?"

"I happened round at Colonel Carvel's this afternoon, and stayed for tea with 'em," he answered, striving to speak casually.

Miss Crane lingered in Mrs. Abner Reed's room later than usual that night.

CHAPTER III

THE SCOURGE OF WAR

"Virginia," said Mrs. Colfax, the next morning on coming downstairs, "I am going back to Bellegarde to-day. I really cannot put up with such a person as Comyn had here to tea last night."

"Very well, Aunt Lillian. At what time shall I order the carriage?"

The lady was surprised. It is safe to say that she had never accurately gauged the force which Virginia's respect for her elders, and affection for her aunt through Clarence, held in check. Only a moment since Mrs. Colfax had beheld her niece. Now there had arisen in front of her a tall person of authority, before whom she deferred instinctively. It was not what Virginia said, for she would not stoop to tirade. Mrs. Colfax sank into a chair, seeing only the blurred lines of a newspaper the girl had thrust into her hand.

"What—what is it?" she gasped. "I cannot read."

"There has been a battle at Wilson's Creek," said Virginia, in an emotionless voice. "General Lyon is killed, for which I suppose we should be thankful. More than seven hundred of the wounded are on their way here. They are bringing them one hundred and twenty miles, from Springfield to Rollo, in rough army wagons, with scarcely anything to eat or drink."

"And—Clarence?"

"His name is not there."

"Thank God!" exclaimed Mrs. Colfax. "Are the Yankees beaten?"

"Yes," said Virginia, coldly. "At what time shall I order the carriage to take you to Bellegarde?"

Mrs. Colfax leaned forward and caught the hem of her niece's gown. "Oh, let me stay," she cried, "let me stay. Clarence may be with them."

Virginia looked down at her without pity.

"As you please, Aunt Lillian," she answered. "You know that you may always stay here. I only beg of you one thing, that when you have anything to complain of, you will bring it to me, and not mention it before Pa. He has enough to worry him."

"Oh, Jinny," sobbed the lady, in tears again, "how can you be so cruel at such a time, when my nerves are all in pieces?"

But she did not lift her voice at dinner, which was very poor indeed for Colonel Carvel's house. All day long Virginia, assisted by Uncle Ben and Aunt Easter, toiled in the stifling kitchen, preparing dainties which she had long denied herself. At evening she went to the station at Fourteenth Street with her father, and stood amongst the people, pressed back by the soldiers, until the trains came in. Alas, the heavy basket which the Colonel carried on his arm was brought home again. The first hundred to arrive, ten hours in a hot car without food or water, were laid groaning on the bottom of great furniture vans, and carted to the new House of Refuge Hospital, two miles to the south of the city.

The next day many good women went there, Rebel and Union alike, to have their hearts wrung. The new and cheap building standing in the hot sun reeked with whitewash and paint. The miserable men lay on the hard floor, still in the matted clothes they had worn in battle. Those were the first days of the war, when the wages of our passions first came to appal us. Many of the wounds had not been tended since they were dressed on the field weeks before.

Mrs. Colfax went too, with the Colonel and her niece, although she declared repeatedly that she could not go through with such an ordeal. She spoke the truth, for Mr. Carvel had to assist her to the waiting-room. Then he went back to the improvised wards to find Virginia busy over a gaunt Arkansan of Price's army, whose pitiful, fever-glazed eyes were following her every motion. His frontiersman's clothes, stained with blackened blood, hung limp over his wasted body. At Virginia's bidding the Colonel ran downstairs for a bucket of fresh water, and she washed the caked dust from his face and hands. It was Mr. Brinsmade who got the surgeon to dress the man's wound, and to prescribe some of the broth from Virginia's basket. For the first time since the war began something of happiness entered her breast.

It was Mr. Brinsmade who was everywhere that day, answering the questions of distracted mothers and fathers and sisters who thronged the place; consulting with the surgeons; helping the few who knew how to work in placing mattresses under the worst cases; or again he might have been seen seated on the bare floor with a pad on his knee, taking down the names of dear ones in distant states,—that he might spend his night writing to them.

They put a mattress under the Arkansan. Virginia did not leave him until he had fallen asleep, and a smile of peace was come upon his sunken face. Dismayed at the fearful sights about her, awed by the groans that rose on every side, she was choosing her way swiftly down the room to join her father and aunt in the carriage below. The panic of flight had seized her. She felt that another little while in this heated, horrible place would drive her mad. She was almost at the door when she came suddenly upon a sight that made her pause.

An elderly lady in widow's black was kneeling beside a man groaning in mortal agony, fanning away the flies already gathering about his face. He wore the uniform of a Union sergeant,—dusty and splotched and torn. A small Testament was clasped convulsively in the fingers of his right hand. The left sleeve was empty. Virginia lingered, whelmed in pity, thrilled by a wonderful womanliness of her who knelt there. Her face the girl had not even seen, for it was bent over the man. The sweetness of her voice held Virginia as in a spell, and the sergeant stopped groaning that he might listen.

"You have a wife?"

"Yes, ma'am."

"And a child?"

The answer came so painfully.

"A boy, ma'am—born the week—before I came—away."

"I shall write to your wife," said the lady, so gently that Virginia could scarce hear, "and tell her that you are cared for. Where does she live?"

He gave the address faintly—some little town in Minnesota. Then he added, "God bless you, lady."

Just then the chief surgeon came and stood over them. The lady turned her face up to him, and tears sparkled in her eyes. Virginia felt them wet in her own. Her worship was not given to many. Nobility, character, efficiency,—all were written on that face. Nobility spoke in the large features, in the generous mouth, in the calm, gray eyes. Virginia had seen her often before, but not until now was the woman revealed to her.

"Doctor, could this man's life be saved if I took him to my home?"

The surgeon got down beside her and took the man's pulse. The eyes closed. For a while the doctor knelt there, shaking his head. "He has fainted," he said.

"Do you think he can be saved?" asked the lady again.

The surgeon smiled,—such a smile as a good man gives after eighteen hours of amputating, of bandaging, of advising,—work which requires a firm hand, a clear eye and brain, and a good heart.

"My dear Mrs. Brice," he said, "I shall be glad to get you permission to take him, but we must first make him worth the taking. Another hour would have been too late." He glanced hurriedly about the busy room, and then added, "We must have one more to help us."

Just then some one touched Virginia's arm. It was her father.

"I am afraid we must go, dear," he said; "your aunt is getting impatient."

"Won't you please go without me, Pa?" she asked. "Perhaps I can be of some use."

The Colonel cast a wondering glance at the limp uniform, and went away. The surgeon, who knew the Carvel family, gave Virginia a look of astonishment. It was Mrs. Brice's searching gaze that brought the color to the girl's face.

"Thank you, my dear," she said simply.

As soon as he could get his sister-in-law off to Locust Street in the carriage, Colonel Carvel came back. For two reeking hours he stood against the newly plastered wall. Even he was surprised at the fortitude and skill Virginia showed from the very first, when she had deftly cut away the stiffened blue cloth, and helped to take off the rough bandages. At length the fearful operation was finished. And the weary surgeon, gathering up his box, expressed with all the energy left to him, his thanks to the two ladies.

Virginia stood up, faint and dizzy. The work of her hands had sustained her while it lasted, but now the ordeal was come. She went down the stairs on her father's arm, and out into the air. All at once she knew that Mrs. Brice was beside her, and had taken her by the hand.

"My dear," she was saying, "God will reward you for this act. You have taught many of us to-day a lesson we should have learned in our Bibles."

Virginia trembled with many emotions, but she answered nothing. The mere presence of this woman had a strange effect upon the girl,—she was filled with a longing unutterable. It was not because Margaret Brice was the mother of him whose life had been so strangely blended with hers— whom she saw in her dreams. And yet now some of Stephen's traits seemed to come to her understanding, as by a revelation. Virginia had labored through the heat of the day by Margaret Brice's side—doing His work, which levels all feuds and makes all women sisters. One brief second had been needful for the spell.

The Colonel bowed with that courtesy and respect which distinguished him, and Mrs. Brice left them to go back into the room of torment, and watch by the sergeant's pallet. Virginia's eyes followed her up the stairs and then she and her father walked slowly to the carriage. With her foot on the step Virginia paused.

"Pa," she said, "do you think it would be possible to get them to let us take that Arkansan into our house?"

"Why, honey, I'll ask Brinsmade if you like," said the Colonel. "Here he comes now, and Anne."

It was Virginia who put the question to him.

"My dear," replied that gentleman, patting her, "I would do anything in the world for you. I'll see General Frémont this very afternoon. Virginia," he added, soberly, "it is such acts as yours to-day that give us courage to live in these times."

Anne kissed her friend.

"Oh, Jinny, I saw what you were doing for one of our men. What am I saying?" she cried. "They are your men, too. This horrible war cannot last. It cannot last."

It was well that Virginia did not see the smile on the face of the commanding general when Mr. Brinsmade at length got to him with her request. This was before the days when the wounded arrived by the thousands, when the zeal of the Southern ladies threatened to throw out of gear the workings of a great system. But the General had had his eye on Mr. Carvel from the first. Therefore he smiled.

"Colonel Carvel," said Mr. Brinsmade, with dignity, "is a gentleman. When he gives his word, it is sacred, sir."

"Even to an enemy," the General put in. "By George, Brinsmade, unless I knew you, I should think that you were half rebel yourself. Well, well, he may have his Arkansan."

Mr. Brinsmade, when he conveyed the news to the Carvel house, did not say that he had wasted a precious afternoon in the attempt to interview his Excellency, the Commander-in-chief. It was like obtaining an audience with the Sultan or the Czar. Citizens who had been prominent in affairs for twenty years, philanthropists and patriotic-spirited men like Mr. Brinsmade, the mayor, and all the ex-mayors mopped their brows in one of the general's anterooms of the big mansion, and wrangled with beardless youths in bright uniforms who were part of the chain.

The General might have been a Richelieu, a Marlborough. His European
notions of uniformed inaccessibility he carried out to the letter. He was
a royal personage, seldom seen, who went abroad in the midst of a glittering guard. It did not seem to weigh with his Excellency that these
simple and democratic gentlemen would not put up with this sort of
thing. That they who had saved the city to the Union were more or less
in communication with a simple and democratic President; that in all
their lives they had never been in the habit of sitting idly for two hours
to mop their brows.

On the other hand, once you got beyond the gold lace and the eti-
quette, you discovered a good man and a patriot. It was far from being
the General's fault that Mr. Hopper and others made money in mules
and worthless army blankets. Such things always have been, and always
will be unavoidable when this great country of ours rises from the deep
sleep of security into which her sons have lulled her, to demand her
sword. We shall never be able to realize that the maintenance of a standing army of comfortable size will save millions in the end. So much for
Democracy when it becomes a catchword.

The General was a good man, had he done nothing else than en-
courage the Western Sanitary Commission, that glorious army of drilled
men and women who gave up all to relieve the suffering which the war
was causing. Would that a novel—a great novel—might be written setting forth with truth its doings. The hero of it could be Calvin Brinsmade, and a nobler hero than he was never under a man's hand. For
the glory of generals fades beside his glory.

It was Mr. Brinsmade's carriage that brought Mrs. Brice home from
her trying day in the hospital. Stephen, just returned from drill at Verandah Hall, met her at the door. She would not listen to his entreaties to
rest, but in the evening, as usual, took her sewing to the porch behind
the house, where there was a little breeze.

"Such a singular thing happened to-day, Stephen," she said. "It was
while we were trying to save the life of a poor sergeant who had lost his
arm. I hope we shall be allowed to have him here. He is suffering horribly."

"What happened, mother?" he asked.

"It was soon after I had come upon this poor fellow," she said. "I saw
the—the flies around him. And as I got down beside him to fan them
away I had such a queer sensation. I knew that some one was standing
behind me. looking at me. Then Dr. Allerdyce came. and I asked him

about the man, and he said there was a chance of saving him if we could only get help. Then some one spoke up,—such a sweet voice. It was that Miss Carvel, my dear, with whom you had such a strange experience when you bought Hester, and to whose party you once went. Do you remember that they offered us their house in Glencoe when the Judge was so ill?"

"Yes," said Stephen.

"She is a wonderful creature," his mother continued. "Such personality, such life! And wasn't it a remarkable offer for a Southern woman to make? They feel so bitterly, and—and I do not blame them." The good lady put down on her lap the night-shirt she was making. "I saw how it happened. The girl was carried away by her pity. And, my dear, her capability astonished me. One might have thought that she had always been a nurse. The experience was a dreadful one for me—what must it have been for her! After the operation was over, I followed her downstairs to where she was standing with her father in front of the building, waiting for their carriage. I felt that I must say something to her, for in all my life I have never seen a nobler thing done. When I saw her there, I scarcely knew what to say. Words seemed so inadequate. It was then three o'clock, and she had been working steadily in that place since morning. I am sure she could not have borne it much longer. Sheer courage carried her through it, I know, for her hand trembled so when I took it, and she was very pale. She usually has color, I believe. Her father, the Colonel, was with her, and he bowed to me with such politeness. He had stood against the wall all the while we had worked, and he brought a mattress for us. I have heard that his house is watched, and that they have him under suspicion for communicating with the Confederate leaders." Mrs. Brice sighed. "He seems such a fine character. I hope they will not get into any trouble."

"I hope not, mother," said Stephen.

It was two mornings later that Judge Whipple and Stephen drove to the Iron Mountain depot, where they found a German company of Home Guards drawn up. On the long wooden platform under the sheds Stephen caught sight of Herr Körner and Herr Hauptmann amid a group of their countrymen. Little Körner came forward to clasp his hands. The tears ran on his cheeks, and he could not speak for emotion. Judge Whipple, grim and silent, stood apart. But he uncovered his head with the others when the train rolled in. Reverently they entered a car where the pine boxes were piled one on another, and they bore out the earthly remains of Captain Carl Richter.

Far from the land of his birth, among those same oaks on Bloody Hill where brave Lyon fell, he had gladly given up his life for the new country and the new cause he had made his own.

That afternoon in the cemetery, as the smoke of the last salute to a hero hung in the flickering light and drifted upward through the great trees, as the still air was yet quivering with the notes of the bugle-call which is the soldiers' requiem, a tall figure, gaunt and bent, stepped out from behind the blue line of the troops. It was that of Judge Whipple. He carried in his hand a wreath of white roses—the first of many to be laid on Richter's grave.

Poor Richter! How sad his life had been! And yet he had not filled it with sadness. For many a month, and many a year, Stephen could not look upon his empty place without a pang. He missed the cheery songs and the earnest presence even more than he had thought. Carl Richter, —as his father before him,—had lived for others. Both had sacrificed their bodies for a cause. One of them might be pictured as he trudged with Father Jahn from door to door through the Rhine country, or shouldering at sixteen a heavy musket in the *Landwehr's* ranks to drive the tyrant Napoleon from the beloved Fatherland. Later, aged before his time, his wife dead of misery, decrepit and prison-worn in the service of a thankless country, his hopes lived again in Carl, the swordsman of Jena. Then came the pitiful Revolution, the sundering of all ties, the elder man left to drag out his few weary days before a shattered altar. In Carl a new aspiration had sprung up, a new patriotism stirred. His, too, had been the sacrifice. Happy in death, for he had helped perpetuate that great Union which should be for all time the refuge of the oppressed.

CHAPTER IV

THE LIST OF SIXTY

ONE chilling day in November, when an icy rain was falling on the black mud of the streets, Virginia looked out of the window. Her eye was caught by two horses which were just skeletons with the skin stretched over them. One had a bad sore on his flank, and was lame. They were pulling a rattle-trap farm wagon with a buckled wheel. On the seat a man, pallid and bent and scantily clad, was holding the reins in his feeble hands, while beside him cowered a child of ten wrapped in a ragged blanket. In the body of the wagon, lying on a mattress pressed down in the midst of broken, cheap furniture and filthy kitchen ware, lay a gaunt woman in the rain. Her eyes were closed, and a hump on the surface of the dirty quilt beside her showed that a child must be there. From such a picture the girl fled in tears. But the sight of it, and of others like it, haunted her for weeks. Through those last dreary days of November, wretched families, which a year since had been in health and prosperity, came to the city, beggars, with the wrecks of their homes. The history of that hideous pilgrimage across a state has never been written. Still they came by the hundred, those families. Some brought little corpses to be buried. The father of one, hale and strong when they started, died of pneumonia in the public lodging-house. The walls of that house could tell many tales to wring the heart. So could Mr. Brinsmade, did he choose to speak of his own charities. He found time, between his labors at the big hospital newly founded, and his correspondence, and his journeys of love,—between early morning and midnight,—to give some hours a day to the refugees.

Throughout December they poured in on the afflicted city, already overtaxed. All the way to Springfield the road was lined with remains of articles once dear—a child's doll, a little rocking-chair, a colored print that had hung in the best room, a Bible text.

Anne Brinsmade, driven by Nicodemus, went from house to house to solicit old clothes, and take them to the crowded place of detention.

315

Christmas was drawing near—a sorry Christmas, in truth. And many of the wanderers were unclothed and unfed.

More battles had been fought; factions had arisen among Union men Another general had come to St. Louis to take charge of the Depart ment, and the other with his wondrous body-guard was gone.

The most serious problem confronting the new general was—how to care for the refugees. A council of citizens was called at headquarters, and the verdict went forth in the never-to-be-forgotten *Orders No. 24*. "Inasmuch," said the General, "as the Secession army had driven these people from their homes, Secession sympathizers should be made to support them." He added that the city was unquestionably full of these. Indignation was rife the day that order was published. Sixty prominent "disloyalists" were to be chosen and assessed to make up a sum of ten thousand dollars.

"They may sell my house over my head before I will pay a cent," cried Mr. Russell. And he meant it. This was the way the others felt. Who were to be on this mysterious list of "Sixty"? That was the all-absorbing question of the town. It was an easy matter to pick the con-spicuous ones. Colonel Carvel was sure to be there, and Mr. Cather-wood and Mr. Russell and Mr. James, and Mr. Worington the lawyer. Mrs. Addison Colfax lived for days in a fermented state of excitement which she declared would break her down; and which, despite her many cares and worries, gave her niece not a little amusement. For Virginia was human, and one morning she went to her aunt's room to read this editorial from the newspaper:—

"For the relief of many palpitating hearts it may be well to state that we understand only two ladies are on the ten thousand dollar list."

"Jinny," she cried, "how can you be so cruel as to read me that, when you know that I am in a state of frenzy now? How does that relieve me? It makes it an absolute certainty that Madame Jules and I will have to pay. We are the only women of importance in the city."

That afternoon she made good her much-uttered threat, and drove to Bellegarde. Only the Colonel and Virginia and Mammy Easter and Ned were left in the big house. Rosetta and Uncle Ben and Jackson had been hired out, and the horses sold,—all save old Dick, who was running, long-haired, in the fields at Glencoe.

Christmas eve was a steel-gray day, and the sleet froze as it fell. Since morning Colonel Carvel had sat poking the sitting-room fire, or pacing the floor restlessly. His occupation was gone. He was observed night and day by Federal detectives. Virginia strove to amuse him, to conceal her anxiety as she watched him. Well she knew that but for her he would long since have fled southward, and often in the bitterness of the night-time she blamed herself for not telling him to go. Ten years had seemed to pass over him since the war had begun.

All day long she had been striving to put away from her the memory of Christmas eves past and gone; of her father's early home-coming from the store, a mysterious smile on his face; of Captain Lige stamping noisily into the house, exchanging uproarious jests with Ned and Jackson. The Captain had always carried under his arm a shapeless bundle which he would confide to Ned with a knowing wink. And then the house would be lighted from top to bottom, and Mr. Russell and Mr. Catherwood and Mr. Brinsmade came in for a long evening with Mr. Carvel over great bowls of apple toddy and egg-nog. And Virginia would have her own friends in the big parlor. That parlor was shut up now, and icy cold.

Then there was Judge Whipple, the joyous event of whose year was his Christmas dinner at Colonel Carvel's house. Virginia pictured him this year at Mrs. Brice's little table, and wondered whether he would miss them as much as they missed him. War may break friendships, but it cannot take away the sacredness of memories.

The sombre daylight was drawing to an early close as the two stood looking out of the sitting-room window. A man's figure muffled in a great-coat slanting carefully across the street caught their eyes. Virginia started. It was the same United States deputy marshal she had seen the day before at Mr. Russell's house.

"Pa," she cried, "do you think he is coming here?"

"I reckon so, honey."

"The brute! Are you going to pay?"

"No, Jinny."

"Then they will take away the furniture."

"I reckon they will."

"Pa, you must promise me to take down the mahogany bed in your room. It—it was mother's. I could not bear to see them take that. Let me put it in the garret."

The Colonel was distressed, but he spoke without a tremor.

"No, Jinny. We must leave this house just as it is." Then he added, strangely enough for him, "God's will be done."

The bell rang sharply. And Ned, who was cook and housemaid, came in with his apron on.

"Does you want to see folks, Marse Comyn?"

The Colonel rose, and went to the door himself. He was an imposing figure as he stood in the windy vestibule, confronting the deputy. Virginia's first impulse was to shrink under the stairs. Then she came out and stood beside her father.

"Are you Colonel Carvel?"

"I reckon I am. Will you come in?"

The officer took off his cap. He was a young man with a smooth face, and a frank brown eye which paid its tribute to Virginia. He did not appear to relish the duty thrust upon him. He fumbled in his coat and drew from his inner pocket a paper.

"Colonel Carvel," said he, "by order of Major General Halleck, I serve you with this notice to pay the sum of three hundred and fifty dollars for the benefit of the destitute families which the Rebels have driven from their homes. In default of payment within a reasonable time such personal articles will be seized and sold at public auctions as will satisfy the demand against you."

The Colonel took the paper. "Very well, sir," he said. "You may tell the General that the articles may be seized. That I will not, while in my right mind, be forced to support persons who have no claim upon me."

It was said in the tone in which he might have refused an invitation to dinner. The deputy marvelled. He had gone into many houses that week; had seen indignation, hysterics, frenzy. He had even heard men and women whose sons and brothers were in the army of secession proclaim their loyalty to the Union. But this dignity, and the quiet scorn of the girl who had stood silent beside them, were new. He bowed, and casting his eyes to the vestibule, was glad to escape from the house.

The Colonel shut the door. Then he turned toward Virginia, thoughtfully pulled his goatee, and laughed gently.

"Lordy, we haven't got three hundred and fifty dollars to our names," said he.

* * * * * * *

The climate of St. Louis is capricious. That fierce valley of the Missouri, which belches fitful blizzards from December to March, is sometimes quiet. Then the hot winds come up from the Gulf, and sleet melts, and windows are opened. In those days the streets will be fetlock deep in soft mud. It is neither summer, nor winter, nor spring, nor anything.

It was such a languorous afternoon in January that a furniture van, accompanied by certain nondescript persons known as United States Police, pulled up at the curb in front of Mr. Carvel's house. Eugénie, watching at the window across the street, ran to tell her father, who came out on his steps and reviled the van with all the fluency of his French ancestors.

Mammy Easter opened the door, and then stood with her arms akimbo, amply filling its place. Her lips protruded, and an expression of defiance hard to describe sat on her honest black face.

"Is this Colonel Carvel's house?"

"Yassir. I 'low you knows dat jes as well as me." An embarrassed silence, and then from Mammy, "Whaffor you laffin at?"

"Is the Colonel at home?"

"Now I reckon you knows dat he ain't. Ef he was, you ain't come here 'quirin' in dat honey voice." (Raising her own voice.) "You tink I dunno whaffor you come? You done come heah to rifle, an' to loot, an' to steal, an' to seize what ain't your'n. You come heah when young Marse ain't to home ter rob him." (Still louder.) "Ned, whaffor you hidin' yonder? Ef yo' ain't man to protect Marse Comyn's prop-ty, jes han' over Marse Comyn's gun."

The marshal and his men had stood, half amused, more than half baffled by this unexpected resistance. Mammy Easter looked so dangerous that it was evident she was not to be passed without extreme bodily discomfort.

"Is your mistress here?"

This question was unfortunate in the extreme.

"You—you white trash!" cried Mammy, bursting with indignation. "Who is you to come heah 'quiring fo' her! I ain't agwine—"

"Mammy!"

"Yas'm! Yas, Miss Jinny." Mammy backed out of the door and clutched at her bandanna.

"Mammy, what is all this noise about?"

The torrent was loosed once more.

"These heah *men*, Miss Jinny, was gwine f'r t' carry away all yo' pa's b'longin's. I jes' tol' 'em dey ain't comin' in ovah dis heah body."

The deputy had his foot on the threshold. He caught sight of the face of Miss Carvel within, and stopped abruptly.

"I have a warrant here from the Provost Marshal, ma'am, to seize personal property to satisfy a claim against Colonel Carvel."

Virginia took the order, read it, and handed it back.

"I do not see how I am to prevent you," she said.

The deputy was plainly abashed.

"I'm sorry, Miss. I—I can't tell you how sorry I am. But it's got to be done."

Virginia nodded coldly. And still the man hesitated.

"What are you waiting for?" she said.

The deputy wiped his muddy feet. He made his men do likewise. Then he entered the chill drawing-room, threw open the blinds and glanced around him.

"I expect all that we want is right here," he said. And at the sight of the great chandelier, with its cut-glass crystals, he whistled. Then he walked over to the big English Rothfield piano and lifted the lid.

The man was a musician. Involuntarily he rested himself on the mahogany stool, and ran his fingers over the keys. They seemed to Virginia, standing motionless in the hall, to give out the very chords of agony.

The piano, too, had been her mother's. It had once stood in the brick house of her grandfather Colfax at Halcyondale. The songs of Beatrice lay on the bottom shelf of the what-not near by. No more, of an evening when they were alone, would Virginia quietly take them out and play them over to the Colonel, as he sat dreaming in the window with his cigar,—dreaming of a field on the borders of a wood, of a young girl who held his hand, and sang them softly to herself as she walked by his side. And, when they reached the house in the October twilight, she had played them for him on this piano. Often he had told Virginia of those days, and walked with her over those paths.

The deputy closed the lid, and sent out to the van for a truck. Virginia stirred. For the first time she heard the words of Mammy Easter.

"Come along upstairs wid yo' Mammy, honey. Dis ain't no place for us, I reckon." Her words were the essence of endearment. And yet, while she pronounced them, she glared unceasingly at the intruders. "Oh, de good Lawd'll burn de wicked!"

The men were removing the carved legs. Virginia went back into the room and stood before the deputy.

"Isn't there something else you could take? Some jewellery?" She flushed. "I have a necklace—"

"No, miss. This warrant's on your father. And there ain't nothing quite so salable as pianos."

She watched them, dry-eyed, as they carried it away. It seemed like a coffin. Only Mammy Easter guessed at the pain in Virginia's breast, and that was because there was pain in her own. They took the rosewood whatnot, but Virginia snatched the songs before the men could touch them, and held them in her arms. They seized the mahogany velvet-bottomed chairs, her uncle's wedding present to her mother; and, last of all, they ruthlessly tore up the Brussels carpet, beginning near the spot where Clarence had spilled ice-cream at one of her children's parties.

She could not bear to look into the dismantled room when they had gone. It was the embodied wreck of her happiness. Ned closed the blinds once more, and she herself turned the key in the lock, and went slowly up the stairs.

CHAPTER V

THE AUCTION

"Stephen," said the Judge, in his abrupt way, "there isn't a great deal doing. Let's go over to the Secesh property sales."

Stephen looked up in surprise. The seizures and intended sale of secession property had stirred up immense bitterness and indignation in the city. There were Unionists (lukewarm) who denounced the measure as unjust and brutal. The feelings of Southerners, avowed and secret, may only be surmised. Rigid ostracism was to be the price of bidding on any goods displayed, and men who bought in handsome furniture on that day because it was cheap have still, after forty years, cause to remember it.

It was not that Stephen feared ostracism. Anne Brinsmade was almost the only girl left to him from among his former circle of acquaintances. Miss Carvel's conduct is known. The Misses Russell showed him very plainly that they disapproved of his politics. The hospitable days at that house were over. Miss Catherwood, when they met on the street, pretended not to see him, and Eugénie Rénault gave him but a timid nod. The loyal families to whose houses he now went were mostly Southerners, in sentiment against forced auctions.

However, he put on his coat, and sallied forth into the sharp air, the Judge leaning on his arm. They walked for some distance in silence.

"Stephen," said he, presently, "I guess I'll do a little bidding."

Stephen did not reply. But he was astonished. He wondered what Mr. Whipple wanted with fine furniture. And, if he really wished to bid, Stephen knew likewise that no consideration would stop him.

"You don't approve of this proceeding, sir, I suppose," said the Judge.

"Yes, sir, on large grounds. War makes many harsh things necessary."

"Then," said the Judge, tartly, "by bidding, we help to support starving Union families. You should not be afraid to bid, sir."

Stephen bit his lip. Sometimes Mr. Whipple made him very angry.

"I am not afraid to bid, Judge Whipple." He did not see the smile on the Judge's face.

"Then you will bid in certain things for me," said Mr. Whipple. Here
he hesitated, and shook free the rest of the sentence with a wrench.
"Colonel Carvel always had a lot of stuff I wanted. Now I've got the
chance to buy it cheap."

There was silence again, for the space of a whole block. Finally, Stephen managed to say:—

"You'll have to excuse me, sir. I do not care to do that."

"What!" cried the Judge, stopping in the middle of a cross-street, so
that a wagon nearly ran over his toes.

"I was once a guest in Colonel Carvel's house, sir. And—"

"And what?"

Neither the young man nor the old knew all it was costing the other
to say these things. The Judge took a grim pleasure in eating his heart.
And as for Stephen, he often went to his office through Locust Street,
which was out of his way, in the hope that he might catch a glimpse of
Virginia. He had guessed much of the privations she had gone through.
He knew that the Colonel had hired out most of his slaves, and he had
actually seen the United States Police drive across Eleventh Street with
the piano that she had played on.

The Judge was laughing quietly,—not a pleasant laugh to hear,—as
they came to Morgan's great warerooms. A crowd blocked the pavement,
and hustled and shoved at the doors,—roughs, and soldiers off duty, and
ladies and gentlemen whom the Judge and Stephen knew, and some of
whom they spoke to. All of these were come out of curiosity, that they
might see for themselves any who had the temerity to bid on a neighbor's household goods. The long hall, which ran from street to street,
was packed, the people surging backward and forward, and falling
roughly against the mahogany pieces; and apologizing, and scolding, and
swearing all in a breath. The Judge, holding tightly to Stephen, pushed
his way fiercely to the stand, vowing over and over that the commotion
was a secession trick to spoil the furniture and stampede the sale. In
truth, it was at the Judge's suggestion that a blue provost's guard was
called in later to protect the seized property.

How many of those mahogany pieces, so ruthlessly tumbled about
before the public eye, meant a heartache! Wedding presents of long ago,
dear to many a bride with silvered hair, had been torn from the corner
where the children had played—children who now, alas, were grown
and gone to war. Yes, that was the Brussels rug that had lain before
the fire, and which the little feet had worn in the corner. Those were

the chairs the little hands had harnessed, four in a row, and fallen on its side was the armchair—the stage coach itself. There were the books, held up to common gaze, that a beloved parent had thumbed with affection. Yes, and here in another part of the hall were the family horses and the family carriage that had gone so often back and forth from church with the happy brood of children, now scattered and gone to war.

As Stephen reached his place beside the Judge, Mr. James's effects were being cried. And, if glances could have killed, many a bidder would have dropped dead. The heavy dining-room table which meant so much to the family went for a song to a young man recently come from Yankeeland, whose open boast it was—like Eliphalet's secret one—that he would one day grow rich enough to snap his fingers in the face of the Southern aristocrats. Mr. James was not there. But Mr. Catherwood, his face haggard and drawn, watched the sideboard he had given his wife on her silver wedding being sold to a pawnbroker.

Stephen looked in vain for Colonel Carvel—for Virginia. He did not want to see them there. He knew by heart the list of things which had been taken from their house. He understood the feeling which had sent the Judge here to bid them in. And Stephen honored him the more.

When the auctioneer came to the Carvel list, and the well-known name was shouted out, the crowd responded with a stir and pressed closer to the stand. And murmurs were plainly heard in more than one direction.

"Now, gentlemen, *and* ladies," said the seller, "this here is a genu-ine English Rothfield piano once belonging to Colonel Carvel, and the celebrated Judge Colfax of Kaintucky." He lingered fondly over the names, that the impression might have time to sink deep. "This here magnificent instrument's worth at the very least" (another pause) "—twelve hundred dollars. What am I bid?"

He struck a base note of the keys, then a treble, and they vibrated 'n the heated air of the big hall. Had he hit the little C of the top octave, the tinkle of that also might have been heard.

"Gentlemen *and* ladies, we have to begin somewheres. What am I bid?"

A menacing murmur gave place to the accusing silence. Some there were who gazed at the Rothfield with longing eyes, but who had no intention of committing social suicide. Suddenly a voice, the rasp of which penetrated to St. Charles Street, came out with a bid. The owner was a seedy man with a straw-colored, drunkard's mustache. He was leaning against the body of Mrs. Russell's barouche (seized for sale), and those about him shrank away as from smallpox. His hundred-dollar offer was followed by a hiss.

What followed next Stephen will always remember. When Judge Whipple drew himself up to his full six feet, that was a warning to those that knew him. As he doubled the bid, the words came out with the aggressive distinctness of a man who through a long life has been used to opposition. He with the gnawed yellow mustache pushed himself clear of the barouche, his smouldering cigar-butt dropping to the floor. But there were no hisses now.

And this is how Judge Whipple braved public opinion once more. As he stood there, defiant, many were the conjectures as to what he could wish to do with the piano of his old friend. Those who knew the Judge (and there were few who did not) pictured to themselves the dingy little apartment where he lived, and smiled. Whatever his detractors might have said of him, no one was ever heard to avow that he had bought or sold anything for gain. A tremor ran through the people. Could it have been of admiration for the fine old man who towered there glaring defiance at those about him? "Give me a strong and consistent enemy," some great personage has said, "rather than a lukewarm friend." Three score and five years the Judge had lived, and now some were beginning to suspect that he had a heart. Verily he had guarded his secret well. But it was let out to many more that day, and they went home praising him who had once pronounced his name with bitterness.

This is what happened. Before he of the yellow mustache could pick up his cigar from the floor and make another bid, the Judge had cried out a sum which was the total of Colonel Carvel's assessment. Many recall to this day how fiercely he frowned when the applause broke forth of itself; and when he turned to go they made a path for him, in admiration, the length of the hall, down which he stalked, looking neither to the right nor left. Stephen followed him, thankful for the day which had brought him into the service of such a man.

And so it came about that the other articles were returned to Colonel Carvel with the marshal's compliments, and put back into the cold parlor where they had stood for many years. The men who brought them offered to put down the carpet, but by Virginia's orders the rolls were stood up in the corner, and the floor left bare. And days passed into weeks, and no sign or message came from Judge Whipple in regard to the piano he had bought. Virginia did not dare mention it to the Colonel.

Where was it? It had been carried by six sweating negroes up the narrow stairs into the Judge's office. Stephen and Shadrach had by Mr. Whipple's orders cleared a corner of his inner office and bedroom of papers and books and rubbish, and there the bulky instrument was finally set up. It occupied one-third of the space. The Judge watched the proceeding grimly, choking now and again from the dust that was raised, yet uttering never a word. He locked the lid when the van man handed him the key, and thrust that in his pocket.

Stephen had of late found enough to do in St. Louis. He was the kind of man to whom promotions came unsought, and without noise. In the autumn he had been made a captain in the Halleck Guards of the State Militia, as a reward for his indefatigable work in the armories and his knowledge of tactics. Twice his company had been called out at night, and once they made a campaign as far as the Merimec and captured a party of recruits who were destined for Jefferson Davis. Some weeks passed before Mr. Brinsmade heard of his promotion and this exploit, and yet scarcely a day went by that he did not see the young man at the big hospital. For Stephen helped in the work of the Sanitary Commission too, and so strove to make up in zeal for the service in the field which he longed to give.

After Christmas Mr. and Mrs. Brinsmade moved out to their place on the Bellefontaine Road. This was to force Anne to take a rest. For the girl was worn out with watching at the hospitals, and with tending the destitute mothers and children from the ranks of the refugees. The Brinsmade place was not far from the Fair Grounds,—now a receiving camp for the crude but eager regiments of the Northern states. To Mr. Brinsmade's, when the day's duty was done, the young Union officers used to ride, and often there would be half a dozen of them to tea. That house, and other great houses on the Bellefontaine Road with which this history has no occasion to deal, were as homes to many a poor fellow who would never see home again. Sometimes Anne would gather together such young ladies of her acquaintance from the neighborhood and the city as their interests and sympathies permitted to waltz with a Union officer, and there would be a little dance. To these dances Stephen Brice was usually invited.

One such occasion occurred on a Friday in January, and Mr. Brinsmade himself called in his buggy and drove Stephen to the country early in the afternoon. He and Anne went for a walk along the river, the surface of which was broken by lumps of yellow ice. Gray clouds hung low in the sky as they picked their way over the frozen furrows of the ploughed fields. The grass was all a yellow-brown, but the north wind which swayed the bare trees brought a touch of color to Anne's cheeks. Before they realized where they were, they had nearly crossed the Bellegarde estate, and the house itself was come into view, standing high on the slope above the withered garden. They halted.

"The shutters are up," said Stephen. "I understood that Mrs. Colfax had come out here not long ago."

"She came out for a day just before Christmas," said Anne, smiling, "and then she ran off to Kentucky. I think she was afraid that she was one of the two women on the list of Sixty."

"It must have been a blow to her pride when she found that she was not," said Stephen, who had a keen remembrance of her conduct upon a certain Sunday not a year gone.

Impelled by the same inclination, they walked in silence to the house and sat down on the edge of the porch. The only motion in the view was the smoke from the slave quarters twisting in the wind, and the hurrying ice in the stream.

"Poor Jinny!" said Anne, with a sigh, "how she loved to romp! What good times we used to have here together!"

"Do you think that she is unhappy?" Stephen demanded, involuntarily.

"Oh, yes," said Anne. "How can you ask? But you could not make her show it. The other morning when she came out to our house I found her sitting at the piano. I am sure there were tears in her eyes, but she would not let me see them. She made some joke about Spencer Catherwood running away. What do you think the Judge will do with that piano, Stephen?"

He shook his head.

"The day after they put it in his room he came in with a great black cloth, which he spread over it. You cannot even see the feet."

There was a silence. And Anne, turning to him timidly, gave him a long, searching look.

"It is growing late," she said. "I think that we ought to go back."

They went out by the long entrance road, through the naked woods. Stephen said little. Only a little while before he had had one of those vivid dreams of Virginia which left their impression, but not their sub-

stance, to haunt him. On those rare days following the dreams her spirit
had its mastery over his. He pictured her then with a glow on her face
which was neither sadness nor mirth,—a glow that ministered to him
alone. And yet, he did not dare to think that he might have won her,
even if politics and war had not divided them.

When the merriment of the dance was at its height that evening,
Stephen stood at the door of the long room, meditatively watching the
bright gowns and the flash of gold on the uniforms as they flitted past.
Presently the opposite door opened, and he heard Mr. Brinsmade's
voice mingling with another, the excitable energy of which recalled
some familiar episode. Almost—so it seemed—at one motion, the owner
of the voice had come out of the door and had seized Stephen's hand in
a warm grasp,—a tall and spare figure in the dress of a senior officer.
The military frock, which fitted the man's character rather than the
man, was carelessly open, laying bare a gold-buttoned white waistcoat
and an expanse of shirt bosom which ended in a black stock tie. The
ends of the collar were apart the width of the red clipped beard, and the
mustache was cropped straight along the line of the upper lip. The forehead rose high, and was brushed carelessly free of the hair. The nose
was almost straight, but combative. A fire fairly burned in the eyes.

"The boy doesn't remember me," said the gentleman, in quick tones,
smiling at Mr. Brinsmade.

"Yes, sir, I do," Stephen made haste to answer. He glanced at the
star on the shoulder strap, and said: "You are General Sherman."

"First rate!" laughed the General, patting him. "First rate!"

"Now in command at Camp Benton, Stephen," Mr. Brinsmade put
in. "Won't you sit down, General?"

"No," said the General, emphatically waving away the chair. "No,
rather stand." Then his keen face suddenly lighted with amusement,—
and mischief, Stephen thought. "So you've heard of me since we met,
sir?"

"Yes, General."

"Humph! Guess you heard I was crazy," said the General, in his
downright way.

Stephen was struck dumb.

"He's been reading the lies in the newspapers too, Brinsmade," the
General went on rapidly. "I'll make 'em eat their newspapers for saying
I was crazy. That's the Secretary of War's doings. Ever tell you what
Cameron did, Brinsmade? He and his party were in Louisville last fall,

when I was serving in Kentucky, and came to my room in the Galt
House. Well, we locked the door, and Miller sent us up a good lunch and
wine. After lunch, the Secretary lay on my bed, and we talked things
over. He asked me what I thought about things in Kentucky. I told him.
I got a map. I said, 'Now, Mr. Secretary, here is the whole Union line
from the Potomac to Kansas. Here's McClellan in the East with one
hundred miles of front. Here Frémont in the West with one hundred
miles. Here we are in Kentucky, in the centre, with three hundred miles
to defend. McClellan has a hundred thousand men, Frémont has sixty
thousand. You give us fellows with over three hundred miles only eighteen thousand.' 'How many do you want?' says Cameron, still on the
bed. '*Two hundred thousand* before we get through,' said I. Cameron
pitched up his hands in the air. 'Great God!' says he, 'where are they to
come from?' 'The northwest is chuck full of regiments you fellows at
Washington won't accept,' said I. 'Mark my words, Mr. Secretary,
you'll need 'em all and more before we get done with this Rebellion.'
Well, sir, he was very friendly before we finished, and I thought the
thing was all thrashed out. No, sir! he goes back to Washington and
gives it out that I'm crazy, and want two hundred thousand men in
Kentucky. Then I am ordered to report to Halleck in Missouri here,
and he calls me back from Sedalia because he believes the lies."

Stephen, who had in truth read the stories in question a month or
two before, could not conceal his embarrassment. He looked at the man
in front of him,—alert, masterful, intelligent, frank to any stranger
who took his fancy,—and wondered how any one who had talked to
him could believe them.

Mr. Brinsmade smiled. "They have to print something, General," he
said.

"I'll give 'em something to print later on," answered the General,
grimly. Then his expression changed. "Brinsmade, you fellows did have
a session with Frémont, didn't you? Anderson sent me over here last
September, and the first man I ran across at the Planters' House was
Appleton. 'What are you in town for?' says he. 'To see Frémont,' I said.
You ought to have heard Appleton laugh. 'You don't think Frémont'll
see *you*, do you?' says he. 'Why not?' 'Well,' says Tom, 'go 'round to
his palace at six to-morrow morning and bribe that Hungarian prince
who runs his body-guard to get you a good place in the line of senators
and governors and first citizens, and before nightfall you may get a
sight of him, since you come from Anderson. Not one man in a hun-

dred,' says Appleton, 'not one man in a hundred, reaches his chief-of-staff.' Next morning," the General continued in a staccato which was often his habit, "had breakfast before daybreak and went 'round there. Place just swarming with Californians—army contracts." (The General sniffed.) "Saw Frémont. Went back to hotel. More Californians, and by gad—old Baron Steinberger with his nose hanging over the register."

"Frémont was a little difficult to get at, General," said Mr. Brinsmade. "Things were confused and discouraged when those first contracts were awarded. Frémont was a good man, and it wasn't his fault that the inexperience of his quartermasters permitted some of those men to get rich."

"No," said the General. "His fault! Certainly not. Good man! To be sure he was—didn't get along with Blair. These court-martials you're having here now have stirred up the whole country. I guess we'll hear now how those fortunes were made. To listen to those witnesses lie about each other on the stand is better than the theatre."

Stephen laughed at the comical and vivid manner in which the General set this matter forth. He himself had been present one day of the sittings of the court-martial when one of the witnesses on the prices of mules was that same seedy man with the straw-colored mustache who had bid for Virginia's piano against the Judge.

"Come, Stephen," said the General, abruptly, "run and snatch one of those pretty girls from my officers. They're having more than their share."

"They deserve more, sir," answered Stephen.

Whereupon the General laid his hand impulsively on the young man's shoulder, divining what Stephen did not say.

"Nonsense!" said he; "you are doing the work in this war, not we. We do the damage—you repair it. If it were not for Mr. Brinsmade and you gentlemen who help him, where would our Western armies be? Don't you go to the front yet a while, young man. We need the best we have in reserve." He glanced critically at Stephen. "You've had military training of some sort?"

"He's a captain in the Halleck Guards, sir," said Mr. Brinsmade, generously, "and the best drillmaster we've had in this city. He's seen service, too, General."

Stephen reddened furiously and started to protest, when the General cried:—

"It's more than I have in this war. Come, come, I knew he was a soldier. Let's see what kind of a strategist he'll make. Brinsmade, have you got such a thing as a map?"

Mr. Brinsmade had, and led the way back into the library. The General shut the door, lighted a cigar with a single vigorous stroke of a match, and began to smoke with quick puffs. Stephen was puzzled how to receive the confidences the General was giving out with such freedom.

When the map was laid on the table, the General drew a pencil from his pocket and pointed to the state of Kentucky. Then he drew a line from Columbus to Bowling Green, through Forts Donelson and Henry.

"Now, Stephen," said he, "there's the Rebel line. Show me the proper place to break it."

Stephen hesitated a while, and then pointed at the centre.

"Good!" said the General. "Very good!" He drew a heavy line across the first, and it ran almost in the bed of the Tennessee River. He swung on Mr. Brinsmade. "Very question Halleck asked me the other day, and that's how I answered it. Now, gentlemen, there's a man named Grant down in that part of the country. Keep your eyes on him. Ever heard of him, Brinsmade? He used to live here once, and a year ago he was less than I was. Now he's a general."

The recollection of the scene in the street by the Arsenal that May morning not a year gone came to Stephen with a shock.

"I saw him," he cried; "he was Captain Grant that lived on the Gravois Road. But surely this can't be the same man who seized Paducah and was in that affair at Belmont."

"By gum!" said the General, laughing. "Don't wonder you're surprised. Grant has stuff in him. They kicked him around Springfield awhile, after the war broke out, for a military carpet-bagger. Then they gave him for a regiment the worst lot of ruffians you ever laid eyes on. He fixed 'em. He made 'em walk the plank. He made 'em march half-way across the state instead of taking the cars the Governor offered. Belmont! I guess he *is* the man that chased the Rebs out of Belmont. Then his boys broke loose when they got into the town. That wasn't Grant's fault. The Rebs came back and chased 'em out into their boats on the river. Brinsmade, you remember hearing about that. Grant did the coolest thing you ever saw. He sat on his horse at the top of the bluff while the boys fell over each other trying to get on the boat. Yes, sir, he sat there, disgusted, on his horse, smoking a cigar, with the Rebs raising pandemonium all around him. And then, sir," cried the Gen-

eral, excitedly, "what do you think he did? Hanged if he didn't force his
horse right on to his haunches, slide down the whole length of the bank
and ride him across a teetering plank on to the steamer. And the Rebs
just stood on the bank and stared. They were so astonished they didn't
even shoot the man. You watch Grant," said the General. "And now,
Stephen," he added, "just you run off and take hold of the prettiest girl
you can find. If any of my boys object, say I sent you."

The next Monday Stephen had a caller. It was little Tiefel, now a
first lieutenant with a bristly beard and tanned face, come to town on
a few days' furlough. He had been with Lyon at Wilson's Creek, and he
had a sad story to tell of how he found poor Richter, lying stark on that
bloody field, with a smile of peace upon his face. Strange that he should
at length have been killed by a sabre!

It was a sad meeting for those two, since each reminded the other of
a dear friend they would see no more on earth. They went out to sup
together in the German style; and gradually, over his beer, Tiefel forgot
his sorrow. Stephen listened with an ache to the little man's tales of
the campaigns he had been through. So that presently Tiefel cried out:—

"Why, my friend, you are melancholy as an owl. I will tell you a funny
story. Did you ever hear of one General Sherman? He that they say is
crazy?"

"He is no more crazy than I am," said Stephen, warmly.

"Is he not?" answered Tiefel, "then I will show you a mistake. You
recall last November he was out to Sedalia to inspect the camp there,
and he sleeps in a little country store where I am quartered. Now up
gets your General Sherman in the middle of the night,—midnight,—
and marches up and down between the counters, and waves his arms.
'So,' says he, 'and so,' says he, 'Sterling Price will be here, and Steele
here, and this column will take that road, and so-and-so's a damned
fool.' Is not that crazy? So he walks up and down for three eternal hours.
Says he, 'Pope has no business to be at Osterville, and Steele here at
Sedalia with his regiments all over the place. They must both go into
camp at La Mine River, and form brigades and divisions, that the
troops may be handled.' "

"If that's insanity," cried Stephen so strongly as to surprise the little
man, "then I wish we had more insane generals. It just shows how a
malicious rumor will spread. What Sherman said about Pope's and
Steele's forces is true as Gospel, and if you ever took the trouble to look

into that situation, Tiefel, you would see it." And Stephen brought down his mug on the table with a crash that made the bystanders jump.

"Himmel!" exclaimed little Tiefel. But he spoke in admiration.

It was not a month after that that Sherman's prophecy of the quiet general who had slid down the bluff at Belmont came true. The whole country hummed with Grant's praises. Moving with great swiftness and secrecy up the Tennessee, in company with the gunboats of Commodore Foote, he had pierced the Confederate line at the very point Sherman had indicated. Fort Henry had fallen, and Grant was even then moving to besiege Donelson.

Mr. Brinsmade prepared to leave at once for the battlefield, taking with him to Paducah physicians and nurses. All day long the boat was loading with sanitary stores and boxes of dainties for the wounded. It was muggy and wet—characteristic of that winter—as Stephen pushed through the drays on the slippery levee to the landing. He had with him a basket his mother had put up. He also bore a message to Mr. Brinsmade from the Judge. It was while he was picking his way along the crowded decks that he ran into General Sherman. The General seized him unceremoniously by the shoulder.

"Good-by, Stephen," he said.

"Good-by, General," said Stephen, shifting his basket to shake hands. "Are you going away?"

"Ordered to Paducah," said the General. He pulled Stephen off the guards into an empty cabin. "Brice," said he, earnestly, "I haven't forgotten how you saved young Brinsmade at Camp Jackson. They tell me that you are useful here. I say, don't go in unless you *have* to. I don't mean force, you understand. But when you feel that you can go in, come to me or write me a letter. That is," he added, seemingly inspecting Stephen's white teeth with approbation, "if you're not afraid to serve under a crazy man."

It has been said that the General liked the lack of effusiveness of Stephen's reply.

CHAPTER VI

ELIPHALET PLAYS HIS TRUMPS

SUMMER was come again. Through interminable days the sun beat down upon the city; and at night the tortured bricks flung back angrily the heat with which he had filled them. Great battles had been fought, and vast armies were drawing breath for greater ones to come.

"Jinny," said the Colonel one day, "as we don't seem to be much use in town, I reckon we may as well go to Glencoe."

Virginia threw her arms around her father's neck. For many months she had seen what the Colonel himself was slow to comprehend—that his usefulness was gone. The days melted into weeks, and Sterling Price and his army of liberation failed to come. The vigilant Union general and his aides had long since closed all avenues to the South. For, one fine morning toward the end of the previous summer, when the Colonel was contemplating a journey, he had read that none might leave the city without a pass, whereupon he went hurriedly to the office of the Provost Marshal. There he had found a number of gentlemen in the same plight, each waving a pass made out by the Provost Marshal's clerks, and waiting for that officer's signature. The Colonel also procured one of these, and fell into line. The Marshal gazed at the crowd, pulled off his coat, and readily put his name to the passes of several gentlemen going east. Next came Mr. Bub Ballington, whom the Colonel knew, but pretended not to.

"Going to Springfield?" asked the Marshal, genially.

"Yes," said Bub.

"Not very profitable to be a minute-man, eh?" in the same tone.

The Marshal signs his name, Mr. Ballington trying not to look indignant as he makes for the door. A small silver bell rings on the Marshal's desk, the one word, "Spot!" breaks the intense silence, which is one way of saying that Mr. Ballington is detained, and will probably be lodged that night at Government expense.

"Well, Colonel Carvel, what can I do for you this morning?" asked the Marshal, genially.

The Colonel pushed back his hat and wiped his brow.

334

"I reckon I'll wait till next week, Captain," said Mr. Carvel. "It's pretty hot to travel just now."

The Provost Marshal smiled sweetly. There were many in the office who would have liked to laugh, but it did not pay to laugh at some people. Colonel Carvel was one of them.

In the proclamation of martial law was much to make life less endurable than ever. All who were convicted by a court-martial of being rebels were to have property confiscated, and slaves set free. Then there was a certain oath to be taken by all citizens who did not wish to have guardians appointed over their actions. There were many who swallowed this oath and never felt any ill effects. Mr. Jacob Cluyme was one, and came away feeling very virtuous. It was not unusual for Mr. Cluyme to feel virtuous. Mr. Hopper did not have indigestion after taking it, but Colonel Carvel would sooner have eaten gooseberry pie, which he had never tasted but once.

That summer had worn away, like a monster which turns and gives hot gasps when you think it has expired. It took the Arkansan just a month, under Virginia's care, to become well enough to be sent to a Northern prison. He was not precisely a Southern gentleman, and he went to sleep over the "Idylls of the King." But he was admiring, and grateful, and wept when he went off to the boat with the provost's guard, destined for a Northern prison. Virginia wept too. He had taken her away from her aunt (who would have nothing to do with him), and had given her occupation. She nor her father never tired of hearing his rough tales of Price's rough army.

His departure was about the time when suspicions were growing set. The favor had caused comment and trouble, hence there was no hope of giving another sufferer the same comfort. The cordon was drawn tighter. One of the mysterious gentlemen who had been seen in the vicinity of Colonel Carvel's house was arrested on the ferry, but he had contrived to be rid of the carpet-sack in which certain precious letters were carried.

Throughout the winter, Mr. Hopper's visits to Locust Street had continued at intervals of painful regularity. It is not necessary to dwell upon his brilliant powers of conversation, nor to repeat the platitudes which he repeated, for there was no significance in Mr. Hopper's tales, not a particle. The Colonel had found that out, and was thankful. His manners were better; his English decidedly better.

It was for her father's sake, of course, that Virginia bore with him. Such is the appointed lot of women. She tried to be just, and it occurred

to her that she had never before been just. Again and again she repeated
to herself that Eliphalet's devotion to the Colonel at this low ebb of his
fortunes had something in it of which she did not suspect him. She had a
class contempt for Mr. Hopper as an uneducated Yankee and a person
of commercial ideals. But now he was showing virtues,—if virtues they
were,—and she tried to give him the benefit of the doubt. With his great
shrewdness and business ability, why did he not take advantage of the
many opportunities the war gave to make a fortune? For Virginia had
of late been going to the store with the Colonel,—who spent his mornings
turning over piles of dusty papers,—and Mr. Hopper had always been
at his desk.

After this, Virginia even strove to be kind to him, but it was uphill
work. The front door never closed after one of his visits that suspicion
was not left behind. Antipathy would assert itself. Could it be that there
was a motive under all this plotting? He struck her inevitably as the kind
who would be content to mine underground to attain an end. The worst
she could think of him was that he wished to ingratiate himself now, in
the hope that, when the war was ended, he might become a partner in
Mr. Carvel's business. She had put even this away as unworthy of her.

Once she had felt compelled to speak to her father on the subject.

"I believe I did him an injustice, Pa," she said. "Not that I like him
any better now. I must be honest about that. I simply *can't* like him. But
I do think that if he had been as unscrupulous as I thought, he would
have deserted you long ago for something more profitable. He would not
be sitting in the office day after day making plans for the business when
the war is over."

She remembered how sadly he had smiled at her over the top of his
paper.

"You are a good girl, Jinny," he said.

Toward the end of July of that second summer riots broke out in the
city, and simultaneously a bright spot appeared on Virginia's horizon.
This took the form, for Northerners, of a guerrilla scare, and an order was
promptly issued for the enrollment of all the able-bodied men in the ten
wards as militia, subject to service in the state, to exterminate the roving
bands. Whereupon her Britannic Majesty became extremely popular,—
even with some who claimed for a birthplace the Emerald Isle. Hundreds
who heretofore had valued but lightly their British citizenship made
haste to renew their allegiance; and many sought the office of the English

Consul whose claims on her Majesty's protection were vague, to say the least. Broken heads and scandal followed. For the first time, when Virginia walked to the store with her father, Eliphalet was not there. It was strange indeed that Virginia defended him.

"I don't blame him for not wanting to fight for the Yankees," she said. The Colonel could not resist a retort.

"Then why doesn't he fight for the South?" he asked.

"Fight for the South!" cried the young lady, scornfully. "Mr. Hopper fight? I reckon the South wouldn't have him."

"I reckon not, too," said the Colonel, dryly.

For the following week curiosity prompted Virginia to take that walk with the Colonel. Mr. Hopper being still absent, she helped him to sort the papers—those grimy reminders of a more prosperous time gone by. Often Mr. Carvel would run across one which seemed to bring some incident to his mind; for he would drop it absently on his desk, his hand seeking his chin, and remain for half an hour lost in thought. Virginia would not disturb him.

Meanwhile there had been inquiries for Mr. Hopper. The Colonel answered them all truthfully—generally with that dangerous suavity for which he was noted. Twice a seedy man with a gnawed yellow mustache had come in to ask Eliphalet's whereabouts. On the second occasion this individual became importunate.

"You don't know nothin' about him, you say?" he demanded.

"No," said the Colonel.

The man took a shuffle forward.

"My name's Ford," he said. "I 'low I kin 'lighten you a little."

"Good day, sir," said the Colonel.

"I guess you'll like to hear what I've got to say."

"Ephum," said Mr. Carvel in his natural voice, "show this man out."

Mr. Ford slunk out without Ephum's assistance. But he half turned at the door, and shot back a look that frightened Virginia.

"Oh, Pa," she cried, in alarm, "what did he mean?"

"I couldn't tell you, Jinny," he answered. But she noticed that he was very thoughtful as they walked home.

The next morning Eliphalet had not returned, but a corporal and guard were waiting to search the store for him. The Colonel read the order, and invited them in with hospitality. He even showed them the way upstairs, and presently Virginia heard them all tramping overhead among the bales. Her eye fell upon the paper they had brought, which lay unfolded on her father's desk. It was signed *Stephen A. Brice, Enrolling Officer.*

That very afternoon they moved to Glencoe, and Ephum was left in sole charge of the store. At Glencoe, far from the hot city and the cruel war, began a routine of peace. Virginia was a child again, romping in the woods and fields beside her father. The color came back to her cheeks once more, and the laughter into her voice. The two of them, and Ned and Mammy, spent a rollicking hour in the pasture the freedom of which Dick had known so long, before the old horse was caught and brought back into bondage. After that Virginia took long drives with her father, and coming home, they would sit in the summer house high above the Merimec, listening to the crickets' chirp, and watching the day fade upon the water. The Colonel, who had always detested pipes, learned to smoke a corncob. He would sit by the hour, with his feet on the rail of the porch and his hat tilted back, while Virginia read to him. Poe and Wordsworth and Scott he liked, but Tennyson was his favorite. Such happiness could not last.

One afternoon when Virginia was sitting in the summer house alone, her thoughts wandering back, as they sometimes did, to another afternoon she had spent there,—it seemed so long ago,—when she saw Mammy Easter coming toward her.

"Honey, dey's comp'ny up to de house. Mister Hopper's done arrived. He's on de po'ch, talkin' to your Pa. Lawsey, look wha he come!"

In truth, the solid figure of Eliphalet himself was on the path some twenty yards behind her. His hat was in his hand; his hair was plastered down more neatly than ever, and his coat was a faultless and sober creation of a Franklin Avenue tailor. He carried a cane, which was unheard of.

Virginia sat upright, and patted her skirts with a gesture of annoyance—what she felt was anger, resentment. Suddenly she rose, swept past Mammy, and met him ten paces from the summer house.

"How-dy-do, Miss Virginia," he cried, pleasantly. "Your father had a notion you might be here." He said *fayther.*

Virginia gave him her hand limply. Her greeting would have frozen a man of ardent temperament. But it was not precisely ardor that Eliphalet showed. The girl paused and examined him swiftly. There was something in the man's air to-day.

"So you were not caught?" she said.

Her words seemed to relieve some tension in him. He laughed noiselessly.

"I just guess I wahn't."

"How did you escape?" she asked, looking at him curiously.

"Well, I did, first of all. You're considerable smart, Miss Jinny, but I'll bet you can't tell me where I was, now."

"I do not care to know. The place might save you again."

He showed his disappointment. "I cal'lated it might interest you to know how I dodged the Sovereign State of Missouri. General Halleck made an order that released a man from enrolling on payment of ten dollars. I paid. Then I was drafted into the Abe Lincoln Volunteers; I paid a substitute. And so here I be, exercising life, and liberty, and the pursuit of happiness."

"So you *bought* yourself free?" said Virginia. "If your substitute gets killed, I suppose you will have cause for congratulation."

Eliphalet laughed, and pulled down his cuffs. "That's his lookout, I cal'late," said he. He glanced at the girl in a way that made her vaguely uneasy. She turned from him, back toward the summer house. Eliphalet's eyes smouldered as they rested upon her figure. He took a step forward.

"Miss Jinny?" he said.

"Yes?"

"I've heard considerable about the beauties of this place. Would you mind showing me 'round a bit?"

Virginia started. It was his tone now. Not since that first evening in Locust Street had it taken on such assurance. And yet she could not be impolite to a guest.

"Certainly not," she replied, but without looking up.

Eliphalet led the way. He came to the summer house, glanced around it with apparent satisfaction, and put his foot on the moss-grown step. Virginia did a surprising thing. She leaped quickly into the doorway before him, and stood facing him, framed in the climbing roses.

"Oh, Mr. Hopper!" she cried. "Please, not in here."

He drew back, staring in astonishment at the crimson in her face.

"Why not?" he asked suspiciously—almost brutally.

She had been groping wildly for excuses, and found none.

"Because," she said, "because I ask you not to." With dignity: "That should be sufficient."

"Well," replied Eliphalet, with an abortive laugh, "that's funny, now. Womenkind get queer notions, which I cal'late we've got to respect and put up with all our lives—eh?"

Her anger flared at his leer and at his broad way of gratifying her whim. And she was more incensed than ever at his air of being at home—it was nothing less. The man's whole manner was an insult. She strove still to hide her resentment.

"There is a walk along the bluff," she said, coldly, "where the view is just as good."

But she purposely drew him into the right-hand path, which led, after a little, back to the house. Despite her pace he pressed forward to her side.

"Miss Jinny," said he, precipitately, "did I ever strike you as a marrying man?"

Virginia stopped, and put her handkerchief to her face, the impulse strong upon her to laugh. Eliphalet was suddenly transformed again into the common commercial Yankee. He was in love, and had come to ask her advice. She might have known it.

"I never thought of you as of the marrying kind, Mr. Hopper," she answered, her voice quivering.

Indeed, he was irresistibly funny as he stood hot and ill at ease. The Sunday coat bore witness to his increasing portliness by creasing across from the buttons; his face, fleshy and perspiring, showed purple veins, and the little eyes receded comically, like a pig's.

"Well, I've been thinking serious of late about getting married," he continued, slashing the rose bushes with his stick. "I don't cal'late to be a sentimental critter. I'm not much on high-sounding phrases, and such things, but I'd give you my word I'd make a good husband."

"Please be careful of those roses, Mr. Hopper."

"Beg pardon," said Eliphalet. He began to lose track of his tenses—that was the only sign he gave of perturbation. "When I come to St. Louis without a cent, Miss Jinny, I made up my mind I'd be a rich man before I left it. If I was to die now, I'd have kept that promise. I'm not thirty-four, and I cal'late I've got as much money in a safe place as a good many men you call rich. I'm not saying what I've got, mind you. All in proper time. I'm a pretty steady kind. I've stopped chewing—there was a time when I done that. And I don't drink nor smoke."

"That is all very commendable, Mr. Hopper," Virginia said, stifling a rebellious titter. "But—but why did you give up chewing?"

"I am informed that the ladies are against it," said Eliphalet,—"dead against it. You wouldn't like it in a husband, now, would you?"

This time the laugh was not to be put down.

"I confess I shouldn't," she said.

"Thought so," he replied, as one versed. His tones took on a nasal twang. "Well, as I was saying, I've about got ready to settle down, and I've had my eye on the lady this seven years."

"Marvel of constancy!" said Virginia. "And the lady?"

"The lady," said Eliphalet, bluntly, "is *you*." He glanced at her bewildered face and went on rapidly: "You pleased me the first day I set eyes on you in the store. I said to myself, 'Hopper, there's the one for you to marry.' I'm plain, but my folks was good people. I set to work right then to make a fortune for you, Miss Jinny. You've just what I need. I'm a plain business man with no frills. You'll do the frills. You're the kind that was raised in the lap of luxury. You'll need a man with a fortune, and a big one; you're the sort to show it off. I've got the foundations of that fortune, and the proof of it right here. And I tell you,"—his jaw was set,—"I tell you that some day Eliphalet Hopper will be one of the richest men in the West."

He had stopped, facing her in the middle of the way, his voice strong, his confidence supreme. At first she had stared at him in dumb wonder. Then, as she began to grasp the meaning of his harangue, astonishment was still dominant,—sheer astonishment. She scarcely listened. But, as he finished, the thatch of the summer house caught her eye. A vision arose of a man beside whom Eliphalet was not worthy to crawl. She thought of Stephen as he had stood that evening in the sunset, and this proposal seemed a degradation. This brute dared to tempt her with money. Scalding words rose to her lips. But she caught the look on Eliphalet's face, and she knew that he would not understand. This was one who rose and fell, who lived and loved and hated and died and was buried by—money.

For a second she looked into his face as one who escapes a pit gazes over the precipice, and shuddered. As for Eliphalet, let it not be thought that he had no passion. This was the moment for which he had lived since the day he had first seen her and been scorned in the store. That type of face, that air,—these were the priceless things he would buy with his money. Crazed with the very violence of his long-pent desire, he seized her hand. She wrung it free again.

"How—how dare you!" she cried.

He staggered back, and stood for a moment motionless, as though stunned. Then, slowly, a light crept into his little eyes which haunted her for many a day.

"You—won't—marry me?" he said.

"Oh, how dare you ask me!" exclaimed Virginia, her face burning with the shame of it. She was standing with her hands behind her, her back against a great walnut trunk, the crusted branches of which hung over the bluff. Even as he looked at her, Eliphalet lost his head, and indiscretion entered his soul.

"You must!" he said hoarsely. "You must! You've got no notion of my money, I say."

"Oh!" she cried, "can't you understand? If you owned the whole of California, I would not marry you."

Suddenly he became very cool. He slipped his hand into a pocket, as one used to such a motion, and drew out some papers.

"I cal'late you ain't got much idea of the situation, Miss Carvel," he said; "the wheels have been a-turning lately. You're poor, but I guess you don't know how poor you are,—eh? The Colonel's a man of honor, ain't he?"

For her life she could not have answered,—nor did she even know why she stayed to listen.

"Well," he said, "after all, there ain't much use in *your* lookin' over them papers. A woman wouldn't know. I'll tell you what they say: they say that if I choose, *I* am Carvel & Company."

The little eyes receded, and he waited a moment, seemingly to prolong a physical delight in the excitement and suffering of a splendid creature. The girl was breathing fast and deep.

"I cal'late you despise me, don't you?" he went on, as if that, too, gave him pleasure. "But I tell you the Colonel's a beggar but for me. Go and ask him if I'm lying. All you've got to do is to say you'll be my wife, and I tear these notes in two. They go over the bluff." (He made the motion with his hands.) "Carvel & Company's an old firm,—a respected firm. You wouldn't care to see it go out of the family, I cal'late."

He paused again, triumphant. But she did none of the things he expected. She said, simply:—

"Will you please follow me, Mr. Hopper?"

And he followed her,—his shrewdness gone, for once. Save for the rise and fall of her shoulders she seemed calm. The path wound through a jungle of waving sunflowers and led into the shade in front of the house.

There was the Colonel sitting on the porch. His pipe lay with its scattered ashes on the boards, and his head was bent forward, as though listening. When he saw the two, he rose expectantly, and went forward to meet them. Virginia stopped before him.

"Pa," she said, "is it true that you have borrowed money from this man?"

Eliphalet had seen Mr. Carvel angry once, and his soul had quivered. Terror, abject terror, seized him now, so that his knees smote together. As well stare into the sun as into the Colonel's face. In one stride he had a hand in the collar of Eliphalet's new coat, the other pointing down the path.

"It takes just a minute to walk to that fence, sir," he said sternly. "If you are any longer about it, I reckon you'll never get past it. You're a cowardly hound, sir!"

Mr. Hopper's gait down the flagstones was an invention of his own. It was neither a walk, nor a trot, nor a run, but a sort of sliding amble, such as is executed in nightmares. Singing in his head was the famous example of the eviction of Babcock from the store,—the only time that the Colonel's bullet had gone wide. And down in the small of his back Eliphalet listened for the crack of a pistol, and feared that a clean hole might be bored there any minute. Once outside, he took to the white road, leaving a trail of dust behind him that a wagon might have raised. Fear lent him wings, but neglected to lift his feet.

The Colonel passed his arm around his daughter, and pulled his goatee thoughtfully. And Virginia, glancing shyly upward, saw a smile in the creases about his mouth. She smiled, too, and then the tears hid him from her.

Strange that the face which in anger withered cowards and made men look grave, was capable of such infinite tenderness,—tenderness and sorrow. The Colonel took Virginia in his arms, and she sobbed against his shoulder, as of old.

"Jinny, did he—?"

"Yes—"

"Lige was right, and—and you, Jinny—I should never have trusted him. The sneak!"

Virginia raised her head. The sun was slanting in yellow bars through the branches of the great trees, and a robin's note rose above the bass chorus of the frogs. In the pauses, as she listened, it seemed as if she could hear the silver sound of the river over the pebbles far below.

"Honey," said the Colonel, "I reckon we're just as poor as white trash."

Virginia smiled through her tears.

"Honey," he said again, after a pause, "I must keep my word and let him have the business."

She did not reproach him.

"There is a little left, a very little," he continued slowly, painfully. "I thank God that it is yours. It was left you by Becky—by your mother. It is in a railroad company in New York, and safe, Jinny."

"Oh, Pa, you know that I do not care," she cried. "It shall be yours and mine together. And we shall live out here and be happy."

But she glanced anxiously at him nevertheless. He was in his familiar posture of thought, his legs slightly apart, his felt hat pushed back, stroking his goatee. But his clear gray eyes were troubled as they sought hers, and she put her hand to her breast.

"Virginia," he said, "I fought for my country once, and I reckon I'm some use yet awhile. It isn't right that I should idle here, while the South needs me. Your Uncle Daniel is fifty-eight, and Colonel of a Pennsylvania regiment.—Jinny, I have to go."

Virginia said nothing. It was in her blood as well as his. The Colonel had left his young wife, to fight in Mexico; he had come home to lay flowers on her grave. She knew that he thought of this; and, too, that his heart was rent at leaving her. She put her hands on his shoulders, and he stooped to kiss her trembling lips.

They walked out together to the summer-house, and stood watching the glory of the light on the western hills.

"Jinny," said the Colonel, "I reckon you will have to go to your Aunt Lillian. It—it will be hard. But I know that my girl can take care of herself. In case—in case I do not come back, or occasion should arise, find Lige. Let him take you to your Uncle Daniel. He is fond of you, and will be all alone in Calvert House when the war is over. And I reckon that is all I have to say. I won't pry into your heart, honey. If you love Clarence, marry him. I like the boy, and I believe he will quiet down into a good man."

Virginia did not answer, but reached out for her father's hand and held its fingers locked tight in her own. From the kitchen the sound of Ned's voice rose in the still evening air.

"Sposin' I was to go to N' Orleans an' take sick and die,
Laik a bird into de country ma spirit would fly."

And after a while down the path the red and yellow of Mammy Easter's bandanna was seen.

"Supper, Miss Jinny. Lawsy, if I ain't ramshacked de premises fo' you
bof. De co'n bread's gittin' cold."

That evening the Colonel and Virginia thrust a few things into her
little leather bag they had chosen together in London. Virginia had found
a cigar, which she hid until they went down to the porch, and there she
gave it to him; when he lighted the match she saw that his hand shook.

Half an hour later he held her in his arms at the gate, and she heard
his firm tread die in the dust of the road. The South had claimed him at
last.

CHAPTER VII

WITH THE ARMIES OF THE WEST

WE are at Memphis,—for a while,—and the Christmas season is approaching once more. And yet we must remember that war recognizes no Christmas, nor Sunday, nor holiday. The brown river, excited by rains, whirled seaward between his banks of yellow clay. Now the weather was crisp and cold, now hazy and depressing, and again a downpour. Memphis had never seen such activity. A spirit possessed the place, a restless spirit called William T. Sherman. He prodded Memphis and laid violent hold of her. She groaned, protested, turned over, and woke up, peopled by a new people. When these walked, they ran, and they wore a blue uniform. They spoke rapidly and were impatient. Rain nor heat nor tempest kept them in. And yet they joked, and Memphis laughed (what was left of her) and recognized a bond of fellowship. The General joked, and the Colonels and the Commissary and the doctors,—down to the sutlers and teamsters and the salt tars under Porter, who cursed the dishwater Mississippi, and also a man named Eads, who had built the newfangled iron boxes officially known as gunboats. The like of these had never before been seen in the waters under the earth.

The loyal citizens—loyal to the South—had been given permission to leave the city. The General told the assistant quartermaster to hire their houses and slaves for the benefit of the Federal Government. Likewise he laid down certain laws to the Memphis papers defining treason. He gave out his mind freely to that other army of occupation, the army of speculation, that flocked thither with permits to trade in cotton. The speculators gave the Confederates gold, which they needed most, for the bales, which they could not use at all.

The forefathers of some of these gentlemen were in old Egypt under Pharaoh—for whom they could have had no greater respect and fear than their descendants had in New Egypt for Grant or Sherman. Yankees were there likewise in abundance. And a certain acquaintance of ours materially added to his fortune by selling in Boston the cotton which cost him fourteen cents, at thirty cents.

One day the shouting and the swearing and the running to and fro came to a climax. Those floating freaks which were all top and drew nothing, were loaded down to the guards with army stores and animals and wood and men,—men who came from every walk in life. Whistles bellowed, horses neighed. The gunboats chased hither and thither, and at length the vast processions paddled down the stream with naval precision, under the watchful eyes of a real admiral.

Residents of Memphis from the river's bank watched the pillar of smoke fade to the southward and ruminated on the fate of Vicksburg. The General paced the deck in thought. A little later he wrote to the Commander-in-Chief at Washington, "The valley of the Mississippi is America."

Vicksburg taken, this vast Confederacy would be chopped in two.

Night fell to the music of the paddles, to the scent of the officers' cigars, to the blood-red vomit of the tall stacks and the smoky flame of the torches. Then Christmas Day dawned, and there was Vicksburg lifted two hundred feet above the fever swamps, her court-house shining in the morning sun. Vicksburg, the well-nigh impregnable key to America's highway. When old Vick made his plantation on the Walnut Hills, he chose a site for a fortress of the future Confederacy that Vauban would have delighted in.

Yes, there were the Walnut Hills, high bluffs separated from the Mississippi by tangled streams and bayous, and on their crests the Parrotts scowled. It was a queer Christmas Day indeed, bright and warm; no snow, no turkeys nor mince pies, no wine, but just hardtack and bacon and foaming brown water.

On the morrow the ill-assorted fleet struggled up the sluggish Yazoo, past impenetrable forests where the cypress clutched at the keels, past long-deserted cottonfields, until it came at last to the black ruins of a home. In due time the great army was landed. It spread out by brigade and division and regiment and company, the men splashing and paddling through the Chickasaw and the swamps toward the bluffs. The Parrotts began to roar. A certain regiment, boldly led, crossed the bayou at a narrow place and swept resistless across the sodden fields to where the bank was steepest. The fire from the battery scorched the hair of their heads. But there they stayed, scooping out the yellow clay with torn hands, while the Parrotts, with lowered muzzles, ploughed the slope with shells. There they stayed, while the blue lines quivered and fell back through the forests on that short winter's afternoon, dragging their

wounded from the stagnant waters. But many were left to die in agony in
the solitude.

Like a tall emblem of energy, General Sherman stood watching the
attack and repulse, his eyes ever alert. He paid no heed to the shells
which tore the limbs from the trees about him, or sent the swamp
water in thick spray over his staff. Now and again a sharp word broke
from his lips, a forceful home thrust at one of the leaders of his columns.

"What regiment stayed under the bank?"

"Sixth Missouri, General," said an aide, promptly.

The General sat late in the Admiral's gunboat that night, but when
he returned to his cabin in the *Forest Queen*, he called for a list of officers
of the Sixth Missouri. His finger slipping down the roll paused at a name
among the new second lieutenants.

"Did the boys get back?" he asked.

"Yes, General, when it fell dark."

"Let me see the casualties,—quick."

That night a fog rolled up from the swamps, and in the morning jackstaff was hid from pilot-house. Before the attack could be renewed, a
political general came down the river with a letter in his pocket from
Washington, by virtue of which he took possession of the three army
corps and their chief, subpœnaed the fleet and the Admiral, and went off
to capture Arkansas Post.

Vicksburg had a breathing spell.

Three weeks later, when the army was resting at Napoleon, Arkansas,
a self-contained man, with a brown beard, arrived from Memphis, and
took command. This was General U. S. Grant. He smoked incessantly in
his cabin. He listened. He spoke but seldom. He had a look in his face
that boded ill to any that might oppose him. Time and labor he counted
as nothing, compared with the accomplishment of an object. Back to
Vicksburg paddled the fleet and transports. Across the river from the
city, on the pasty mud behind the levee's bank, were dumped Sherman's
regiments, condemned to weeks of ditch-digging, that the gunboats might
arrive at the bend of the Mississippi below by a canal, out of reach of the
batteries. Day in and day out they labored, officers and men. Sawing off
stumps under the water, knocking poisonous snakes by scores from the
branches, while the river rose and rose and rose, and the rain crept by
inches under their tent flies, and the enemy walked the parapets of Vicksburg and laughed. Two gunboats accomplished the feat of running the
batteries, that their smiles might be sobered.

To the young officers who were soiling their uniforms with the grease of saws, whose only fighting was against fever and water snakes, the news of an expedition into the Vicksburg side of the river was hailed with caps in the air. To be sure, the saw and axe, and likewise the levee and the snakes, were to be there, too. But there was likely to be a little fighting. The rest of the corps that was to stay watched grimly as the detachment put off in the little *Diligence* and *Silver Wave*.

All the night the smoke-pipes were batting against the boughs of oak and cottonwood, and snapping the trailing vines. Some other regiments went by another route. The ironclads, followed in hot haste by General Sherman in a navy tug, had gone ahead, and were even then shoving with their noses great trunks of trees in their eagerness to get behind the Rebels. The Missouri regiment spread out along the waters, and were soon waist deep, hewing a path for the heavier transports to come. Presently the General came back to a plantation half under water, where Black Bayou joins Deer Creek, to hurry the work in cleaning out that Bayou. The light transports meanwhile were bringing up more troops from a second detachment. All through the Friday the navy great guns were heard booming in the distance, growing quicker and quicker, until the quivering air shook the hanging things in that vast jungle. Saws stopped, and axes were poised over shoulders, and many times that day the General lifted his head anxiously. As he sat down in the evening in a slave cabin redolent with corn pone and bacon, the sound still hovered among the trees and rolled along the still waters.

The General slept lightly. It was three o'clock Saturday morning when the sharp challenge of a sentry broke the silence. A negro, white eyed, bedraggled, and muddy, stood in the candle light under the charge of a young lieutenant. The officer saluted, and handed the General a roll of tobacco.

"I found this man in the swamp, sir. He has a message from the Admiral—"

The General tore open the roll and took from it a piece of tissue paper which he spread out and held under the candle. He turned to a staff officer who had jumped from his bed and was hurrying into his coat.

"Porter's surrounded," he said. The order came in a flash. "Kilby Smith and all men here across creek to relief at once. I'll take canoe through bayou to Hill's and hurry reënforcements."

The staff officer paused, his hand on the latch of the door.

"But your escort, General. You're not going through that sewer in a canoe without an escort!"

"I guess they won't look for a needle in that haystack," the General answered. For a brief second he eyed the lieutenant. "Get back to your regiment, Brice, if you want to go," he said.

Stephen saluted and went out. All through the painful march that followed, though soaked in swamp water and bruised by cypress knees, he thought of Sherman in his canoe, winding unprotected through the black labyrinth, risking his life that more men might be brought to the rescue of the gunboats.

The story of that rescue has been told most graphically by Sherman himself. How he picked up the men at work on the bayou and marched them on a coal barge; how he hitched the barge to a navy tug; how he met the little transport with a fresh load of troops, and Captain Elijah Brent's reply when the General asked if he would follow him. "As long as the boat holds *together*, General." And he kept his word. The boughs hammered at the smoke-pipes until they went by the board, and the pilot-house fell like a pack of cards on the deck before they had gone three miles and a half. Then the indomitable Sherman disembarked, a lighted candle in his hand, and led a stiff march through thicket and swamp and breast-deep backwater, where the little drummer boys carried their drums on their heads. At length, when they were come to some Indian mounds, they found a picket of three companies of the force which had reached the flat the day before, and had been sent down to prevent the enemy from obstructing further the stream below the fleet.

"The Admiral's in a bad way, sir," said the Colonel who rode up to meet the General. "He's landlocked. Those clumsy ironclads of his can't move backward or forward, and the Rebs have been peppering him for two days."

Just then a fusillade broke from the thickets, nipping the branches from the cottonwoods about them.

"Form your line," said the General. "Drive 'em out."

The force swept forward, with the three picket companies in the swamp on the right. And presently they came in sight of the shapeless ironclads with their funnels belching smoke, a most remarkable spectacle. How Porter had pushed them there was one of the miracles of the war.

Then followed one of a thousand memorable incidents in the life of a memorable man. General Sherman, jumping on the bare back of a scrawny horse, cantered through the fields. And the bluejackets, at sight of that familiar figure, roared out a cheer that might have shaken the drops from the wet boughs. The Admiral and the General stood together on the deck, their hands clasped. And the Colonel astutely remarked, as he rode up in answer to a summons, that if Porter was the only man whose daring could have pushed a fleet to that position, Sherman was certainly the only man who could have got him out of it.

"Colonel," said the General, "that move was well executed, sir. Admiral, did the Rebs put a bullet through your rum casks? We're just a little tired. And now," he added, wheeling on the Colonel when each had a glass in his hand, "who was in command of that company on the right, in the swamp? He handled them like a regular."

"He's a second lieutenant, General, in the Sixth Missouri. Captain wounded at Hindman, and first lieutenant fell out down below. His name is Brice, I believe."

"I thought so," said the General.

Some few days afterward, when the troops were slopping around again at Young's Point, opposite Vicksburg, a gentleman arrived on a boat from St. Louis. He paused on the levee to survey with concern and astonishment the flood of waters behind it, and then asked an officer the way to General Sherman's headquarters. The officer, who was greatly impressed by the gentleman's looks, led him at once to a trestle bridge which spanned the distance from the levee bank over the flood to a house up to its first floor in the backwaters. The orderly saluted.

"Who shall I say, sir?"

The officer looked inquiringly at the gentleman, who gave his name.

The officer could not repress a smile at the next thing that happened. Out hurried the General himself, with both hands outstretched.

"Bless my soul!" he cried, "if it isn't Brinsmade. Come right in, come right in and take dinner. The boys will be glad to see you. I'll send and tell Grant you're here. Brinsmade, if it wasn't for you and your friends on the Western Sanitary Commission, we'd all have been dead of fever and bad food long ago." The General sobered abruptly. "I guess a good many of the boys are laid up now," he added.

"I've come down to do what I can, General," responded Mr. Brinsmade, gravely. "I want to go through all the hospitals to see that our nurses are doing their duty and that the stores are properly distributed."

"You shall, sir, this minute," said the General. He dropped instantly the affairs which he had on hand, and without waiting for dinner the two gentlemen went together through the wards where the fever raged. The

General surprised his visitor by recognizing private after private in the cots, and he always had a brief word of cheer to brighten their faces, to make them follow him with wistful eyes as he passed beyond them. "That's poor Craig," he would say, "corporal, Third Michigan. They tell me he can't live," and "That's Olcott, Eleventh Indiana. Good God!" cried the General, when they were out in the air again, "how I wish some of these cotton traders could get a taste of this fever. They keep well—the vultures! And by the way, Brinsmade, the man who gave me no peace at all at Memphis was from your city. Why, I had to keep a whole corps on duty to watch him."

"What was his name, sir?" Mr. Brinsmade asked.

"Hopper!" cried the General, with feeling. "Eliphalet Hopper. As long as I live I shall never forget it. How the devil did he get a permit? What are they about at Washington?"

"You surprise me," said Mr. Brinsmade. "He has always seemed inoffensive, and I believe he is a prominent member of one of our churches."

"I guess that's so," answered the General, dryly. "If ever I set eyes on him again, he's clapped into the guard house. He knows it, too."

"Speaking of St. Louis, General," said Mr. Brinsmade, presently, "have you ever heard of Stephen Brice? He joined your army last autumn. You may remember talking to him one evening at my house."

"He's one of my boys!" cried the General. "Remember him? Guess I do!" He paused on the very brink of relating again the incident at Camp Jackson, when Stephen had saved the life of Mr. Brinsmade's own son. "Brinsmade, for three days I've had it on my mind to send for that boy. I'll have him at headquarters now. I like him," cried General Sherman, with tone and gesture there was no mistaking. And good Mr. Brinsmade, who liked Stephen, too, rejoiced at the story he would have to tell the widow. "He has spirit, Brinsmade. I told him to let me know when he was ready to go to war. No such thing. He never came near me. The first thing I hear of him is that he's digging holes in the clay of Chickasaw Bluff, and his cap is fanned off by the blast of a Parrott six feet above his head. Next thing he turns up on that little expedition we took to get Porter to sea again. When we got to the gunboats, there was Brice's company on the flank. He handled those men surprisingly, sir—surprisingly. I shouldn't have blamed the boy if one or two Rebs got by him. But no, he swept the place clean." By this time they had come back to the bridge leading to headquarters, and the General beckoned quickly to an orderly.

"My compliments to Lieutenant Stephen Brice, Sixth Missouri, and ask him to report here at once. At once, you understand!"

"Yes, General."

It so happened that Mr. Brice's company were swinging axes when the orderly arrived, and Mr. Brice had an axe himself, and was up to his boot tops in yellow mud. The orderly, who had once been an Iowa farmer, was near grinning when he gave the General's message and saw the lieutenant gazing ruefully at his clothes.

Entering headquarters, Stephen paused at the doorway of the big room where the officers of the different staffs were scattered about, smoking, while the negro servants were removing the dishes from the table. The sunlight, reflected from the rippling water outside, danced on the ceiling. At the end of the room sat General Sherman, his uniform, as always, a trifle awry. His soft felt hat with the gold braid was tilted forward, and his feet, booted and spurred, were crossed. Small wonder that the Englishman who sought the typical American found him in Sherman.

The sound that had caught Stephen's attention was the General's voice, somewhat high-pitched, in the key that he used in telling a story. These were his closing words:—

"Sin gives you a pretty square deal, boys, after all. Generally a man says, 'Well, I *can* resist, but I'll have my fun just this once.' That's the way it happens. They tell you that temptation comes irresistibly. Don't believe it. Do you, Mr. Brice? Come over here, sir. Here's a friend of yours."

Stephen made his way to the General, whose bright eyes wandered rapidly over him as he added:—

"This is the condition my officers report in, Brinsmade,—mud from head to heel."

Stephen had sense enough to say nothing, but the staff officers laughed, and Mr. Brinsmade smiled as he rose and took Stephen's hand.

"I am delighted to see that you are well, sir," said he, with that formal kindliness which endeared him to all. "Your mother will be rejoiced at my news of you. You will be glad to hear that I left her well, Stephen."

Stephen inquired for Mrs. Brinsmade and Anne.

"They are well, sir, and took pleasure in adding to a little box which your mother sent. Judge Whipple put in a box of fine cigars, although he deplores the use of tobacco."

"And the Judge, Mr. Brinsmade—how is he?"

The good gentleman's face fell.

"He is ailing, sir, it grieves me to say. He is in bed, sir. But he is ably looked after. Your mother desired to have him moved to her house, but he is difficult to stir from his ways, and he would not leave his little room. He is ably nursed. We have got old Nancy, Hester's mother, to stay with him at night, and Mrs. Brice divides the day with Miss Jinny Carvel, who comes in from Bellegarde every afternoon."

"Miss Carvel?" exclaimed Stephen, wondering if he heard aright. And at the mention of her name he tingled.

"None other, sir," answered Mr. Brinsmade. "She has been much honored for it. You may remember that the Judge was a close friend of her father's before the war. And—well, they quarrelled, sir. The Colonel went South, you know."

"When—when was the Judge taken ill, Mr. Brinsmade?" Stephen asked. The thought of Virginia and his mother caring for him together was strangely sweet.

"Two days before I left, sir, Dr. Polk had warned him not to do so much. But the Doctor tells me that he can see no dangerous symptoms."

Stephen inquired now of Mr. Brinsmade how long he was to be with them.

"I am going on to the other camps this afternoon," said he. "But I should like a glimpse of your quarters, Stephen, if you will invite me. Your mother would like a careful account of you, and Mr. Whipple, and —your many friends in St. Louis."

"You will find my tent a little wet, sir," replied Stephen, touched.

Here the General, who had been sitting by watching them with a very curious expression, spoke up.

"That's hospitality for you, Brinsmade!"

Stephen and Mr. Brinsmade made their way across plank and bridge to Stephen's tent, and his mess servant arrived in due time with the package from home. But presently, while they sat talking of many things, the canvas of the fly was thrust back with a quick movement, and who should come stooping in but General Sherman himself. He sat down on a cracker box. Stephen rose confusedly.

"Well, well, Brice," said the General, winking at Mr. Brinsmade, "I think you might have invited me to the feast. Where are those cigars Mr. Brinsmade was talking about?"

Stephen opened the box with alacrity. The General chose one and lighted it.

"Don't smoke, eh?" he inquired.

"Why, yes, sir, when I can."

"Then light up, sir," said the General, "and sit down. I've been think-ing lately of court-martialling you, but I decided to come 'round and talk it over with you first. That isn't strictly according to the rules of the service. Look here, Mr. Brice, why did you leave St. Louis?"

"They began to draft, sir, and I couldn't stand it any longer."

"But you wouldn't have been drafted. You were in the Home Guards, if I remember right. And Mr. Brinsmade tells me you were useful in many ways. What was your rank in the Home Guards?"

"Lieutenant colonel, sir."

"And what are you here?"

"A second lieutenant in temporary command, General."

"You have commanded men?"

"Not in action, sir. I felt that that was different."

"Couldn't they do better for you than a second-lieutenancy?"

Stephen did not reply at once. Mr. Brinsmade spoke up.

"They offered him a lieutenant-colonelcy."

The General was silent a moment. Then he said: "Do you remember meeting me on the boat when I was leaving St. Louis, after the capture of Fort Henry?"

Stephen smiled. "Very well, General," he replied.

General Sherman leaned forward.

"And do you remember I said to you, 'Brice, when you get ready to come into this war, let me know.' Why didn't you do it?"

Stephen thought a minute. Then he said gravely, but with just a sus-picion of humor about his mouth:—

"General, if I had done that, you wouldn't be here in my tent to-day."

Like lightning the General was on his feet, his hand on Stephen's shoulder.

"By gad, sir," he cried, delighted, "so I wouldn't."

CHAPTER VIII

A STRANGE MEETING

THE story of the capture of Vicksburg is the old, old story of failure turned into success, by which man is made immortal. It involves the history of a general who never retraced his steps, who cared neither for mugwump murmurs nor political cabals, who took both blame and praise with equanimity. Through month after month of discouragement, and work gone for naught, and fever and death, his eyes never left his goal. And by grace of the wisdom of that President who himself knew sorrow and suffering and defeat and unjust censure, General Grant won.

Boldness did it. The canal abandoned, one red night fleet and transports swept around the bend and passed the city's heights, on a red river. The Parrotts and the Dahlgrens roared, and the high bluffs flung out the sound over the empty swamp land.

Then there came the landing below, and the cutting loose from a base —unheard of. Corps behind cursed corps ahead for sweeping the country clear of forage. Battles were fought. Confederate generals in Mississippi were bewildered.

One night, while crossing with his regiment a pontoon bridge, Stephen Brice heard a shout raised on the farther shore. Sitting together on a log under a torch, two men in slouch hats were silhouetted. That one talking with rapid gestures was General Sherman. The impassive profile of the other,—the close-cropped beard and the firmly held cigar that seemed to go with it,—Stephen recognized as that of the strange Captain Grant who had stood beside him in the street by the Arsenal. He had not changed a whit. Motionless, he watched corps after corps splash by, artillery, cavalry, and infantry, nor gave any sign that he heard their plaudits.

At length the army came up behind the city to a place primeval, where the face of the earth was sore and tortured, worn into deep gorges by the rains, and flung up in great mounds. Stripped of the green magnolias and the cane, the banks of clay stood forth in hideous yellow nakedness, save

356

for a lonely stunted growth, or a bare trunk that still stood tottering on the edge of a bank, its pitiful withered roots reaching out below. The May weather was already sickly hot.

First of all there was a murderous assault, and a still more murderous repulse. Three times the besiegers charged, sank their color staffs into the redoubts, and three times were driven back. Then the blue army settled into the earth and folded into the ravines. Three days in that narrow space between the lines lay the dead and wounded suffering untold agonies in the moist heat. Then came a truce to bury the dead, to bring back what was left of the living.

The doomed city had no rest. Like clockwork from the Mississippi's banks beyond came the boom and shriek of the coehorns on the barges. The big shells hung for an instant in the air like birds of prey, and then could be seen swooping down here and there, while now and anon a shaft of smoke rose straight to the sky, the black monument of a home.

Here was work in the trenches, digging the flying sap by night and deepening it by day, for officers and men alike. From heaven a host of blue ants could be seen toiling in zigzags forward, ever forward, along the rude water-cuts and through the hills. A waiting carrion from her vantage point on high marked one spot and then another where the blue ants disappeared, and again one by one came out of the burrow to hurry down the trench,—each with his ball of clay.

In due time the ring of metal and sepulchred voices rumbled in the ground beneath the besieged. Counter-mines were started, and through the narrow walls of earth commands and curses came. Above ground the saps were so near that a strange converse became the rule. It was "Hello, Reb!" "Howdy, Yank!" Both sides were starving, the one for tobacco and the other for hardtack and bacon. These necessities were tossed across, sometimes wrapped in the Vicksburg news-sheet printed on the white side of a homely green wall paper. At other times other amenities were indulged in. Hand-grenades were thrown and shells with lighted fuses rolled down on the heads of acquaintances of the night before, who replied from wooden coehorns hooped with iron.

The Union generals learned (common item in a siege) that the citizens of Vicksburg were eating mule meat.

Not an officer or private in the Vicksburg armies who does not remember the 25th of June, and the hour of three in an afternoon of pitiless heat. Silently the long blue files wound into position behind the earth barriers which hid them from the enemy, coiled and ready to strike when the towering redoubt on the Jackson road should rise heavenwards. By common consent the rifle crack of day and night was hushed, and even the Parrotts were silent. Stillness closed around the white house of Shirley once more, but not the stillness it had known in its peaceful homestead days. This was the stillness of the death-prayer. Eyes staring at the big redoubt were dimmed. At last, to those near, a little wisp of blue smoke crept out.

Then the earth opened with a quake. The sun was darkened, and a hot blast fanned the upturned faces. In the sky, through the film of shattered clay, little black dots scurried, poised, and fell again as arms and legs and headless trunks and shapeless bits of wood and iron. Scarcely had the dust settled when the sun caught the light of fifty thousand bayonets, and a hundred shells were shrieking across the crater's edge. Earth to earth, alas, and dust to dust! Men who ran across that rim of a summer's afternoon died in torture under tier upon tier of their comrades— and so the hole was filled.

An upright cannon marks the spot where a scrawny oak once stood on a scarred and baked hillside, outside of the Confederate lines at Vicksburg. Under the scanty shade of that tree, on the eve of the Nation's birthday, stood two men who typified the future and the past. As at Donelson, a trick of Fortune's had delivered one comrade of old into the hands of another. Now she chose to kiss the one upon whom she had heaped obscurity and poverty and contumely. He had ceased to think or care about Fortune. And hence, being born a woman, she favored him.

The two armies watched and were still. They noted the friendly greeting of old comrades, and after that they saw the self-contained Northerner biting his cigar, as one to whom the pleasantries of life were past and gone. The South saw her General turn on his heel. The bitterness of his life was come. Both sides honored him for the fight he had made. But war does not reward a man according to his deserts.

The next day—the day our sundered nation was born—Vicksburg surrendered: the obstinate man with the mighty force had conquered. See the gray regiments marching silently in the tropic heat into the folds of that blue army whose grip has choked them at last. Silently, too, the blue coats stand, pity and admiration on the brick-red faces. The arms are stacked and surrendered, officers and men are to be paroled when the counting is finished. The formations melt away, and those who for months have sought each other's lives are grouped in friendly talk.

The coarse army bread is drawn eagerly from the knapsacks of the blue, smoke quivers above a hundred fires, and the smell of frying bacon brings a wistful look into the gaunt faces. Tears stand in the eyes of many a man as he eats the food his Yankee brothers have given him on the birthday of their country.

Within the city it is the same. Stephen Brice, now a captain in General Lauman's brigade, sees with thanksgiving the stars and stripes flutter from the dome of that court-house which he had so long watched from afar. Later on, down a side street, he pauses before a house with its face blown away. On the verge of one of its jagged floors is an old four-posted bed, and beside it a child's cot is standing pitifully,—the tiny pillow still at the head and the little sheets thrown across the foot. So much for one of the navy's shells.

While he was thinking of the sadness of it all, a little scene was acted: the side door of the house opened, a weeping woman came out, and with her was a tall Confederate Colonel of cavalry. Gallantly giving her his arm, he escorted her as far as the little gate, where she bade him good-by with much feeling. With an impulsive movement he drew some money from his pocket, thrust it upon her, and started hurriedly away that he might not listen to her thanks. Such was his preoccupation that he actually brushed into Stephen, who was standing beside a tree. He stopped and bowed.

"Excuse me, seh," he said contritely. "I beg your pardon, seh."

"Certainly," said Stephen, smiling; "it was my fault for getting in your way."

"Not at all, seh," said the cavalry Colonel; "my clumsiness, seh." He did not pass on, but stood pulling with some violence a very long mustache. "Damn you Yankees," he continued, in the same amiable tone, "you've brought us a heap of misfortune. Why, seh, in another week we'd been fo'ced to eat *niggers*."

The Colonel made such a wry face that Stephen laughed in spite of himself. He had marked the man's charitable action, and admired his attempt to cover it. The Colonel seemed to be all breadth, like a card. His shoulders were incredible. The face was scant, perchance from lack of food, the nose large, with a curved rim, and the eyes blue gray. He wore clay-flecked cavalry boots, and was six feet five if an inch, so that Stephen's six seemed insignificant beside him.

"Captain," he said, taking in Stephen's rank, "we won't qua'l as to who's host heah. One thing's suah," he added, with a twinkle, "I've been

heah longest. Seems like ten yeahs since I saw the wife and children down
in the Palmetto State. I can't offer you a dinner, seh. We've eaten all
the mules and rats and sugar cane in town." (His eye seemed to interpo-
late that Stephen wouldn't be there otherwise.) "But I can offer you
something choicer than you have in the No'th."

Whereupon he drew from his hip a dented silver flask. The Colonel
remarked that Stephen's eyes fell on the coat of arms.

"Prope'ty of my grandfather, seh, of Washington's Army. My name
is Jennison,—Catesby Jennison, at your service, seh," he said. "You
have the advantage of me, Captain."

"My name is Brice," said Stephen.

The big Colonel bowed decorously, held out a great, wide hand, and
thereupon unscrewed the flask. Now Stephen had never learned to like
straight whiskey, but he took down his share without a face. The exploit
seemed to please the Colonel, who, after he likewise had done the liquor
justice, screwed on the lid with ceremony, offered Stephen his arm with
still greater ceremony, and they walked off down the street together.
Stephen drew from his pocket several of Judge Whipple's cigars, to which
his new friend gave unqualified praise.

On every hand Vicksburg showed signs of hard usage. Houses with
gaping chasms in their sides, others mere heaps of black ruins; great
trees felled, cabins demolished, and here and there the sidewalk ploughed
across from curb to fence.

"Lordy," exclaimed the Colonel. "Lordy! how my ears ache since
your damned coehorns have stopped. The noise got to be silence with us,
seh, and yesterday I reckoned a hundred volcanoes had bust. Tell me,"
said he: "when the redoubt over the Jackson road was blown up, they
said a nigger came down in your lines alive. Is that so?"

"Yes," said Stephen, smiling; "he struck near the place where my
company was stationed. His head ached a bit. That seemed to be all."

"I reckon he fell on it," said Colonel Catesby Jennison, as if it were a
matter of no special note.

"And now tell me something," said Stephen. "How did you burn our
sap-rollers?"

This time the Colonel stopped, and gave himself up to hearty laughter.

"Why, that *was* a Yankee trick, sure enough," he cried. "Some ingenious cuss soaked port fire in turpentine, and shot the wad in a large-
bore musket."

"We thought you used explosive bullets."

The Colonel laughed again, still more heartily.

"Explosive bullets! Good Lord, it was all we could do to get percussion caps. Do you know how we got percussion caps, seh? Three of our officers—dare-devils, seh—floated down the Mississippi on logs. One fellow made his way back with two hundred thousand. He's the pride of our Vicksburg army. Not afraid of hell. A chivalrous man, a forlorn-hope man. The night you ran the batteries he and some others went across to your side in skiffs—in skiffs, seh, I say—and set fire to the houses in De Soto, that we might see to shoot. And then he came back in the face of our own batteries and your guns. That man was wounded by a trick of fate, by a cussed bit of shell from your coehorns while eating his dinner in Vicksburg. He's pretty low, now, poor fellow," added the Colonel, sadly.

"Where is he?" demanded Stephen, fired with a desire to see the man.

"Well, he ain't a great ways from here," said the Colonel. "Perhaps you might be able to do something for him," he continued thoughtfully. "I'd hate to see him die. The doctor says he'll pull through if he can get care and good air and good food." He seized Stephen's arm in a fierce grip. "You ain't fooling?" he said.

"Indeed I am not," said Stephen.

"No," said the Colonel, thoughtfully, as to himself, "you don't look like the man to fool."

Whereupon he set out with great strides, in marked contrast to his former languorous gait, and after a while they came to a sort of gorge, where the street ran between high banks of clay. There Stephen saw the magazines which the Confederates had dug out, and of which he had heard. But he saw something, too, of which he had not heard. Colonel Catesby Jennison stopped before an open doorway in the yellow bank and knocked. A woman's voice called softly to him to enter.

They went into a room hewn out of the solid clay. Carpet was stretched on the floor, paper was on the walls, and even a picture. There was a little window cut like a port in a prison cell, and under it a bed, beside which a middle-aged lady was seated. She had a kindly face which seemed to Stephen a little pinched as she turned to them with a gesture of restraint. She pointed to the bed, where a sheet lay limply over the angles of a wasted frame. The face was to the wall.

"Hush!" said the lady, "it is the first time in two days that he has slept."

But the sleeper stirred wearily, and woke with a start. He turned over. The face, so yellow and peaked, was of the type that grows even more handsome in sickness, and in the great fever-stricken eyes a high spirit burned. For an instant only the man stared at Stephen, and then he dragged himself to the wall.

The eyes of the other two were both fixed on the young Union Captain.

"My God!" cried Jennison, seizing Stephen's rigid arm, "does he look as bad as that? We've seen him every day."

"I—I know him," answered Stephen. He stepped quickly to the bedside, and bent over it. "Colfax!" he said. "Colfax!"

"This is too much, Jennison," came from the bed a voice that was pitifully weak; "why do you bring Yankees in here?"

"Captain Brice is a friend of yours, Colfax," said the Colonel, tugging at his mustache.

"Brice?" repeated Clarence, "Brice? Does he come from St. Louis?"

"Do you come from St. Louis, sir?"

"Yes. I have met Captain Colfax—"

"Colonel, sir."

"Colonel Colfax, before the war. And if he would like to go to St. Louis, I think I can have it arranged at once."

In silence they waited for Clarence's answer. Stephen well knew what was passing in his mind, and guessed at his repugnance to accept a favor from a Yankee. He wondered whether there was in this case a special detestation. And so his mind was carried far to the northward to the memory of that day in the summer-house on the Meramec heights. Virginia had not loved her cousin then—of that Stephen was sure. But now,—now that the Vicksburg army was ringing with his praise, now that he was unfortunate—Stephen sighed. His comfort was that he would be the instrument.

The lady in her uneasiness smoothed the single sheet that covered the sick man. From afar came the sound of cheering, and it was this that seemed to rouse him. He faced them again, impatiently.

"I have reason to remember Mr. Brice," he said steadily. And then, with some vehemence, "What is he doing in Vicksburg?"

Stephen looked at Jennison, who winced.

"The city has surrendered," said that officer.

They counted on a burst of anger. Colfax only groaned.

"Then you can afford to be generous," he said, with a bitter laugh.

"But you haven't whipped us yet, by a good deal. Jennison," he cried, "Jennison, why in hell did you give up?"

"Colfax," said Stephen, coming forward, "you're too sick a man to talk. I'll look up the General. It may be that I can have you sent North to-day."

"You can do as you please," said Clarence, coldly, "with a prisoner."

The blood rushed to Stephen's face. Bowing to the lady, he strode out of the room. Colonel Jennison, running after him, caught him in the street.

"You're not offended, Brice?" he said. "He's sick—and God Almighty, he's proud—I reckon," he added with a touch of humility that went straight to Stephen's heart. "I reckon that some of us are too derned proud—But we ain't *cold*."

Stephen grasped his hand.

"Offended!" he said. "I admire the man. I'll go to the General directly. But just let me thank you. And I hope, Colonel, that we may meet again—as friends."

"Hold on, seh," said Colonel Catesby Jennison; "we may as well drink to that."

Fortunately, as Stephen drew near the Court House, he caught sight of a group of officers seated on its steps, and among them he was quick to recognize General Sherman.

"Brice," said the General, returning his salute, "been celebrating this glorious Fourth with some of our Rebel friends?"

"Yes, sir," answered Stephen, "and I came to ask a favor for one of them." Seeing that the General's genial, interested expression did not change, he was emboldened to go on. "This is one of their colonels, sir. You may have heard of him. He is the man who floated down the river on a log and brought back two hundred thousand percussion caps—"

"Good Lord," interrupted the General, "I guess we all heard of him after that. What else has he done to endear himself?" he asked, with a smile.

"Well, General, he rowed across the river in a skiff the night we ran these batteries, and set fire to De Soto to make targets for their gunners."

"I'd like to see that man," said the General, in his eager way. "Where is he?"

"What I was going to tell you, sir. After he went through all this, he was hit by a piece of mortar shell, while sitting at his dinner. He's rather far gone now, General, and they say he can't live unless he can be sent North. I—I know who he is in St. Louis. And I thought that as long as the officers are to be paroled I might get your permission to send him up to-day."

"What's his name?"

"Colfax, sir."

The General laughed. "I know the breed," said he. "I'll bet he didn't thank you."

"No, sir, he didn't."

"I like his grit," said the General, emphatically. "These young bloods are the backbone of this rebellion, Brice. They were made for war. They never did anything except horse-racing and cock-fighting. They ride like the devil, fight like the devil, but don't care a picayune for anything. Walker had some of 'em. Crittenden had some. And, good Lord, how they hate a Yankee! I know this Colfax, too. He's a cousin of that fine-looking girl Brinsmade spoke of. They say he's engaged to her. Be a pity to disappoint her—eh?"

"Yes, General."

"Why, Captain, I believe you would like to marry her yourself! Take my advice, sir, and don't try to tame any wildcats."

"I'm glad to do a favor for that young man," said the General, when Stephen had gone off with the slip of paper he had given him. "I like to do that kind of a favor for any officer, when I can. Did you notice how he flared up when I mentioned the girl?"

This is why Clarence Colfax found himself that evening on a hospital steamer of the Sanitary Commission, bound north for St. Louis.

CHAPTER IX

BELLEGARDE ONCE MORE

SUPPER at Bellegarde was not the simple meal it had been for a year past at Colonel Carvel's house in town. Mrs. Colfax was proud of her table, proud of her fried chickens and corn fritters and her desserts. How Virginia chafed at those suppers, and how she despised the guests whom her aunt was in the habit of inviting to some of them! And when none was present, she was forced to listen to Mrs. Colfax's prattle about the fashions, her tirades against the Yankees.

"I'm sure he must be dead," said that lady, one sultry evening in July. Her tone, however, was not one of conviction. A lazy wind from the river stirred the lawn of Virginia's gown. The girl, with her hand on the wicker back of the chair, was watching a storm gather to the east- ward, across the Illinois prairie.

"I don't see why you say that, Aunt Lillian," she replied. "Bad news travels faster than good."

"And not a word from Comyn. It is cruel of him not to send us a line, telling us where his regiment is."

Virginia did not reply. She had long since learned that the wisdom of silence was the best for her aunt's unreasonableness. Certainly, if Clar- ence's letters could not pass the close lines of the Federal troops, news of her father's Texas regiment could not come from Red River.

"How was Judge Whipple to-day?" asked Mrs. Colfax, presently.

"Very weak. He doesn't seem to improve much."

"I can't see why Mrs. Brice,—isn't that her name?—doesn't take him to her house. Yankee women are such prudes."

Virginia began to rock slowly, and her foot tapped the porch.

"Mrs. Brice has begged the Judge to come to her. But he says he has lived in those rooms, and that he will die there,—when the time comes."

"How you worship that woman, Virginia! You have become quite a Yankee yourself, I believe, spending whole days with her, nursing that old man."

"The Judge is an old friend of my father's; I think he would wish it," replied the girl, in a lifeless voice.

Her speech did not reveal all the pain and resentment she felt. She thought of the old man racked with pain and suffering in the heat, lying patient on his narrow bed, the only light of life remaining the presence of the two women. They came day by day, and often Margaret Brice had taken the place of the old negress who sat with him at night. Worship Margaret Brice! Yes, it was worship; it had been worship since the day she and her father had gone to the little whitewashed hospital. Providence had brought them together at the Judge's bedside. The marvellous quiet power of the older woman had laid hold of the girl in spite of all barriers.

Often when the Judge's pain was eased sufficiently for him to talk, he would speak of Stephen. The mother never spoke of her son, but a light would come into her eyes at this praise of him which thrilled Virginia to see. And when the good lady was gone, and the Judge had fallen into slumber, it would still haunt her.

Was it out of consideration for her that Mrs. Brice would turn the Judge from this topic which he seemed to love best? Virginia could not admit to herself that she resented this. She had heard Stephen's letters to the Judge. They came every week. Strong and manly they were, with plenty of praises for the Southern defenders of Vicksburg. Only yesterday Virginia had read one of these to Mr. Whipple, her face burning. Well that his face was turned to the window, and that Stephen's mother was not there!

"He says very little about himself," Mr. Whipple complained. "Had it not been for Brinsmade, we should never know that Sherman had his eye on him, and had promoted him. We should never have known of that exploit at Chickasaw Bluff. But what a glorious victory was Grant's capture of Vicksburg, on the Fourth of July! I guess we'll make short work of the Rebels now."

No, the Judge had not changed much, even in illness. He would never change. Virginia laid the letter down, and tears started to her eyes as she repressed a retort. It was not the first time this had happened. At every Union victory Mr. Whipple would loose his tongue. How strange that, with all his thought of others, he should fall short here!

One day, after unusual forbearance, Mrs. Brice had overtaken Virginia on the stairway. Well she knew the girl's nature, and how difficult she must have found repression. Margaret Brice had taken her hand.

"My dear," she had said, "you are a wonderful woman."

That was all. But Virginia had driven back to Bellegarde with a strange elation in her heart.

Some things the Judge had forborne to mention, and for this Virginia was thankful. One was the piano. But she had overheard Shadrach telling old Nancy how Mrs. Brice had pleaded with him to move it, that he might have more room and air. He had been obdurate. And Colonel Carvel's name had never once passed his lips.

Many a night the girl had lain awake listening to the steamboats as they toiled against the river's current, while horror held her. Horror lest her father at that moment be in mortal agony amongst the heaps left by the battle's surges; heaps in which, like mounds of ashes, the fire was not yet dead. Fearful tales she had heard in the prison hospitals of wounded men lying for days in the Southern sun between the trenches at Vicksburg, or freezing amidst the snow and sleet at Donelson.

Was her bitterness against the North not just? What a life had been Colonel Carvel's! It had dawned brightly. One war had cost him his wife. Another, and he had lost his fortune, his home, his friends, all that was dear to him. And that daughter, whom he loved best in all the world, he was perchance to see no more.

Mrs. Colfax, yawning, had taken a book and gone to bed. Still Virginia sat on the porch, while the frogs sang of rain, and the lightning quivered across the eastern sky. She heard the crunch of wheels in the gravel.

A bar of light, peopled by moths, slanted out of the doorway and fell on a closed carriage. A gentleman slowly ascended the steps. Virginia recognized him as Mr. Brinsmade.

"Your cousin Clarence has come home, my dear," he said. "He was among the captured at Vicksburg, and is paroled by General Grant."

Virginia gave a little cry and started forward. But he held her hands.

"He has been wounded!"

"Yes," she exclaimed, "yes. Oh, tell me, Mr. Brinsmade, tell me—all—"

"No, he is not dead, but he is very low. Mr. Russell has been kind enough to come with me."

She hurried to call the servants. But they were all there in the light, in African postures of terror,—Alfred, and Sambo, and Mammy Easter, and Ned. They lifted the limp figure in gray, and carried it into the hall chamber, his eyes closed, his face waxen under a beard brown and shaggy. Heavily, Virginia climbed the stairs to break the news to her aunt.

There is little need to dwell on the dark days which followed—Clarence hanging between life and death. That his life was saved was due to Virginia and to Mammy Easter, and in no particle to his mother Mrs. Colfax flew in the face of all the known laws of nursing, until Virginia was driven to desperation, and held a council of war with Dr. Polk. Then her aunt grew jealous, talked of a conspiracy, and threatened to send for Dr. Brown—which Dr. Polk implored her to do. By spells she wept, when they quietly pushed her from the room and locked the door. She would creep in to him in the night during Mammy Easter's watches and talk him into a raging fever. But Virginia slept lightly and took the alarm. More than one scene these two had in the small hours, while Ned was riding post haste over the black road to town for the Doctor.

By the same trusty messenger did Virginia contrive to send a note to Mrs. Brice, begging her to explain her absence to Judge Whipple. By day or night Virginia did not leave Bellegarde. And once Dr. Polk, while walking in the garden, found the girl fast asleep on a bench, her sewing on her lap. Would that a master had painted his face as he looked down at her!

'Twas he who brought Virginia daily news of Judge Whipple. Bad news, alas! for he seemed to miss her greatly. He had become more querulous and exacting with patient Mrs. Brice, and inquired for her continually. She would not go. But often, when he got into his buggy, the Doctor found the seat filled with roses and fresh fruit. Well he knew where to carry them.

What Virginia's feelings were at this time no one will ever know. God had mercifully given her occupation, first with the Judge, and later, when she needed it more, with Clarence. It was she whom he recognized first of all, whose name was on his lips in his waking moments. With the petulance of returning reason, he pushed his mother away. Unless Virginia was at his bedside when he awoke, his fever rose. He put his hot hand into her cool one, and it rested there sometimes for hours. Then and only then, did he seem contented.

The wonder was that her health did not fail. People who saw her during that fearful summer, fresh and with color in her cheeks, marvelled. Great-hearted Puss Russell, who came frequently to inquire, was quieted before her friend, and the frank and jesting tongue was silent in that presence. Anne Brinsmade came with her father and wondered. A miracle had changed Virginia. Her poise, her gentleness, her dignity, were the effects which people saw. Her force people felt. And this is why we cannot of ourselves add one cubit to our stature. It is God who changes,—who cleanses us of our levity with the fire of trial. Happy, thrice happy, those whom He chasteneth.

And yet how many are there who could not bear the fire—who would cry out at the flame!

Little by little Clarence mended, until he came to sit out on the porch in the cool of the afternoon. Then he would watch for hours the tassels stirring over the green fields of corn and the river running beyond, while the two women sat by. At times, when Mrs. Colfax's headaches came on, and Virginia was alone with him, he would talk of the war; sometimes of their childhood, of the mad pranks they played here at Bellegarde, of their friends. Only when Virginia read to him the Northern account of the battles would he emerge from a calm sadness into excitement; and he clenched his fists and tried to rise when he heard of the capture of Jackson and the fall of Port Hudson. Of love he spoke not a word, and now that he was better he ceased to hold her hand. But often when she looked up from her book, she would surprise his dark eyes fixed upon her, and a look in them of but one interpretation. She was troubled.

The Doctor came but every other day now, in the afternoon. It was his custom to sit for a while on the porch chatting cheerily with Virginia, his stout frame filling the rocking-chair. Dr. Polk's indulgence was gossip—though always of a harmless nature: how Mr. Cluyme always managed to squirm over to the side which was in favor, and how Maude Catherwood's love-letter to a certain dashing officer of the Confederate army had been captured and ruthlessly published in the hateful *Democrat*. It was the Doctor who gave Virginia news of the Judge, and sometimes he would mention Mrs. Brice. Then Clarence would raise his head; and once (she saw with trepidation) he had opened his lips to speak.

One day the Doctor came, and Virginia looked into his face and divined that he had something to tell her. He sat but a few moments, and when he arose to go he took her hand.

"I have a favor to beg of you, Jinny," he said. "The Judge has lost his nurse. Do you think Clarence could spare you for a little while every day? I shouldn't ask it," Dr. Polk continued, somewhat hurriedly for him, "but the Judge cannot bear a stranger near him. And I am afraid to have him excited while in this condition."

"Mrs. Brice is ill?" she cried. And Clarence, watching, saw her color go.

"No," replied Dr. Polk, "but her son Stephen has come home from the army. He was transferred to Lauman's brigade, and then he was wounded." He jangled the keys in his pocket and continued: "It seems that he had no business in the battle. Johnston in his retreat had driven animals into all the ponds and shot them, and in the hot weather the water was soon poisoned. Mr. Brice was scarcely well enough to stand when they made the charge, and he is now in a dreadful condition. He is a fine fellow," added the Doctor, with a sigh. "General Sherman sent a special physician to the boat with him. He is—"

Subconsciously the Doctor's arm sought Virginia's back, as though he felt her swaying. But he was looking at Clarence, who had jerked himself forward in his chair, his thin hands convulsively clutching at the arms of it. He did not appear to see Virginia.

"Stephen Brice, did you say?" he cried; "will he die?"

In his astonishment the Doctor passed his palm across his brow, and for a moment he did not answer. Virginia had taken a step from him, and was standing motionless, almost rigid, her eyes on his face.

"Die?" he said, repeating the word mechanically; "my God, I hope not. The danger is over, and he is resting easily. If he were not," he said quickly and forcibly, "I should not be here."

The Doctor's mare passed more than one fleet-footed trotter on the road to town that day. And the Doctor's black servant heard his master utter the word "fool" twice, and with great emphasis.

For a long time Virginia stood on the end of the porch until the heaving of the buggy harness died on the soft road. She felt Clarence's gaze upon her before she turned to face him.

"Virginia!" He had called her so of late.

"Yes, dear."

"Virginia, sit here a moment; I have something to tell you."

She came and took the chair beside him, her heart beating, her breast rising and falling. She looked into his eyes, and her own lashes fell before the hopelessness there. But he put out his fingers wasted by illness, and she took them in her own.

He began slowly, as if every word cost him pain.

"Virginia, we were children together here. I cannot remember the time when I did not love you, when I did not think of you as my wife. All I did when we played together was to try to win your applause. That was my nature. I could not help it. Do you remember the day I climbed out on the rotten branch of the big pear tree yonder to get you that pear—when I fell on the roof of Alfred's cabin? I did not feel the pain. It was because you kissed it and cried over me. You are crying now," he said tenderly. "Don't, Jinny. It isn't to make you sad that I am saying this.

"I have had a great deal of time to think lately, Jinny. I was not brought up seriously,—to be a man. I have been thinking of that day just before you were eighteen, when you rode out here. How well I remember it! It was a purple day. The grapes were purple, and a purple haze was over there across the river. You had been cruel to me. You were grown a woman then, and I was still nothing but a boy. Do you remember the doe coming out of the forest, and how she ran screaming when I tried to kiss you? You told me I was good for nothing. Please don't interrupt me. It was true what you said, that I was wild and utterly useless. I had never served or pleased any but myself,—and you. I had never studied or worked. You were right when you told me I must learn something,—do something,—become of some account in the world. I am just as useless to-day."

"Oh, Clarence, after what you have done for the South?"

He smiled with peculiar bitterness.

"What have I done for her?" he added. "Crossed the river and burned houses. I could not build them again. Floated down the river on a log after a few percussion caps. That did not save Vicksburg."

"And how many had the courage to do that?" she exclaimed.

"Pooh," he said, "courage! the whole South has it. Courage! If I did not have that, I would send Sambo to my father's room for his ebony box, and blow my brains out. No, Jinny, I am nothing but a soldier of fortune. I never possessed any quality but a wild spirit for adventure, to shirk work. I wanted to go with Walker, you remember. I wanted to go to Kansas. I wanted to distinguish myself," he added with a gesture. "But that is all gone now, Jinny. I wanted to distinguish myself for you. Now I see how an earnest life might have won you. No, I have not done yet."

She raised her head, frightened, and looked at him searchingly.

"One day," he said, "one day a good many years ago you and I and Uncle Comyn were walking along Market Street in front of Judge

Whipple's office, and a slave auction was going on. A girl was being sold on whom you had set your heart. There was some one in the crowd, a Yankee, who bid her in and set her free. Do you remember him?"

He saw her profile, her lips parted, her look far away. She inclined her head.

"Yes," said her cousin, "so do I remember him. He has crossed my path many times since, Virginia. And mark what I say—it was *he* whom you had in mind on that birthday when you implored me to make something of myself. It was Stephen Brice."

Her eyes flashed upon him quickly.

"Oh, how dare you?" she cried.

"I dare anything, Virginia," he answered quietly. "I am not blaming you. And I am sure that you did not realize that he was the ideal which you had in mind. The impression of him has never left it. Fate is in it. Again, that night at the Brinsmades', when we were in fancy dress, I felt that I had lost you when I got back. He had been there when I was away, and gone again. And—and—you never told me."

"It was a horrible mistake, Max," she faltered. "I was waiting for you down the road, and stopped his horse instead. It—it was nothing—"

"It was fate, Jinny. In that half-hour I lost you. How I hated that man!" he cried, "how I hated him!"

"Hated!" exclaimed Virginia, involuntarily. "Oh, no!"

"Yes," he said, "*hated!* I would have killed him if I could. But now—"

"But now?"

"Now he has saved my life. I have not—I could not tell you before. He came into the place where I was lying in Vicksburg, and they told him that my only chance was to come North. I turned my back upon him, insulted him. Yet he went to Sherman and had me brought home— to you, Virginia. If he loves you,—and I have long suspected that he does—"

"Oh, no," she cried, hiding her face. "No."

"I know he loves you, Jinny," her cousin continued calmly, inexorably. "And you know that he does. You must feel that he does. It was a brave thing to do, and a generous. He knew that you were engaged to me. He thought that he was saving me for you. He was giving up the hope of marrying you himself."

Virginia sprang to her feet. Unless you had seen her then, you had never known the woman in her glory.

"Marry a Yankee!" she cried. "Clarence Colfax, have you known and loved me all my life that you might accuse me of this? Never, never, *never!*"

Transformed, he looked incredulous admiration.

"Jinny, do you mean it?" he cried.

In answer she bent down with all that gentleness and grace that was hers, and pressed her lips to his forehead. Long after she had disappeared in the door he sat staring after her.

But later, when Mammy Easter went to call her mistress for supper, she found her with her face buried in the pillows.

CHAPTER X

IN JUDGE WHIPPLE'S OFFICE

AFTER this Virginia went to the Judge's bedside every day, in the morning, when Clarence took his sleep. She read his newspapers to him when he was well enough. She read the detested *Missouri Democrat*, which I think was the greatest trial Virginia ever had to put up with. To have her beloved South abused, to have her heroes ridiculed, was more than she could bear. Once, when the Judge was perceptibly better, she flung the paper out of the window, and left the room. He called her back penitently.

"My dear," he said, smiling admiration, "forgive an old bear. A selfish old bear, Jinny; my only excuse is my love for the Union. When you are not here, I lie in agony, lest she has suffered some mortal blow unknown to me, Jinny. And if God sees fit to spare our great country, the day will come when you will go down on your knees and thank Him for the inheritance which He saved for your children. You are a good woman, my dear, and a strong one. I have hoped that you will see the right. That you will marry a great citizen, one unwavering in his service and devotion to our Republic."

The Judge's voice trembled with earnestness as he spoke. And the gray eyes under the shaggy brows were alight with the sacred fire of his life's purpose. Undaunted as her spirit was, she could not answer him then.

Once, only once, he said to her: "Virginia, I loved your father better than any man I ever knew. Please God I may see him again before I die."

He never spoke of the piano. But sometimes at twilight his eyes would rest on the black cloth that hid it. Virginia herself never touched that cloth. To her it seemed the shroud upon a life of happiness that was dead and gone.

Virginia had not been with Judge Whipple during the critical week after Stephen was brought home. But Anne had told her that his anxiety was a pitiful thing to see, and that it had left him perceptibly weaker.

Certain it was that he was failing fast. So fast that on some days Virginia, watching him, would send Ned or Shadrach in hot haste for Dr. Polk.

At noon Anne would relieve Virginia,—Anne or her mother,—and frequently Mr. Brinsmade would come likewise. For it is those who have the most to do who find the most time for charitable deeds. As the hour for their coming drew near, the Judge would be seeking the clock, and scarce did Anne's figure appear in the doorway before the question had arisen to his lips:—

"And how is my young Captain to-day?"

That is what he called him,—"my young Captain."

Virginia's choice of her cousin, and her devotion to him, while seemingly natural enough, had drawn many a sigh from Anne. She thought it strange that Virginia herself had never once asked her about Stephen's condition, and she spoke of this one day to the Judge with as much warmth as she was capable of.

"Jinny's heart is like steel where a Yankee is concerned. If her best friend were a Yankee—"

Judge Whipple checked her, smiling.

"She has been very good to one Yankee I know of," he said. "And as for Mrs. Brice, I believe she worships her."

"But when I said that Stephen was much better to-day she swept out of the room as if she did not care whether he lived or died."

"Well, Anne," the Judge had answered, "you women are a puzzle to me. I guess you don't understand yourselves," he added.

That was a strange month in the life of Clarence Colfax,—the last of his recovery, while he was waiting for the news of his exchange. Bellegarde was never more beautiful, for Mrs. Colfax had no whim of letting the place run down because a great war was in progress. Though devoted to the South, she did not consecrate her fortune to it. Clarence gave as much as he could.

Whole afternoons Virginia and he would sit in the shaded arbor seat; or at the cool of the day descend to the bench on the lower tier of the summer garden, to steep, as it were, in the blended perfumes of the roses and the mignonettes and the pinks. He was soberer than of old. Often through the night he pondered on the change in her. She, too, was grave. But he was troubled to analyze her gravity, her dignity. Was this merely strength of character, the natural result of the trials through

which she had passed, the habit acquired of being the helper and com-
forter instead of the helped and comforted? Long years afterward the
brightly colored portrait of her remained in his eye,—the simple linen
gown of pink or white, the brown hair shining in the sunlight, the graceful poise of the head. And the background of flowers—flowers everywhere, far from the field of war.

Sometimes, when she brought his breakfast on a tray in the morning,
there was laughter in her eyes. In the days gone by they had been all
laughter.

They were engaged. She was to be his wife. He said it over to himself many, many times in the day. He would sit for a space, feasting his
eyes upon her until she lifted her look to his, and the rich color flooded
her face. He was not a lover to sit quietly by, was Clarence. And yet, as
the winged days flew on, that is what he did. It was not that she did not
respond to his advances: he did not make them. Nor could he have told
why. Was it the chivalry inherited from a long line of Colfaxes who
were gentlemen? Not wholly. Something of awe had crept into his feeling for her.

As the month wore on, and the time drew near for him to go back to
the war, a state that was not quite estrangement, and yet something
very like it, set in. Poor Clarence! Doubts bothered him, and he dared
not give them voice. By night he would plan his speeches,—impassioned,
imploring. To see her in her marvellous severity was to strike him
dumb. Horrible thought! Whether she loved him, whether she did not
love him, she would not give him up. Through the long years of their lives
together, he would never know. He was not a weak man now, was Clarence Colfax. He was merely a man possessed of a devil, enchained by
the power of self-repression come upon her whom he loved.

And day by day that power seemed to grow more intense,—invulnerable. Among her friends and in the little household it had raised Virginia to heights which she herself did not seem to realize. She was become the mistress of Bellegarde. Mrs. Colfax was under its sway, and
doubly miserable because Clarence would listen to her tirades no more.

"When are you to be married?" she had ventured to ask him once.
Nor had she taken pains to hide the sarcasm in her voice.

His answer, bringing with it her remembrance of her husband at certain times when it was not safe to question him, had silenced her. Addison Colfax had not been a quiet man. When he was quiet he was
dangerous.

"Whenever Virginia is ready, mother," he had replied.

Whenever Virginia was ready! He knew in his heart that if he were to ask her permission to send for Dr. Posthelwaite to-morrow that she would say yes. To-morrow came,—and with it a great envelope, an official answer to Clarence's report that he was fit for duty once more. He had been exchanged. He was to proceed to Cairo, there to await the arrival of the transport *Indianapolis,* which was to carry five hundred officers and men from Sandusky Prison, who were going back to fight once more for the Confederacy. O that they might have seen the North, all those brave men who made that sacrifice! That they might have realized the numbers and the resources and the wealth arrayed against them!

It was a cool day for September, a perfect day, an auspicious day, and yet it went the way of the others before it. This was the very fulness of the year. the earth giving out the sweetness of her maturity, the corn in martial ranks, with golden plumes nodding. The forest still in its glory of green. They walked in silence the familiar paths, and Alfred, clipping the late roses for the supper table, shook his white head as they passed him. The sun, who had begun to hurry on his southward journey, went to bed at six. The few clothes Clarence was to take with him had been packed by Virginia in his bag, and the two were standing in the twilight on the steps of the house, when Ned came around the corner. He called his young mistress by name, but she did not hear him. He called again.

"Miss Jinny!"

She started as from a sleep, and paused.

"Yes, Mr. Johnson," said she, and smiled. He wore that air of mystery so dear to darkeys.

"Gemmen to see you, Miss Jinny."

"A gentleman!" she said in surprise. "Where?"

The negro pointed to the lilac shrubbery.

"Thar!"

"What's all this nonsense, Ned?" said Clarence, sharply. "If a man is there, bring him here at once."

"Reckon he won't come, Marse Cla'ence," said Ned. "He fearful skeered ob de light ob day. He got suthin' very pertickler fo' Miss Jinny."

"Do you know him?" Clarence demanded.

"No sah—yessah—leastwise I'be seed 'um. Name's Robinson."

The word was hardly out of his mouth before Virginia had leaped down the four feet from the porch to the flower-bed and was running across the lawn toward the shrubbery. Parting the bushes after her, Clarence found his cousin confronting a large man, whom he recognized as the carrier who brought messages from the South.

"What's the matter, Jinny?" he demanded.

"Pa has got through the lines," she said breathlessly. "He—he came up to see me. Where is he, Robinson?"

"He went to Judge Whipple's rooms, ma'am. They say the Judge is dying. I reckoned you knew it, Miss Jinny," Robinson added contritely.

"Clarence," she said, "I must go at once."

"I will go with you," he said; "you cannot go alone."

In a twinkling Ned and Sambo had the swift pair of horses harnessed, and the light carriage was flying over the soft clay road toward the city. As they passed Mr. Brinsmade's place, the moon hung like a great round lantern under the spreading trees about the house. Clarence caught a glimpse of his cousin's face in the light. She was leaning forward, her gaze fixed intently on the stone posts which stood like monuments between the bushes at the entrance. Then she drew back again into the dark corner of the barouche. She was startled by a sharp challenge, and the carriage stopped. Looking out, she saw the provost's guard like black card figures on the road, and Ned fumbling for his pass.

On they drove into the city streets until the dark bulk of the Court House loomed in front of them, and Ned drew rein at the little stairway which led to the Judge's rooms. Virginia, leaping out of the carriage, flew up the steps and into the outer office, and landed in the Colonel's arms.

"Jinny!"

"Oh, Pa!" she cried. "Why do you risk your life in this way? If the Yankees catch you—"

"They won't catch me, honey," he answered, kissing her. Then he held her out at arm's length and gazed earnestly into her face. Trembling, she searched his own.

"Pa, how old you look!"

"I'm not precisely young, my dear," he said, smiling.

His hair was nearly white, and his face seared. But he was a fine erect figure of a man, despite the shabby clothes he wore, and the mud-bespattered boots.

"Pa," she whispered, "it was foolhardy to come *here*. Why did you come to St. Louis at all?"

"I came to see you, Jinny, I reckon. And when I got home to-night and heard Silas was dying, I just couldn't resist. He's the oldest friend I've got in St. Louis, honey, and now—now—"

"Pa, you've been in battle?"

"Yes," he said.

"And you weren't hurt; I thank God for that," she whispered. After a while: "Is Uncle Silas dying?"

"Yes, Jinny; Dr. Polk is in there now, and says that he can't last through the night. Silas has been asking for you, honey, over and over. He says you were very good to him,—that you and Mrs. Brice gave up everything to nurse him."

"She did," Virginia faltered. "She was here night and day until her son came home. She is a noble woman—"

"Her son?" repeated the Colonel. "Stephen Brice? Silas has done nothing the last half-hour but call his name. He says he must see the boy before he dies. Polk says he is not strong enough to come."

"Oh, no, he is not strong enough," cried Virginia.

The colonel looked down at her queerly.

"Where is Clarence?" he asked.

She had not thought of Clarence. She turned hurriedly, glanced around the room, and then peered down the dark stairway.

"Why, he came in with me. I wonder why he did not follow me up?"

"Virginia."

"Yes, Pa."

"Virginia, are you happy?"

"Why, yes, Pa."

"Are you going to marry Clarence?" he asked.

"I have promised," she said simply.

Then after a long pause, seeing her father said nothing, she added, "Perhaps he was waiting for you to see me alone. I will go down to see if he is in the carriage."

The Colonel started with her, but she pulled him back in alarm.

"You will be seen, Pa," she cried. "How can you be so reckless?"

He stayed at the top of the passage, holding open the door that she might have light. When she reached the sidewalk, there was Ned standing beside the horses, and the carriage empty.

"Ned!"

"Yass'm, Miss Jinny."

"Where's Mr. Clarence?"

"He done gone, Miss Jinny."

"Gone?"

"Yass'm. Fust I seed was a man plump out'n Willums's, Miss Jinny. He was a-gwine shufflin' up de street when Marse Cla'ence put out after him, pos' has'e. Den he run."

She stood for a moment on the pavement in thought, and paused on the stairs again, wondering whether it were best to tell her father. Perhaps Clarence had seen—she caught her breath at the thought and pushed open the door.

"Oh, Pa, do you think you are safe here?" she cried.

"Why, yes, honey, I reckon so," he answered. "Where's Clarence?"

"Ned says he ran after a man who was hiding in an entrance. Pa, I am afraid they are watching the place."

"I don't think so, Jinny. I came here with Polk, in his buggy, after dark."

Virginia, listening, heard footsteps on the stairs, and seized her father's sleeve.

"Think of the risk you are running, Pa," she whispered. She would have dragged him to the closet. But it was too late. The door opened, and Mr. Brinsmade entered, and with him a lady veiled.

At sight of Mr. Carvel, Mr. Brinsmade started back in surprise. How long he stared at his old friend Virginia could not say. It seemed to her an eternity. But Mrs. Brice has often told since how straight the Colonel stood, his fine head thrown back, as he returned the glance. Then Mr. Brinsmade came forward, with his hand outstretched.

"Comyn," said he, his voice breaking a little, "I have known you these many years as a man of unstained honor. You are safe with me. I ask no questions. God will judge whether I have done my duty."

Mr. Carvel took his friend's hand. "Thank you, Calvin," he said. "I give you my word of honor as a gentleman that I came into this city for no other reason than to see my daughter. And hearing that my old friend was dying, I could not resist the temptation, sir—"

Mr. Brinsmade finished for him. And his voice shook.

"To come to his bedside. How many men do you think would risk their lives so, Mrs. Brice?"

"Not many, indeed, Mr. Brinsmade," she answered. "Thank God he will now die happy. I know it has been much on his mind."

The Colonel bowed over her hand.

"And in his name, madam,—in the name of my oldest and best friend, —I thank you for what you have done for him. I trust that you will allow me to add that I have learned from my daughter to respect and admire you. I hope that your son is doing well."

"He is, thank you, Colonel Carvel. If he but knew that the Judge were dying, I could not have kept him at home. Dr. Polk says that he must not leave the house, or undergo any excitement."

Just then the door of the inner room opened, and Dr. Polk came out. He bowed gravely to Mrs. Brice and Mr. Brinsmade, and he patted Virginia.

"The Judge is still asleep," he said gently. "And—he may not wake up in this world."

Silently, sadly, they went together into that little room where so much of Judge Whipple's life had been spent. How little it was! And how completely they filled it,—these five people and the big Rothfield covered with the black cloth. Virginia pressed her father's arm as they leaned against it, and brushed her eyes. The Doctor turned the wick of the night-lamp.

What was that upon the sleeper's face from which they drew back? A smile? Yes, and a light. The divine light which is shed upon those who have lived for others, who have denied themselves the lusts of the flesh. For a long space, perhaps an hour, they stayed, silent save for a low word now and again from the Doctor as he felt the Judge's heart. Tableaux from the past floated before Virginia's eyes. Of the old days of the happy days in Locust Street, of the Judge quarrelling with her father, and she and Captain Lige smiling near by. And she remembered how sometimes when the controversy was finished the Judge would rub his nose and say:—

"It's my turn now, Lige."

Whereupon the Captain would open the piano, and she would play the hymn that he liked best. It was "Lead, Kindly Light."

What was it in Silas Whipple's nature that courted the pain of memories? What pleasure could it have been all through his illness to look upon this silent and cruel reminder of days gone by forever? She had heard that Stephen Brice had been with the Judge when he had bid it in. She wondered that he had allowed it, for they said that he was the only one who had ever been known to break the Judge's will. Virginia's eyes rested on Margaret Brice, who was seated at the head of the bed smoothing the pillows. The strength of Stephen's features were in hers, but not the ruggedness. Her features were large, indeed, yet stanch and softened. The widow, as if feeling Virginia's look upon her, glanced up from the Judge's face and smiled at her. The girl colored with pleasure, and again at the thought which she had had of the likeness between mother and son.

Still the Judge slept on, while they watched. And at length the thought of Clarence crossed Virginia's mind. Why had he not returned? Perhaps he was in the office without. Whispering to her father, she stole out on tip-toe. The office was empty. Descending to the street, she was unable to gain any news of Clarence from Ned, who was becoming alarmed likewise.

Perplexed and troubled, she climbed the stairs again. No sound came from the Judge's room. Perhaps Clarence would be back at any moment. Perhaps her father was in danger. She sat down to think,—her elbows on the desk in front of her, her chin in her hand, her eyes at the level of a line of books which stood on end—*Chitty's Pleadings, Blackstone, Greenleaf on Evidence*. Absently, as a person whose mind is in trouble, she reached out and took one of them down and opened it. Across the fly-leaf, in a high and bold hand, was written the name, *Stephen Atterbury Brice*.

It was his desk! She was sitting in his chair!

She dropped the book, and, rising abruptly, crossed quickly to the other side of the room. Then she turned, hesitatingly, and went back. This was his desk—his chair, in which he had worked so faithfully for the man who lay dying beyond the door. For him whom they all loved— whose last hours they were here to soothe. Wars and schisms may part our bodies, but stronger ties unite our souls. Through Silas Whipple, through his mother, Virginia knew that she was woven of one piece with Stephen Brice. In a thousand ways she was reminded, lest she drive it from her belief. She might marry another, and that would not matter.

She sank again into his chair, and gave herself over to the thoughts crowding in her heart. How the threads of his life ran next to hers, and crossed and recrossed them! The slave auction, her dance with him, the Fair, the meeting at Mr. Brinsmade's gate,—she knew them all. Her love and admiration for his mother. Her dreams of him—for she did dream of him. And now he had saved Clarence's life that she might marry her cousin. Was it true that she would marry Clarence? That seemed to her only a dream. It had never seemed real. Again she glanced at the signature in the book, as if fascinated by the very strength of it. She turned over a few pages of the book. "Supposing the defendant's counsel essays to prove by means of—" that was his writing again, a marginal note. There were marginal notes on every page; even the last was covered with them. And then at the end, "First reading, February, 1858. Second reading, July, 1858. Bought with some of money obtained by first article for M.D." That capacity for work, incomparable gift, was what she had always coveted the most. Again she rested her elbows on the desk and her chin on her hands, and sighed unconsciously.

She had not heard the step on the stair. She had not seen the door open. She did not know that any one was in the room until she heard his voice, and then she thought that she was dreaming.

"Miss Carvel!"

"Yes?" Her head did not move.

He took a step toward her.

"Miss Carvel!"

Slowly she raised her face to his, unbelief and wonder in her eyes,— unbelief and wonder and fright. No; it could not be he. But when she met the quality of his look, the grave tenderness of it, she trembled, and surrendered her own to the page where his handwriting quivered and became a blur.

He never knew the effort it cost her to rise and confront him. She herself had not measured or fathomed the power which his very person exhaled. It seemed to have come upon him suddenly. He needed not to have spoken for her to have felt that. What it was she could not tell. She knew alone that it was nigh irresistible, and she grasped the back of the chair as though material support might sustain her.

"Is he—dead?"

She was breathing hard.

"No," she said. "Not—not yet. They are waiting—for the end."

"And you?" he asked in grave surprise, glancing at the door of the Judge's room.

Then she remembered Clarence.

"I am waiting for my cousin," she said.

Even as she spoke she was with this man again at the Brinsmade gate. Those had been her very words! Intuition told her that he, too, was thinking of that time. Now he had found her at his desk, and, as if that were not humiliation enough, with one of his books taken down and laid open at his signature. Suffused, she groped for words to carry her on. "I am waiting for Clarence, Mr. Brice. He was here, and is gone somewhere."

He did not seem to take account of the speech. And his silence—goad to indiscretion—pressed her to add:—

"You saved him, Mr. Brice. I—we all—thank you so much. And that is not all I want to say. It is a poor enough acknowledgment of what you did,—for we have not always treated you well." Her voice faltered almost to faintness, as he raised his hand in pained protest. But she continued: "I shall regard it as a debt I can never repay. It is not likely that in my life to come I can ever help you, but I shall pray for that opportunity."

He interrupted her.

"I did nothing, Miss Carvel, nothing that the most unfeeling man in our army would not do. Nothing that I would not have done for the merest stranger."

"You saved him for me," she said.

O fateful words that spoke of themselves! She turned away from him for very shame, and yet she heard him saying:—

"Yes, I saved him for you."

His voice was in the very note of the sadness which has the strength to suffer, to put aside the thought of self. A note to which her soul responded with anguish when she turned to him with the natural cry of woman.

"Oh, you ought not to have come here to-night. Why did you come? The Doctor forbade it. The consequences may kill you."

"It does not matter much," he answered. "The Judge was dying."

"How did you know?"

"I guessed it,—because my mother had left me."

"Oh, you ought not to have come!" she said again.

"The Judge has been my benefactor," he answered quietly. "I could walk, and it was my duty to come."

"You did not walk!" she gasped.

He smiled.

"I had no carriage," he said.

With the instinct of her sex she seized the chair and placed it under him. "You must sit down at once," she cried.

"But I am not tired," he replied.

"Oh, you must sit down, you *must*, Captain Brice." He started at the title, which came so prettily from her lips.

"Won't you please?" she said pleadingly.

He sat down. And, as the sun peeps out of a troubled sky, she smiled.

"It is your chair," she said.

He glanced at the book, and the bit of sky was crimson. But still he said nothing.

"It is your book," she stammered. "I did not know that it was yours when I took it down. I—I was looking at it while I was waiting for Clarence."

"It is dry reading," he remarked, which was not what he wished to say.

"And yet—"

"Yes?"

"And yet you have read it twice." The confession had slipped to her lips.

She was sitting on the edge of his desk, looking down at him. Still he did not look at her. All the will that was left him averted his head. And the seal of honor was upon his speech. And he wondered if man were ever more tempted.

Then the evil spread its wings, and soared away into the night. And the moment was past. Peace seemed to come upon them both, quieting the tumult in their hearts, and giving them back their reason. Respect likewise came to the girl,—respect that was akin to awe. It was he who spoke first.

"My mother has told me how faithfully you nursed the Judge, Miss Carvel. It was a very noble thing to do."

"Not noble at all," she replied hastily. "Your mother did the most of it. And he is an old friend of my father—"

"It was none the less noble," said Stephen, warmly. "And he quarrelled with Colonel Carvel."

"My father quarrelled with him," she corrected. "It was well that I should make some atonement. And yet mine was no atonement. I love Judge Whipple. It was a—a privilege to see your mother every day— oh, how he would talk of you! I think he loves you better than any one on this earth."

"Tell me about him," said Stephen, gently.

Virginia told him, and into the narrative she threw the whole of her pent-up self. How patient the Judge had been, and the joy he had de- rived from Stephen's letters. "You were very good to write to him so often," she said. It seemed like a dream to Stephen, like one of the many dreams of her, the mystery of which was of the inner life beyond our ken. He could not recall a time when she had not been rebellious, antagonistic. And now—as he listened to her voice, with its exquisite low tones and modulations, as he sat there in this sacred intimacy, perchance to be the last in his life, he became dazed. His eyes, softened, with supreme eloquence cried out that she was his, forever and forever. The magnetic force which God uses to tie the worlds together was pulling him to her. And yet the Puritan resisted—

Then the door swung open, and Clarence Colfax, out of breath, ran into the room. He stopped short when he saw them, his hand fell to his sides, and his words died on his lips. Virginia did not stir.

It was Stephen who rose to meet him, and with her eyes the girl followed his motions. The broad and loosely built frame of the Northerner, his shoulders slightly stooping, contrasted with Clarence's slighter figure, erect, compact, springy. The Southerner's eye, for that moment, was flint struck with the spark from the steel. Stephen's face, thinned by illness, was grave. The eyes kindly, yet penetrating. For an instant they stood thus regarding each other, neither offering a hand. It was Stephen who spoke first, and if there was a trace of emotion in his voice, one who was listening intently failed to mark it.

"I am glad to see that you have recovered, Colonel Colfax," he said.

"I should indeed be without gratitude if I did not thank Captain Brice for my life," answered Clarence.

Virginia flushed. She had detected the undue accent on her cousin's last words, and she glanced apprehensively at Stephen. His forceful reply surprised them both.

"Miss Carvel has already thanked me sufficiently, sir," he said. "I am happy to have been able to have done you a good turn, and at the same time to have served her so well. It was she who saved your life. It is to her your thanks are chiefly due. I believe that I am not going too far, Colonel Colfax," he added, "when I congratulate you both."

Before her cousin could recover, Virginia slid down from the desk and had come between them. How her eyes shone and her lip trembled as she gazed at him, Stephen has never forgotten. What a woman she was as she took her cousin's arm and made him a curtsey.

"What you have done may seem a light thing to you, Captain Brice," she said. "That is apt to be the way with those who have big hearts. You have put upon Colonel Colfax, and upon me, a life's obligation."

When she began to speak, Clarence raised his head. As he glanced, incredulous, from her to Stephen, his look gradually softened, and when she had finished, his manner had become again frank, boyish, impetuous —nay, penitent. He seized Stephen's hand.

"Forgive me, Brice," he cried. "Forgive me. I should have known better. I—I did you an injustice, and you, Virginia. I was a fool—a scoundrel."

Stephen shook his head.

"No, you were neither," he said. Then upon his face came the smile of one who has the strength to renounce all that is dearest to him—that smile of the unselfish, sweetest of all. It brought tears to Virginia. She was to see it once again, upon the features of one who bore a cross,— Abraham Lincoln. Clarence looked, and then he turned away toward the door to the stairway, as one who walks blindly, in a sorrow.

His hand was on the knob when Virginia seemed to awake. She flew after him.

"Wait!" she whispered.

Then she raised her eyes, slowly, to Stephen, who was standing motionless beside his chair.

"Captain Brice!"

"Yes," he answered.

"My father is in the Judge's room," she said.

"Your father!" he exclaimed. "I thought—"

"That he was an officer in the Confederate Army. So he is." Her head went up as she spoke.

Stephen stared at her, troubled. Suddenly her manner changed. She took a step toward him, appealingly.

"Oh, he is not a spy," she cried. "He has given Mr. Brinsmade his word that he came here for no other purpose than to see me. Then he heard that the Judge was dying—"

"He has given his word to Mr. Brinsmade?"

"Yes."

"Then," said Stephen, "what Mr. Brinsmade sanctions is not for me to question."

She gave him yet another look, a fleeting one which he did not see. Then she softly opened the door and passed into the room of the dying man. Stephen followed her.

As for Clarence, he stood for a space staring after them. Then he went noiselessly down the stairs into the street.

CHAPTER XI

LEAD, KINDLY LIGHT

WHEN the Judge opened his eyes for the last time in this world, they fell first upon the face of his old friend, Colonel Carvel. Twice he tried to speak his name, and twice he failed. The third time he said it faintly.

"Comyn!"

"Yes, Silas."

"Comyn, what are you doing here?"

"I reckon I came to see you, Silas," answered the Colonel.

"To see me die," said the Judge, grimly.

Colonel Carvel's face twitched, and the silence in that little room seemed to throb.

"Comyn," said the Judge again. "I heard that you had gone South to fight against your country. I see you here. Can it be that you have at last returned in your allegiance, to the flag for which your forefathers died?"

Poor Colonel Carvel!

"I am still of the same mind, Silas," he said.

The Judge turned his face away, his thin lips moving as in prayer. But they knew that he was not praying.

"Silas," said Mr. Carvel, "we were friends for twenty years. Let us be friends again, before—"

"Before I die," the Judge interrupted. "I am ready to die. Yes, I am ready. I have had a hard life, Comyn, and few friends. It was my fault. I—I did not know how to make them. Yet no man ever valued those few more than I. But," he cried, the stern fire unquenched to the last, "I would that God had spared me to see this Rebellion stamped out. For it will be stamped out." To those watching, his eyes seemed fixed on a distant point, and the light of prophecy was in them. "I would that God had spared me to see this Union supreme once more. Yes, it will be supreme. A high destiny is reserved for this nation—I think the highest of all on this earth."

Amid profound silence he leaned back on the pillows from which he

388

had risen, his breath coming fast. None dared look at the neighbor beside them.

It was Stephen's mother who spoke. "Would you not like to see a clergyman, Judge?" she asked.

The look on his face softened as he turned to her.

"No, madam," he answered; "you are clergyman enough for me. You are near enough to God—there is no one in this room who is not worthy to stand in the presence of death. Yet I wish that a clergyman were here, that he might listen to one thing I have to say. When I was a boy I worked my way down the river to New York, to see the city. I met a bishop there. He said to me, 'Sit down, my son, I want to talk to you. I know your father in Albany. You are Senator Whipple's son.' I said to him, 'No, sir, I am not Senator Whipple's son. I am no relation of his.' If the bishop had wished to talk to me after that, Mrs. Brice, he might have made my life a little easier—a little sweeter. I know that they are not all like that. But it was by just such things that I was embittered when I was a boy." He stopped, and when he spoke again, it was more slowly, more gently, than any of them had heard him speak in all his life before. "I wish that some of the blessings which I am leaving now had come to me then—when I was a boy. I might have done my little share in making the world a brighter place to live in, as all of you have done. Yes, as all of you are now doing for me. I am leaving the world with a better opinion of it than I ever held in life. God hid the sun from me when I was a little child. Margaret Brice," he said, "if I had had such a mother as you, I would have been softened then. I thank God that He sent you when He did."

The widow bowed her head, and a tear fell upon his pillow.

"I have done nothing," she murmured, "nothing."

"So shall they answer at the last whom He has chosen," said the Judge. "I was sick, and ye visited me. He has promised to remember those who do that. Hold up your head, my daughter. God has been good to you. He has given you a son whom all men may look in the face, of whom you need never be ashamed. Stephen," said the Judge, "come here."

Stephen made his way to the bedside, but because of the moisture in his eyes he saw but dimly the gaunt face. And yet he shrank back in awe at the change in it. So must all of the martyrs have looked when the fire of the faggots licked their feet. So must John Bunyan have stared through his prison bars at the sky.

"Stephen," he said, "you have been faithful in a few things. So shall you be made ruler over many things. The little I have I leave to you, and the chief of this is an untarnished name. I know that you will be true to it because I have tried your strength. Listen carefully to what I have to say, for I have thought over it long. In the days gone by our fathers worked for the good of the people, and they had no thought of gain. A time is coming when we shall need that blood and that bone in this Republic. Wealth not yet dreamed of will flow out of this land, and the waters of it will rot all save the pure, and corrupt all save the incorruptible. Half-tried men will go down before that flood. You and those like you will remember how your fathers governed,—strongly, sternly, justly. It was so that they governed themselves. Be vigilant. Serve your city, serve your state, but above all serve your country."

He paused to catch his breath, which was coming painfully now, and reached out his bony hand to seek Stephen's.

"I was harsh with you at first, my son," he went on. "I wished to try you. And when I had tried you I wished your mind to open, to keep pace with the growth of this nation. I sent you to see Abraham Lincoln—that you might be born again—in the West. You were born again. I saw it when you came back. I saw it in your face. O God," he cried, with sudden eloquence, "would that his hands—Abraham Lincoln's hands—might be laid upon all who complain and cavil and criticise, and think of the little things in life! Would that his spirit might possess their spirit!"

He stopped again. They marvelled and were awed, for never in all his days had such speech broken from this man.

"Good-by, Stephen," he said, when they thought he was not to speak again. "Hold the image of Abraham Lincoln in front of you. Never forget him. You—you are a man after his own heart—and—and mine."

The last word was scarcely audible. They started forward, for his eyes were closed. But presently he stirred again, and opened them.

"Brinsmade," he said. "Brinsmade, take care of my orphan girls. Send Shadrach here."

The negro came forth, shuffling and sobbing, from the doorway.

"You ain't gwine away, Marse Jedge?"

"Yes, Shadrach, good-by. You have served me well. I have left you provided for."

Shadrach kissed the hand of whose secret charity he knew so much. Then the Judge withdrew it, and motioned to him to rise. He called his oldest friend by name. And Colonel Carvel came from the corner where he had been listening, with his face drawn.

"Good-by, Comyn. You were my friend when there was none other. You were true to me when the hand of every man was against me. You—you have risked your life to come to me here. May God spare it for Virginia."

At the sound of her name, the girl started. She came and bent over him. And when she kissed him on the forehead, he trembled.

"Uncle Silas!" she faltered.

Weakly he reached up and put his hands on her shoulders. He whispered in her ear. The tears came and lay wet upon her lashes as she undid the button at his throat. There, on a piece of cotton twine, hung a little key. She took it off, but still his hands held her.

"I have saved it for you, my dear," he said. "God bless you—" why did his eyes seek Stephen's?—"and make your life happy. Virginia—will you play my—hymn—once more—once more?"

They lifted the night lamp from the piano, and the medicine. It was Stephen who stripped it of the black cloth it had worn, who stood by Virginia ready to lift the lid when she had turned the lock. The girl's exaltation gave a trembling touch divine to the well-remembered chords, and those who heard were lifted, lifted far above and beyond the power of earthly spell.

> "Lead, Kindly Light, amid the encircling gloom,
>   Lead Thou me on!
> The night is dark, and I am far from home,
>   Lead Thou me on.
> Keep Thou my feet! I do not ask to see
> The distant scene; one step enough for me."

A sigh shook Silas Whipple's wasted frame, and so he died.

CHAPTER XII

THE LAST CARD

MR. BRINSMADE and the Doctor were the first to leave the little room where Silas Whipple had lived and worked and died, Mr. Brinsmade bent upon one of those errands which claimed him at all times. He took Shadrach with him. Virginia sat on, a vague fear haunting her,—a fear for her father's safety. Where was Clarence? What had he seen? Was the place watched? These questions, at first intruding upon her sorrow, remained to torture her.

Softly she stirred from the chair where she had sat before the piano, and opened the door of the outer office. A clock in a steeple near by was striking twelve. The Colonel did not raise his head. Only Stephen saw her go; she felt his eyes following her, and as she slipped out lifted hers to meet them for a brief instant through the opening of the door. Then it closed behind her.

First of all she knew that the light in the outer office was burning dimly, and the discovery gave her a shock. Who had turned it down? Had Clarence? Was he here? Fearfully searching the room for him, her gaze was held by a figure in the recess of the window at the back of the room. A solid, bulky figure it was, and, though uncertainly outlined in the semi-darkness, she knew it. She took a step nearer, and a cry escaped her.

The man was Eliphalet Hopper. He got down from the sill with a motion at once sheepish and stealthy. Her breath caught, and instinctively she gave back toward the door, as if to open it again.

"Hold on!" he said. "I've got something I want to say to you, Miss Virginia."

His tones seemed strangely natural. They were not brutal. But she shivered and paused, horrified at the thought of what she was about to do. Her father was in that room—and Stephen. She must keep them there, and get this man away. She must not show fright before him, and yet she could not trust her voice to speak just then. She must not let him know that she was afraid of him—this she kept repeating to herself. But how to act? Suddenly an idea flashed upon her.

Virginia never knew how she gathered the courage to pass him, even swiftly, and turn up the gas. He started back, blinking as the jet flared. For a moment she stood beside it, with her head high, confronting him and striving to steady herself for speech.

"Why have you come here?" she said. "Judge Whipple—died—to-night."

The dominating note in his answer was a whine, as if, in spite of himself, he were awed.

"I ain't here to see the Judge."

She was pale, and quite motionless. And she faltered now. She felt her lips moving, but knew not whether the words had come.

"What do you mean?"

He gained confidence. The look in his little eyes was the filmy look of those of an animal feasting.

"I came here to see you," he said,—"*you.*" She was staring at him now, in horror. "And if you don't give me what I want, I cal'late to see some one else—in there," said Mr. Hopper.

He smiled, for she was swaying, her lids half closed. By a supreme effort she conquered her terror and looked at him. The look was in his eyes still, intensified now.

"How dare you speak to me after what has happened!" she said. "If Colonel Carvel were here, he would—kill you."

He flinched at the name and the word, involuntarily. He wiped his forehead, hot at the very thought.

"I want to know!" he exclaimed, in faint-hearted irony. Then, remembering his advantage, he stepped close to her. "He is here," he said, intense now. "He is here, in that there room." He seized her wrists. Virginia struggled, and yet she refrained from crying out. "He never leaves this city without I choose. I can have him hung if I choose," he whispered, next to her.

"Oh!" she cried; "oh, if you choose!"

Still his body crept closer, and his face closer. And her strength was going.

"There's but one price to pay," he said hoarsely, "there's but one price to pay, and that's you—*you.* I cal'late you'll marry me now."

Delirious at the touch of her, he did not hear the door open. Her

senses were strained for that very sound. She heard it close again, and a
footstep across the room. She knew the step—she knew the voice, and
her heart leaped at the sound of it in anger. An arm in a blue sleeve came
between them, and Eliphalet Hopper staggered and fell across the books
on the table, his hand to his face. Above him towered Stephen Brice.
Towered was the impression that came to Virginia then, and so she
thought of the scene ever afterward. Small bits, like points of tempered
steel, glittered in Stephen's eyes, and his hands following up the mastery
he had given them clutched Mr. Hopper's shoulders. Twice Stephen
shook him so that his head beat upon the table.

"You—you beast!" he cried, but he kept his voice low. And then, as if
he expected Hopper to reply: "Shall I kill you?"

Again he shook him violently. He felt Virginia's touch on his arm.

"Stephen!" she cried, "your wounds! Be careful! Oh, do be careful!"

She had called him *Stephen*. He turned slowly, and his hands fell from
Mr. Hopper's cowering form as his eyes met hers. Even he could not
fathom the appeal, the yearning, in their dark blue depths. And yet what
he saw there made him tremble. She turned away, trembling too.

"Please sit down," she entreated. "He—he won't touch me again while
you are here."

Eliphalet Hopper raised himself from the desk, and one of the big
books fell with a crash to the floor. Then they saw him shrink, his eyes
fixed upon some one behind them. Before the Judge's door stood Colonel
Carvel, in calm, familiar posture, his feet apart, and his head bent forward as he pulled at his goatee.

"What is this man doing here, Virginia?" he asked.

She did not answer him, nor did speech seem to come easily to Mr.
Hopper in that instant. Perhaps the sight of Colonel Carvel had brought
before him too vividly the memory of that afternoon at Glencoe.

All at once Virginia grasped the fulness of the power in this man's
hands. At a word from him her father would be shot as a spy—and Stephen Brice, perhaps, as a traitor. But if Colonel Carvel should learn that
he had seized her,—here was the terrible danger of the situation. Well
she knew what the Colonel would do. Would Stephen tell him? She
trusted in his coolness that he would not.

Before a word of reply came from any of the three, a noise was heard
on the stairway. Some one was coming up. There followed four seconds
of suspense, and then Clarence came in. She saw that his face wore a

worried, dejected look. It changed instantly when he glanced about him, and an oath broke from his lips as he singled out Eliphalet Hopper standing in sullen aggressiveness beside the table.

"So you're the spy, are you?" he said in disgust. Then he turned his back and faced his uncle. "I saw him in Williams's entry as we drove up. He got away from me."

A thought seemed to strike him. He strode to the open window at the back of the office, and looked out. There was a roof under it.

"The sneak got in here," he said. "He knew I was waiting for him in the street. So you're the spy, are you?"

Mr. Hopper passed a heavy hand across the cheek where Stephen had struck him.

"No, I ain't *the* spy," he said, with a meaning glance at the Colonel.

"Then what are you doing here?" demanded Clarence, fiercely.

"I cal'late that *he* knows," Eliphalet replied, jerking his head toward Colonel Carvel. "Where's his Confederate uniform? What's to prevent my calling up the provost's guard below?" he continued, with a smile that was hideous on his swelling face.

It was the Colonel who answered him, very quickly and very clearly.

"Nothing whatever, Mr. Hopper," he said. "This is the way out." He pointed at the door. Stephen, who was watching him, could not tell whether it were a grim smile that creased the corners of the Colonel's mouth as he added, "You might prefer the window."

Mr. Hopper did not move, but his eyes shifted to Virginia's form. Stephen deliberately thrust himself between them that he might not see her.

"What are you waiting for?" said the Colonel, in the mild voice that should have been an ominous warning.

Still Mr. Hopper did not move. It was clear that he had not reckoned upon all of this; that he had waited in the window to deal with Virginia alone. But now the very force of a desire which had gathered strength in many years made him reckless. His voice took on the oily quality in which he was wont to bargain.

"Let's be calm about this business, Colonel," he said. "We won't say anything about the past. But I ain't set on having you shot. There's a consideration that would stop me, and I cal'late you know what it is."

Then the Colonel made a motion. But before he had taken a step Virginia had crossed the room swiftly, and flung herself upon him.

"Oh, don't, Pa!" she cried. "Don't! Tell him that I will agree to it. Yes, I will. I can't have you—shot." The last word came falteringly, faintly.

"Let me go,—honey," whispered the Colonel, gently. His eyes did not leave Eliphalet. He tried to disengage himself, but her fingers were clasped about his neck in a passion of fear and love. And then, while she clung to him, her head was raised to listen. The sound of Stephen Brice's voice held her as in a spell. His words were coming coldly, deliberately, and yet so sharply that each seemed to fall like a lash.

"Mr. Hopper, if ever I hear of your repeating what you have seen or heard in this room, I will make this city and this state too hot for you to live in. I know you. I know how you hide in areas, how you talk sedition in private, how you have made money out of other men's misery. And, what is more, I can prove that you have had traitorous dealings with the Confederacy. General Sherman has been good enough to call himself a friend of mine, and if he prosecutes you for your dealings in Memphis, you will get a term in a Government prison. You ought to be hung. Colonel Carvel has shown you the door. Now go."

And Mr. Hopper went.

CHAPTER XIII

FROM THE LETTERS OF MAJOR STEPHEN BRICE

*Of the Staff of General Sherman on the March to the Sea,
and on the March from Savannah Northward*

HEADQUARTERS MILITARY DIVISION OF THE MISSISSIPPI
GOLDSBORO, N.C.   MARCH 24, 1865.

DEAR MOTHER: The South Carolina Campaign is a thing of the past.
I pause as I write these words—they seem so incredible to me. We have
marched the four hundred and twenty-five miles in fifty days, and the
General himself has said that it is the longest and most important march
ever made by an organized army in a civilized country. I know that you
will not be misled by the words "civilized country." Not until the history
of this campaign is written will the public realize the wide rivers and all
but impassable swamps we have crossed with our baggage trains and
artillery. The roads (by courtesy so called) were a sea of molasses; and
every mile of them has had to be corduroyed. For fear of worrying you I
did not write you from Savannah how they laughed at us for starting at
that season of the year. They said we would not go ten miles, and I most
solemnly believe that no one but "Uncle Billy" and an army organized
and equipped by him could have gone ten miles. Nothing seems to stop
him. You have probably remarked in the tone of my letters ever since we
left Kingston for the sea, a growing admiration for "my General."

It seems very strange that this wonderful tactician can be the same
man I met that day going to the Arsenal in the street car, and again at
Camp Jackson. I am sure that history will give him a high place among
the commanders of the world. Certainly none was ever more tireless than
he. He never fights a battle when it can be avoided, and his march into
Columbia while threatening Charleston and Augusta was certainly a
master stroke of strategy.

I think his simplicity his most remarkable trait. You should see him as
he rides through the army, an erect figure, with his clothes all angular
and awry, and an expanse of white sock showing above his low shoes.

You can hear his name running from file to file; and sometimes the new regiments can't resist cheering. He generally says to the Colonel:—

"Stop that noise, sir. Don't like it."

On our march to the sea, if the orders were ever given to turn northward, "the boys" would get very much depressed. One moonlight night I was walking my horse close to the General's over the pine needles, when we overheard this conversation between two soldiers:—

"Say, John," said one, "I guess Uncle Billy don't know our corps is goin' north."

"I wonder if he does," said John. "If I could only get a sight of them white socks, I'd know it was all right."

The General rode past without a word, but I heard him telling the story to Mower the next day.

I can find little if any change in his manner since I knew him first. He is brusque, but kindly, and he has the same comradeship with officers and men—and even the negroes who flock to our army. But few dare to take advantage of it, and they never do so twice. I have been very near to him, and have tried not to worry him or ask many foolish questions. Sometimes on the march he will beckon me to close up to him, and we have a conversation something on this order:—

"There's Kenesaw, Brice."

"Yes, sir."

Pointing with his arm.

"Went beyond lines there with small party. Rebel battery on summit. Had to git. Fired on. Next day I thought Rebels would leave in the night. Got up before daylight, fixed telescope on stand, and waited. Watched top of Kenesaw. No Rebel. Saw one blue man creep up, very cautious, looked around, waved his hat. Rebels gone. Thought so."

This gives you but a faint idea of the vividness of his talk. When we make a halt for any time, the general officers and their staffs flock to headquarters to listen to his stories. When anything goes wrong, his perception of it is like a lightning flash,—and he acts as quickly.

By the way, I have just found the letter he wrote me, offering this staff position. Please keep it carefully, as it is something I shall value all my life.

GAYLESVILLE, ALABAMA, October 25, 1864.

MAJOR STEPHEN A. BRICE:

Dear Sir,—The world goes on, and wicked men sound asleep. Davis has sworn to destroy my army, and Beauregard has come to do the work,

—so if you expect to share in our calamity, come down. I offer you this last chance for staff duty, and hope you have had enough in the field. I do not wish to hurry you, but you can't get aboard a ship at sea. So if you want to make the trip, come to Chattanooga and take your chances of meeting me.

Yours truly,

W. T. SHERMAN, *Major General.*

One night—at Cheraw, I think it was—he sent for me to talk to him. I found him lying on a bed of Spanish moss they had made for him. He asked me a great many questions about St. Louis, and praised Mr. Brinsmade, especially his management of the Sanitary Commission.

"Brice," he said, after a while, "you remember when Grant sent me to beat off Joe Johnston's army from Vicksburg. You were wounded then, by the way, in that dash Lauman made. Grant thought he ought to warn me against Johnston.

" 'He's wily, Sherman,' said he. 'He's a dangerous man.'

" 'Grant,' said I, 'you give me men enough and time enough to look over the ground, and I'm not afraid of the devil.' "

Nothing could sum up the man better than that. And now what a trick of fate it is that he has Johnston before him again, in what we hope will prove the last gasp of the war! He likes Johnston, by the way, and has the greatest respect for him.

I wish you could have peeped into our camp once in a while. In the rare bursts of sunshine on this march our premises have been decorated with gay red blankets, and sombre gray ones brought from the quartermasters, and white Hudson's Bay blankets (not so white now), all being between forked sticks. It is wonderful how the pitching of a few tents, and the busy crackle of a few fires, and the sound of voices—sometimes merry, sometimes sad, depending on the weather, will change the look of a lonely pine knoll. You ask me how we fare. I should be heartily ashamed if a word of complaint ever fell from my lips. But the men! Whenever I wake up at night with my feet in a puddle between the blankets, I think of the men. The corduroy roads which our horses stumble over through the mud, they make as well as march on. Our flies are carried in wagons, and our utensils and provisions. They must often bear on their backs the little dog-tents, under which, put up by their own labor, they crawl to sleep, wrapped in a blanket they have carried all day, perhaps waist deep in water. The food they eat has been in their haversacks for many a weary mile, and is cooked in the little skillet and pot which have also been a part of their burden. Then they have their musket and accoutrements, and the "forty rounds" at their backs. Patiently, cheerily tramping along, going they know not where, nor care much either, so it be not in retreat. Ready to make roads, throw up works, tear up railroads, or hew out and build wooden bridges; or, best of all, to go for the Johnnies under hot sun or heavy rain, through swamp and mire and quicksand. They marched ten miles to storm Fort McAllister. And how the cheers broke from them when the *pop pop pop* of the skirmish line began after we came in sight of Savannah! No man who has seen but not shared their life may talk of personal hardship.

We arrived at this pretty little town yesterday, so effecting a junction with Schofield, who got in with the 23d Corps the day before. I am writing at General Schofield's headquarters. There was a bit of a battle on Tuesday at Bentonville, and we have come hither in smoke, as usual. But this time we thank Heaven that it is not the smoke of burning homes,— only some resin the "Johnnies" set on fire before they left.

I must close. General Sherman has just sent for me.

ON BOARD DESPATCH BOAT "MARTIN."
AT SEA, March 25, 1865.

DEAR MOTHER: A most curious thing has happened. But I may as well begin at the beginning. When I stopped writing last evening at the summons of the General, I was about to tell you something of the battle of Bentonville on Tuesday last. Mower charged through as bad a piece of wood and swamp as I ever saw, and got within one hundred yards of Johnston himself, who was at the bridge across Mill Creek. Of course we did not know this at the time, and learned it from prisoners.

As I have written you, I have been under fire very little since coming to the staff. When the battle opened, however, I saw that if I stayed with the General (who was then behind the reserves) I would see little or nothing; I went ahead "to get information" beyond the line of battle into the woods. I did not find these favorable to landscape views, and just as I was turning my horse back again I caught sight of a commotion some distance to my right. The Rebel skirmish line had fallen back just that instant, two of our skirmishers were grappling with a third man, who was fighting desperately. It struck me as singular that the fellow was not in gray, but had on some sort of dark clothes.

I could not reach them in the swamp on horseback, and was in the act of dismounting when the man fell, and then they set out to carry him

to the rear, still farther to my right, beyond the swamp. I shouted, and
one of the skirmishers came up. I asked him what the matter was.

"We've got a spy, sir," he said excitedly.

"A spy! Here?"

"Yes, Major. He was hid in the thicket yonder, lying flat on his face.
He reckoned that our boys would run right over him and that he'd get
into our lines that way. Tim Foley stumbled on him, and he put up as
good a fight with his fists as any man I ever saw."

Just then a regiment swept past us. That night I told the General, who
sent over to the headquarters of the 17th Corps to inquire. The word
came back that the man's name was Addison, and he claimed to be a
Union sympathizer who owned a plantation near by. He declared that he
had been conscripted by the Rebels, wounded, sent back home, and was
now about to be pressed in again. He had taken this method of escaping
to our lines. It was a common story enough, but General Mower added
in his message that he thought the story fishy. This was because the
man's appearance was very striking, and he seemed the type of Confederate fighter who would do and dare anything. He had a wound, which
had been a bad one, evidently got from a piece of shell. But they had
been able to find nothing on him. Sherman sent back word to keep the
man until he could see him in person.

It was about nine o'clock last night when I reached the house the General has taken. A prisoner's guard was resting outside, and the hall was
full of officers. They said that the General was awaiting me, and pointed
to the closed door of a room that had been the dining room. I opened it.

Two candles were burning in pewter sticks on the bare mahogany
table. There was the General sitting beside them, with his legs crossed,
holding some crumpled tissue paper very near his eyes, and reading. He
did not look up when I entered. I was aware of a man standing, tall and
straight, just out of range of the candles' rays. He wore the easy dress of
a Southern planter, with the broad felt hat. The head was flung back so
that there was just a patch of light on the chin, and the lids of the eyes
in the shadow were half closed.

My sensations are worth noting. For the moment I felt precisely as I
had when I was hit by that bullet in Lauman's charge. I was aware of
something very like pain, yet I could not place the cause of it. But this is
what since has made me feel queer: you doubtless remember staying at
Hollingdean, when I was a boy, and hearing the story of Lord Northwell's
daredevil Royalist ancestor,—the one with the lace collar over the dull-

gold velvet, and the pointed chin, and the lazy scorn in the eyes. Those eyes are painted with drooping lids. The first time I saw Clarence Colfax I thought of that picture—and now I thought of the picture first.

The General's voice startled me.

"Major Brice, do you know this gentleman?" he asked.

"Yes, General."

"Who is he?"

"His name is Colfax, sir—Colonel Colfax, I think."

"Thought so," said the General.

I have thought much of that scene since, as I am steaming northward over green seas and under cloudless skies, and it has seemed very unreal. I should almost say supernatural when I reflect how I have run across this man again and again, and always opposing him. I can recall just how he looked at the slave auction, which seems so long ago: very handsome, very boyish, and yet with the air of one to be deferred to. It was sufficiently remarkable that I should have found him in Vicksburg. But now—to be brought face to face with him in this old dining room in Goldsboro'! And he a prisoner—a spy.

He had not moved. I did not know how he would act, but I went up to him and held out my hand, and said:—

"How do you do, Colonel Colfax?"

I am sure that my voice was not very steady, for I cannot help liking him. And then his face lighted up and he gave me his hand. And he smiled at me and again at the General, as much as to say that it was all over. He has a wonderful smile.

"We seem to run into each other, Major Brice," said he.

The pluck of the man was superb. I could see that the General, too, was moved, from the way he looked at him. And he speaks a little more abruptly at such times.

"Guess that settles it, Colonel," he said.

"I reckon it does, General," said Clarence, still smiling.

The General turned from him to the table with a kind of jerk and clapped his hand on the tissue paper.

"These speak for themselves, sir," he said. "It is very plain that they would have reached the prominent citizens for whom they were intended if you had succeeded in your enterprise. You were captured out of uniform. You know enough of war to appreciate the risk you ran. Any statement to make?"

"No, sir."

"Call Captain Vaughan, Brice, and ask him to conduct the prisoner back."

"May I speak to him, General?" I asked. The General nodded.

I asked him if I could write home for him—or do anything else. That seemed to touch him. Some day I shall tell you what he said.

Then Vaughan took him out, and I heard the guard shoulder arms and tramp away in the night. The General and I were left alone with the mahogany table between us, and a family portrait of somebody looking down on us from the shadow on the wall. A moist spring air came in at the open windows, and the candles flickered. After a silence, I ventured to say:—

"I hope he won't be shot, General."

"Don't know, Brice," he answered. "Can't tell now. Hate to shoot him, but war is war. Magnificent class he belongs to—pity we should have to fight those fellows." He paused, and drummed on the table. "Brice," said he, "I'm going to send you to General Grant at City Point with despatches. I'm sorry Dunn went back yesterday, but it can't be helped. Can you start in half an hour?"

"Yes, sir."

"You'll have to ride to Kinston. The railroad won't be through until to-morrow. I'll telegraph there, and to General Easton at Morehead City. He'll have a boat for you. Tell Grant I expect to run up there in a day or two myself, when things are arranged here. You may wait until I come."

"Yes, sir."

I turned to go, but Clarence Colfax was on my mind.

"General?"

"Eh! what?"

"General, could you hold Colonel Colfax until I see you again?"

It was a bold thing to say, and I quaked. And he looked at me in his keen way, through and through.

"You saved his life once before, didn't you?"

"You allowed me to have him sent home from Vicksburg, sir."

He answered with one of his jokes—apropos of something he said on the Court House steps at Vicksburg. Perhaps I shall tell it to you sometime.

"Well, well," he said, "I'll see, I'll see. Thank God this war is pretty near over. I'll let you know, Brice, before I shoot him."

I rode the thirty odd miles to Kinston in a little more than three hours. A locomotive was waiting for me, and I jumped into a cab with a friendly engineer. Soon we were roaring seaward through the vast pine forests. It was a lonely journey, and you were much in my mind. My greatest apprehension was that we might be derailed and the despatches captured; for as fast as our army had advanced, the track of it had closed again, like the wake of a ship at sea. Guerillas were roving about, tearing up ties and destroying bridges.

There was one five-minute interval of excitement when, far down the tunnel through the forest, we saw a light gleaming. The engineer said there was no house there—that it must be a fire. But we did not slacken our speed, and gradually the leaping flames grew larger and redder until we were upon them.

Not one gaunt figure stood between them and us. Not one shot broke the stillness of the night. As dawn broke I beheld the flat, gray waters of the Sound stretching away to the eastward, and there was the boat at the desolate wharf beside the warehouse, her steam rising white in the chill morning air.

CHAPTER XIV

THE SAME, CONTINUED

HEADQUARTERS ARMIES OF THE UNITED STATES
CITY POINT, VIRGINIA, March 28, 1865.

DEAR MOTHER: I arrived here safely the day before yesterday, and I hope that you will soon receive some of the letters I forwarded on that day. It is an extraordinary place, this City Point; a military city sprung up like a mushroom in a winter. And my breath was quite taken away when I first caught sight of it on the high table-land. The great bay in front of it, which the Appomattox helps to make, is a maze of rigging and smoke-pipes, like the harbor of a prosperous seaport. There are gunboats and supply boats, schooners and square-riggers and steamers, all huddled together, and our captain pointed out to me the *Malvern* flying Admiral Porter's flag. Barges were tied up at the long wharves, and these were piled high with wares and flanked by squat warehouses. Although it was Sunday, a locomotive was puffing and panting along the foot of the ragged bank.

High above, on the flat promontory between the two rivers, is the city of tents and wooden huts, the great trees in their fresh faint green towering above the low roofs. At the point of the bluff a large flag drooped against its staff, and I did not have to be told that this was General Grant's headquarters.

There was a fine steamboat lying at the wharf, and I had hardly stepped ashore before they told me she was President Lincoln's. I read the name on her—the *River Queen*. Yes, the President is here, too, with his wife and family.

There are many fellows here with whom I was brought up in Boston. I am living with Jack Hancock, whom you will remember well. He is a captain now, and has a beard.

But I must go on with my story. I went straight to General Grant's headquarters,—just a plain, rough slat house such as a contractor might build for a temporary residence. Only the high flagstaff and the Stars and

Stripes distinguish it from many others of the same kind. A group of officers stood chatting outside of it, and they told me that the General had walked over to get his mail. He is just as unassuming and democratic as "my general." General Rankin took me into the office, a rude room, and we sat down at the long table there. Presently the door opened, and a man came in with a slouch hat on and his coat unbuttoned. He was smoking a cigar. We rose to our feet, and I saluted.

It was the general-in-chief. He stared at me, but said nothing.

"General, this is Major Brice of General Sherman's staff. He has brought despatches from Goldsboro'," said Rankin.

He nodded, took off his hat and laid it on the table and reached out for the despatches. While reading them he did not move, except to light another cigar. I am getting hardened to unrealities,—perhaps I should say *marvels*, now. Our country abounds in them. It did not seem so strange that this silent General with the baggy trousers was the man who had risen by leaps and bounds in four years to be general-in-chief of our armies. His face looks older and more sunken than it did on that day in the street near the Arsenal, in St. Louis, when he was just a military carpet-bagger out of a job. He is not changed otherwise. But how different the impressions made by the man in authority and the same man out of authority!

He made a sufficient impression upon me then, as I told you at the time. That was because I overheard his well-merited rebuke to Hopper. But I little dreamed that I was looking on the man who was to come out of the West and save this country from disunion. And how quietly and simply he has done it, without parade or pomp or vainglory. Of all those who, with every means at their disposal, have tried to conquer Lee, he is the only one who has in any manner succeeded. He has been able to hold him fettered while Sherman has swept the Confederacy. And these are the two men who were unknown when the war began.

When the General had finished reading the despatches, he folded them quickly and put them in his pocket.

"Sit down and tell me about this last campaign of yours, Major," he said.

I talked with him for about half an hour. I should rather say *talked to him*. He is a marked contrast to Sherman in this respect. I believe that he only opened his lips to ask two questions. You may well believe that they were worth the asking, and they revealed an intimate knowledge of our march from Savannah. I was interrupted many times by the arrival of different generals, aides, etc. He sat there smoking, imperturbable. Sometimes he said "yes" or "no," but oftener he merely nodded his head. Once he astounded by a brief question an excitable young lieutenant, who floundered. The General seemed to know more than he about the matter he had in hand.

When I left him, he asked me where I was quartered, and said he hoped I would be comfortable.

Jack Hancock was waiting for me, and we walked around the city, which even has barber shops. Everywhere were signs of preparation, for the roads are getting dry, and the General preparing for a final campaign against Lee. Poor Lee! What a marvellous fight he has made with his material. I think that he will be reckoned among the greatest generals of our race.

Of course, I was very anxious to get a glimpse of the President, and so we went down to the wharf, where we heard that he had gone off for a horseback ride. They say that he rides nearly every day, over the corduroy roads and through the swamps, and wherever the boys see that tall hat they cheer. They know it as well as the lookout tower on the flats of Bermuda Hundred. He lingers at the campfires and swaps stories with the officers, and entertains the sick and wounded in the hospitals. Isn't it like him?

He hasn't changed, either. I believe that the great men don't change. Away with your Napoleons and your Marlboroughs and your Stuarts. These are the days of simple men who command by force of character, as well as knowledge. Thank God for the American! I believe that he will change the world, and strip it of its vainglory and hypocrisy.

In the evening, as we were sitting around Hancock's fire, an officer came in.

"Is Major Brice here?" he asked.

I jumped up.

"The President sends his compliments, Major, and wants to know if you would care to pay him a little visit."

If I would care to pay him a little visit! That officer had to hurry to keep up with me as I walked to the wharf. He led me aboard the *River Queen,* and stopped at the door of the after-cabin.

Mr. Lincoln was sitting under the lamp, slouched down in his chair, in the position I remembered so well. It was as if I had left him but yesterday. He was whittling, and he had made some little toy for his son Tad, who ran out as I entered.

When he saw me, the President rose to his great height, a sombre, towering figure in black. He wears a scraggly beard now. But the sad smile, the kindly eyes in their dark caverns, the voice—all were just the same. I stopped when I looked upon the face. It was sad and lined when I had known it, but now all the agony endured by the millions, North and South, seemed written on it.

"Don't you remember me, Major?" he asked.

The wonder was that he had remembered me! I took his big bony hand, which reminded me of Judge Whipple's. Yes, it was just as if I had been with him always, and he were still the gaunt country lawyer.

"Yes, sir," I said, "indeed I do."

He looked at me with that queer expression of mirth he sometimes has.

"Are these Boston ways, Steve?" he asked. "They're tenacious. I didn't think that any man could travel so close to Sherman and keep 'em."

"They're unfortunate ways, sir," I said, "if they lead you to misjudge me."

He laid his hand on my shoulder, just as he had done at Freeport.

"I know you, Steve," he said. "I shuck an ear of corn before I buy it. I've kept tab on you a little the last five years, and when I heard Sherman had sent a Major Brice up here, I sent for you."

What I said was boyish. "I tried very hard to get a glimpse of you to-day, Mr. Lincoln. I wanted to see you again."

He was plainly pleased.

"I'm glad to hear it, Steve," he said. "Then you haven't joined the ranks of the grumblers? You haven't been one of those who would have liked to try running this country for a day or two, just to show me how to do it?"

"No, sir," I said, laughing.

"Good!" he cried, slapping his knee. "I didn't think you were that kind, Steve. Now sit down and tell me about this General of mine who wears seven-leagued boots. What was it—four hundred and twenty miles in fifty days? How many navigable rivers did he step across?" He began to count on those long fingers of his. "The Edisto, the Broad, the Catawba, the Pedee, and—?"

"The Cape Fear," I said.

"Is—is the General a nice man?" asked Mr. Lincoln, his eyes twinkling.

"Yes, sir, he is that," I answered heartily. "And not a man in the army wants anything when he is around. You should see that Army of the Mississippi, sir. They arrived in Goldsboro' in splendid condition."

He got up and gathered his coat-tails under his arms, and began to walk up and down the cabin.

"What do the boys call the General?" he asked.

I told him "Uncle Billy." And, thinking the story of the white socks might amuse him, I told him that. It did amuse him.

"Well, now," he said, "any man that has a nickname like that is all right. That's the best recommendation you can give the General—just say 'Uncle Billy.' " He put one lip over the other. "You've given 'Uncle Billy' a good recommendation, Steve," he said. "Did you ever hear the story of Mr. Wallace's Irish gardener?"

"No, sir."

"Well, when Wallace was hiring his gardener he asked him whom he had been living with.

" 'Misther Dalton, sorr.'

" 'Have you a recommendation, Terence?'

" 'A ricommindation is it, sorr? Sure I have nothing agin Misther Dalton, though he moightn't be knowing just the respict the likes of a first-class garthener is entitled to.' "

He did not laugh. He seldom does, it seems, at his own stories. But I could not help laughing over the "ricommindation" I had given the General. He knew that I was embarrassed, and said kindly:—

"Now tell me something about 'Uncle Billy's Bummers.' I hear that they have a most effectual way of tearing up railroads."

I told him of Poe's contrivance of the hook and chain, and how the heaviest rails were easily overturned with it, and how the ties were piled and fired and the rails twisted out of shape. The President listened to every word with intense interest.

"By Jing!" he exclaimed, "we *have* got a general. Cæsar burnt his bridges behind him, but Sherman burns his *rails*. Now tell me some more."

He helped me along by asking questions. Then I began to tell him how the negroes had flocked into our camps, and how simply and plainly the General had talked to them, advising them against violence of any kind, and explaining to them that "Freedom" meant only the liberty to earn their own living in their own way, and not freedom from work.

"We have got a general, sure enough," he cried. "He talks to them plainly, does he, so that they understand? I say to you, Brice," he went on earnestly, "the importance of plain talk can't be overestimated. Any thought, however abstruse, can be put in speech that a boy or a negro can grasp. Any book, however deep, can be written in terms that everybody can comprehend, if a man only tries hard enough. When I was a boy I used to hear the neighbors talking, and it bothered me so because I could not understand them that I used to sit up half the night thinking things out for myself. I remember that I did not know what the word *demonstrate* meant. So I stopped my studies then and there and got a volume of Euclid. Before I got through I could *demonstrate* everything in it, and I have never been bothered with *demonstrate* since."

I thought of those wonderfully limpid speeches of his: of the Freeport debates, and of the contrast between his style and Douglas's. And I understood the reason for it at last. I understood the supreme mind that had conceived the Freeport Question. And as I stood before him then, at the close of this fearful war, the words of the Gospel were in my mind. "So the last shall be first, and the first, last; for many be called, but few chosen."

How I wished that all those who have maligned and tortured him could talk with him as I had talked with him. To know his great heart would disarm them of all antagonism. They would feel, as I feel, that his life is so much nobler than theirs, and his burdens so much heavier, that they would go away ashamed of their criticism.

He said to me once: "Brice, I hope we are in sight of the end, now. I hope that we may get through without any more fighting. I don't want to see any more of our countrymen killed. And then," he said, as if talking to himself, "and then we must show them mercy—mercy."

I thought it a good time to mention Colfax's case. He has been on my mind ever since. Mr. Lincoln listened attentively. Once he sighed, and he was winding his long fingers around each other while I talked.

"I saw the man captured, Mr. Lincoln," I concluded. "And if a technicality will help him out, he was actually within his own skirmish line at the time. The Rebel skirmishers had not fallen back on each side of him."

"Brice," he said, with that sorrowful smile, "a technicality might save Colfax, but it won't save me. Is this man a friend of yours?" he asked.

That was a poser.

"I think he is, Mr. Lincoln. I should like to call him so. I admire him." And I went on to tell of what he had done at Vicksburg, leaving out, however, my instrumentality in having him sent north. The President used almost Sherman's words.

"By Jing!" he exclaimed. (That seems to be a favorite expression of his.) "Those fellows were born to fight. If it wasn't for them, the South would have quit long ago." Then he looked at me in his funny way, and said, "See here, Steve, if this Colfax isn't exactly a friend of yours, there must be some reason why you are pleading for him in this way."

"Well, sir," I said, at length, "I should like to get him off on account of his cousin, Miss Virginia Carvel." And I told him something about Miss Carvel, and how she had helped you with the Union sergeant that day in the hot hospital. And how she had nursed Judge Whipple."

"She's a fine woman," he said. "Those women have helped those men to prolong this war about three years. And yet we must save them for the nation's sake. They are to be the mothers of our patriots in days to come. Is she a friend of yours, too, Steve?"

What was I to say?

"Not especially, sir," I answered finally. "I have had to offend her rather often. But I know that she likes my mother."

"Why!" he cried, jumping up, "she's a daughter of Colonel Carvel. I always had an admiration for that man. An ideal Southern gentleman of the old school,—courteous, as honorable and open as the day, and as brave as a lion. You've heard the story of how he threw a man named Babcock out of his store, who tried to bribe him?"

"I heard you tell it in that tavern, sir. And I have heard it since." It did me good to hear the Colonel praised.

"I always liked that story," he said. "By the way, what's become of the Colonel?"

"He got away—South, sir," I answered. "He couldn't stand it. He hasn't been heard of since the summer of '63. They think he was killed in Texas. But they are not positive. They probably never will be," I added.

He was silent awhile.

"Too bad!" he said. "Too bad. What stuff those men are made of! And so you want me to pardon this Colfax?"

"It would be presumptuous in me to go that far, sir," I replied. "But I hoped you might speak of it to the General when he comes. And I would be glad of the opportunity to testify."

He took a few strides up and down the room.

"Well, well," he said, "that's my vice—pardoning, saying yes. It's always one more drink with me. It—" he smiled—"it makes me sleep better. I've pardoned enough Rebels to populate New Orleans. Why," he continued, with his whimsical look, "just before I left Washington, in comes one of your Missouri senators with a list of Rebels who are shut up in McDowell's and Alton. I said:—

" 'Senator, you're not going to ask me to turn loose all those at once?'

"He said just what you said when you were speaking of Missouri a while ago, that he was afraid of guerilla warfare, and that the war was nearly over. I signed 'em. And then what does he do but pull out another batch longer than the first! And those were worse than the first.

" 'What! you don't want me to turn these loose, too?'

" 'Yes, I do, Mr. President. I think it will pay to be merciful.'

" 'Then durned if I don't,' I said, and I signed 'em."

Steamer "River Queen."

On the Potomac, April 9, 1865.

Dear Mother: I am glad that the telegrams I have been able to send reached you safely. I have not had time to write, and this will be but a short letter.

You will be surprised to see this heading. I am on the President's boat, in the President's party, bound with him for Washington. And this is how it happened: The very afternoon of the day I wrote you, General Sherman himself arrived at City Point on the steamer *Russia*. I heard the salutes, and was on the wharf to meet him. That same afternoon he and General Grant and Admiral Porter went aboard the *River Queen* to see the President. How I should have liked to be present at that interview!

After it was over they all came out of the cabin together: General Grant silent, and smoking, as usual; General Sherman talking vivaciously; and Lincoln and the Admiral smiling and listening. That was historic! I shall never expect to see such a sight again in all my days. You can imagine my surprise when the President called me from where I was standing at some distance with the other officers. He put his hand on my shoulder then and there, and turned to General Sherman.

"Major Brice is a friend of mine, General," he said. "I knew him in Illinois."

"He never told me that," said the General.

"I guess he's got a great many important things shut up inside of him," said Mr. Lincoln, banteringly. "But he gave you a good recommendation, Sherman. He said that you wore white socks, and that the boys liked you and called you 'Uncle Billy.' And I told him that was the best recommendation he could give anybody."

I was frightened. But the General only looked at me with those eyes that go through everything, and then he laughed.

"Brice," he said, "you'll have my reputation ruined."

"Sherman," said Mr. Lincoln, "you don't want the Major right away, do you? Let him stay around here for a while with me. I think he'll find it interesting." He looked at the general-in-chief, who was smiling just a little bit. "I've got a sneaking notion that Grant's going to do something."

Then they all laughed.

"Certainly, Mr. Lincoln," said my General, "you may have Brice. Be careful he doesn't talk you to death—he's said too much already."

That is how I came to stay.

I have no time now to tell you all that I have seen and heard. I have ridden with the President, and have gone with him on errands of mercy and errands of cheer. I have been almost within sight of what we hope is the last struggle of this frightful war. I have listened to the guns of Five Forks, where Sheridan and Warren bore their own colors in the front of the charge. I was with Mr. Lincoln while the battle of Petersburg was raging, and there were tears in his eyes.

Then came the retreat of Lee and the instant pursuit of Grant, and—Richmond. The quiet General did not so much as turn aside to enter the smoking city he had besieged for so long. But I went there, with the President. And if I had one incident in my life to live over again, I should choose this. As we were going up the river, a disabled steamer lay across the passage in the obstruction of piles the Confederates had built. Mr. Lincoln would not wait. There were but a few of us in his party, and we stepped into Admiral Porter's twelve-oared barge and were rowed to Richmond, the smoke of the fires still darkening the sky. We landed within a block of Libby Prison.

With the little guard of ten sailors he marched the mile and a half to General Weitzel's headquarters,—the presidential mansion of the Confederacy. You can imagine our anxiety. I shall remember him always as I saw him that day, a tall, black figure of sorrow, with the high silk hat we have learned to love. Unafraid, his heart rent with pity, he walked unharmed amid such tumult as I have rarely seen. The windows filled, the streets ahead of us became choked, as the word that the President was coming ran on like quick-fire. The mob shouted and pushed. Drunken men reeled against him. The negroes wept aloud and cried hosannas.

They pressed upon him that they might touch the hem of his coat, and one threw himself on his knees and kissed the President's feet.

Still he walked on unharmed, past the ashes and the ruins. Not as a conqueror was he come, to march in triumph. Not to destroy, but to heal. Though there were many times when we had to fight for a path through the crowds, he did not seem to feel the danger.

Was it because he knew that his hour was not yet come?

To-day, on the boat, as we were steaming between the green shores of the Potomac, I overheard him reading to Mr. Sumner:—

> "Duncan is in his grave;
> After life's fitful fever he sleeps well;
> Treason has done his worst; nor steel, nor poison,
> Malice domestic, foreign levy, nothing,
> Can touch him further."

WILLARD'S HOTEL, WASHINGTON, April 10, 1865.

I have looked up the passage, and have written it in above. It haunts me.

CHAPTER XV

THE MAN OF SORROWS

THE train was late—very late. It was Virginia who first caught sight of the new dome of the Capitol through the slanting rain, but she merely pressed her lips together and said nothing. In the dingy brick station of the Baltimore and Ohio Railroad more than one person paused to look after them, and a kind-hearted lady who had been in the car kissed the girl good-by.

"You think that you can find your uncle's house, my dear?" she asked, glancing at Virginia with concern. Through all of that long journey she had worn a look apart. "Do you think you can find your uncle's house?"

Virginia started. And then she smiled as she looked at the honest, alert, and squarely built gentleman beside her.

"Captain Brent can, Mrs. Ware," she said. "He can find anything."

Whereupon the kind lady gave the Captain her hand.

"You look as if you could, Captain," said she. "Remember, if General Carvel is out of town, you promised to bring her to me."

"Yes, ma'am," said Captain Lige, "and so I *shall*."

"Kerridge, kerridge! Right dis-a-way! No sah, dat ain't de kerridge you wants. Dat's it, lady, you'se lookin' at it. Kerridge, kerridge, ker-ridge!"

Virginia tried bravely to smile, but she was very near to tears as she stood on the uneven pavement and looked at the scrawny horses stand-ing patiently in the steady down pour. All sorts of people were coming and going,—army officers and navy officers and citizens of states and territories, driving up and driving away.

And this was Washington!

She was thinking then of the multitude who came here with aching hearts,—with heavier hearts than was hers that day. How many of the throng hurrying by would not flee, if they could, back to the peaceful homes they had left? But perhaps those homes were gone now. De-stroyed, like her own, by the war. Women with children at their breasts, and mothers bowed with sorrow, had sought this city in their agony.

415

Young men and old had come hither, striving to keep back the thoughts of dear ones left behind, whom they might never see again. And by the thousands, and tens of thousands they had passed from here to the places of blood beyond.

"Kerridge, sah! Kerridge!"

"Do you know where General Daniel Carvel lives?"

"Yes, sah, reckon I does. I Street, sah. Jump right in, sah."

Virginia sank back on the stuffy cushions of the rattletrap, and then sat upright again and stared out of the window at the dismal scene. They were splashing through a sea of mud. Ever since they had left St. Louis, Captain Lige had done his best to cheer her, and he did not intend to desist now.

"This beats all," he cried. "So this is Washington! Why, it don't compare to St. Louis, except we haven't got the White House and the Capitol. Jinny, it would take a scow to get across the street, and we don't have ramshackly stores and nigger cabins bang up against fine houses like that. This is ragged. That's what it is, *ragged*. We don't have any dirty pickaninnies dodging among the horses in our residence streets. I declare, Jinny, if those aren't *pigs!*"

Virginia laughed. She could not help it.

"Poor Lige!" she said. "I hope Uncle Daniel has some breakfast for you. You've had a good deal to put up with on this trip."

"Lordy, Jinny," said the Captain, "I'd put up with a good deal more than this for the sake of going anywhere with you."

"Even to such a doleful place as this?" she sighed.

"This is all right, if the sun'll only come out and dry things up and let us see the green on those trees," he said. "Lordy, how I do love to see the spring green in the sunlight!"

She put out her hand over his.

"Lige," she said, "you know you're just trying to keep up my spirits. You've been doing that ever since we left home."

"No such thing," he replied with vehemence. "There's nothing for you to be cast down about."

"Oh, but there is!" she cried. "Suppose I can't make your Black Republican President pardon Clarence!"

"Pooh!" said the Captain, squeezing her hand and trying to appear unconcerned. "Your Uncle Daniel knows Mr. Lincoln. He'll have that arranged."

Just then the rattletrap pulled up at the sidewalk, the wheels of the near side in four inches of mud, and the Captain leaped out and spread the umbrella. They were in front of a rather imposing house of brick, flanked on one side by a house just like it, and on the other by a series of dreary vacant lots where the rain had collected in pools. They climbed the steps and rang the bell. In due time the door was opened by a smiling yellow butler in black.

"Does General Carvel live here?"

"Yas, miss. But he ain't to home now. Done gone to New York."

"Oh," faltered Virginia. "Didn't he get my telegram day before yesterday? I sent it to the War Department."

"He's done gone since Saturday, miss." And then, evidently impressed by the young lady's looks, he added hospitably, "Kin I do anything fo' you, miss?"

"I'm his niece, Miss Virginia Carvel, and this is Captain Brent."

The yellow butler's face lighted up.

"Come right in, Miss Jinny. Done heerd de General speak of you often —yas'm. De General'll be to home dis a'ternoon, suah. 'Twill do him good ter see you, Miss Jinny. He's been mighty lonesome. Walk right in, Cap'n, and make yo'selves at home. Lizbeth—Lizbeth!" A yellow maid came running down the stairs. "Heah's Miss Jinny."

"Lan' of goodness!" cried Lizbeth. "I knows Miss Jinny. Done seed her at Calve't House. How *is* you, Miss Jinny?"

"Very well, Lizbeth," said Virginia, listlessly sitting down on the hall sofa. "Can you give us some breakfast?"

"Yas'm," said Lizbeth, "jes' reckon we kin." She ushered them into a walnut dining room, big and high and sombre, with plush-bottomed chairs placed about—walnut also; for that was the fashion in those days. But the Captain had no sooner seated himself than he shot up again and started out.

"Where are you going, Lige?"

"To pay off the carriage driver," he said.

"Let him wait," said Virginia. "I'm going to the White House in a little while."

"What—what for?" he gasped.

"To see your Black Republican President," she replied, with alarming calmness.

"Now, Jinny," he cried, in excited appeal, "don't go doin' any such fool trick as that. Your Uncle Dan'l will be here this afternoon. *He* knows the President. And then the thing'll be fixed all right, and no *mistake.*"

Her reply was in the same tone—almost a monotone—which she had used for three days. It made the Captain very uneasy, for he knew when she spoke in that way that her will was in it.

"And to lose that time," she answered, "may be to have him shot."

"But you can't get to the President without credentials," he objected.

"What," she flashed, "hasn't any one a right to see the President? You mean to say that he will not see a woman in trouble? Then all these pretty stories I hear of him are false. They are made up by the Yankees."

Poor Captain Lige! He had some notion of the multitude of calls upon Mr. Lincoln, especially at that time. But he could not, he dared not, remind her of the principal reason for this,—Lee's surrender and the approaching end of the war. And then the Captain had never seen Mr. Lincoln. In the distant valley of the Mississippi he had only heard of the President very conflicting things. He had heard him criticised and reviled and praised, just as is every man who goes to the White House, be he saint or sinner. And, during an administration, no man at a distance may come at a President's true character and worth. The Captain had seen Lincoln caricatured vilely. And again he had read and heard the pleasant anecdotes of which Virginia had spoken, until he did not know what to believe.

As for Virginia, he knew her partisanship to, and undying love for, the South; he knew the class prejudice which was bound to assert itself, and he had seen enough in the girl's demeanor to fear that she was going to demand rather than implore. She did not come of a race that was wont to bend the knee.

"Well, well," he said despairingly, "you must eat some breakfast first, Jinny."

She waited with an ominous calmness until it was brought in, and then she took a part of a roll and some coffee.

"This won't do," exclaimed the Captain. "Why, why, that won't get you halfway to Mr. Lincoln."

She shook her head, half smiling.

"You must eat enough, Lige," she said.

He was finished in an incredibly short time, and amid the protestations of Lizbeth and the yellow butler they got into the carriage again, and splashed and rattled toward the White House. Once Virginia glanced out, and catching sight of the bedraggled flags on the houses in honor of Lee's surrender, a look of pain crossed her face. The Captain could not repress a note of warning.

"Jinny," said he, "I have an idea that you'll find the President a good deal of a *man*. Now if you're allowed to see him, don't get him *mad*, Jinny, whatever you do."

Virginia stared straight ahead.

"If he is something of a man, Lige, he will not lose his temper with a woman."

Captain Lige subsided. And just then they came in sight of the house of the Presidents, with its beautiful portico and its broad wings. And they turned in under the dripping trees of the grounds. A carriage with a black coachman and footman was ahead of them, and they saw two stately gentlemen descend from it and pass the guard at the door. Then their turn came. The Captain helped her out in his best manner, and gave some money to the driver.

"I reckon he needn't wait for us this time, Jinny," said he.

She shook her head and went in, he following, and they were directed to the anteroom of the President's office on the second floor. There were many people in the corridors, and one or two young officers in blue who stared at her. She passed them with her head high.

But her spirits sank when they came to the anteroom. It was full of all sorts of people. Politicians, both prosperous and seedy, full faced and keen faced, seeking office; women, officers, and a one-armed soldier sitting in the corner. He was among the men who offered Virginia their seats, and the only one whom she thanked. But she walked directly to the doorkeeper at the end of the room. Captain Lige was beside her.

"Can we see the President?" he asked.

"Have you got an appointment?" said the old man.

"No."

"Then you'll have to wait your turn, sir," he said, shaking his head and looking at Virginia. And he added: "It's slow work waiting your turn, there's so many governors and generals and senators, although the session's over. It's a busy time, miss."

Virginia went very close to him.

"Oh, can't you do something?" she said. And added, with an inspiration, "I *must* see him. It's a matter of life and death."

She saw instantly, with a woman's instinct, that her words had had their effect. The old man glanced at her again, as if demurring.

"You're sure, miss, it's life and death?" he said.

"Oh, why should I say so if it were not?" she cried.

"The orders are very strict," he said. "But the President told me to give precedence to cases when a life is in question. Just you wait a minute, miss, until Governor Doddridge comes out, and I'll see what I can do for you. Give me your name, please, miss."

She remained standing where she was. In a little while the heavy door opened, and a portly, rubicund man came out with a smile on his face. He broke into a laugh, when halfway across the room, as if the memory of what he had heard were too much for his gravity. The door-keeper slipped into the room, and there was a silent, anxious interval. Then he came out again.

"The President will see you, miss."

Captain Lige started forward with her, but she restrained him.

"Wait for me here, Lige," she said.

She swept in alone, and the door closed softly after her. The room was a big one, and there were maps on the table, with pins sticking in them. She saw that much, and then—!

Could this fantastically tall, stooping figure before her be that of the President of the United States? She stopped, as from the shock he gave her. The lean, yellow face with the mask-like lines all up and down, the unkempt, tousled hair, the beard—why, he was a hundred times more ridiculous than his caricatures. He might have stood for many of the poor white trash farmers she had seen in Kentucky—save for the long black coat.

"Is—is this Mr. Lincoln?" she asked, her breath taken away.

He bowed and smiled down at her. Somehow that smile changed his face a little.

"I guess I'll have to own up," he answered.

"My name is Virginia Carvel," she said. "I have come all the way from St. Louis to see you."

"Miss Carvel," said the President, looking at her intently, "I have rarely been so flattered in my life. I—I hope I have not disappointed you."

Virginia was justly angry.

"Oh, you haven't," she cried, her eyes flashing, "because I am what you would call a Rebel."

The mirth in the dark corners of his eyes disturbed her more and more. And then she saw that the President was laughing.

"And have you a better name for it, Miss Carvel?" he asked. "Because I am searching for a better name—just now."

She was silent—sternly silent. And she tapped her foot on the carpet. What manner of man was this?

"Won't you sit down?" said the President, kindly. "You must be tired after your journey." And he put forth a chair.

"No, thank you," said Virginia; "I think that I can say what I have come to say better standing."

"Well," said Mr. Lincoln, "that's not strange. I'm that way, too. The words seem to come out better. That reminds me of a story they tell about General Buck Tanner. Ever heard of Buck, Miss Carvel? No? Well, Buck was a character. He got his title in the Mormon war. One day the boys asked him over to the square to make a speech. The General was a little uneasy.

" 'I'm all right when I get standing up, Liza,' he said to his wife. 'Then the words come right along. Only trouble is they come too cussed fast. How'm I going to stop 'em when I want to?'

" 'Well, I du declare, Buck,' said she, 'I gave you credit for some sense. All you've got to do is to set down. That'll end it, I reckon.'

"So the General went over to the square and talked for about an hour and a half, and then a Chicago man shouted to him to dry up. The General looked pained.

" 'Boys,' said he, 'it's jest every bit as bad for me as it is for you. You'll have to hand up a chair, boys, because I'm never going to get shet of this goldarned speech any other way.' "

Mr. Lincoln had told this so comically that Virginia was forced to laugh, and she immediately hated herself. A man who could joke at such a time certainly could not feel the cares and responsibilities of his office. He should have been a comedian. And yet this was the President who had conducted the war, whose generals had conquered the Confederacy. And she was come to ask him a favor.

Virginia swallowed her pride.

"Mr. Lincoln," she began, "I have come to talk to you about my cousin, Colonel Clarence Colfax."

"I shall be happy to talk to you about your cousin, Colonel Colfax, Miss Carvel. Is he your third or fourth cousin?"

"He is my first cousin," she retorted.

"Is he in the city?" asked Mr. Lincoln, innocently. "Why didn't he come with you?"

"Oh, haven't you heard?" she cried. "He is Clarence Colfax of St. Louis, now a Colonel in the army of the Confederate States."

"Which army?" asked Mr. Lincoln.

Virginia tossed her head in exasperation.

"In General Joseph Johnston's army," she replied, trying to be patient. "But now," she gulped, "now he has been arrested as a spy by General Sherman's army."

"That's too bad," answered Mr. Lincoln.

"And—and they are going to shoot him."

"That's worse," said Mr. Lincoln, gravely. "But I expect he deserves it."

"Oh, no, he doesn't," she cried. "You don't know how brave he is! He floated down the Mississippi on a log, out of Vicksburg, and brought back thousands and thousands of percussion caps. He rowed across the river when the Yankee fleet was going down, and set fire to De Soto so that they could see to shoot."

"Well," said Mr. Lincoln, "that's a good starter."

Then he looked thoughtful.

"Miss Carvel," said he, "that argument reminds me of a story about a man I used to know in the old days in Illinois. His name was McNeil, and he was a lawyer. One day he was defending a prisoner for assault and battery before Judge Drake.

" 'Judge,' says McNeil, 'you oughtn't to lock this man up. It was a fair fight, and he's the best man in the state in a fair fight. And, what's more, he's never been licked in a fair fight in his life.'

" 'And if your honor does lock me up,' the prisoner put in, 'I'll give your honor a thunderin' big lickin' when I get out.'

"The Judge took off his coat.

" 'Gentlemen,' said he, 'it's a powerful queer argument, but the Court will admit it on its merits. The prisoner will please to step out on the grass.' "

This time Virginia contrived merely to smile. She was striving against something, she knew not what. Her breath was coming deeply, and she was dangerously near to tears. Why? She could not tell. She had come into this man's presence despising herself for having to ask him a favor. The sight of his face she had ridiculed. Now she could not look into it without an odd sensation. What was in it? Sorrow? Yes, that was nearest it.

What had the man done? Told her a few funny stories—given quizzical answers to some of her questions. Quizzical, yes; but she could not be sure then there was not wisdom in them, and that humiliated her. She

had never conceived of such a man. And, be it added gratuitously, Virginia deemed herself something of an adept in dealing with men.

"And now," said Mr. Lincoln, "to continue for the defence, I believe
that Colonel Colfax first distinguished himself at the time of Camp Jackson, when of all the prisoners he refused to accept a parole."

Startled, she looked up at him swiftly, and then down again. "Yes,"
she answered, "yes. But oh, Mr. Lincoln, please don't hold that against
him."

If she could only have seen his face then. But her lashes were
dropped.

"My dear young lady," replied the President, "I honor him for it. I
was merely elaborating the argument which you have begun. On the
other hand, it is a pity that he should have taken off that uniform which
he adorned, and attempted to enter General Sherman's lines as a civilian,
—as a spy."

He had spoken these last words very gently, but she was too excited
to heed his gentleness. She drew herself up, a gleam in her eyes like the
crest of a blue wave in a storm.

"A spy!" she cried; "it takes more courage to be a spy than anything
else in war. Then he will be shot. You are not content in the North with
what you have gained. You are not content with depriving us of our
rights, and our fortunes, with forcing us back to an allegiance we despise.
You are not content with humiliating our generals and putting innocent
men in prisons. But now I suppose you will shoot us all. And all this
mercy that I have heard about means nothing—nothing—"

Why did she falter and stop?

"Miss Carvel," said the President, "I am afraid from what I have
heard just now, that it means nothing."

Oh, the sadness of that voice,—the ineffable sadness,—the sadness
and the woe of a great nation! And the sorrow in those eyes, the sorrow
of a heavy cross borne meekly,—how heavy none will ever know. The
pain of a crown of thorns worn for a world that did not understand.

No wonder Virginia faltered and was silent. She looked at Abraham
Lincoln standing there, bent and sorrowful, and it was as if a light had
fallen upon him. But strangest of all in that strange moment was that
she felt his strength. It was the same strength she had felt in Stephen
Brice. This was the thought that came to her.

Slowly she walked to the window and looked out across the green
grounds where the wind was shaking the wet trees, past the unfinished

monument to the Father of her country, and across the broad Potomac to Alexandria in the hazy distance. The rain beat upon the panes, and then she knew that she was crying softly to herself. She had met a force that she could not conquer, she had looked upon a sorrow that she could not fathom, albeit she had known sorrow.

Presently she felt him near. She turned and looked through her tears at his face that was all compassion. And now she was unashamed. He had placed a chair behind her.

"Sit down, Virginia," he said. Even the name fell from him naturally. She obeyed him then like a child. He remained standing.

"Tell me about your cousin," he said; "are you going to marry him?"

She hung an instant on her answer. Would that save Clarence? But in that moment she could not have spoken anything but the truth to save her soul.

"No, Mr. Lincoln," she said; "I was—but I did not love him. I—I think that was one reason why he was so reckless."

Mr. Lincoln smiled.

"The officer who happened to see Colonel Colfax captured is now in Washington. When your name was given to me, I sent for him. Perhaps he is in the anteroom now. I should like to tell you, first of all, that this officer defended your cousin and asked me to pardon him."

"He defended him! He asked you to pardon him! Who is he?" she exclaimed.

Again Mr. Lincoln smiled. He strode to the bell-cord, and spoke a few words to the usher who answered his ring. The usher went out. Then the door opened, and a young officer, spare, erect, came quickly into the room, and bowed respectfully to the President. But Mr. Lincoln's eyes were not on him. They were on the girl. He saw her head lifted, timidly. He saw her lips part and the color come flooding into her face. But she did not rise.

The President sighed. But the light in her eyes was reflected in his own. It has been truly said that Abraham Lincoln knew the human heart.

The officer still stood facing the President, the girl staring at his profile. The door closed behind him.

"Major Brice," said Mr. Lincoln, "when you asked me to pardon Colonel Colfax, I believe that you told me he was inside his own skirmish lines when he was captured."

"Yes, sir, he was."

Suddenly Stephen turned, as if impelled by the President's gaze, and so his eyes met Virginia's. He forgot time and place,—for the while even this man whom he revered above all men. He saw her hand tighten on the arm of her chair. He took a step toward her, and stopped. Mr. Lincoln was speaking again.

"He put in a plea, a lawyer's plea, wholly unworthy of him, Miss Virginia. He asked me to let your cousin off on a technicality. What do you think of that?"

"Oh!" said Virginia. Just the exclamation escaped her—nothing more. The crimson that had betrayed her deepened on her cheeks. Slowly the eyes she had yielded to Stephen came back again and rested on the President. And now her wonder was that an ugly man could be so beautiful.

"I wish it understood, Mr. Lawyer," the President continued, "that I am not letting off Colonel Colfax on a technicality. I am sparing his life," he said slowly, "because the time for which we have been waiting and longing for four years is now at hand—the time to be merciful. Let us all thank God for it."

Virginia had risen now. She crossed the room, her head lifted, her heart lifted, to where this man of sorrows stood smiling down at her.

"Mr. Lincoln," she faltered, "I did not know you when I came here. I should have known you, for I had heard him—I had heard Major Brice praise you. Oh," she cried, "how I wish that every man and woman and child in the South might come here and see you as I have seen you to-day. I think—I think that some of their bitterness might be taken away."

Abraham Lincoln laid his hands upon the girl. And Stephen, watching, knew that he was looking upon a benediction.

"Virginia," said Mr. Lincoln, "I have not suffered by the South, I have suffered *with* the South. Your sorrow has been my sorrow, and your pain has been my pain. What you have lost, I have lost. And what you have gained," he added sublimely, "I have gained."

He led her gently to the window. The clouds were flying before the wind, and a patch of blue sky shone above the Potomac. With his long arm he pointed across the river to the southeast, and as if by a miracle a shaft of sunlight fell on the white houses of Alexandria.

"In the first days of the war," he said, "a flag flew there in sight of the place where George Washington lived and died. I used to watch that flag, and thank God that Washington had not lived to see it. And sometimes,—sometimes I wondered if God had allowed it to be put in irony just there." His voice seemed to catch. "That was wrong," he continued.

"I should have known that this was our punishment—that the sight of it was my punishment. Before we could become the great nation He has destined us to be, our sins must be wiped out in blood. You loved that flag, Virginia. You love it still. I say in all sincerity, may you always love it. May the day come when this Nation, North and South, may look back upon it with reverence. Thousands upon thousands of brave Americans have died under it for what they believed was right. But may the day come again when you will love that flag you see there now—Washington's flag—better still."

He stopped, and the tears were wet upon Virginia's lashes. She could not have spoken then.

Mr. Lincoln went over to his desk and sat down before it. Then he began to write, slouched forward, one knee resting on the floor, his lips moving at the same time. When he got up again he seemed taller than ever.

"There!" he said, "I guess that will fix it. I'll have that sent to Sherman. I have already spoken to him about the matter."

They did not thank him. It was beyond them both. He turned to Stephen with that quizzical look on his face he had so often seen him wear.

"Steve," he said, "I'll tell you a story. The other night Harlan was here making a speech to a crowd out of the window, and my boy Tad was sitting behind him.

" 'What shall we do with the Rebels?' said Harlan to the crowd.

" 'Hang 'em!' cried the people.

" 'No,' says Tad, 'hang on to 'em.'

"And the boy was right. That is what we intend to do,—hang on to 'em. And, Steve," said Mr. Lincoln, putting his hand again on Virginia's shoulder, "if you have the sense I think you have, you'll hang on, too."

For an instant he stood smiling at their blushes,—he to whom the power was given to set apart his cares and his troubles and partake of the happiness of others. For of such was his happiness.

Then the President drew out his watch. "Bless me!" he said, "I am ten minutes behind my appointment at the Department. Miss Virginia, you may care to thank the Major for the little service he has done you. You can do so undisturbed here. Make yourselves at home."

As he opened the door he paused and looked back at them. The smile passed from his face, and an ineffable expression of longing—longing and tenderness—came upon it.

Then he was gone.

For a space, while his spell was upon them, they did not stir. Then Stephen sought her eyes that had been so long denied him. They were not denied him now. It was Virginia who first found her voice, and she called him by his name.

"Oh, Stephen," she said, "how sad he looked!"

He was close to her, at her side. And he answered her in the earnest tone which she knew so well.

"Virginia, if I could have had what I most wished for in the world, I should have asked that you should know Abraham Lincoln."

Then she dropped her eyes, and her breath came quickly.

"I—I might have known," she answered, "I might have known what he was. I had heard you talk of him. I had seen him in you, and I did not know. Do you remember that day when we were in the summer-house together at Glencoe, long ago? When you had come back from seeing him?"

"As yesterday," he said.

"You were changed then," she said bravely. "I saw it. Now I under· stand. It was because you had seen Mr. Lincoln."

"When I saw him," said Stephen, reverently, "I knew how little and narrow I was."

Then, overcome by the incense of her presence, he drew her to him until her heart beat against his own. She did not resist, but lifted her face to him, and he kissed her.

"You love me, Virginia!" he cried.

"Yes, Stephen," she answered, low, more wonderful in her surrender than ever before. "Yes—dear." Then she hid her face against his blue coat. "I—I cannot help it. Oh, Stephen, how I have struggled against it! How I have tried to hate you, and couldn't. No, I couldn't. I tried to insult you, I did insult you. And when I saw how splendidly you bore it, I used to cry."

He kissed her brown hair.

"I loved you through it all," he said. "Virginia!"

"Yes, dearest."

"Virginia, did you dream of me?"

She raised her head quickly, and awe was in her eyes.

"How did you know?"

"Because I dreamed of you," he answered. "And those dreams used to linger with me half the day as I went about my work. I used to think of them as I sat in the saddle on the march."

"I, too, treasured them," she said. "And I hated myself for doing it."

"Virginia, will you marry me?"

"Yes."

"To-morrow?"

"Yes, dear, to-morrow." Faintly, "I—I have no one but you—now." Once more he drew her to him, and she gloried in his strength.

"God help me to cherish you, dear," he said, "and guard you well."

She drew away from him, gently, and turned toward the window.

"See, Stephen," she cried, "the sun has come out at last."

For a while they were silent, looking out; the drops glistened on blade and leaf, and the joyous new green of the earth entered into their hearts.

CHAPTER XVI

ANNAPOLIS

It was Virginia's wish, and was therefore sacred. As for Stephen, he little cared whither they went. And so they found themselves on that bright afternoon in mid-April under the great trees that arch the unpaved streets of old Annapolis.

They stopped by direction at a gate, and behind it was a green cluster of lilac bushes, which lined the walk to the big plum-colored house which Lionel Carvel had built. Virginia remembered that down this walk on a certain day in June, a hundred years agone, Richard Carvel had led Dorothy Manners.

They climbed the steps, tottering now with age and disuse, and Virginia playfully raised the big brass knocker, brown now, that Scipio had been wont to polish until it shone. Stephen took from his pocket the clumsy key that General Carvel had given him, and turned it in the rusty lock. The door swung open, and Virginia stood in the hall of her ancestors.

It was musty and damp this day as the day when Richard had come back from England and found it vacant and his grandfather dead. But there, at the parting of the stairs, was the triple-arched window which he had described. Through it the yellow afternoon light was flooding now, even as then, checkered by the branches in their first fringe of green. But the tall clock which Lionel Carvel used to wind was at Calvert House, with many another treasure.

They went up the stairs, and reverently they walked over the bare floors, their footfalls echoing through the silent house. A score of scenes in her great-grandfather's life came to Virginia. Here was the room—the corner one at the back of the main building, which looked out over the deserted garden—that had been Richard's mother's. She recalled how he had stolen into it on that summer's day after his return, and had flung open the shutters. They were open now, for their locks were off. The prie-dieu was gone, and the dresser. But the high bed was there, stripped of its poppy counterpane and white curtains; and the steps by which she had entered it.

And next they went into the great square room that had been Lionel Carvel's, and there, too, was the roomy bed on which the old gentleman had lain with the gout, while Richard read to him from the *Spectator*. One side of it looked out on the trees in Freshwater Lane, and the other across the roof of the low house opposite to where the sun danced on the blue and white waters of the Chesapeake.

"Honey," said Virginia, as they stood in the deep recess of the window, "wouldn't it be nice if we could live here always, away from the world? Just we two! But you would never be content to do that," she said, smiling reproachfully. "You are the kind of man who must be in the midst of things. In a little while you will have far more besides me to think about."

He was quick to catch the note of sadness in her voice. And he drew her to him.

"We all have our duty to perform in the world, dear," he answered. "It cannot be all pleasure."

"You—you Puritan!" she cried. "To think that I should have married a Puritan! What would my great-great-great-great-grandfather say, who was such a stanch Royalist? Why, I think I can see him frowning at me now, from the door, in his blue velvet coat and silver-laced waistcoat."

"He was well punished," retorted Stephen; "his own grandson was a Whig, and seems to have married a woman of spirit."

"She *had* spirit," said Virginia. "I am sure that she did not allow my great-grandfather to kiss her—unless she wanted to."

And she looked up at him, half smiling, half pouting, altogether bewitching.

"From what I hear of him, he was something of a man," said Stephen. "Perhaps he did it anyway."

"I am glad that Marlborough Street isn't a crowded thoroughfare," said Virginia.

When they had seen the dining-room, with its carved mantel and silver door-knobs, and the ballroom in the wing, they came out, and Stephen locked the door again. They walked around the house, and stood looking down the terraces,—once stately, but crumbled now,—where Dorothy had danced on the green on Richard's birthday. Beyond and below was the spring-house, and there was the place where the brook dived under the ruined wall,—where Dorothy had wound into her hair the lilies of the valley before she sailed for London.

The remains of a wall that had once held a balustrade marked the outlines of the formal garden. The trim hedges, for seventy years neglected, had grown incontinent. The garden itself was full of wild green things coming up through the brown of last season's growth. But in the grass the blue violets nestled, and Virginia picked some of these and put them in Stephen's coat.

"You must keep them always," she said, "because we got them here."

They spied a seat beside a hoary trunk. There on many a spring day Lionel Carvel had sat reading his *Gazette*. And there they rested now. The sun hung low over the old-world gables in the street beyond the wall, and in the level rays was an apple tree dazzling white, like a bride. The sweet fragrance which the day draws from the earth lingered in the air.

It was Virginia who broke the silence.

"Stephen, do you remember that fearful afternoon of the panic, when you came over from Anne Brinsmade's to reassure me?"

"Yes, dear," he said. "But what made you think of it now?"

She did not answer him directly.

"I believed what you said, Stephen. But you were so strong, so calm, so sure of yourself. I think that made me angry when I thought how ridiculous I must have been."

He pressed her hand.

"You were not ridiculous, Jinny."

She laughed.

"I was not as ridiculous as Mr. Cluyme with his bronze clock. But do you know what I had under my arm—what I was saving of all the things I owned?"

"No," he answered; "but I have often wondered."

She blushed.

"This house—this place made me think of it. It was Dorothy Manners's gown, and her necklace. I could not leave them. They were all the remembrance I had of that night at Mr. Brinsmade's gate, when we came so near to each other."

"Virginia," he said, "some force that we cannot understand has brought us together, some force that we could not hinder. It is foolish for me to say so, but on that day of the slave auction, when I first saw you, I had a premonition about you that I have never admitted until now even to myself."

She started.

"Why, Stephen," she cried, "I felt the same way!"

"And then," he continued quickly, "it was strange that I should have gone to Judge Whipple, who was an intimate of your father's—such a singular intimate. And then came your party, and Glencoe, and that curious incident at the Fair."

"When I was talking to the Prince, and looked up and saw you among all those people."

He laughed.

"That was the most uncomfortable of all, for me."

"Stephen," she said, stirring the leaves at her feet, "you might have taken me in your arms the night Judge Whipple died—if you had wanted to. But you were strong enough to resist. I love you all the more for that."

Again she said:—

"It was through your mother, dearest, that we were most strongly drawn together. I worshipped her from the day I saw her in the hospital. I believe that was the beginning of my charity toward the North."

"My mother would have chosen you above all women, Virginia," he answered.

*   *   *   *   *   *   *

In the morning came to them the news of Abraham Lincoln's death. And the same thought was in both their hearts, who had known him as it was given to few to know him. How he had lived in sorrow; how he had died a martyr on the very day of Christ's death upon the cross. And they believed that Abraham Lincoln gave his life for his country even as Christ gave his for the world.

And so must we believe that God has reserved for this Nation a destiny high upon the earth.

Many years afterward Stephen Brice read again to his wife those sublime closing words of the second inaugural:—

"With malice toward none, with charity for all, with firmness in the right as God gives us to see the right, let us strive on to finish the work we are in, to bind up the nation's wounds, to care for him who shall have borne the battle, and for his widow and his children—to do all which may achieve and cherish a just and lasting peace among ourselves and with all nations."

AFTERWORD

THE author has chosen St. Louis for the principal scene of this story
for many reasons. Grant and Sherman were living there before the Civil
War, and Abraham Lincoln was an unknown lawyer in the neighboring
state of Illinois. It has been one of the aims of this book to show the remarkable contrasts in the lives of these great men who came out of the
West. This old city of St. Louis, which was founded by Laclede in 1765,
likewise became the principal meeting-place of two great streams of
emigration which had been separated, more or less, since Cromwell's day.
To be sure, they were not all Cavaliers who settled in the tidewater
Colonies. There were Puritan settlements in both Maryland and Virginia.
But the life in the Southern states took on the more liberal tinge which
had characterized that of the Royalists, even to the extent of affecting
the Scotch Calvinists, while the asceticism of the Roundheads was the
keynote of the Puritan character in New England. When this great
country of ours began to develop, the streams moved westward; one over
what became the plain states of Ohio and Indiana and Illinois, and the
other across the Blue Ridge Mountains into Kentucky and Tennessee.
They mixed along the line of the Ohio River. They met at St. Louis, and,
farther west, in Kansas.

Nor can the German element in St. Louis be ignored. The part played
by this people in the Civil War is a matter of history. The scope of this
book has not permitted the author to introduce the peasantry and trad-
ing classes which formed the mass in this movement. But Richter, the
type of the university-bred revolutionist which emigrated after '48, is
drawn more or less from life. And the duel described actually took place
in Berlin.

St. Louis is the author's birthplace, and his home,—the home of those
friends whom he has known from childhood and who have always treated
him with unfaltering kindness. He begs that they will believe him when
he says that only such characters as he loves are reminiscent of those he
has known there. The city has a large population,—large enough to
include all the types that are to be found in the middle West.

One word more. This book is written of a time when feeling ran high.

433

It has been necessary to put strong speech into the mouths of the characters. The breach that threatened our country's existence is healed now. There is no side but Abraham Lincoln's side. And this side, with all reverence and patriotism, the author has tried to take.

Abraham Lincoln loved the South as well as the North.